D0327242

AN AMERICAN BRAT

Also by Bapsi Sidhwa

The Bride
Cracking India
(*originally titled* Ice-Candy Man)
The Crow Eaters

AN AMERICAN BRAT

Bapsi Sidhwa

MILKWEED EDITIONS

r

Milkweed Editions, 430 First Avenue North, Suite 400, Minneapolis, MN 55401

Printed in the United States of America
Published in 1993 by Milkweed Editions

93 94 95 96 97   5 4 3 2 1

First Edition

Publication of this book is made possible in part by grants provided by the Jerome
Foundation; the Minnesota State Arts Board through an appropriation by the
Minnesota State Legislature; and the Literature Program of the National Endowment
for the Arts. Additional support has been provided by the Dayton Hudson Foundation
for Dayton's and Target Stores; First Bank System Foundation; General Mills
Foundation; Honeywell Foundation; The McKnight Foundation; Andrew W. Mellon
Foundation; Northwest Area Foundation; I. A. O'Shaughnessy Foundation; Star
Tribune/Cowles Media Foundation; Surdna Foundation; Lila Wallace-Reader's Digest
Literary Publishers Marketing Development Program, funded through a grant to the
Council of Literary Magazines and Small Presses; and generous individuals.

Library of Congress Cataloging-in-Publication Data

Sidhwa, Bapsi.
    An American brat / Bapsi Sidhwa. — 1st ed.
      p.   cm.
    ISBN 0-915943-73-5 (cloth)
    1. Pakistanis—Travel—United States—Fiction. 2. Teenage girls—
United States—Fiction. I. Title
PR9540.9.S53A82 1993
823—dc20   93-27523
                                                                CIP

For
Noshir
Minoo
Feroze (alias Fred)
And in memory of Laurie Colwin.

AN
AMERICAN
BRAT

Chapter 1

Zareen Ginwalla hurried into the hall when the bell rang, waved the cook who had popped out back into the kitchen, and opened the portals of their home to her husband. Zareen never thought of the entrance as a mere ingress. The ancient door, grooved by the centuries and touched by vestiges of faded dyes, was too resplendent to allow for that.

But as Zareen stretched to her toes to kiss Cyrus, the usual lift to her spirits that the antique conferred was missing. She dutifully helped her husband out of his navy blue blazer and, as she handed him his cardigan, gave vent to the emotion that had been agitating her all afternoon.

"I'm really worried about Feroza."

Cyrus, whose canny instincts had registered the clouds lurking behind his wife's abstracted welcome, at once grew wary. In any event it was not customary for Zareen to greet him at the door, cardigan in hand.

Guarding his eyes Cyrus raised his chin — ostensibly to loosen his tie — and wondered if their daughter had told Zareen what had happened a few evenings back, when he'd been constrained to put his fatherly foot down. If so, he'd better watch out. His shoulders stiffened; it was purely reflexive, accustomed as he was to attack before his wife got him on the defensive. On the other hand, if Feroza had said nothing, which it occurred to him was more likely, he'd better be circumspect.

"What's wrong?" Cyrus inquired cautiously, his voice conveying just the right tinge of mild concern.

"She's becoming more and more backward every day."

Set in tight-lipped censure, Zareen's face betrayed the hours spent in solitary brooding and the dark anxieties her brooding had spawned. Cyrus, who thought his daughter was if anything too forward, maintained his guard. He examined his fingernails cursorily, made a discreet sound in the back of his throat, and raised his eyebrows a fraction.

"She won't even answer the phone anymore! 'What if it's someone I don't know?' " Zareen mimicked her daughter in English. "I told her — don't be silly. No one's going to jump out of the phone to bite you!"

Her high-heeled slippers clicking determinedly beneath the hem of the printed silk caftan she usually wore in the house, Zareen followed her husband into the bedroom. She always wore high heels, "to measure up to my husband," and removed them only when she got into bed or stepped into her bath.

It had been a typically gorgeous winter's day, bracing, bright, and windless — except for an occasional breeze that sighed through the chrysanthemums in their neighborhood and masked the reek of exhaust fumes from the buses and rickshaws on the road. Even though the sun was about to set and most of the gas heaters were off, Zareen did not feel the need of a shawl.

Cyrus sat on the bed to remove his shoes, avoiding contact with the film of Lahore's ubiquitous dust that veiled their polish, and Zareen fetched his pajamas and slippers from the dressing room.

She continued: "I went to bring Feroza from school today. I was chatting with Mother Superior on the veranda — she was out enjoying the sun — and I had removed my cardigan. Feroza pretended she didn't know me.

"In the car she said: 'Mummy, please don't come to school dressed like that.' She objected to my sleeveless sari-blouse! Really, this narrow-minded attitude touted by General Zia is infecting her, too. I told her: 'Look, we're Parsee, everybody knows we dress differently.'

"When I was her age, I wore frocks and cycled to Kinnaird College. And that was in '59 and '60 — fifteen years after Partition! Can she wear frocks? No. Women mustn't show their legs, women shouldn't dress like this, and women shouldn't act like that. Girls mustn't play hockey or sing or dance! If everything corrupts their pious little minds so easily, then the *mullahs* should wear *burqas* and stay within the four walls of their houses!"

When alone, Zareen and Cyrus conversed mostly in Gujrati,

interspersed with odd snatches in English. That their most trivial conversations often took a political turn was not surprising. In Pakistan, politics, with its special brew of martial law and religion, influenced every aspect of day-to-day living.

Cyrus had stretched his lank, pajamaed frame on the bed and locked his hands behind his head. Zareen fretted about the room, plumping pillows, shifting magazines, talking as she unnecessarily tidied the immaculately ordered room.

"It's absurd how things have changed. I was really hopeful when Bhutto was elected. For the first time I felt it didn't matter that I was not a Muslim, or that I was a woman. You remember when he told the women in Peshawar to sit with the men? That took guts!"

They had watched the rally on television. Zulfikar Ali Bhutto, riding the crest of his popularity, had dared to fault the gender segregation practiced by his volatile tribal supporters in Northwest Frontier.

"Even Ayah and the sweeper's wife asked, 'What are these *women's rights?'* Our women's committees were making real progress. He was open-minded — didn't force religion down everybody's throat. Now it is as if none of that happened.

"Could you imagine Feroza cycling to school now? She'd be a freak! Those *goondas* would make vulgar noises and bump into her, and the *mullahs* would tell her to cover her head. Instead of moving forward, we are moving backward. What I could do in '59 and '60, my daughter can't do in 1978! Our Parsee children in Lahore won't know how to mix with Parsee kids in Karachi or Bombay."

"Don't worry," Cyrus said. "When the time comes, they'll learn in two minutes. Everybody's feeling frustrated, not only women. Your Bhutto also let us down, asking the army to control law and order! Didn't he know he was inviting martial law? Nationalizing even the cotton gins, ruining the economy."

Cyrus spoke bitterly, reflecting the sense of betrayal that straddled the country. Bottled up for thirteen years of martial law, their dreams had soared like genii with Bhutto's electoral victory. The return to democracy had made Pakistanis feel proud again, a part of the modern world community.

"And the idiot prohibited drinking in clubs!" Cyrus said, as if this measure capped all offenses. Lately political discussions with Cyrus took this turn.

"What do you mean *my* Bhutto; he was as much yours then! He was forced to by the *fundos*," Zareen retorted. "You know what he said when they accused him of drinking: 'Yes, I drink! Yes, I drink whiskey: not the blood of poor people!' " Zareen sounded absurdly theatrical even to herself.

Cyrus struck his forehead and groaned. "If you repeat that once more, you'll turn into a green parrot and fly away — or I'll commit suicide."

Surprisingly, the enforcement of prohibition was also a sore point with the wives in their intimate circle of affluent Muslim friends. Unable to congregate over drinks at the Punjab and Gymkhana clubs, the men drank instead at each others' homes. Since the men didn't drink after dinner, the food was served late — around midnight. The resentful wives sustained themselves on juices, sodas, and soup until then. Like Zareen, they felt they were forced to chaperone their men on an endless round of evening binges.

"It might do you all good to drink less," Zareen said, pursuing this train of association to its conclusion.

"I thought we were talking about Feroza," Cyrus said mildly, directing his wife to less hazardous ground. "Let's stick to that. I think Feroza is confused by these sudden switches in attitude. She probably feels she has to conform, be like her Muslim friends. There are hardly any Parsee girls her age. She wants you to be like her friends' mothers, that's all.

"I'll tell you one thing, though." Cyrus twisted his neck to follow Zareen's restless passage across the room. "Zia or no Zia, I'd much prefer she stay narrow-minded and decently dressed than go romping about looking fast and loose."

"What d'you mean?" demanded Zareen, turning from straightening the portrait of Zarathustra to glower threateningly at her recumbent spouse.

Cyrus lay back and shut his eyes.

"It's okay for you to run around getting drunk every evening, but I must stop wearing sleeveless blouses." Zareen's voice sawed like an infuriated bee's. She would have much preferred to shout, but she was conscious of the servants in the kitchen. "I know you think my sari-blouses are short, but they're not half as short as your sister's *cholis*. At least I don't run around flashing my belly button."

While Zareen paused to marshal her inflamed thoughts, her gaze fell on her husband's hapless shoes. She picked them up by their laces and dropped them, clattering, outside the door for the cook or ayah to clean. "If you think I'm going to cater to this . . . this *mullah*-ish mentality of yours, you're mistaken," she said, slamming the door shut. "I'll dress the way my mother dresses, and I'll dress the way my grandmothers dressed! And no one's ever called the Junglewalla women indecent!"

Zareen marched across the room and looked down at Cyrus. "More than can be said for this *mullah* lying on my bed. Get out of my bed, you *mullah!*"

At the sudden increase in the volume of her voice, Cyrus opened startled eyes and winced to see his diminutive spouse towering over him, arm flung out and finger pointed at the door.

Cyrus raised his head from the pillow, partly to defend himself against his wife's unexpectedly belligerent posture, and partly to display his hurt countenance. "I never said anything like that. Of course you're all one-hundred-percent decent women. They're my family, too, damn it. And you're my wife!"

He spoke with such vehement conviction and injured pride that Zareen became confused. She imperiously raised her chin — and found herself glaring sternly through the window at their gardener's bald head.

A ragged turban partially covering his baldness, the gardener stood on the tips of his bare toes on a rickety stool. He was trimming the gardenia hedge with a hefty pair of shears.

Zareen made a mental note to get him a pair of tennis shoes. She had also been late in getting the servants their yearly supply of coats and sweaters from Landa Bazaar, that bonanza of secondhand American garments that rained on Lahore every winter and clothed its freezing populace to bizarre effect. One occasionally saw bearded clergy and hardy villagers floating about in outmoded women's coats in startling colors.

"So?" Cyrus inquired amiably, stacking the pillows behind his back to sit up. The question was meant both to recall Zareen to her initial mission and to offer her a chance to disclose the strategy she had evidently worked out to countermand Feroza's alarming backwardness.

Zareen made an effort to compose herself. She bent to adjust the knob of the gas heater and, steering her thoughts back to their original track, sat down on the bed facing her husband. Her hands in her lap, her dark eyes filled with candor, she tilted forward. So intent was she on her choice of words that she was unconscious of the silken thrust of her caftaned bosom and its effect on her husband.

Cyrus slyly lowered his eyelids.

"Jana," Zareen used the endearment persuasively, "I think we should send Feroza to America for a short holiday. She'll be taking her matric exams in a few days. She's been so depressed lately. You're right, it's these politics." When Dorab Patel, one of the seven judges on the supreme court bench who was distantly related to Cyrus, had told them how Bhutto was being treated in jail, and how thin he'd become, they had all been depressed.

"I think Feroza must get away," Zareen continued. "Just for three or four months. Manek can look after her. Travel will broaden her outlook, get this puritanical rubbish out of her head."

Manek was Zareen's younger brother, only six years older than her daughter Feroza. Considering the furthest Feroza or Zareen had ever traveled was across the border to Bombay, the suggestion to send their daughter off by herself to the United States was audacious. Zareen looked at her husband anxiously.

Cyrus shifted his position to settle a little lower amidst the pillows. "Okay, I'll think about it," he said, and Zareen, who had expected a flat "no," was so taken aback that she walked meekly into the bathroom, bolted the door, and collapsed weak-kneed on the pot (as was her wont when she sought seclusion) to ponder the consequences of her anxieties.

She, of course, had no notion how relieved Cyrus was that Feroza hadn't told her mother anything about the incident

14

involving the young man. Cyrus wrapped a scarf cut from an old satin sari round his eyes and, curling up to a soft pillow, his mind full of silken images of his wife, drifted into sleep.

Almost a week earlier, Cyrus had driven home from his sporting goods store on the Mall to see his daughter talking to an unknown young man, a rugged-looking fellow with shirt cuffs rolled up to display broad wrists and thick forearms.

The winter days in Lahore are short. It was dark enough that February evening for Cyrus to look through the net screening into the sitting room without being seen. Feroza and the muscular youth sat across the room from each other, a large Persian carpet demarcating a salutary space between them. Feroza sat back in her stuffed chair demurely enough, but Cyrus did not like the way the young man leaned forward, sitting on the very edge of the three-piece sofa. His black leather jacket, crumpled and carelessly cast aside, looked reptilian and lewd.

By the time Cyrus had tiptoed past the window and entered the kitchen from the side of the house, his fertile imagination had bridged the distance between them. He envisaged the man's face close to his daughter's, his rough-trousered knees touching hers.

Zareen was out, and the bedroom lights had not been switched on. Cyrus parted the bedroom curtains in the dark and peeped through the split in the sitting-room curtains. They sat exactly as he had left them: Feroza well back in her chair, attentively listening, the young man on the edge of the sofa, earnestly talking.

The fellow was persuading Feroza to act in the annual Government College play. Obviously Feroza had refused, but the lout persisted. Couldn't he take "no" for an answer? Would he ask his own sister to act in front of that mob of sex-starved hoodlums?

Suddenly Cyrus sensed Feroza's hesitation, and before she might imprudently commit herself, he thrust his neck and fiercely scowling features through the curtains. Holding the maroon fabric clenched beneath his chin, he rumbled, "Who is this fat man? Tell him to get out!"

The young man, who was no fatter than any other weight-pumping Punjabi, was so startled by the apparition glaring at him out of the curtains that he froze on the edge of his seat. Feroza likewise froze against the back of hers.

Cyrus stared at the petrified youth for an interminable moment and then swiveled his fearsome eyes to Feroza. Some trick of light had turned them into sunken hollows and his own long, craggily handsome face chalky.

As abruptly as it had appeared, her father's hideously grimacing and pallid face disappeared.

Feroza shot out of her chair. "I think you'd better go," she mumbled, breathless, flushing with embarrassment.

The youth, gray behind his inherent tan, stood up looking dazed. Collecting his black leather jacket, he meekly followed Feroza through the double doors and down the veranda steps.

The young man's bicycle appeared to be perilously close to Cyrus's menacingly parked Volkswagen — as if the angry little beetle had been restrained at the very last moment from mangling the cycle to pulp.

Feroza fiddled with the shawl covering her chest and shoulders. Twisting on the balls of her feet, she finally looked up at the handsome youth. Her eyes unnaturally bright, her face abnormally red, she said, "I'm sorry, I don't think I'll be able to act in the play. You know how it is — my father won't like it. Please don't come again. Don't phone, please."

She sounded so formally correct, so hopelessly resigned, that, recovering his poise at this trusting display of her embarrassment and misery, the young man said, "I understand."

He looked into the almond brilliance of Feroza's eyes longer than he ought. Hearing a man clear his throat and cough significantly, the young man sighed. Almost shuddering with the effort, he slid his arms into the leather sleeves of his jacket and turned away to do up the zipper.

Feroza stood wretchedly as the wide-shouldered figure mounted his bicycle and, without once turning to look back, rode forever out of her life.

Chapter 2

Cyrus was glad Feroza had not discussed the incident with Zareen. Alarmed as Zareen was by Feroza's sudden timidities, she might not have agreed with his stand. But he would not have his daughter fool around with Muslim boys — or any boys.

Zareen did not know the way the men talked about women. He remembered how the boys at Saint Anthony's, his old school, and later at the Hailey College of Commerce had talked about bold girls who acted in Government College plays. He knew Zareen would be as irreconcilably opposed to their daughter marrying outside the faith as himself. But in her sudden crusade to champion "forwardness," Zareen might be complacent about Feroza's taking part in a play, believing their daughter would come out of the experience unscathed to marry a suitable Parsee boy at the proper time.

After seventeen years of marriage, Cyrus felt he understood his wife well enough. Zareen's complacence stemmed from her confidence in Feroza's upbringing. Every Parsee girl grew up warned of the catastrophe that could take the shape of a good-looking non-Parsee man. Marrying outside her community could exclude the girl from community matters and certainly bar her from her faith.

Further, Zareen was an innocent. Eleven years younger than Cyrus, she had married too young, at seventeen, to have any concept of the vagaries of the sexual drive and the tyranny of restrained passions.

And Cyrus had noticed Feroza's reaction to the husky youth. Although she was a year younger than Zareen was when she married Cyrus, Feroza seemed, somehow, more sexually ripe. What with the onslaught of television and the American and British videos, it was hard to keep young girls as innocent as one might wish. Despite all their careful indoctrination — Zareen's, her grandmothers', her aunts' — it would not be as easy to keep Feroza out of harm's way as they had presumed when, in keeping with the times, they had decided to let Feroza graduate before getting her married.

જ

The morning after Zareen had voiced her concern and presented her strategy to her husband, she was racked by doubt. Perhaps her suggestion had been too extreme. She developed one of her splitting headaches.

Zareen swallowed a couple of aspirins and, after instructing her ayah to see that no one disturbed her, lay down with a dark green silk scarf over her eyes. She took a few deep breaths and forced herself to become still and quiet. Muffled spurts of gnashing sound came from the gardener, who was mowing the lawn. Sparrows were creating a din in the gardenia hedge, and other birds whistled and trilled with astonishing sweetness. She heard them only when she shut her eyes. What did these birds look like, Zareen wondered.

Tires squealing, a car careened madly round and round the Main Gulberg Market traffic circle. Zareen awoke with a start. The shrill ferocity of the noise made her heart pound. The "Toyota crowd," Cyrus called them: the show-off newly moneyed. Although the title was apt, Zareen suspected her mother's new Toyota had contributed to her husband's inspiration.

In the quiet that followed, as if sleeping on the issue had helped solve her problem, it occurred to Zareen that she was in need of loftier counsel than the rational consolations Cyrus had served up. She recalled guiltily that she had not visited Data Gunj Baksh's shrine since Cyrus's appendectomy more than a year ago.

Zareen silently begged the Muslim saint's forgiveness for the neglect and, mentally ticking them off, prudently thanked him for his past kindnesses. Then, without thinking it the least bit strange, she switched to her own faith and said a short Zoroastrian prayer, invoking Sarosh Ejud, the Angel of Success Who Protects Mankind With Effective Weapons.

Given the medley of religions that exist cheek-by-jowl in the subcontinent and the spiritual impulse that sustains them, people of all faiths flock to each other's shrines and cathedrals. They came to the fifteenth-century *sufi*'s shrine from all over Pakistan, and before Partition they came from all over northern India. When Sikh and Hindu pilgrims from across the border in India visit the temples and *gurdwaras* in Pakistan, they never fail to "pay their respects" to the Muslim mystic known for his miraculous power to grant wishes.

By the time Feroza returned from school, Zareen's headache had been banished by her resolve to visit the shrine.

Zareen waited impatiently for Feroza to finish her tea and, saying, "Your matric exams are close. I think it's time we went to Data Sahib," hauled her daughter off to the mystic's tomb.

While they waited for the driver to park the car, Zareen and Feroza walked to the gargantuan vats of cooked rice lined up on the dirt path that ran along the rutted parking lot. The fine dust churned up by the cars had spread over the whole area and hung suspended in the air like a mist.

The stout, scruffy-looking man Zareen always dealt with greeted her. He shooed away the other salesmen crowding them and, pulling his vest down over his massive stomach and greasy *lungi*, led his customers to his stall.

Zareen stretched her neck and expertly sniffed as the man slid back the immense copper lids from the steaming vats of aromatic rice for her inspection.

The large yard in front of the green-domed shrine was as always teeming with pilgrims and beggars. A group of about ten Quawali singers, idly circled in front by squatting villagers, were vigorously clapping their hands and singing devotional songs in praise of the saint and his Beloved. Zareen and Feroza wondered if it was one of the more famous groups who performed on TV, but their salesman didn't think it was.

Holding aloft and punching a gigantic pair of tongs, a longhaired holy man, intoxicated by Godly fervor, twirled and circled the ring of onlookers, his dancing feet raising little puffs of dust.

Zareen selected one vat of sweetened yellow rice and one of aromatic rice with chick-peas. They covered their heads with their *dopattas* and stood to one side as a rapidly forming line of beggars, daily-wage laborers, and poor pilgrims held out their ragged shirt-flaps and veils for the ladled rice. After a few minutes, Zareen left the driver to oversee the distribution, and the women went into the lane of flowers and shrine shawls.

Carrying small newspaper-bags filled with rose petals and garlands, they were walking towards the steep flight of steps that led to the women's section when the news zipped through the premises like an electric charge that Zulfikar Ali, Bhutto's sister, was at the tomb.

Caught up in the swell of a sudden crowd, Zareen and Feroza were sucked deeper into the fragrant lane of flowers and gaudy shawls. They pulled their veils forward over their faces and draped them to cover their chests. Zareen held on to Feroza, her eyes stern and darting, warning off any mischief.

The men around them appeared to be well behaved. They kept their eyes averted and their hands to themselves. Ahead of them Zareen noticed three or four foreigners making their way, their light heads bare, and she recognized the profile of the woman from the American consulate. They often met at parties. The woman turned slightly and spotted Zareen. They smiled at each other, shrugging, and made good-natured, bemused faces at their common predicament.

Hanging on to each other, mother and daughter were swept to a place where the lane widened to form a square in front of the shrine. It was a side entrance to the saint's tomb that they had not known about.

The crowd was already quite large. Feroza and Zareen backed up to where a knot of women, their sympathetic, uplifted gazes intently focused, were holding their own against the pull and sway of the crowd. Zareen and Feroza raised their faces, and their eyes automatically fastened on the object of the crowd's intense scrutiny.

There was no mistaking her. The jailed prime minister's sister was standing at the top of an abrupt flight of steps. She had a thick, straight, tall body and the same features and glowing complexion as Bhutto's, except that the mold of her countenance was washed by a resigned melancholy they could not even bring themselves to conceive on her brother's confident and handsome face.

Her pain wrenched their hearts. Her head covered by a dun-colored *shatoose*, the woman clung to the latticework of a wide, ornate silver door. It had been installed by Bhutto some years ago, when he was prime minister, as a mark of his gratitude to the saint.

His sister's eyes were closed, and her lips trembled in prayer. The concentrated intensity of the crowd's focus appeared to form a nimbus about her, and her pale profile was clearly visible as she turned her head from side to side to press one cheek and then the other to the ornate gate.

The shouting and talking that had accompanied them in the narrow lane was muted in the square. The press and the restless movements of the assembly were also stilled.

In some form or other, the motley crowd standing in the square had heard the elite bitterly complain that Bhutto had aroused aspirations he could not fulfill. He had promised them *roti, kapra, makan* — bread, clothes, shelter — which he could not provide.

The images from the television screens, from posters, newspapers, and public rostrums, from the fermenting cauldron of the rumor mills, swirled in the minds of the crowd.

Some men shouted, "Bhutto Zindabad! Long live Bhutto!" and old women, bandy-legged in their loose *shalwars,* with labored, crablike movements, lumbered up the steps to pass their gnarled hands over his sister's shawl and sigh, "We pray for your brother. Don't fret, he will be free. Allah is merciful!"

∽

Feroza banged shut bedroom doors, whipped open car doors, and smashed shuttlecocks over the net at her startled adversaries. She avoided meeting her parents' evening guests, who had become almost a part of her extended family, and stopped listening to the political arguments that became so heated over dinner. On the few occasions she sat with them, she ventured to speak out, a contribution not encouraged in someone her age.

Their guests wrangled about Bhutto's deeds and misdeeds during his prime ministership, the Islamization of state institutions by

21

General Zia, and which way the verdict in the Bhutto trial for the murder of a political rival would go.

The arguments turned into acrimonious screeching sessions as the trial progressed. Every so often one of the guests would bang down on the table and loudly proclaim, "I'll never eat in this house again!" and promptly turn up the next evening.

They debated which of the panel of seven supreme court judges hearing the case were for Bhutto and which were opposed. A judge believed to be unbiased, one of the few whom Bhutto's paranoia had not antagonized, had a stroke and later died. Another reached the age of retirement.

One of the diners and imbibers asserted that the defending lawyer was in cahoots with the prosecution. Why else would Yahyah Bakhtiyar drag the trial on and on? Another confided that a Bangladeshi holy man had advised Bhutto's wife, Nusrat, and his daughter, Benazir, that Bhutto's stars would dramatically improve if the trial stretched into the New Year.

The day after their visit to Data Sahib's tomb, Feroza heard her mother's passionate voice above the squabbling. "It's immaterial whether the court finds him guilty or not guilty. The trial's a farce — the death sentence has already been passed. He will become a martyr!"

Feroza understood her mother. She had also witnessed the emotion of the crowd at the shrine.

The lawyer Feroza had always known as Uncle Anwar, tall, long-faced, bespectacled, the pace of the tic in his left eye betraying his emotion, shouted, "So what? Don't you know the bastard had drawn up a hit list? I was on it! You'll be surprised at those who were on it: many of them our friends. I'll see to it the bastard's hanged." He was the chief prosecuting attorney.

Feroza shut her ears. She was racked by the discord in her perceptions. Uncle Anwar was an old family friend, someone she trusted and couldn't bear to think of on anyone's hit list.

But a martyr's claim exerts its own logic. When Zareen came into her room to persuade Feroza to join them for dinner, Feroza told her, "I don't want to see their faces!"

Feroza spent the weekends at her grandmother's and most evenings at the houses of her classmates. She spent more and more time sulking and reading romances and detective stories in her room when she was home. She locked her door.

Zareen was used to Feroza's flashes of temper, which vanished soon after they appeared, but she was perplexed by the acceleration of her fury and the duration of her prolonged rages. Neither the pressure of the exams nor the political situation could account for her behavior. Feroza had usually taken her exams with an aplomb that had perturbed her parents. Politics, considering how it affected each individual's personal life, was a national passion. But previously the shared passion had always drawn the family together.

Cyrus guessed that Feroza's sulks and truculence might have as much to do with the expulsion of that Government College lout as with politics. But he kept his own counsel and prudently permitted his wife to fret and hypothesize.

Feroza's behavior recalled Zareen to the trials of Feroza's childhood, which she had all but (and gratefully at that) forgotten.

Feroza had been a stubborn child — with a streak of pride bordering on arrogance that compelled consideration not always due a child. Awed, Zareen often wondered where she got her pride.

Driven to exasperation, Cyrus had once spanked Feroza when she was about four. He stopped only when he noticed the blood on her tiny clenched lips. He never struck her again. It was a contest of wills over some trifling matter, and Cyrus had wanted his daughter to apologize. "Say sorry . . . say sorry," he had demanded, shaking her, pausing, and striking her. Lynx eyes blazing in her furious little face, Feroza did not cry or even wince. When he saw the blood, he gave up, horrified to have lost control over himself.

By this time Feroza was being invited to an increasing number of birthday parties, and Zareen discovered that she was also antisocial. Invariably the anxious hostess called the next day to inquire if she or someone else had offended the child? Feroza had stayed in her corner with her ayah and couldn't be coaxed to play games. She had not come to the table, even when the candles were blown out and the cake cut. No matter how hard they all tried, Feroza did not smile or say a single word all evening. At the end of this litany, the caller invariably sounded more aggrieved than anxious.

Zareen was mortified. She knew exactly what Feroza had put the callers through. Feroza's steady gaze and queenly composure was disconcerting in a four-year-old.

Zareen bought increasingly expensive birthday presents.

Then Feroza bit one child, scratched another, tore an earring off a little girl at school with part of her ear still in it, and Zareen's tepid belief in astrology became passionate. She discovered Linda Goodman's *Love Signs,* and the book became her gospel. The text appealed to her mind because it advised the mother of a Scorpio child to buy a strong playpen and stock up on vitamins, and to her heart because it instructed the mother to sit in the playpen taking vitamins, while the child wreaked whatever havoc it was destined to.

Absorbing the spirit of the text, Zareen barricaded herself behind the mental equivalent of a stout playpen. She learned to keep in the good graces of her daughter, bolting at the first hint of debate, and left the disciplining entirely to her mother. Cyrus had in any case decided to keep his hands, and will, off their daughter.

But Khutlibai, notoriously short on patience, could summon up oceanic reserves of that virtue where it concerned her granddaughter. And she lavished on Feroza a devotion that turned her youngest son, Manek, into an embittered delinquent and an implacable enemy of his pampered niece. With only six years between them, Manek and Feroza grew up more as siblings than as uncle and niece. Their hostilities often assumed epic proportions.

By the time Feroza was eleven, she had been forged by the alchemy of her uncle's sinister ingenuity, the burgeoning strength of her resourceful genes, and the extravagant care lavished on her by her grandmother into a wise, winning, and, at least overtly, malleable child.

Chapter 3

For three successive evenings, they waited for the urgent trunk call to America to materialize. Each time Zareen booked the call, the rushed operator gave her a cryptic number and informed her that she was thirtieth or fortieth in line. By the time Zareen finished asking, "How long will it take?" the operator had hung up.

On the fourth evening, Cyrus took matters in hand.

"Operator," he said with solemn authority, "there's been a death in the family. I need to speak to the party at once. His mother's died."

"I'll try my best, sir." The operator was properly grave and respectful of the bereaved family's feelings and of their need for urgency.

"You shouldn't have said that." Zareen's dark eyes were filled with reproach.

"Look," Cyrus said. "Do you want the call, or not? You have to be smart, that's all."

"If you're so damn smart, you could have got rid of your own mother. You won't feel so smart if mine finds out."

But before Cyrus could come back with a rejoinder, the phone rang. Zareen pounced on it. She heard the operator's remote voice say, "Call from Pakistan, sir," and Manek was on the line.

"We are sending Feroza to you," Zareen said.

"You don't have to shout just because you're twenty thousand miles away. I can hear you as if you were next door." Then, abruptly, Manek asked, "Why?"

"What d'you mean 'why'! For a holiday, what else. Just for two or three months . . . Is it okay? Will you look after her?"

"Yes, yes," he said. Taken aback by the unexpected call, and the even more unexpected nature of the call, Manek didn't sound as enthusiastic as he might have.

Zareen's heart sank. She had counted on his three years in the

New World to change him. He hadn't changed one bit. "What do you mean, 'yes-yes,' " she said. "I'm not sending my child so far if you're not going to look after her."

"I'll look after her. Don't worry, just send her." Manek had by now digested the news, and he sounded as hearteningly eager as Zareen could have hoped. She at once detected the new warm note in his voice and was as elated as she had been despondent a moment earlier.

"I'll look after her. Let me know when she's coming. I'll go to New York to meet her."

Having been away almost three years, Manek was eager to see anyone from home. He was overwhelmed by an entirely unexpected surge of affection for Feroza.

"Here," Zareen said, speaking into the receiver, as astonished by his sudden enthusiasm as she was by her conviction of his sincerity. "Talk to Feroza."

Feroza glowed. "I'm so excited," she shouted.

"Don't yell," Manek said. "You're puncturing my eardrum. Why do you Third World Pakis shout so much? Everybody's not deaf."

Feroza directed a bloodcurdling shriek into the receiver.

"Stupid girl. D'you know how much your screeches are costing your parents?"

"So? You're not paying. And what do you mean, 'Paki.' What're you, some snow-white Englishman?"

"Oh God . . . Please don't bring your *gora* complex with you."

"Why should I have a *gora* complex? I'm quite light-skinned."

"If that's what you think, you're in for a big shock."

"Black, brown, white are all the same to me," Feroza said, adopting her grandmother's expedient piety. "We are all God's creatures."

"Stop it. And listen — get rid of your 'white-man' complex before you come to America."

Feroza hugged and kissed her parents. She sought out her ayah and hugged her until the old woman trilled, "Stop it, *bus kar* — you'll squash my bones and ribs."

They heard the gentle click of the latch when Feroza finally went into her room; she did not lock her door.

Feroza slipped under her quilt fully dressed, her eyes wide open, her mind throbbing with elation. She was going to America! She found it difficult to believe. She repeated to herself, "I'm going to America, I'm going to America!" until her doubts slowly ebbed and her certainty, too, caught the rhythm of her happiness.

To the land of glossy magazines, of "Bewitched" and "Star Trek," of rock stars and jeans . . .

A week later Cyrus came home with a fat envelope containing the green-and-white Pakistan International Airlines ticket for Feroza. Feroza clutched the envelope to her heart, whirling with pleasure. And then, glancing at Zareen and Cyrus, she asked, "Why am I a Paki Third Worlder?"

∾

Zareen heard two sharp blasts of the horn; it was her mother's Toyota. By the time Khutlibai, shepherded by her chauffeur and bundled up in sari and overcoat, got out of the car, the welcoming committee of servants had flung wide the portals of the house and lined up to receive her.

The cook, the gardener, the ayah, and sundry children from the servants' quarters salaamed and fussed over Khutlibai with broad, affectionate grins. Zareen moved forward to kiss her mother on her discreetly rouged cheek.

Khutlibai received the kiss coolly. She inquired about each servant's health and their families' welfare, sharing good news with gladness, commiserating with misfortune, when she noticed the inflamed sty that almost shut the sweeper's son's eye. "Let me look at it," she said, putting on her half-moon glasses and beckoning to the boy, who was shivering in a lilac ladies' cardigan. Khutlibai placed her hand beneath his icy chin and peered at the sty. "How long have you had it?"

Embarrassed by the unexpected attention, the boy shuffled his bare feet and said, "It's been . . . maybe . . . a month."

The cook said, "I told his father to bathe his eyes with salt and hot water — "

"Not salt. Boric powder," Zareen asserted, attempting to stem the flow of advice. She knew how easily it could turn into a bizarre and uncontrollable flood.

Zareen had become averse to advice on medical issues ever since she'd had a kicking, braying, and protesting donkey milked for six consecutive days. This horror had been perpetrated at Khutlibai's insistence when Feroza had whooping cough. The Gulberg Market populace had gathered for half an hour each morning to witness the hazardous and noisy extraction of the two measly tablespoons of milk. Whoever said Cleopatra bathed in asses' milk didn't know what they were talking about. The daily pandemonium would have wrecked the pyramids and turned the Egyptians into twitching idiots.

The donkey's milk had proved no more effective than the rides in a glider advised by Feroza's pediatrician, Dr. Anwar. Zareen and Feroza had glided, petrified, in the eerie silence of the rarefied air above Lahore for an hour each day for ten days.

The whooping cough had run its course and petered out at the end of its natural cycle of six months.

"I know a remedy," the ayah piped up, transferring the shivering boy's chin to her calloused hand and squinting shortsightedly at the inflamed sty. "In my village we rub it with the sole of an old shoe."

"That too," Khutlibai agreed, "but the only sure cure I know is to tie a black thread on the opposite toe. Which eye is the sty in?" She drew the boy to her. "It's in the right eye." Turning to the ayah, she instructed, "Tie black thread — ordinary sewing thread will do — round his left big toe."

The sty disposed of, Khutlibai proceeded to issue the latest Junglewalla news bulletins. Her brother might visit next month from Karachi. Her cousin Sillamai had undertaken to construct a fire temple in Delhi. Her granddaughter Bunny had been second in her class; Behram had called from Rawalpindi to give her the good news, but the credit went entirely to her daughter-in-law Jeroo. She supervised the children's homework every single day. The comment was not lost on Zareen, who had no reason to doubt that her mother disapproved of the way she brought up Feroza.

Then, responding to the servants' queries about her health, Khutlibai said she was as well, by God's grace, as could be expected at her age. The cold hurt her old joints. Her heart sometimes beat too fast and sometimes too slow, but she did not complain. It was His will.

Khutlibai cast faintly skeptical gold-flecked eyes at the clear sky to indicate His whimsy and finally turned her attention to Zareen.

"Is your husband home?"

"He had his lunch and went back to the shop," Zareen said, alluding to Cyrus's sporting-goods business.

"Good." Khutlibai nodded, approving more her own timing in avoiding him than his diligence.

"Feroza hasn't come back from school, has she?" she inquired next.

"It's only two-thirty; her school is over at four." Zareen was wary now.

"Good, good," Khutlibai nodded cryptically. "I want to talk to you alone," she said and headed straight for the bedroom.

It was severely cold. That morning the grass on the lawn had been silvered with frost, and a fine crust of ice had formed on the Volkswagen. The gas fire was on in the bedroom. Zareen helped Khutlibai out of her coat, drew back the quilt on the bed closest to the heater, and, pushing the pillows against the headboard, prepared a snug roost for her mother. Khutlibai sank into the bed with a sigh. Removing her feet from her flat, black velvet slippers, she lifted them laboriously onto the bed. She leaned back on the pillows, and Zareen drew the goose-down quilt up to her waist.

Zareen sat down on the bed, facing her mother expectantly, and Khutlibai closed her eyes to indicate her exhaustion.

The frail old ayah, tightly wound up in her white cotton sari, had followed them into the room with a small bowl for Khutlibai's dentures. Khutlibai liked to remove them when she napped, which she sometimes did when visiting in the afternoon. The ayah asked if she could get Khutlibai some tea, or would she prefer hot soup?

"What kind of soup?"

"Chicken," Zareen cut in impatiently, and peremptorily dismissed the ayah with instructions to bring two cups.

Khutlibai's slightly protuberant brown eyes grew sharp in her foxlike face. She had light skin to match the eyes and wavy brown streaks in her graying hair. In a community where light color is at a premium, she had been considered beautiful in her youth. She was still a handsome woman in a comfortably corpulent yet imposing way. Her back, supported on the protruding pedestal of her ample rump — of which her deceased husband, Sorabjee Junglewalla, was reputed to have been both proud and fond — was broad and stately.

"What's this I hear," Khutlibai said, coming straight to the point and fixing Zareen with a challenging and retaliatory look, "Ping-Pong is sending my granddaughter to America?"

"Yes," Zareen said, "we are," ignoring the humor at her husband's expense and the jibe at his sporting-goods business. She knew Khutlibai used the nickname when she wanted to be particularly offensive, and Zareen's brusque dismissal of the ayah had offended her.

"Oh, it's *we*, is it? And Ping-Pong and *we* don't bother to consult with our elders or our older brother?"

"Mumma," Zareen was firm, "I'm the one who's keen that Feroza should go. Not Cyrus. I've had a hard enough time persuading him, and don't you give me a hard time too! You've no idea how difficult Feroza's been of late. All this talk about Islam, and how women should dress, and how women should behave, is turning her quite strange. And you know how Bhutto's trial is getting to her."

Knowing that nothing would alter Khutlibai's opinion as conclusively as her son-in-law's opposition to a plan, Zareen had looked straight at her mother and glibly lied.

"Is the poor child's behavior so unpardonable that you have to banish her from the country? If you can't bear to keep her, I will," Khutlibai said, rejecting the bait. The matter was of too much moment for her to be so easily diverted. "She's too innocent and young to be sent *there*."

The *there* was pregnant with unspeakable knowledge of the sexual license allowed American girls and the perils of drink and drugs. Compounding the danger were vivid images of rapists looming in dark alleys to entice, molest, and murder young girls.

"Where's the hurry to get rid of her? You'll be rid of her anyway once she's married."

"She's only going for three or four months, Mumma!" Zareen protested and explained at greater length how upsettingly timid and narrow-minded Feroza was becoming.

But Khutlibai had her own ideas about what was narrow-minded and what was not. And she was aggravated by Zareen's interpretation of events. "You've never shown much sense where Feroza's upbringing is concerned. Jumping into this committee with Nusrat Bhutto, and that committee with Mumtaz Karamat, and not bothering about the child. And then you get her all fired up with this political nonsense. Who is this Bhutto to you that you get so worked up? If I hadn't been around, God knows who'd have taught my granddaughter to pray. You've stopped wearing your *sudra* and *kusti;* you prefer to show your skin at the waist. What kind of example are you setting for your child?"

"Mumma, even Cyrus's sisters don't wear *sudras* beneath sari-blouses any more."

"If they jump into a well, must you also jump into the well?"

This was Khutlibai's standard rejoinder to arguments of this nature. She had an arsenal of favorite Gujrati homilies that she hauled out and fired like heat-seeking missiles at her stewing daughter. However standard or clichéd the homily was, it never failed to swamp Zareen's mind with crushing memories of childhood routs. Her eyes began to smart.

"But this I did not expect, even from you," Khutlibai continued. "Instead of guiding your daughter correctly and checking her behavior, you are encouraging her to go wrong! Thank God she has shown more sense than you, that's all I can say."

It was amazing how her mother could still turn her into a whiny little four-year-old. Zareen's lips were quivering. She cast her eyes down, sniffed, and stood up.

"Here, sit down," Khutlibai ordered, but the ayah came in just then with the soup, and Zareen escaped to the bathroom.

Zareen blew her nose and splashed her face. She looked into the mirror and was filled with pity for her reflection. Although her eyes

31

were puffy and her nose red, it was still an adequate face. Zareen turned slightly to look at the delicate curve of her cheek and jaw, at the slight bump broadening her nose just where it should to give her fine eyes an erotic quality, and was gradually reassured. She touched up her lipstick, sprayed herself with perfume, and, her heels sounding her resolution on the bathroom and dressing room floors, marched into the bedroom.

Zareen noted that her mother had removed her dentures. They lay on the bedside table in the bowl provided by the ayah. Zareen dragged the rocking chair forward and, maintaining a formal distance between them, sat down, defiantly rocking.

Khutlibai had poured her soup into the saucer and was making a blubbery sound as she drew in air with the scalding broth.

"Stop making that disgusting noise, Mumma." The rocking chair and her mother's dentureless mouth gave Zareen an advantage. "I hate it; it makes me feel sick. Sometimes I feel so ashamed of you."

Khutlibai stared at Zareen in utter amazement. She averted her eyes and sat forward, her back stiff. "I never expected to be insulted in my son-in-law's house!"

Khutlibai swung her feet off the bed and stood up with a swiftness remarkable in one who had sunk into it so heavily a short while before. Drawing herself up to her full five feet two inches, the lower edge of her shawl resting on the projecting shelf of her bottom, Khutlibai trudged with tragic and affronted majesty to the door.

Hastily putting her cup down and full of contrition, Zareen rushed to block her exit.

Khutlibai gave her daughter a brief hurt-puppy look and, moving her legs in a stiff, pistonlike gait that was curiously submissive and hopeless, trudged back to the bed. She sat down abruptly, her feet dangling, her shoulders fallen, her mouth collapsed, looking unbearably wounded, sapped, and mortified.

"Mumma," Zareen said, thoroughly abashed, holding out the cup with dregs of the broth still in it. "Here, finish this."

Her mouth slightly gaping, Khutlibai eyed Zareen meekly and obediently drained the contents.

Zareen sat down next to her and put her arm round her mother's shoulders. She pressed her wet cheek to Khutlibai's and, in an awkward, sideways motion, kissed her eyebrow and the hollow near her temple. Zareen felt her mother's cheek twitch with a persistent tic; it was as if the altercation had reversed their roles.

Zareen felt intolerably sad.

೮೨

At word of Khutlibai's imminent departure, the bearded cook, the sweeper, and the balding gardener, sporting new tennis shoes but no socks, gathered outside the main door.

Bundled up in her coat, shawl, and muffler, Khutlibai emerged from the bedroom, preceded by Zareen and followed by the ayah.

The sweeper, very dark and stocky with a mop of straight hair slanting rakishly across his forehead, clicked his heels, saluted, and stood at grinning attention. The message of Khutlibai's remedy had been conveyed to him. The boy stood next to his father, shivering in his ladies' cardigan, the black thread conspicuous on his left big toe.

Instead of her usual chuckles and affectionate banter, Khutlibai smiled in wan approval at the toe, which was beginning to swell on account of the tourniquet and was turning blue in the cold.

The dejected angle of Khutlibai's head, and the motion she made to touch it, indicated to the sweeper that though she appreciated his antic attention, she was unable to respond as she usually did because of unwonted circumstance.

The sweeper at once became serious and, gesturing with reassuring, open-palmed motions of his hands, inquired, "Is everything all right, *baijee*? You are visiting after so long; have you forgotten us? If we have offended in some way, I beg forgiveness."

Khutlibai affectionately stroked the grubby jacket covering his arm, saying only, "Live long, son." Then, gathering all the servants in the orbit of her tragic gaze, she commented, "You know how it is. It is not good policy to visit a son-in-law's house too often. It is better for all concerned this way. Our elders knew what they were about when they made such traditions. May God never show us the

33

day when we might need to depend on our married daughters and son-in-laws."

The servants murmured agreement and deferentially touched their foreheads. The blast of a musical horn from a passing minibus on the road appeared to further salute the wisdom of her utterance. Zareen looked away, prim and remote.

Khutlibai reached into her handbag and, licking the tips of thumb and forefinger to separate the crisp fifty-rupee notes, distributed them among the servants. The blue-eyed Pathan chauffeur, who had the fierce loyalty and light skin of the tribes in the northern areas, shepherded his charge into the car, lifted her shawl clear of the door, and shut it.

The servants hung around to wave good-bye. Zareen stood a little apart, unsmiling, and, as soon as the car began to move, strode inside.

Cyrus's car turned into the drive almost immediately after. The cook opened the Volkswagen door, salaamed, and took the briefcase from him.

Cyrus located his wife in the bedroom. "Old lady's been visiting?" he inquired, removing his jacket and tie.

"Umm."

"Had a bit of an accident I think . . . Her blue-eyed boy knocked down a cyclist. I heard him swearing."

Zareen glanced at him briefly to indicate her interest.

"Don't think he was hurt," Cyrus assured her.

Zareen stopped paying attention and picked up his jacket.

"You're in a good mood," Cyrus remarked. "What's the old woman been up to?"

"What can she be 'up to'?" Zareen's tart voice expressed her displeasure.

"From the grins on the servants' faces, Queen Victoria's been dispensing largess."

"You can't grudge them the odd tip."

"I don't grudge them anything. It's just that every time she comes and goes, there's a minor insurrection. Last time the sweeper asked for a raise. Before then the cook demanded a new stove. God knows what it'll be today. The gardener will probably ask for more manure."

"Poor thing, she hardly comes because this is how you talk!"

"You know I'm always polite to her. Next time I won't rush about trying to make her comfortable if this is your reaction to the effort I make."

"You think she doesn't know how you talk behind her back? She's more sensitive than you think."

"Sensitive!" On his way to slipping into his pajamas, Cyrus briefly flashed his bottom at his spouse to express his opinion of his mother-in-law's sensitivity. He resumed his seat on the bed, darkly saying, "This house is chock-full of her spies!"

"Look, I'm not interested in your paranoia!" Zareen shouted. Banging the dressing room door shut, she darted into the bathroom and occupied her all-purpose perch.

☙

Khutlibai phoned the next morning. Could Zareen visit her? She would have come, but it wasn't proper to visit a married daughter day after day.

"Mumma," Zareen said. "Nobody cares about such things anymore."

"Whether they do or do not, I will do what is right."

"You know Cyrus loves to see you," Zareen said warmly. "We don't care much for old-fashioned thinking; you know that."

"Yes, yes. You and your Ping-Pong are the only modern ones in the whole world . . . We are all stupids."

Zareen was relieved. Her mother had recovered from her heart-rending docility of the day before.

But when Zareen drove to the sprawling old colonial brick house on Punj-Mahal Road the next afternoon, Khutlibai greeted her on the whitewashed veranda in a subdued and chastened manner. Although she had grown up in the old bungalow, Zareen did not feel comfortable in it anymore. In fact she could not bear to be in the narrow room with the tall walls that had been hers for so many years; it had been completely repossessed by a gloomy battalion of Khutlibai's old cupboards.

Khutlibai and Sorabji Junglewalla had moved into the house, which was brand-new and considered modern then, straight from their honeymoon in Kashmir in 1940. The house had been completely renovated in two phases, once during Sorabji's last years and once after his death, when a portion of the dining room roof, with its parallel rafters, came crashing down on a summer's night.

Zareen followed her mother inside. Khutlibai was being hospitable and was treating her daughter with the consideration she reserved for friends and acquaintances. She was also wearing her dentures, something she often neglected to do if only her daughter was visiting.

Khutlibai bustled about in her velvet slippers, fetching and slicing the cottage cheese she had made from buffalo's milk that very morning, opening cabinet drawers to pick out the best silver and the daintiest napkins. Ordering her ancient cook, Kalay Khan, who looked like a butler left over from the Raj in his white tunic and red cummerbund, to bring tea and onion *pakoras,* Khutlibai ushered her daughter into what she preferred to call the drawing room.

The walls of the drawing room were decorated with dour portraits of dead ancestors, and the massive round-topped gold frames were hung with fragrant jasmine garlands. As always Zareen stopped before the arresting portrait of her great-grandmother Putlibai.

The life-size face tipped forward almost at the level of Zareen's eye. The photographer had caught the yellow eyes in the gaunt, high-cheekboned face in a miraculous shaft of light, and the magnified irises glowed as if alive. The piercing eyes dominated the portrait, the room, and the aged house with their eerie amber luminosity.

Zareen respectfully touched her bowed head to the icon. Raising her eyes, she saluted also her arrestingly handsome and noble-looking great-grandfather Faredoon Junglewalla, whose larger portrait hung above Putlibai's, safeguarding her in death as he had in life.

Both figures were enshrined in family legend. The pioneering couple, accompanied by Putlibai's mother, Jerbanoo (a remarkably tempestuous lady whom Khutlibai was said to take after), had traveled from their ancestral village in Central India to Lahore by bullock cart at the turn of the century. The family business, a provision and wine store, was founded by Faredoon Junglewalla during the British Raj, its fortune vastly augmented by his son, Behram. Zareen muttered a short prayer for the benefit of all her ancestors' souls.

When the two women were comfortably ensconced on the drawing room sofa before their TV trays, Khutlibai again broached the subject that occupied all her thoughts: when was Feroza going to America?

"Next Friday," Zareen said, giving her mother a stealthy sideways look. She was sure Khutlibai already had all the information she required from Feroza. She must also know how eager Feroza was to go, and how excited. Zareen waited for her mother to direct the dialogue to suit her sense of occasion.

"And where will she stay? Who'll look after her? I'm so worried: a raw, unmarried girl traveling so far by herself. Have you made proper arrangements? Will she stay in a good, safe hotel?"

"Of course not." Raising supercilious eyebrows to mark her irritation, Zareen looked away deliberately. "Why should she stay in a hotel when she can stay with her uncle? She will stay with Manek. I have talked to him. He will come to New York to receive her. He'll take good care of her. Now don't worry."

Zareen was aware, at the periphery of her vision, of the slowly dawning creases of astonishment beginning to wreathe her mother's mobile features. She braced herself.

"Manek?" Khutlibai sounded astounded. "You're going to leave her care to Manek? God help the child!"

And Khutlibai brought her considerable histrionic abilities to bear as well on what she said next. "Don't you remember how he chased her all over the neighborhood with a shotgun? Luckily she wasn't seriously injured. And how he made her run round and round the compound, cracking that hunter's whip of his? Ask me how many times I've had to save her from being maimed. I didn't tell you this, but one time he helped her up a tree and began sawing off the branch she was sitting on! I'll tell you how he will look after her. He'll push her into the nearest well!"

"I doubt there are any wells in America," Zareen said dryly. She was already beginning to feel battle-weary.

But Khutlibai was in full throttle. "With no one to look out for her, he will bully her to his heart's content. No," she switched to emphatic English, "I will not permit it to happen. I will put my foot down!" Khutlibai raised a leaden leg and clumsily thudded it down. The flimsy TV table tipped precariously. Zareen and Khutlibai both reached out to prevent the dishes from crashing.

"It's all right, Mumma, I'll get it." Zareen said, bending swiftly to retrieve the teaspoons, forks, and spilled *pakoras* from the carpet.

Khutlibai looked on, flustered and contrite.

Quick to grab the unexpected advantage she had suddenly gained and in the same warm tone of voice and reassuring manner, Zareen said, "Mumma, I wish you could have heard Manek yourself; if only it weren't so difficult to get through to America. I could tell he's changed! He sounded quite *responsible* and *dependable*. I think he has *matured!*"

Zareen's liberal and impressive use of English words, and the conviction vibrant in her voice, communicated to her mother some part of the excitement and awe she had felt after her conversation with Manek.

"I think he's going to surprise us all," Zareen said, surprised by the emotional charge in her voice. Simultaneously her eyes filled with tears of relief and thankfulness at the thought of the alteration America had wrought in her brother.

The new subtleties Zareen had detected in the modulation of Manek's voice had indicated self-reliance, a novel consideration for her anxieties and feelings, and an even less-expected ability to actually reassure her and convince her of the sincerity of his intent to look after Feroza. These nuances in the inflection of his vocal cords had been absorbed by Zareen's eager ears as promising signs of the evolution that a stay in the mind-broadening and character-building horizons abroad was meant to confer upon the unrefined native sensibility.

All this was quite apart from the blooming of genius an expensive education (in Manek's case at M.I.T.) was expected to ensure.

All Parsee boys, by virtue of their demanding roles as men, were presumed to be geniuses until they proved themselves nincompoops. And since the community's understanding of genius was inextricably knit with the facility to make money and acquire a certain standing — even if only within the community — the men generally measured up. The community bristled with financial, business, engineering, doctoring, accounting, stockbrokering, computing, and researching geniuses.

Not being burdened with similar expectations, the girls were not required to study abroad. If they persisted, and if the family could afford it, they might be affectionately indulged. It was also expedient sometimes to send them to finishing schools in Europe, either to prepare them for or divert them from marriage.

Chapter 4

They had phoned Manek with the flight details two weeks before
Feroza was due to leave. Manek assured them he would be at
Kennedy Airport when she arrived and would take good care of her.
He instructed Feroza to do her duty-free shopping at Dubai
Airport, since it was the cheapest. He did not require much persua-
sion to disclose what he would like, namely a cassette player and a
camera. He gave her the brand names and particulars of each.

Like most Parsees, who know very little about their religion,
Feroza had a comfortable relationship with the faith she was born
into; she accepted it as she did the color of her eyes or the length
of her limbs. The day before her departure, Feroza drove their blue
Volkswagen to the trendy new *agyari* in the Parsee colony. She
visited the fire temple about four or five times a year: on the three
New Years the Parsees celebrate according to different calendars;
on Pateti, which is the last day of the year; and on special occasions,
like her impending voyage.

Zareen could not accompany her because she was having her
period; her presence would pollute the temple.

The *atash* — the consecrated fire in the *agyari* that is never permitted to go out — had been lovingly tended for eighty years by
mobed Antia and his son, who was also a *mobed*. The holy fire had
been moved about two years ago, with due reverence and ceremony, to be housed in the new *agyari* near the fashionable Liberty
Market in Gulberg. The old location behind the Small-Causes
Court had become congested, and the traffic of tongas, bullock
carts, and lorries that jammed the narrow lanes made the approach
difficult.

Feroza honked to alert the priest of her presence. He lived in
special quarters built right next to the temple. As she walked past,
Feroza noticed the large padlock on his door and was disappointed.

Feroza liked to hear the priest chant her family's names during the *Tandarosti* prayer for good health. He recited the prayer slowly and with a solemn majesty that caused each word to resonate with sacred significance beneath the dome of the inner sanctum and the soaring vault of the hall.

Feroza also liked to watch the priest, luminous in a froth of starched white robes, decorously feed the fire with offerings of sandalwood from a long-handled silver ladle.

The narrow side door of the *agyari* was open. Feroza covered her head with a scarf, daubed her eyes with water from a silver jar, and performed her *kusti* in the lobby. As she unwound the sacred thread girdling her waist and retied the knots in the front and the back, she asked Ahura Mazda's forgiveness for every ignoble thought, word, and deed she was guilty of and prayed that she might have the good thoughts, the eloquent tongue, and the strength to perform the deeds that would advance His Divine Plan. Having thus girded her loins in the service of the Lord, she entered the circular hall fragrant with sandalwood smoke and frankincense.

Feroza lit an oil lamp and saluted the enormous framed portraits of departed Lahori Parsees and, removing her shoes, knelt before the marble threshold of the inner sanctum. The walls and dome of the small, round room imbued the space with a mystic aura and provided an appropriate foil for the *atash* as the manifestation of God's energy.

Feroza lay her forehead on the cool marble and requested the Almighty to protect her during her long journey overseas and to make her visit to America happy and successful. Then she solicited His blessings for herself and for all members of her family. Taking a pinch of ash from a ladle placed on the marble step, Feroza daubed her forehead with it; she already felt as if she had shed all impure thoughts.

Feroza took a few steps backwards and, holding her palms together, raised her eyes to the *atash*. The holy fire glowed serenely on its bed of pale ashes in a round tray on top of the fire altar. The altar was like a gigantic, long-stemmed silver eggcup with a turned-out lip. The embers of the larger logs gleamed through a lattice-work of freshly arranged sticks of sandalwood at the level of her eye. Someone had made an offering, Feroza thought; the priest must have left just before she came.

Feroza whispered her prayers and gazed devoutly at the small flames licking the crisscross of sandalwood, and, suddenly, she felt the spiritual power of the fire reach out from its divine depths to encompass her with its pure energy. She was at once buoyant, fearless, secure in her humanity. And as the lucid flame of the holy vision illumed her mind and was absorbed into her heart, she felt herself being suffused with God's presence. She felt He was speaking to her, acknowledging her prayers.

Feroza's spirits leapt with exultation. Bowing her head in gratitude, she moved to a side window and, pressing her radiant face to the polished brass bars, chanted the happy little *Jasa-me-avanghe Mazda* prayer. Although she recited it in the hallowed Avastan language of the Gathas, she knew its meaning from the English translation in her prayer book:

> Come to my help, O Ahura-Mazda!
> Give me victory, power, and the joy of life.

&

Seven cars drove up the cemented drive to the welcoming portals of the Ginwalla residence at approximately eleven o'clock the following morning. Set deep in its carved frame, the door had been painstakingly transported a couple of years ago from the neglected *haveli* of bygone *nawabs* to grace the Ginwallas' new residence. Zareen had hung her prized possession with strings of white roses and decorated the entrance with festive designs of fish and flowers pressed from small perforated tin trays containing powdered chalk.

Since it was Friday, the Muslim sabbath, Cyrus was home. Debonair in an ivory raw silk *shalwar-kamiz* and matching woolen waistcoat, Cyrus led the guests — mostly relatives, Parsee friends, and a sprinkling of close Muslim friends from their nightly round of parties — into the front lawn, boxed in by thick gardenia and rose hedges. The farewell was an almost ceremonial occasion and, as such, an essentially Parsee affair.

42

Feroza sat amidst her well-wishers, too excited to touch the food in the plate on her lap. Behind her the white roses, their velvet petals still cradling dew, gleamed against the bottle-green hedges as if fashioned from mother-of-pearl. Her younger cousins, particularly the girls, gaped at her in awe — when they were not running around noisily — made bashful by her sudden importance.

Feroza's voluble aunts looked proud and exhilarated, as if they had a share in the adventure she was embarked upon. Their loud, cheerful voices drowned out the clamor of the scooter-rickshaws and minibuses and the cries of the hawkers and of men brawling on the street. The Ginwalla bungalow was just off the enormous roundabout of the Gulberg Main Market.

A formation of parrots streaked overhead in a chutney-green flurry and disappeared in the thick foliage of a mango tree next door. A couple of crows hopped on the garden wall, alertly turning their heads this way and that, their beady eyes on the food table. They cawed raucously, and two other crows joined the party on the wall. Between them they set up such a racket, spreading news of the banquet to sundry other crows, that Cyrus, withdrawing from his pocket a large cambric handkerchief and waving it, loped to the wall shouting, "Shoo, shoo!"

A few guests were gathered at the long buffet table covered with lace tablecloths. Armed with a duster, her stiletto heels sinking in the grass, Zareen kept the flies off one end of the table and her eye cocked on the kites wheeling high above like vigilantes of the enormous azure sky. She hoped the duster and the crowd would keep the kites, which up close were as big as chickens, from swooping down on the food.

Zareen had wrapped the rich *palu* end of her yellow *tanchoi* sari round her neck to free her movements. Except for her gold bangles, her shapely arms as well as her velvety midriff were defiantly bare. Since Feroza was too excited and Khutlibai and Cyrus too busy talking to and serving the guests to notice or comment, Zareen did not get to deliver the retorts she had prepared.

The wizened little ayah whisked the flies at the other end of the long table. She obligingly lifted the net doilies, trimmed with beads, from the dishes when the guests wished to help themselves to the food. It was the usual auspicious-occasion fare: sweet vermicelli sprinkled with fried raisins and almonds, thick slices of spicy fried salmon, and fruit. Round stainless steel platters contained yogurt as firm as jelly, upon which a thick skin of clotted cream had formed. The yogurt had been sweetened and set the night before and strewn with red rose petals just before the dish was carried out. Deep silver dishes heaped with plain white rice and the special-occasion yellow pureed lentil — the combination known as *dhan-dar* — formed the main course. The aroma of the fried fish and spices hung in the scented air, whetting appetites. Emptied dishes were promptly replenished by the bearded and harried cook, whose portly frame was mummified in a white apron that reached almost to his ankles, specially stitched for the occasion by the nearsighted ayah.

The children ran everywhere, drinking colored sodas directly from the bottles, and the women, flaunting a slightly risqué air, drank Murree-beer-and-7UP shandies. Cyrus's unabashedly fat sister-in-law, Freny, who lived twenty-five miles from Lahore in Kot Lakpat, persuaded Khutlibai, who hated beer, to try a little of the mixed brew.

The men strutted on the lawn with their froth-topped beer mugs as if they were toting weapons. They had the jaunty, faintly guilty mien of men who are up to mischief — and that despite the Drink Permits in their pockets.

Once the food and drinks were consumed, the bustle to and from the garden increased. Feroza went in to brush her teeth and check her last-minute packing. Her two bulging suitcases stood in a corner of her room. She slipped a cardboard cylinder containing a handsome poster of Bhutto, right arm raised and mouth arrested mid-speech, into one of them.

Zareen examined the silver prayer-tray to ascertain that it contained everything needed for the auspicious *sagan* and placed it on the small, brass-inlaid hall table.

In the garden, Khutlibai was regaling relatives with the latest family health and news bulletins. Cyrus's mother, Soonamai, a thin, bamboo-straight, wonderfully dignified, and tactful lady, sat next to Khutlibai, obviously enjoying her company. The two shrewd old women got on very well when they saw each other, which, by tacit agreement, was not often.

Soonamai visited Cyrus and Zareen only rarely because of her dependence on Rohinton, her eldest son, to transport her from Kot Lakpat, where she lived with him and his redoubtable wife with so much discretion that Freny considered her mother-in-law her best friend.

Suddenly an indefinable noise stopped their breaths. Almost at once they realized that the Market mosque's stereo system was being tested. The air was blasted by a cough. And when the assistant *maulvi* cleared his throat in a loud "ahun-haam!" with impressive squelchy undertones, the feat was broadcast from the eight most powerful stereo amplifiers in Lahore, mounted right on top of the mosque's minaret.

The *maulvi* made a few announcements that rent the peaceful afternoon, "A girl, age five, who answers to the name of Shameem, is missing. She is wearing a red cardigan and gold earrings . . . A boy, age three, who answers to the name of Akhtar, is missing. He is wearing a white shirt and blue knickers . . . ," and then the Main Market *maulvi* proceeded to shred the afternoon completely, when, accompanied by a children's choir, he began to sing religious songs.

The guests gathered on the Ginwalla lawn all had their own street-corner mosques with their own resident *maulvis* and stereo systems, but they had never heard such a nasal, grating voice or been subjected to such uninhibited disregard for the esthetics of a tune. The assault on their ears was intolerable. They could hardly hear themselves speak. Since it was Friday, the head *maulvi*, his invited cronies, and sundry bearded cheerleaders could be counted on to keep the stereo system booming all afternoon.

It was pointless sitting outside. Led by Khutlibai, followed by Soonamai, the party drifted indoors. In any case, it was time they thought about leaving for the airport.

In her trendy new denim *shalwar-kamiz* and cashmere cardigan, Feroza stood on the little wooden pallet in the sitting room, happily receiving travel money envelopes and hugs.

Khutlibai, who had modestly hung back because she was a widow, was persuaded by Zareen and Soonamai to launch the good-luck ceremony. She stood before her granddaughter while Zareen stood at hand, holding the prayer-tray. Khutlibai put her thumb into the red paste in a silver container and left her imprint on Feroza's forehead. Feroza leaned forward accommodatingly, and Khutlibai pressed the rice she held in her palm on Feroza's forehead. Quite a few grains stuck to the drying paste, and Khutlibai was pleased. It meant as many blessings on the child.

She next popped a lump of crystallized sugar into Feroza's mouth, handed her a coconut, and bestowed a long list of specific blessings. May you return home safe and soon. May you marry a rare diamond among men. May you have many children and become a grandmother and a great-grandmother, and live in contentment and happiness with all your children and their children. May you live a hundred years and always be lucky like me, and happy and God-blessed . . . Aa-meen!

Then she garlanded Feroza and finally, expertly cracking her knuckles on her own temples to remove the envious and evil eye from her lovely granddaughter, stepped back.

Soonamai's turn was next. One by one the aunts came up, performing a much shorter version of the ceremony, mainly blessing and hugging Feroza and presenting envelopes anointed with the auspicious red paste and thick with cash. The uncles also gave her hugs, while the cousins, fingers stuck in mouths and noses, looked on with envy.

At a little after two o'clock, a stately cavalcade of nine cars, their chassis swinging low from the loads of passengers and luggage, drove out of the gates of the Ginwalla residence.

Feroza sat snugly ensconced between her grandmothers in the Toyota. Covering their heads with their saris, stroking Feroza's arms and thighs, the two old women prayed for her safety during her dangerous voyage and for her protection from unknown perils once she reached her destination. She knew from their sibilant whispers and inclination to rock that they were going through the proscribed seven *Yathas* and five *Ashem Vahoos* for the benefit of the traveler.

Sudden tears welled in Feroza's eyes. She brushed them away impatiently. It wouldn't do to have a pink nose and swollen eyes before all the people coming to see her off at the airport. She looked out the window to divert her attention, and all at once it struck her that she was going far from Lahore, from the sights, the sounds, and the fragrances that were dear to her, from the people she loved and had taken for granted. Her vision grew inward and, in a strange dreamlike way, expanded to accommodate a kaleidoscope of images of the entire city and its surrounding green fields.

The sky was still a deep, translucent blue, paling only round the sun, and in the imaginatively telescoped collage of her insight, the sun's amber light nestled on the brown waters of the shallow Ravi and glowed on the marble domes and minarets of the Badshahi Mosque. It shone on the warren of narrow streets and on the wooden balconies of dilapidated buildings, and just as the glowing *atash* in the temple had sunk into her heart and filled it with its holy warmth the day before, Feroza felt that the dazzling sun today warmed the hearts and bronzed bodies of Lahore's seven million inhabitants.

The brand-new, tree-lined boulevards and palatial bungalows, the ancient Moghul fort and the ancient mausoleums, the new gardens with new fountains, floated radiant in Feroza's multidimensional vision. It was her city. A beautiful, lushly green and luminous city, and she would miss it. Feroza felt the warmth of the sun nestle on the back of her head. She would miss Lahore, and her family.

But there were many splendid cities beneath the same caressing sun that she wanted to look at, many new faces in the teeming world she wished to know and love as much as she loved her classmates and her family.

Feroza shut her eyes and recited the ancient prayers from the Avesta that her grandmothers had taught her, her heart already in a tumult of nostalgia and fantastic anticipation. Even though she had not understood a word of the extinct language of the Sacred Book, Feroza had blind faith in the power of its verses and imbued them with whatever exalted concepts and spiritual longing her soul and emotions periodically required. Her maternal uncle, Behram, had given her an Avesta in Roman English, with an English translation of her prayers, on her fourteenth birthday. Feroza was enchanted by their poetry and not the least bit disappointed by the meaning, despite the esoteric significance with which her imagination had endowed the words. In fact the translated verses embodied her inarticulate exaltation.

A little clutch of schoolgirls from the Convent of the Sacred Heart was already waiting at the airport. They held delicate strings of pearly jasmine buds that curiously matched their own aura of pristine innocence. They clung together, shy smiles twitching on their lips and in their eyes, leaning on one another as if each was incapable of walking by herself, the little bunch a unified entity. Some were bolder, and the painfully shy ones clustered behind them. They were all holding onto or in some way touching each other, fiddling with clothes, adjusting their long, chiffon *dopattas,* pushing back and smoothing stray wisps of dark hair.

With twittering, birdlike cries, they welcomed Feroza and absorbed her into their collective midst as soon as she got out of the car, their slender fingers with painted tips fluttering above her head like beige butterflies, messing her fine hair as they hung the jasmine garlands on her. They giggled, nervously remembering to restrain their improper merriment, aware of the eyes attracted like magnets to their sheltered youth and the wealth that burnished so much unattainable loveliness. Every short while, one or the other would exclaim "*Hai!*" or a shocked "*Alllll-ah!*" or "*Hai Allah!*" and let escape a peal of quickly constrained laughter. Everyone could tell their talk was full of wicked mischief and innuendo. They spoke in Urdu, with the odd word or sentence in English tossed in so naturally it blended with the rhythm and the consonants of Urdu.

By an odd coincidence, most of the girls had a touch of green, gold, gray in their gorgeous eyes, and the same shy collective light shone out of Feroza's tawny irises as they leaned on each other like yielding saplings, touching, touching.

The party from the house formed another cluster near them and watched Feroza's friends and Feroza with tender smiles and alert, protective expressions. Suddenly Cyrus's brother Rohinton, a huge, stern, and taciturn man, took a couple of determined strides and planted himself in front of two men who were picking their teeth and ogling the girls with brash, kohl-rimmed eyes.

The men moved away, more stolid than docile. As custodian of the girls, the uncle was within his rights. Next Rohinton, accompanied by Zareen's brother Behram who had turned up from Rawalpindi with Jeroo, stalked a wide circle round the girls, demarcating perimeters. Their austere, threatening glares peremptorily dispersed the oglers and loafers.

Arms akimbo, massive chest thrust out, Freny also stood guard. Behram's sleek wife, Jeroo, who was addicted to chiffon saris and to fiddling with her pearls, stood with her, primly glaring about and on the lookout. They noticed a bunch of college students staring at the girls and making remarks. Mimicking the girls' gestures, two young men draped themselves about their giggling friends, smoothing their cropped hair as if they were long tresses and adjusting their imaginary scarves.

The aunts marched up to them. "Oye, shamelesses! Don't you have mothers and sisters? Go stare at them!"

The students ducked and, pretending to scold and thump their comrades, facetiously saying, "Sorry an-tee, sorry an-tee," pushed and shoved each other away, quickly dissolving in the crowd.

They were all grouped in a huge hall, with bunches of people gathered round departing kin like orbiting satellites. Since they were all taking the same flight to Karachi — from where some, like Feroza, would fly to other countries — there was a mad and tearful scramble to say good-bye when the flight was announced. The girls' hands reached out, reluctant to let go as Feroza pulled away, giving the impression of stretched, elasticized bodies being torn apart.

Feroza was kissed and hugged and whispered to by every member of the Ginwalla party and was now absorbed into the Parsee pack. Feroza put an arm each round Zareen and Khutlibai. Soonamai stood near them, straight and dignified. She had already hugged Feroza and held her granddaughter's small hand and pliant fingers pressed to her wet eyes. No one was dry-eyed. Zareen and Khutlibai daubed their eyes with soggy handkerchiefs; and Cyrus, who had wound his long arms round all three, briefly removed them to blow his imposing nose.

Khutlibai, Zareen, and the aunts were whispering breathlessly, as if Feroza's fate hung on the flurry of last-minute instructions they were imparting: "Don't talk to strangers; and never, ever look into their eyes!"

"A man asked your uncle Behram, 'What is the time?' and when your uncle looked at his watch, he hit him on the head and took away his watch and wallet."

"Someone asked your Rohinton *kaka* for a cigarette, and when he stopped to say, 'Look, my good man' — you know how your *kaka* talks — 'I am a Parsee; Parsees don't smoke,' the ruffian pointed a knife at his fly and took away his watch, wallet, and Bally shoes!"

"If anyone talks to you, just look straight ahead and act deaf."

"Don't accept anything to eat or drink from strangers. It may be drugged. God knows what they will do to you."

"Give Manek the letter first thing you do . . . and don't worry, he'll take good care of you," said Zareen, and Khutlibai promptly added, "If he doesn't, *sock him one!*" She winked, causing a rivulet of tears to run down her soggy cheeks.

Feroza laughed and hugged her grandmother, wondering where she'd gotten that from — one of the American series featured on TV, most likely.

Cyrus had already given Feroza one hundred American dollars (purchased on the black market), and so had Khutlibai. The khaki-clad porter wheeled Feroza's suitcases past the security men at the checkpoint and signaled to her to follow. Feroza showed her ticket, and as she went past the uniformed men Cyrus's last message — in English except for one Gujrati word — rang out: "I've sent Manek enough *doria* for you. Take it from him."

Few in Lahore understand Gujrati, so Parsees use it as a secret language when the occasion demands. Conversation about dollars purchased on the black market in the presence of security men is such an occasion.

Feroza's happy little face suddenly grew theatrically wan. She shook her head in dismay and spread her hands in a hopelessly defeated gesture. She mouthed the words, "Why him?" and, in a dumb charade, pointing at her breastbone, delivered the message that was clear to Cyrus, "*You should have given it to me; you know how difficult Manek can be.*"

Cyrus made a sheepish and contrite face, and Zareen lightly spanked his shoulder twice for Feroza's benefit.

Other passengers were crowding behind her. Weighted down with hand luggage and travel documents, Feroza was pushed away, frantically waving good-bye.

Chapter 5

Feroza hugged the adventure of her travel to America to herself throughout the flight. As she hurtled through space, she became conscious also of the gravitational pull of the country she was leaving behind. Her sense of self, enlarged by the osmosis of identity with her community and with her group of school friends, stayed with her like a permanence — like the support that ocean basins provide the wind- and moon-generated vagaries of its waters. And this cushioning stilled her fear of the unknown: an unconscious panic that lay coiled somewhere between her navel and her ribs and was just beginning to manifest itself in a fleeting irregularity of her heartbeat.

Feroza beamed at the women passengers and directed at the air-hostesses a gratitude that infused their drudging routine with the glamour that had attracted them to the profession in the first place. They were delicately pretty girls, their smiling faces framed by fawn scarves edged with orange, expressly designed for them by Pierre Cardin in Paris.

The PIA flight touched down at Dubai, Paris, and Frankfurt. Feroza bought the cassette player and camera for Manek at the Dubai Duty-Free. Later that evening they landed at Heathrow Airport in London. The transit passengers were instructed to leave the plane with all their hand luggage and proceed to the transit lounge. The flight for New York would take off at two in the morning: a layover of six hours.

Feroza was juggling her hand luggage and the duty-free packages, wondering how she would carry them all off the plane, when a properly polite Pakistani voice addressed her in English:

"*Jee*, can I help you carry something, *jee?*"

"It's all right." Feroza glanced at the well-built youth for the briefest moment before sternly averting her face to address again the problem of her multitudinous hand luggage.

Just as Feroza concluded she'd been too cavalier in refusing the proffered help, the polite voice said, "Excuse me, *jee*," and a navy blue cardiganed arm shot out beneath her nose to hoist the shoulder bag and cassette player from her seat.

The youth stood back, holding Feroza's bags and restraining the tide of passengers banked behind him, and Feroza stepped into the aisle with the insouciance of one accustomed to such homage. This austere and regal behavior was expected of her. A more amiable attitude might be misconstrued.

Feroza was engrossed in an Agatha Christie murder mystery in the transit lounge when a familiar, tentative voice said, "*Jee* . . ."

Feroza looked up with a start. The brawny youth in the navy blue cardigan, accompanied by another properly respectful young man, stood before her.

"Can we get you something to drink, *jee*? A Coke, or tea? A sandwich?"

An ominous bell, accompanied by her grandmother's voice, sounded an alarm. Feroza at once said, "No." And a split second later, "Thank you."

They did not look like the kind of strangers who'd spike her Coke with drugs.

"It's a long wait, *jee*." The youth was unobtrusively insistent. "We wondered if you'd care to join us for a *gup-shup*? It'll help pass the time?"

"I'm reading. Thank you," Feroza said primly, and at once regretted her decision.

Nose ostensibly buried in the Agatha Christie paperback, Feroza sat in the lounge feeling lonely. The transit lounge hummed with subdued conversations and the fretful cries of children. It wasn't long before Feroza drifted into a romantic daydream of the swarthy young man with the reptilian leather jacket who had been so peremptorily banished by her father from their sitting room. Her adolescent fantasy cast him in the role of her persistent fellow traveler, and the traveler in the role of the insistent Government College student. As the competing images of the young men alternated and the imagined relationships passionately intensified, the time whizzed by.

Feroza slept very little during the twenty-nine hours it took to arrive at Kennedy Airport. For the last eight-hour lap of their flight from London to New York, they had picked up a different set of passengers. Mainly American and European. Most of the Pakistanis who had boarded the plane with her in Karachi had disembarked in London. Already the space within the aircraft, the atmosphere, had changed, become foreign. And the barely acknowledged anxiety which had assailed her the past few days, that the trip might not after all materialize, vanished. She knew she had made it to America!

By the time the plane landed and Feroza nervously stepped from the fluted corridor into the airport lounge, she was triumphant and glowing. The orderly traffic of rushing people, the bright lights and warmed air, the extraordinary cleanliness and sheen on floors and furnishings, the audacious immensity of the glass-and-steel enclosed spaces dazzled her. Burdened and awkward with her belongings, she tramped behind the other passengers, faithfully following them to the lines that had formed at the passport check. She did not see the proper young Pakistani again; he must have been swallowed up and ingested by one of the myriad lines.

It seemed to Feroza that the sallow, unsmiling officer hunched behind the counter handled her passport with aggravation. Her Pakistani passport opened from the wrong end. There was a moment of confusion. Then, starting from the back, he leafed through the pages, studying them minutely. He asked her how long she'd stay, where she'd stay, who'd support her. When Feroza told him she would stay with her uncle, who'd naturally support her, he became very inquisitive about her uncle. Was he a United States citizen, resident, visitor? How old was he, what did he do?

Feroza suddenly became aware of the pale green, almost colorless eyes studying her with startling intentness. The official repeated the question: How would her uncle support her? Feroza was barely conscious of what she said. An odd expression flitted across the hostile man's sallow face. Thereafter he appeared to doubt everything she said with chilling implacability.

It was Feroza's first moment of realization — she was in a strange country amidst strangers. She became quite breathless. The line behind her was getting restive; some in it were already looking at her with the distrust and hostility reserved for miscreants.

"What's your uncle's name?" the man asked. He placed a slip of paper on the counter. "Write it down."

Feroza wrote: Mr. Manek Junglewalla.

The man tried to pronounce the name. Feroza smiled nervously and tried to help him with the pronunciation. There was no answering smile in the cold, unblinking eyes staring at her, or any change in the professional set of the stern mouth.

The official carefully wrote something on a white slip and tucked it into her passport.

"Show this after you collect your luggage. You must go for secondary inspection."

Without looking at Feroza, he handed back her passport.

Utterly confused by the cryptic instruction, her legs trembling, Feroza followed the other passengers towards the baggage claim section.

And, finding herself suddenly confronted by a moving staircase, she came to a dead stop.

A few people pushed past her to step on the escalator.

An elderly American couple, their cameras and reading glasses dangling from their creased necks, appeared to understand her predicament. They had square jaws and gentle, undefined lips with faint lines running up from them, and, as married couples often do, they looked alike. They smiled, sympathetic and tentative, and asked Feroza if she understood English.

At her nod and her diffident answering smile, the man took the duty-free packages from her hand and stepped onto the escalator. The woman took hold of Feroza's arm and, telling her to mind the cracks before the steps fell away, escorted her down the escalator. "Now get ready to get off," she said and held Feroza firmly round the waist. Taken unawares by the continuing momentum, Feroza all but tumbled when they got off.

Feroza laughed, apologetic, embarrassed, delighted by the unexpected adventure. And, after her chilling reception by the passport officer, deeply touched by the kindness. The woman gave her arm a squeeze, and, infected by the spirit of Feroza's wonder as her eyes again locked on the descending human cargo, the woman and her husband turned also to gaze upon the marvelously plunging staircase.

"Will someone be there to meet you, hon?" the woman asked as they neared the crush of passengers waiting by the conveyor belt.

"Oh, yes. My uncle," Feroza said confidently.

The husband spotted their luggage and pushed through the crowd.

"You sure, hon?" The woman was concerned, but anxious also to help her husband.

Feroza nodded quickly, gratefully.

"Now, you take care, honey," the woman said and, giving Feroza a quick hug, barreled into the thicket.

Feroza found her path to the conveyor belt blocked. Every time she tried to push through, someone or some piece of luggage intruded into the space, and she felt obliged to step back. She hovered on the fringe of the press, looking out for her luggage.

The crowd thinned as more people wheeled away their belongings. Feroza once again saw her gentle elderly friends. They were pushing their carts past parallel rows of ribbonlike customs counters. She followed their awkward, chunky figures with misting eyes and, in her heightened state of excitement and nervousness, an aching sense of loss.

Feroza's eye caught the stately progression of her outsize suitcases on the conveyor belt. Afraid they might disappear, Feroza quickly slipped through the crowd that had by now thinned and hauled them off. She was staggered by their weight. It was the first time she had needed to handle her suitcases. She wondered what her mother had stuffed into them to make them so heavy. She remembered the books and magazines Manek had asked for, and the heavy onyx gifts Zareen had wrapped in newspaper and carefully inserted among her clothes to prevent them from breaking.

After some moments of confusion, Feroza timidly approached an immensely tall black porter with a large cart, explaining, "My bags are very heavy . . . Can you . . . ?"

The porter barely deigned to flicker his lids. Gazing over her head, he trundled his cart to an elegant set of matching luggage spread before a woman in a discreetly gleaming white mink.

Feroza wondered if he had heard her.

She finally gathered the courage to ask another gray-haired woman, who appeared to bear a resemblance to the couple who had befriended her, where she had gotten her cart. The woman hastily pointed out a shining caterpillar of stacked carts.

Feroza was struggling to extract one when a breezy young man inserted a dollar bill in a slot and calmly walked away with the cart. Feroza stared at the slot-box in bewilderment. When another young man in patched jeans hustled up with the same intent, Feroza stepped right in front of the box, barring access:

"It's my turn!"

The slight, sunny haired youth's sneakers squeaked as he came to an astonished halt.

Feroza realized how strange and rude she must sound. She caught hold of the cart handle. "I don't know how to get this," she explained, half apologetic, half appealing for help. "Can you show me?"

The young man bent his sunny head to catch her breathy rush of words.

Feroza delved into her purse and fetched up a small wad of dollar bills of different denominations. She held them out for his inspection.

The lean young man's smoky gray eyes were appraising her with the kind of interest and candor that would have fetched him a bullet from any self-respecting Pakistani father.

Feroza lowered her lids in confusion and unwittingly acquired a haughty air. He was half a foot taller than her five feet four inches. He appeared to her a great deal taller.

Teasingly attempting to look into her eyes, aware of her embarrassment, the youth leaned closer. He smiled flirtatiously, warmly, and, talking in an accent she found difficult to follow but pleasing, showed her how to insert the dollar bill.

Feroza loaded her suitcases and hand luggage on the cart. Her mind was now filled with images of the slender young American and his candid, admiring eyes. How easily he had talked to her, his gestures open, confident. She wished she could have responded to his readiness to be friends, but she was too self-conscious.

That was it: the word she was seeking to define her new experience. He was unself-conscious. And, busy with their own concerns, none of the people moving about them had even bothered to glance their way or stare at her, as they would have in Pakistan.

Her wide-open eyes soaking in the new impressions as she pushed the cart, a strange awareness seeped into Feroza: She knew no one, and no one knew her! It was a heady feeling to be suddenly so free — for the moment, at least — of the thousand constraints that governed her life.

The two panels of a heavy exit door at the far end opened to allow a stack of crates to pass, and, suddenly, Feroza saw Manek leaning against the demarcation railing just outside the exit. One ankle comfortably crossed over the other, arms patiently folded, Manek had peered into the abruptly revealed interior also.

After an initial start, and without the slightest change in his laid-back posture, he at once contorted his features to display a gamut of scatty emotions — surprise, confusion, helplessness — to reflect Feroza's presumed condition. At the same time, he raised a languid forearm from the elbow and waved his hand from side to side like a mechanical paw.

Feroza squealed and waved her whole arm and, with a huge grin on her face, steered the cart towards him. She was so excited, and also relieved, to see him. Even from the distance, his skin looked lighter, his face fuller. He had grown a mustache. Knowing him as she did, his deliberate insouciance and the regal wave of the mechanical paw filled her with delight. He hadn't changed as much as her mother had imagined. He was the same old Manek, except he was really glad to see her. Three years of separation have a mellowing effect, make remembered ways dearer. Feroza's heart filled with affection for her former tormentor. Having no brothers, she hadn't realized how much she missed him.

A woman in a blue uniform, stationed at a counter to the left of

Feroza's path, checked her. "Hey! You can't leave the terminal. Your passport, please." She held out her hand.

The woman read the white slip inserted in the passport. She looked sternly at Feroza. "You must go for secondary inspection." Again the cryptic instruction.

The woman said something to a man in a white shirt and navy pants standing by her. She showed him the slip and gave him Feroza's passport.

Feroza noticed the "Immigration" badge pinned to the man's shirt. He motioned to her.

As she followed him, Feroza quickly glanced back at the exit to see if Manek was still there, but the heavy metal panels were closed. An inset door in one of the panels opened just enough to let the passengers and their carts through, one at a time.

Feroza followed the immigration officer past the row of ribbon-like wooden counters. A few open suitcases lay on them at uneven distances. These were being searched by absorbed customs inspectors who acted as if they had all the time in the world at their disposal. The weary passengers standing before their disarrayed possessions looked subdued and, as happens when law-abiding citizens are accosted with unwarranted suspicion, unaccountably guilty.

The man led her to the very last counter and told her to place her bags on it.

Applying leverage with her legs, struggling with the stiff leather straps that bound the suitcases, Feroza hoisted the bags, one by one, to the counter.

"Are you a student?" he asked.

"What?" The officer leaned forward in response to Feroza's nervous mumbling and cupped his ear. He had slightly bulging, watery blue eyes and a moist, pale face that called to Feroza's mind images of soft-boiled eggs.

"What're you speaking — English? Do you want an interpreter?"

"No." Feroza shook her head and, managing a somewhat louder pitch, breathlessly repeated, "I'm a tourist."

"I'm an officer of the United States Immigration and Naturalization Service, authorized by law to take testimony."

The man spoke gravely, and it took Feroza a while to realize he was reciting something he must have parroted hundreds of times.

"I desire to take your sworn statement regarding your application for entering the United States. Are you willing to answer my questions at this time?"

"Y-es," Feroza stammered, her voice a doubtful quaver.

Why was she being asked to give sworn statements? Was it normal procedure?

"Do you swear that all the statements you are about to make will be the truth, the whole truth, and nothing but the truth, so help you God?"

Feroza looked at the man, speechless, then numbly nodded. "Yes."

"If you give false testimony in this proceeding, you may be prosecuted for perjury. If you are convicted of perjury, you can be fined two thousand dollars or imprisoned for not more than five years, or both. Do you understand?"

"Y-yes." By now Feroza's pulse was throbbing.

"Please speak up. What is your complete and correct name?"

"Feroza Cyrus Ginwalla."

"Are you known by any other name?"

"No."

"What is your date of birth?"

"November 19, 1961."

He asked her where she was born, what her nationality was, her Pakistan address, her parents' address. Had her parents ever applied for U.S. citizenship? Was she single or married? Did she have any relatives in the United States? Anyone else besides her uncle?

"How long do you wish to stay in the United States?"

"Two or three months."

"What'll it be? Two months or three months? Don't you know?"

"Probably three months."

"Probably?"

The officer had placed a trim, booted foot on the counter; her green passport was open on his knee. His soft-boiled, lashless eyes were looking at Feroza with such humiliating mistrust that Feroza's posture instinctively assumed the stolid sheath of dignity that had served her so well since childhood.

"Where will you reside in the United States?" The officer appeared edgy, provoked by her haughty air.

An olive-skinned Hispanic customs inspector in a pale gray uniform sauntered up to them. He had rebellious, straight black hair that fell over his narrow, close-set eyes.

"With my uncle," Feroza said.

"*Where* will you stay . . . What is the *address?*"

The officer spoke with exaggerated patience, as if asking the question for the tenth time of an idiot.

"I don't know," Feroza answered, her offended expression concealing how stupid she felt, how intimidated.

"You don't know?" The man appeared to be suddenly in a rage. "You should know!"

But why was he so angry?

The Hispanic customs inspector with the unruly hair indicated a suitcase with a thrust of his chin. "Open it." He sounded crude and discomfitingly foreign to Feroza.

Rummaging in her handbag, Feroza withdrew a tiny key and tried clumsily to fit it into the lock.

"What is your uncle's occupation?" her interrogator asked. "Can he support you?"

"He's a student. But he also works at two other jobs to make extra money."

She had stepped into the trap. Didn't she know it was a crime for foreign students to work, he asked. Her uncle would be hauled before an immigration judge and, most likely, deported. She would have to go back on the next available flight. He knew she was a liar. She had no uncle in America. Her so-called "uncle" was in fact her fiancé. He wished to point out that she was making false statements; would she now speak the truth?

Feroza could not credit what her ears heard. Her eyes were smarting. The fear that had lain dormant during the flight, manifesting itself only in an unnoticed flutter of her heart, now sprang into her consciousness like a wild beast and made her heart pound. "I'm telling you the truth," she said shakily.

Sensing that some people were staring at them, Feroza cast her eyes down and took a small step, backing away from the luggage, wishing to disassociate herself from the intolerable scene the man was creating. The key dangled in the tiny lock.

"Open your bags," the customs inspector said, intent on his duty. He sounded hostile.

Feroza fumbled with the lock again. She unbuckled the leather straps, pressed open the snaps, and lifted the lid. She opened the other suitcase.

The contents had been neatly packed by Zareen, and Feroza drew courage from the well-ordered stacks of clothes, the neat parcels containing her shoes, the little plastic pouches holding her toiletries.

Like a shark attacking in calm waters, the customs inspector with the discomfiting accent plunged his hands into one suitcase after the other and rummaged callously among the contents. Odd bits of clothing spilled over the sides: a slippery stack of nylon underwear, a cardigan.

The man held up one of the parcels: "What's this?"

"Shoes."

He dug out copper wall plaques, heavy onyx bookends and ash-trays, the books and magazines Manek had asked for, a sanitary pad. He felt it as if searching for something concealed in it.

He brutally caricatured Feroza's shocked expression.

Feroza shut her mouth and looked steadily at the inspector — but hers was the steadfast gaze of a mesmerized kitten.

The man fished out and examined small vests, a brassiere.

Feroza became hatefully conscious of the tears sliding down her burning cheeks.

"What's the matter, officer? Can I help you?"

It was Manek. He was accompanied by another immigration officer.

"Who're you?"

"He's my uncle," Feroza said, gasping on an intake of air that was like a shuddering sigh. Faint with relief to have Manek with her, she gave his arm a squeeze and clung to it.

How was Feroza to know that Manek had been paged, his name announced over the loudspeakers in the reception lobby, interrogated? She sensed, though, that she had unwittingly incriminated him with her naive answers to the questions fired at her, and she was petrified.

"He's your uncle?" Feroza's cross-examiner looked incredulous. He turned to the officer with Manek, a moist-skinned, oval-faced man with a scanty thatch of damp blond hair. They could be brothers. "Does he look like her uncle?"

The officer with Manek twisted his glistening lips in a fastidious grimace: "No."

"I'm her uncle, officer," Manek asserted. He appeared composed, reliable, trustworthy.

Feroza was amazed. She could never have expected the Manek she knew to project these sterling qualities. And, at the same time, she was unutterably glad to have this confidence-inspiring new manifestation of her uncle at her side.

"No, you're not. You're too young to be her uncle. You're her fiancé. How old are you?"

"I'm twenty-two, officer." There he was again: meek, composed, worthy.

"What's the status of your visa?"

"I'm a student, sir. At M.I.T. I'm studying chemical engineering. I have an F-1 visa."

From his manner of speaking, Feroza guessed that he had been separately questioned. She was appalled at the official perfidy, and at herself for not having sensed it earlier.

"This woman just told me you work at two different jobs. The F-1 visa does not permit you to work. You have broken the law. You will have to face charges . . . You'll be deported."

"I work in the university cafeteria and at other odd jobs there, officer. She's just arrived, she doesn't know. I receive enough money from home for my tuition and living expenses. I can show you my bank drafts and statements to prove it. I can get a letter from my university. I work only for them. I'm permitted that."

The officer was skeptical. He turned to Feroza and, at the sight of her, at once reverted to his aspect of demon prosecutor.

"You are not eligible to enter the United States. You and your 'uncle' have concealed the truth. You're both lying. Isn't this man your fiancé? Aren't you here to marry him?"

Bewildered and scared, Feroza could not fathom what it was about her that got this pale man with his soft-boiled eyes so riled. She stared at him with her mesmerized kitten's eyes and shook her head.

"She's lying." The officer shifted his righteous, watery blue stare to his colleague, seeking confirmation.

His colleague nodded grimly.

"Aren't you engaged to him? Come on . . . you've come to the United States to marry your fiancé! You both plan to live here illegally. We know how to get at the truth. Stop lying!"

"I'm her uncle, officer. I cannot marry my niece."

"Are you kidding? We know y'all marry your cousins."

"Yes, officer; but not our nieces."

Feroza was crying again. Her whole body shook with her sobs and the effort to contain them: to restrict the ugly scene to their small circle and not advertise her misery and humiliation.

Meanwhile the customs inspector was holding up a lacy pink nylon nightie he had fished out of the bag. It looked obscene pinched between his spatulate fingers.

"Ah-ha!" Feroza's interrogator sounded triumphant. "The wedding negligee!"

Both immigration officers leered at the nightgown Zareen had packed at the last minute as if it was an incriminating weapon discovered at the scene of a crime.

"It's no use, your lying. Here's the evidence!"

The inspector repeatedly stabbed a soggy-looking, tapered finger at the offending garment.

Feroza, who had only heard of seeing "red," felt a crimson rush of blood blur her vision. Her tears, scorched by her rage, dried up. In a swift, feline gesture, she snatched her mother's nightgown from the Hispanic's stubby, desecrating fingers and said, "To hell with you and your damn country. I'll go back!"

Feroza flung the soft pink apparel into the bag and began stashing her other belongings on the swollen mound of disheveled clothes.

The inspector, who had displayed the nightdress and had it snatched from his hand, turned as if what was happening was no concern of his and drifted away.

Feroza's immigration officer had surprise stamped all over his soft, shiny face. By the looks of it, he might have exceeded his bounds.

"*Choop kar,*" Manek hissed into Feroza's ear, warning his niece to shut up.

"Look, officer, I guarantee she'll go back at the end of three months, or whenever her visa finishes." Manek turned to the immigration officer who had accompanied him. "I can get a letter certifying she's my niece. Here's my visiting card. I promise to send you a copy of my passport and visa and a letter from the university stating I don't work anywhere else. I will send you copies of the bank drafts from Pakistan."

The officer took the proffered card. Manek signed a form acknowledging that his statements had been correctly recorded. He was sternly advised to provide proof of his assertions as soon as possible.

Feroza also signed a form. The officer who had treated her so vilely just a few moments back was now conciliatory. Shaken by the yellow blaze of fury emanating from the eyes Feroza had inherited from Khutlibai, and confounded by the fierce dignity imparted to her genes by Soonamai, he even stashed a few of her belongings into her turbulent suitcase.

Once all the contents were back in, the officer brought the lid forward, marked it with chalk, and, after stamping Feroza's passport, handed it back to her.

Chapter 6

As the taxi drove out of Kennedy Airport, speaking in Gujrati Manek said, "You're the same old *uloo*. That was a damn silly way to behave. What if those chaps had packed us back to Lahore? You're in America now: you have to learn to control your temper. There are no grannies or mummy-daddies here to bail you out!"

What rubbish! Feroza thought. What had she ever done that might require her grandmothers or parents to bail her out of prison?

Aloud she said, "He insulted my mother! I couldn't stand the way that creep handled her nightgown."

"You'll have to learn to stand a lot of things in this world."

"Look. You didn't stand up for your sister's honor. So don't shout at me for defending her *izzat*."

"I'm not shouting," said Manek, managing with difficulty to keep his voice low and sound reasonable. "And you'd better forget this honor-shonor business. Nobody bothers about that here."

They remained silent in their respective places in the rear of the taxi. Feroza's profile, silhouetted against the wintry night outside, was a study in aristocratic umbrage.

"So, how's everyone at home?" Manek asked, after a while.

"Fine."

"Look, I've missed you all," Manek said. "Talk to me properly."

Impulsively he sought Feroza's hand in the dark and gripped it. It was icy cold and surprisingly soft, almost fragile.

Manek did something else he had never done before — he put his arm, stiff and awkward, round her shoulders.

"Are you feeling cold? Look, don't worry," he said with unaccustomed kindness, "it's all right. Immigration gives everyone a hard time. You should hear some of the stories! But that's behind us. We're going to have a great time. You'll love New York. I've planned it so we can spend a week here. Then we'll get back to Cambridge. If I get the time, we'll even go to Disneyland."

Immediately Feroza noticed the garlands of lights outlining the iron rhythm of the bridge they were racing along, the sumptuous red taillights of the cars ahead. Then she realized they had driven over other bridges, equally long.

And then they were climbing into a futuristic spaghetti of curving and incredibly suspended roads, mile upon looping mile of wide highway that weaved in and out of the sky at all angles so that sometimes they descended to the level of the horizon of lights in the distance that Manek told her was Manhattan, and sometimes they appeared to be aiming at the sky. Feroza saw ships in an incredible river. How deep the river must be to hold the ships.

Feroza couldn't credit everything her eyes saw. And, as excitement gripped her, she laughed, a clear laugh with modulations that suddenly informed Manek, more than the bodily changes he had noticed, that Feroza had grown into a woman — a desirable and passionate woman — in the three years he'd been away, and he'd have to look out for her.

He felt proud of his niece, happy and awkward.

"Vekh! Vekh! Sher-di-batian!" Feroza said in exuberant Punjabi, mimicking excited yokels pointing out the bright city lights from bullock carts. It was an old joke they shared with their young friends and cousins, except she now used it to express her own excitement at the extravagant display.

The sky and the air appeared to her to be lit up in a perennial glow that dispelled night and darkness and sleep, banished all things that did not participate in the happy, wakeful celebration of life.

It was almost two in the morning by the time the taxi deposited Manek and Feroza at the YMCA on Broadway.

Once they were in their room on the fifteenth floor, Manek, utterly exhausted, got into his pajamas and slipped into bed.

Feroza pushed the heavier of the two suitcase against the wall. "I don't need to open this till we get to Cambridge. It's got lots of gifts and things for you, but you'll have to wait."

Manek agreed: he had no wish to see its contents strewn about in the tiny room, or to repack the bulky suitcase. He knew what he'd asked for and the gifts could wait.

Feroza unzipped a canvas carryall, removed a nightdress and her robe, and began rummaging through its contents.

"Look, don't be so *pora-chora* at this time of night," he said, slipping into his old bullying tone. "Turn off the light and go to sleep. You can unpack in the morning."

Feroza fished out an intricately patterned fawn-and-blue cardigan and, saying, "Catch, it's for you," threw it to Manek.

Manek sat up in bed and spread it out on his comforter. "Not bad," he said.

"Your sister got swollen eyes knitting the Fair Isle pattern for you, and all you can say is 'Not bad'?"

"Very nice," Manek said, running his hand appreciatively over the soft wool; it had been a long time since anyone had bothered to pamper him.

Feroza, who had expected him to make disparaging comments, checked a caustic remark and tried not to show how surprised she was by his uncharacteristic behavior. She switched off the light and discreetly changed into her nightdress.

Just before getting into bed, Feroza slipped a gray-and-white snakeskin wallet under Manek's pillow. "It's from your mother," she said, but Manek was already asleep.

Outside their room, the night was full of unfamiliar smells and alien sounds that kept Feroza's eyes wide awake and her breath tentative. She fell asleep to the shrill, eerie cry of the sirens that patrol New York, just when she was convinced she would never sleep at all.

ભ

Manek slept late himself and permitted Feroza to sleep in her lumpy twin bed till noon. When he decided it was time she woke up, he sprang into an energetic bustle of noisy activity, accompanied by a stream of incessant chatter in Gujrati. Manek had not spoken Gujrati in so long. He relished each word and enjoyed the sound of his voice uttering the funny little phrases that have crept into the language since the Parsees adopted it almost fourteen hundred years ago, when they fled to India as religious refugees after the Arab invasion of Persia.

"Come, come, *boochimai*, up, up!" He called Feroza *boochimai*, an archaic Gujrati word for "little girl" she hated. "If you spread yourself out all broad and flat like this, your arms and legs will become loose." Imitating his mother's dulcet tones when Khutlibai indulged her granddaughter, he trilled, "Should I tell Kalay Khan to bring my sweetie tea and toast in bed?" and bullied and bundled his niece into her printed robe.

"Move your trotters, move your trotters," Manek prompted Feroza, as, groggy with jet lag and numbed by his chatter, she permitted herself to be shepherded towards the women's bathrooms.

When he had booked into the YMCA the day before, Manek had discovered that the fifteenth floor was reserved for married couples. The receptionist had asked him if he was going to occupy the room with his wife. Thinking on his nimble feet, Manek quickly said, "Yes."

The twenty-second floor was for women only. The rest of the building appeared to have been taken over by weirdos and winos, of various shades and races, who hung out on all the levels.

Armed with her toilet bag, Feroza tottered into the empty restroom and locked herself in a vacant cubicle. She heard a flush, but when she emerged she was alone. Feroza headed for one of the washbasins lined up against the wall and splashed her face with cold water. She removed her toiletries from the plastic bag and, leaning over the basin, began to brush her teeth.

All at once Feroza felt uneasy, menaced, as if she were being observed by someone or something dangerous. She had rolled up the sleeves of her robe, and the fine hair on her arms stood up. Feroza had not heard any sounds to indicate that another person was using the facilities. Assuming her imagination was playing tricks in her new surroundings and to dispel her irrational fear, she raised her head and looked into the mirror.

Feroza stood transfixed. A man's bloodshot eyes, his dark reflection, was staring at her. The face in the mirror was unself-conscious, speculative, hideously examining her not as a woman but as a specimen of the female gender. Feroza whirled around, swallowing her toothpaste.

The man's face suddenly broke into a cunning, lewd, brown-toothed grin. "How ya doin', baby? Ya wanna poke?"

Gripping the toothbrush like a weapon, Feroza reflexively scanned the room, looking for a route of escape. Her eyes lit on a pair of dark, very long feet. The bony toes, resting in shoddy rubber thongs, protruded from a toilet cubicle. The hairy shins disappeared abruptly behind the partly open half-door, giving the legs an eerily disembodied quality.

Hardly aware of what she was doing, Feroza snatched up her bag and tried to dodge past the threatening figure.

The man moved to block her path. "Howja like it if I rub it up against ya?" he said softly, his rank breath and strong body smell striking her like physical blows.

Feroza swerved and, banging against one of the half-doors, dodged past him. His hand brushed her back, but it was as if he touched to frighten rather than stop her.

Feroza took several wrong turns in the halls before she located their room. Completely out of breath, she hurtled in and gasped, "It was the men's bathroom!"

Manek was at the desk. Taken by surprise, he looked unsure. Then he said, speaking with quiet certainty, "I went to the men's room after leaving you. It's across the hall."

Once again Manek escorted Feroza to the door marked WOMEN. Feroza peered in cautiously. A short, middle-aged black woman was applying lipstick. Feroza's toothpaste tube lay where she had abandoned it.

Feroza quickly rinsed her mouth, brushed her hair, and applied Vaseline to her chapped lips. The woman, wiping her hands near the paper towel dispenser, smiled when Feroza looked at her and said, "How're you, honey?"

"Hi," Feroza said and added: "There was a man in the washroom. Two men. Just a little while ago."

"You tell the management, honey. There sure are creeps hangin' around. They talk mighty dirty, too. Now, you take care, honey."

Her drawling southern accent and syntax were hard to follow, but Feroza picked up enough words to understand the drift of what was said.

And sure enough, Feroza soon discovered that when she passed close to the men hanging around in the building, it was more likely than not they would mutter something obscene, fill her ears with the kind of abusive talk the man in the restroom had frightened her with.

Chapter 7

After a leisurely hamburger lunch at McDonald's, which left Feroza struck with wonder at the quick service and the quantities of fries, ketchup, and the ice in the Coke, Manek hauled Feroza off on a tour of New York. They rode the ferry to the Statue of Liberty and explored the iron innards of the stern figure presiding over the ocean. They gaped giddily from atop the Empire State Building midtown and the twin World Trade towers at the tip of the island. They strolled with the nannies and babies through the zoo at Central Park, marveling each time they lifted their incredulous eyes from the wild animals in their native habitats to the shimmering glass and steel embankments of the Manhattan skyline reflecting the sunlight.

And saying "Lift your trotters, lift your trotters," Manek hurried Feroza past the enticing window displays of dresses, shoes, sportswear, and jewelry on Fifth Avenue and Madison.

The next morning while Feroza was still in bed, Manek warned her that he was going to take her to a very special place.

Feroza took pains with her outfit, and after a frugal breakfast of bagels and cream cheese at the YMCA cafeteria, they rushed off to catch a bus.

Manek trotted Feroza in her high heels, turquoise *shalwar-kamiz*, and red overcoat through the narrow limestone-and-granite gorge of Wall Street. His face was radiant with an expression one expects to see only in holy places. "Do you know, more money changes hands here in one hour than in a whole year in Pakistan?"

"Really?"

Later that afternoon, when they inadvertently found themselves on Lexington Avenue outside Bloomingdale's, Feroza glued her nose to the plate glass, enchanted by the apparel on the skinny mannequins, the colorful patent-leather shoes, and the gleaming handbags. She refused to budge.

Exasperated and impatient, Manek said, "I wish you wouldn't waste my time gaping at junk."

"You call this junk?"

Feroza's voice was hushed with awe, and when she turned to him, her face was as reverent as his had been on Wall Street.

Feroza went into Bloomingdale's. It was like entering a surreal world of hushed opulence festooned by all manner of hats propped up on stands and scarves and belts draped here and there like fabulous confetti. The subtle lighting enhanced the plush shimmer of wool and leather and the glowing colors of the silk. Feroza felt she had never seen such luxuriant textures or known the vibrant gloss of true colors. And it was merely the entrance foyer that had affected her so.

Feroza moved amidst the dazzling wares, oblivious of Manek's grumbling rumbles. Disconsolate and defeated, he limped behind her like a weary ghost. It was hot inside. Manek removed his coat and glumly followed the direction of Feroza's gaze as she sought out other vistas, bewitched by further displays of merchandise that appeared to attract his witless niece with a suctionlike force. His heart sinking, Manek followed Feroza into the disorienting maze that he knew was specifically designed to snare harebrained spendthrifts like his obdurate charge.

"There's no logic to this place," he grumbled. "We could lose each other here. The damned place is like a spider's web, luring you in." And as Feroza, insensible of his counsel, floated deeper and deeper into the web of racks and counters, in desperation he cautioned, "Look, don't panic if you lose me. Just ask someone to point out the Lexington Avenue entrance and stand outside it. Will you remember that? Lexington Avenue."

Feroza nodded absently, and Manek's gloom deepened.

All at once Manek's nostrils flared and twitched. Slightly knitting his brow he sniffed, once, twice, like a bloodhound who has unexpectedly lit upon a promising trail, and with profound certitude he announced: "I can smell a *desi!*"

Feroza paid him scant attention.

"I bet there's an Indian or Paki in the room. One can smell a native from a mile." Again his nose twitched. "You wait here, I'll be

73

back soon," he instructed, and sleuthed off to prowl the twilight periphery of the elegantly embellished space.

Having carefully scouted the area with his nose, like a hound on a promising trail, Manek found himself exactly where he'd started.

"It's you," he said to Feroza, surprised. "You're the smelly *desi!*"

Feroza was shocked out of her trance by the accusation. She looked at Manek startled and uncomprehending. Her red coat lay on a stack of marked-down purses on a table, and dark stains marked the cloth under her arms.

"Don't you use deodorant?"

Feroza raised her arm and ducked quickly to sniff.

"I can't smell anything."

"You can't smell your own smell, stupid; people are going to start fainting any minute."

"It's this damned nylon-satin *kamiz*," Feroza said matter-of-factly. "It starts smelling if it becomes hot. I can't help it. As if you never sweat!"

"That's the trouble with you *desis*. You don't even know what a deodorant is, and you want to make an atom bomb!"

How could Feroza tell him of the countless times her mother and grandmother had soaked the underarms of her garments in an ammonia solution to get rid of the odor that clung to her clothes even after they were washed? It was an odor she was accustomed to, accepted by her young friends as natural to their years, and in summer they showered twice and sometimes even thrice a day.

Two hours later Feroza emerged with a pair of Gloria Vanderbilt jeans, a navy blue polka-dotted shirt, and a stick of deodorant.

ᥱᏽ

"I wish you'd learn to keep your eyes on things that'll benefit your brain," Manek said after he had dragged Feroza out of Bloomingdale's, "instead of clogging it with passing fancies and expensive habits. Did you have to buy Gloria Vanderbilt? Will anyone even notice the tag? Cheaper jeans would fit you just as well."

And, determined to indoctrinate his niece with culture and improve her mind, Manek quick-marched Feroza through a whirlwind tour of all the major museums in New York. Each time they were "done" with a museum, he scratched it off the tourist guide list with the ballpoint he kept tucked behind his ear.

They embarked on the cultural mission by covering a strip along Fifth Avenue, from about One-hundred-and-fortieth Street to the Sixties, and Manek pointed out the mansions of the famous that look out on Central Park. Feroza, who had heard of the Vanderbilts and the Carnegies ever since she could remember, was duly impressed.

Manek pointed out, with a trace of irony, that many of the elegant mansions had been made over into museums, and that the Museum of the City of New York had been built from scratch to resemble the made-over mansions.

They visited the Museo el Barrio, devoted to Hispanic-American art, and the Jewish Museum in the Warburg Mansion. The spectacular Guggenheim, with its impressive spiraling interior, delighted Feroza more than the paintings on its curving walls. They took a bus to the Museum of Modern Art and even dashed off to the Military Museum in the permanently docked aircraft carrier *Intrepid* on the West Side.

Manek and Feroza would begin the tour of each museum by exploring the main lobby, then peek into a few rooms leading from it, and hunt out the restrooms and snack bars.

Then they would walk or take a bus, preferring either means of locomotion to the sinister labyrinths of the subways, and rush off to another museum.

Feroza enjoyed the escalators they rode up and down, and delighted in being treated to a cup of tea in the Palm Room at the Plaza Hotel as much as she appreciated the length of the foot-long hot dogs in the cafeterias and delis.

If a display caught her eye or her imagination, as it did in the Egyptian and African sections in the magnificent Metropolitan Museum of Art, Manek became impatient and hurried her to some other section or work of art, remarking, "If you go into a trance in front of everything, we won't see New York in a hundred years. I'm not spending good money on your stay in the YMCA just so that you can vegetate. You'll have plenty of time to turn into a cauliflower or an okra once you're back in Lahore."

Manek was much more tolerant of her dalliance before the

dinosaurs and stuffed gorillas at the American Museum of Natural History on the other side of Central Park. In fact, at one point, Feroza gave him a little nudge and slyly remarked, "Let's move on before you turn into a gorilla or something."

Feroza, still disoriented by her sudden swing from Lahore to New York — a trajectory that appeared to have pitched her into the next century — and the ten-hour lag she had not yet adjusted to, had a surrealistic impression of blurred images: a kaleidoscope of perceptions in which paintings, dinosaurs, American Indian artifacts, and Egyptian mummies mingled with hamburgers, pretzels, sapphire earrings, deodorants, and glamorous window displays.

On the fourth day of her tour of New York, Feroza balked at the thought of visiting yet another museum and stubbornly insisted on window-shopping on Fifth Avenue and ogling the strands of pearls and diamonds displayed at Tiffany's. Manek, dragging her away by the scruff of her red-coated neck, preached her a catechism on the value Americans placed on time.

"Why is Pakistan so backward?" he asked.

Feroza knew better than to answer.

"Are we stuck in the Middle Ages because we were colonized? Because we are illiterate? Because we don't have enough technology to make atom bombs?"

Feroza, distracted by the elegant skirts and jackets displayed at Christian Dior's and worn by the assured women stepping briskly past in a variety of sneakers, started guiltily. Manek was looking at her with a curious expression. She promptly and obligingly agreed: "Yup."

"What's this new 'yup-yup' business you've learned? You're not a puppy!" Manek appeared to be disgusted and hurt. "You've not listened to one word I've said."

Feroza hastily caught his arm. The echo of his words lingered somewhere in her mind. "We're backward because we can't make atom bombs?"

"No," Manek said, instantly mollified, and happily continued airing his views as they were jostled among the throng of shoppers, office workers, pooper-scooping dog-walkers, and vendors on the pavement.

"It's because we squander time! It is the single most precious commodity besides money, and we act as if we are millionaires in eternity. But time is running out . . . and time will catch up with you. Then you'll say — "

Manek slowed down, hunched his shoulders, and, acting out his impersonation of an old and palsied Feroza, wrung agitated hands beneath his penitently bowed head: "Oh, Manek, I wish I'd done thissss . . . ! Oh, Manek, I wish I'd done thaaat, instead of wasting my precious time and money on idiotic baubles . . . Oh, Manek, I wish I'd listened to you!"

Manek was completely intoxicated by the rich brew of humor, wisdom, and histrionic talent he projected. A few alarmed tourists gaped at him because of the high-pitched and quavering sounds he emitted — no doubt wondering, Feroza thought, if he was one of the lunatics forced out of the notoriously over-full asylums of New York. But the native New Yorkers, pledged to their purpose, saw him only as an obstruction and swerved past, unheeding.

"By which time you will be toothless and penniless," continued Manek, "and it will be too late. You'll have squandered your life!"

Feroza was irritated by the gradual switch from the general to specifically herself. And embarrassed.

"Behave yourself," she scolded, turning round and stepping away from him. "People are looking at us."

"Oh, no!" Manek exclaimed in the same shrill, breathless contralto in which he had warbled earlier and ended his impersonation on the same quavering, indeterminate note: "They are Americans. They will not waste their time on ussss. Only illiterate natives like you, from Third World countries, waste time . . . "

Feroza felt her face flush. She aimed a swift kick at his shins, and when he cried, "Ouch! What're you doing?" she hissed. "You Third World native yourself! It's my time, and my life, and I'm answerable to no one but my parents and my God!"

And later that evening, when Feroza adopted the classic pose of the bemused New York tourist and bent back awkwardly to ogle the skyscrapers beginning to blaze their lights, Manek preened and glowed as if he were the architect of the fabulous city.

It dawned on Feroza that Manek was not showing her around

as much as showing off America. She observed him from the corner of her eye for a while, and, with the impact of a zap of lightning, it struck her that Manek might not want to return to Pakistan. She felt an unexpected and almost tragic sense of loss.

Feroza carried the conviction of Manek's impending severance like an ache within her as they ambled through the streets and avenues, heading in the general direction of the Y. Feroza found herself wanting to indulge Manek. She glanced at him frequently out of sad, affectionate eyes and cast the same melancholy gaze upon the very different world they had suddenly stumbled upon on Eighth Avenue.

It took a few moments for the difference to register, and when it did, Feroza's native curiosity became at once alert. She absorbed the sleazy atmosphere, rife with titillation and novelty, through all her excited and amplified senses.

Their spirit of daring and adventure heightened by a voyeuristic sense of guilt, Manek and Feroza walked past small dark video parlors flashing lewd advertising, interspersed by grubby pawn shops, cheap hotels, and bars. Manek knew the delis had sold the beer in brown bags to the furtive men who drank it slyly on the street.

"Look after your purse," Manek cautioned, and Feroza clutched her odds-and-ends-swollen handbag to her stomach as if it were a football and she the center forward about to be tackled.

"Not like that, idiot," Manek said, "someone will think you've got thousands of dollars in it . . . Just remain alert. Keep your eyes open, we are in a very interesting part of New York . . . See that fellow wiggling his bottom in the tight jeans?" With a slight inclination of his head, Manek directed Feroza's attention to a young man drifting ahead of them aimlessly. "He's a male prostitute."

Hugely satisfied by the astonishment unhinging his niece's jaw, he cryptically said, "You've a lot to learn, *boochimai*."

After a little while, it occurred to Manek that the lissome women with the plunging necklines and fabulous bosoms strutting about so gorgeously on high heels were transvestites. He nudged Feroza and, with an unobtrusive movement of his chin in their direction, whispered, "I think these are American-style *heejras*."

Feroza looked about with eyes widened to absorb knowledge nothing had prepared her for. Feroza was woolly about the distinction between eunuchs and transvestites, and the *heejras* in Lahore were about as different from these glamorous creatures as earthworms are from butterflies. The Lahori variety looked much more like men with long hair, many of them balding, dressed up as women. This made their coy antics ludicrous and amusing, perhaps only because she had been accustomed to seeing them as clownish figures since childhood.

Whether it was a mad June noon or a freezing midnight in December, come earthquake, flood, tear gas, or riots, if a son was born in a palace, hovel, or hospital, the *heejras* would materialize clapping hands, and hoarsely singing their congratulations. And sometimes they would claim a child as their own: they would know, no matter how secretly the baby was delivered, if it was a *heejra*, a fifty-fifty.

As they walked further, Feroza felt she had gained so much knowledge — of the type denied her in Lahore — in the past few days that Manek did not need to point out the pimps with their gold chains and open shirt collars or the miniskirted prostitutes who were decidedly less alluring than the elegant transvestites. Feroza also began to notice odd embraces and movements in shadowed spaces.

"What're you doing?" Manek said. "Don't stare, it's dangerous— they don't like it."

Standing in a dark corner, a young man in jeans, wearing a hooded jacket over his T-shirt, caught her attention. She noticed him because, unlike most people on the sidewalk, he was not merely loitering. He looked like he was there for a purpose: focused, alert as a panther — and as dangerous.

She observed other young men in their twenties and thirties, wearing jeans, sneakers, windbreakers, and warm-up jackets, occupying corners and recessed doorways, some of them darting from one place to another making brief contacts. It was like surveying a clandestine army of commandos. People seemed to converge suddenly on key figures and as swiftly move away, as if quick transactions were being accomplished.

Feroza felt a sinister prickling in her spine. She felt she had descended into a pit and was looking at something she was not meant to see.

A young man with a white face loomed abruptly towards her out of a dark doorway, and though his eyes were not clearly visible, she could tell they were fixed on her with such wariness and menace that she involuntarily gasped.

And then Manek had his arm round her and was quickening his stride to rush forward, pushing her to cross the street, saying, "Don't look at him. Don't look back. Try to behave normally."

It was not possible to cross the street because of the traffic. They had scuttled along the road some ways, and when they felt they were safely past the dangerous territory, they got back on the sidewalk.

Manek slid his eyes about furtively by way of example. "I told you, don't stare at people! Especially if they're doing something funny — it's an invitation to attack. They feel you're snooping, or violating their privacy. At least don't let them know you're looking. Avoid eye contact. That fellow was a drug dealer—very dangerous."

As Manek told her about lookouts, runners, and drug dealers — whatever little he knew about them embellished by his imagination — Feroza realized her earlier instinct to liken the young men to commandos was accurate. She had witnessed a subterranean army of the drug Mafia.

Except for a marked increase in the number of the human derelicts, who, Manek explained, were "bag ladies" and the homeless, Manek and Feroza were surrounded by the same cast of seedy characters as before.

Still on Eighth Avenue, they crossed Forty-second Street to the Port Authority bus terminal. The interior of the terminal appeared stark in the neon lighting, and from its squalid center sprang a fetid stench that made Feroza reel. She sensed the terminal was the infested hub of poverty from which the homeless and the discarded spiraled all over the shadier sidewalks of New York. Ragged and filthy men and women were spreading scores of flattened cardboard boxes to sleep on in the bus terminal.

Feroza was used to the odor of filth, the reek of poverty: sweat, urine, open drains, rotting carrion, vegetables, and the other debris that the poor in Pakistan had become inured to.

But those were smells and sights she was accustomed to and had developed a tolerance for. This was an alien filth, a compost reeking of vomit and alcoholic belches, of neglected old age and sickness, of drugged exhalations and the malodorous ferment of other sub-stances she could not decipher. The smells disturbed her psyche; it seemed to her they personified the callous heart of the rich country that allowed such savage neglect to occur. The fetid smell made her want to throw up. She ran out of the building, and, leaning against the wall of the terminal, began to retch.

"What's the matter?" Manek asked, and when Feroza raised her face for an instant, he saw the horror and compassion that mingled with her physical misery. She began to retch again, and Manek said, "Don't do that, you'll make me vomit too." He took her arm. "Come on, let's cross the street while the light's green."

They turned right on Forty-second Street, and Manek said, "So, you've seen now, America is not all Saks and skyscrapers."

Feroza blinked in the sudden glare of light from the cinema mar-quees advertising their titles: *Lustful Lucy Bangs the Boys, Behind the Green Door, Virgin Lust, Deep Throat.*

Forty-second Street appeared to have its own distinct character. A couple of shifty-eyed young men walked sideways besides them, furtively dangling gold chains and wristwatches. From the way Manek quickened his step, Feroza guessed they were selling stolen goods.

A grubby, bulky man with sloping shoulders sidled up to Manek and pushed a dog-eared flyer at him. He whispered something and Manek said, "I'm not interested, sir."

The man hurried his pace to keep up with them and continued shoving the flyer at Manek until he took it. Feroza glimpsed the words "massage" and "sauna" in bold type. The man frightened her. "Let's get out of here," she said, clutching Manek's arm.

"What's there to be afraid of?" Manek said, assuming an

exaggerated nonchalance. As another unsavory character made eye contact and started walking towards them, he said, "There's a bus stop a little further up — let's go."

They climbed aboard a bus and moved toward the empty seats at the back. The last row was occupied by a solitary bag lady with scraggly blond and gray hair and an unbuttoned overcoat. They backed off at once. The raggedy lady, wearing layer upon layer of unwashed clothing, was flanked by two large shopping bags that sat on either side of her like overstuffed watchdogs, and she gave off a tidal wave of an aroma that staggered them. The noxious smell staked out her domain as surely as an animal's territorial scent warns off intruders.

As she reeled forward between the aisles, Feroza again elongated her neck and made alarming retching noises. Manek hung back, preferring not to know her.

The bus was fairly full with a batch of middle-aged Eastern European and Russian immigrant women who cleaned the skyscrapers every night and couples on their way home from the theater or a restaurant. Manek and Feroza found seats in front.

They had barely settled down when the bus took a sharp turn and suddenly they were bathed in a shower of lights. Soaring billboards flashed their neon dazzle in blue, red, and green. Legitimate theaters advertised their fare, and Feroza noticed the billboards for *A Chorus Line* and *Cats* — remote and legendary musicals she had heard about and never even dreamed of seeing. White and yellow light spilled from restaurants and souvenir shops.

Feroza felt as if a stage set had been flipped around to reveal the glitzy and glamorous side of the ugliness and tawdry scenes they had witnessed on Eighth Avenue and on Forty-second Street.

"It's Times Square!" Manek announced, leaning across Feroza to look out the window. He turned his bright face to hers, and his eyes were shining.

Feroza was glad to be sharing her adventures with her uncle: Manek seemed to have shed the last vestiges of his adolescent jealousy of her. Her melancholy and fear flew out the window, and her lightened heart thrilled to the rhythm of the garish lights, to the

sight of Japanese tourists taking photographs, the vendors displaying jewelry, scarves, tacky T-shirts, and buttons. Feroza felt it all
represented a rich slice of the life and experience she had come to
America to explore.

A new lot of passengers climbed aboard the bus. Some, tourists
like themselves, were mildly drunk and flushed with excitement.
There were a couple of middle-aged, drunken men with tattoos.

Manek observed a respectable-looking family with teenage children. Manek had sold Bibles in the South one summer, and he
guessed right away that they were from the Bible Belt. After a tiring
day spent sightseeing, they appeared agog, stunned by their glimpse
of Sodom. The rest of the passengers consisted of some stoned kids,
flamboyant toughs who were also stoned, their shaved heads, black
leather accouterments and earrings proclaiming their sub-caste as
distinctly as caste marks on a Brahmin's forehead declares his. It was
a racially impartial mixture of black and white.

A tall, rail-thin young man lurched up the aisle and fell into the
two empty seats in front of Feroza and Manek. He appeared restless. The bus braked and then pitched forward, jolting back the
youth's blond head. He balanced himself by spreading his long arms
in an expansive, good-humored gesture, and at the same time, he
turned and glanced back.

He had an open, pleasant face, and Feroza noted with surprise
the distended pupils shadowing his light eyes. The kid was about
her age; he couldn't be more than sixteen. He smiled at Feroza, his
eyes wandering slightly, and said, "Hey, lady, I haven't eaten in a
week. D'you have any change so I can get some breakfast?"

Was he also addressing the passengers behind them? Feroza
wasn't sure. The indulgence and affection she had felt for Manek
earlier, when her heart had ached at the thought of his severance
from Lahore, was instantly transferred to the hungry kid. Again his
eyes wandered and, of their own accord, kept rolling up, showing
anemic white crescents as if he was about to faint from weakness.

Feroza reached into her handbag and stretched out her hand
with a dollar bill.

"He's spaced out," Manek remarked, eyeing the clear-cut profile of the emaciated youth with disgust and disapproval.

"Shush!" Feroza said, embarrassed.

"Why?" Manek asked. "Are you afraid of hurting his feelings? I'm not in awe of these trashy whites like you are." And, able to belch at will, Manek belched loudly, twice.

"I'm not sitting near you if this is how you're going to behave." Feroza stood up from the window seat and tried to edge past.

Manek pulled her down by the tail of her polka-dotted shirt from Bloomingdale's. "Sit, stupid. You must get over your *gora* complex. Once you know enough whites, you'll realize how ignorant and dirty they are, and you'll stop feeling sorry for bastards like him."

Meanwhile the emaciated young man stood up. Balancing his slender shanks against the seat, he spread his hands as if embracing all the passengers with his affectionate gesture. "Gee, lady," he said to Feroza with such rapture that he appeared to be lit up from within. "People are so nice!" He lurched past them, his dimples twinkling in little pools of reflected light.

"Thanks, pal," Feroza heard him say behind her and wondered how much someone else had given him.

"Would you give anything to a drugged *afeemi* back home? No, only a nice little kick in the balls."

Although Manek spoke quietly, Feroza was quite sure people could hear him. She turned away, furious. Manek glanced at her profile gone rigid with embarrassment and emitted a series of loud, chastising belches.

Chapter 8

Feroza insisted she would sleep late the next morning.

Feroza insisted on sleeping late every morning, but Manek, assuming the role of both lion and lion tamer, roared and growled until he awakened her. The previous morning, he had twisted his bed sheet into a rope and cracked it in the air until, reminded of the whip he used to chase her with, Feroza threw off her blanket and, grumbling, shoved her arms into her robe.

Manek accompanied her to the ladies' rest room and stood vigil outside while Feroza made sure there were no suspicious-looking legs lurking in the cubicles. Manek hung around for a few moments, warning off potential attackers with his presence. Sometimes he waited till she came out, particularly at night.

This morning, too, she mumbled and whined her protests.

When she finally unglued her eyes at Manek's insistence, Feroza found herself, from a distance of less than two inches, peering at a whorl of dark hair in Manek's left armpit. Manek hung above her nose, stretched out diagonally like an awkward gymnast.

Feroza promptly shut her eyes.

"Smell anything?" he asked.

"No. Get away."

Feeble with sleep, Feroza tried to push him. She felt the pressure ease from the mattress as Manek stood up.

"I want you to open your eyes for just one minute, then you can go back to sleep."

Feroza did not believe him.

"I'll pour water on your face if you don't."

Resistance was futile. Feroza discreetly opened an eye.

"Watch me." Manek quickly rubbed the deodorant stick into his hairy armpit. "This is how you use it. Then put on your clothes. Okay?"

Feroza nodded.

"Okay. You can go back to sleep."

Surprised at her unexpected reprieve, Feroza sat up in bed to mumble sarcastically, "Thank you!" and promptly ducked beneath her comforter.

"I'll have breakfast, get some papers photocopied, and be back in an hour."

Feroza's head jiggled beneath the comforter to indicate she had heard.

She was dressed by the time Manek returned.

He told her it was time he wrote to his university and the banks to sort out the trouble with the immigration authorities at the airport. He also needed to work on a neglected term paper. He suggested that Feroza have her breakfast, window-shop around the YMCA, and return by one-thirty. He would then treat her to a tour of an art gallery.

By now Feroza was longing to saunter into shops and browse at her own pace in New York instead of rushing from museum to museum. She gave a yelp of pure joy, and Manek prudently removed the larger bills from her purse, saying, "Now be alert. Don't get lost. And don't look dopey, or someone like that white monkey you squandered your wealth on yesterday will mug you."

"I can look after myself, uncle dear," Feroza asserted with so much confidence that Manek leaped out of the chair, grabbed his niece by the arm and warned, "Look, don't show off. If something happens to you, I won't know what to do. You'd better stay close. If you get lost, raise your hand like this and wave it for a taxi. Tell the driver to take you to the YMCA at Broadway and Sixty-third Street. Remember that."

He quickly scribbled the address on a scrap of paper. "Here, put this in your purse. There are twenty other YMCAs and you could end up in the Bronx or someplace."

"I know, I know, *baba*," Feroza said, trying to conceal her irritation. "I won't go far."

Feroza walked up and down the streets, a sharp wind flattening the loose *shalwar* against her shins and causing the excess material to flutter like flags behind her legs. Lured by the windows of the small shops as if by magnets, she barely felt the cold. Manek had explained the grid system to her, but with him in haste and her in tow, she had not quite understood what he meant. Discovering the beauty and the simplicity of its logic for herself, noting street numbers and the names of the avenues, Feroza struck out with mounting confidence and researched the area in a widening square around the YMCA.

Satisfied by her exploration of the shops, Feroza bought, after much deliberation and heart searching, a Cross pen and a knitted red beret to match her coat. The deliberation and heart searching were occasioned by the conversion rate of eleven rupees to the dollar. To spend twenty dollars on a pen and cap was an extravagance. Many families in Pakistan lived on less each month. Feroza had not considered costs, or comparisons like these, while Manek did the spending, but digging into her own purse and handling the currency weighted her down with responsibility. She walked out of the small store wearing the cap at a jaunty angle.

Feroza returned to the YMCA at around one o'clock. Manek and Feroza had been out most afternoons and Feroza had never returned so early. She was surprised by the long lines of people waiting for the elevators. Feroza looked around, perplexed, wondering which one to stand in, and hastily positioned herself in a line that was being rapidly absorbed through open doors into an elevator.

Feroza realized only when they sailed past the fifteenth floor that the elevator did not stop on her floor but on the twenty-second floor, the level reserved for women.

She stepped out with the others wondering what she should do. She glanced around but she couldn't see any sign of a door leading to the staircase.

Her smile twitching, embarrassed, Feroza turned to a cheerful-looking woman who had got off with her and was observing her confusion with friendly, inquiring eyes. Feroza explained what had happened.

"The elevators stop at different levels, didn't you know?" the woman asked, voicing her surprise.

Feroza colored and apologetically mumbled, "I wasn't sure."

"You'll have to go down again, get into the correct line, and take the elevator that goes to the fifteenth floor. Read the numbers that are marked on top, or ask someone."

The woman spoke rapidly, and although she exuded a daunting air of confidence, she was sympathetic and pleasant. She wore no makeup and her short, wavy brown hair with its sun-bleached highlights gave her a reliable, wholesome air.

Feroza found herself warming to the woman's no-nonsense charm and considerate manner. "That'll take another hour," she confided ruefully, discouraged at the thought of all that going up and down and standing in line again.

"There's another way," the amiable woman said. "Come, I'll show you."

Feroza almost ran to keep up with the brisk figure walking down the hall. She was evidently in a hurry, and Feroza felt grateful that she was sparing the time for her.

The woman opened a heavy, green metal door. "Here," she said with a indulgent smile, "just run down to the fifteenth floor."

Feroza stepped inside the door hesitantly. There appeared to be no light. She wondered if she had not better use the elevators after all.

The woman gave her an almost impatient shove.

"Go on, it's all right," she said and shut the door.

It was instantly very dark and quiet, as if in closing the door, the amiable woman had shut Feroza out of New York.

It was also much colder. Feroza felt disoriented, confused for a moment about where she was. The air was rank with the odor of stale cigarette smoke and food. She got a whiff of urine and of decaying refuse.

Feroza stood still, blinking, trying to accustom her eyes to the darkness and adjust them to the weak cone of light from a bulb hanging over the landing. Soon she was able to make out the tarnished surface of a rod running across the center of the door. The rod ended in a curved projection that she guessed must be the handle.

Fearing that the woman who had been so kind to her might still be in the hall and think she was not only ungrateful but also a coward, Feroza waited a minute and then tried the handle quietly to see if the door would open.

It didn't.

The bulb dangling from an exposed length of wire showed the unswept cement floor of the landing. Some debris had accumulated in a corner — cigarette butts, food cartons, a grimy plastic bag with something in it.

Feroza noticed the beginning of a wrought-iron balustrade running along some concrete steps. She moved cautiously to peer down. The shallow steps appeared to dissolve in the darkness. Feroza took hold of the railing and slowly, tentatively, began her descent.

It became so dark she had to feel her way with the tip of her sneakers, then plant both feet before negotiating the next step. The bulb on the next landing must have died. At certain places the bannister had become loose in its moorings and wobbled beneath her hand. She couldn't see anything. What if some part of the balustrade were missing — as happened in nightmares — or a section of it came away where the concrete had crumbled, and she plunged into the void? She moved closer to the wall, and an unsettling weakness crept into her legs.

A little further down, following the steps round a sharp angle, Feroza saw the opaque glow from a dust coated bulb forming a pale oval of light on the next landing. She quickened her pace.

Again the handle wouldn't give. She exerted more pressure and pressed her shoulder hard against the door. She knocked tentatively. There was no responsive sound.

Feroza stood by the door to collect her thoughts and became aware of her rapidly beating heart. She must not panic. She was glad she had on sneakers. Although part of her craved to shout and bang on the door, a stronger instinct warned her to conceal her presence — to assess her situation before making a noise. To be more in control.

Perhaps the woman knew the door on the fifteenth floor would open.

Treading carefully lest the grit on the steps should crunch

beneath her feet and echo in the unknown space through which she was descending, Feroza went down another flight of steps and another. She lost count.

Was this the fifteenth floor? It must be. Feroza felt completely disoriented. She tried the knob, pulling and pushing. She shoved her shoulder against the door's solid mass. It was immovable.

Feroza suddenly found it difficult to breath. The wave of fear she had managed to bank so far broke through her defenses. She slammed the door with the flat of her hand and shrieked, "Can anybody hear me? Is anyone there? Open the door . . . Somebody, please, open the door!"

She waited, listening, eyes enlarged and intent, terrified at the noise she had just made.

There was only silence.

Feroza stood trembling at the periphery of the pale light, hemmed in by darkness. She was inside a nightmare — only it was real. She would not be able to struggle out of it by reciting the *Kemna Mazda* prayer as she usually did. She forced her eyes shut and, her blood throbbing, said it anyway: "Who shall protect us when the vengeful harm of the wicked threatens us but Thee, O Mazda! May the Evil utterly vanish and never destroy Your Creation . . ."

But the prayer did not help. When she opened her eyes, her world had unaccountably shrunk, as if nothing existed outside the stairwell. America assumed a ruthless, hollow, cylindrical shape without beginning or end, without sunlight, an unfathomable concrete tube inhabited by her fear. She was sure something monstrous was crouched in the impervious shadows that patrolled this alien domain — ferocious sewer rats, a brutish Doberman — breathing softly, waiting patiently.

Feroza felt the skin on her scalp tighten and lift the roots of her hair. She tried to dispel the dreadful illusions her fear had bred by deliberately recalling images of the well-lit halls, the building crowded with people, the bustle on the streets, and the acres of shops stretched round the YMCA. She whispered the one hundred and one names of Ahura Mazda like an incantation: One Who Relieves

Pain and Suffering, The Lord of Desire, The Causeless Cause, The Cause of Everything, The Creator of All That is Spiritual, The Undeceived, The Forgiving . . .

Then her panic gave way to a more focused fear: a self-preserving fear that permitted her to assess her situation.

Someone was bound to hear her sooner or later. She had no other recourse. She banged on the door again and, more in control, shouted, "Is anyone there? I'm locked in the stairway. Can anyone hear me? Open the door, somebody."

She couldn't just stand there. Driven by her need for action, she went down more flights of endless steps. Her feet by now were sure, her descent down the shallow steps quick. She knocked on the door at each landing. The odor of rot was getting stronger, and there was a new sweetish reek of alcohol and vomit she recognized from their evening on Eighth Avenue. Again, it made her want to throw up. She visualized the concrete stairwell drilling down and down, dwindling to a narrow point deep in the dank bowels of the earth. She was buried alive — sealed in a crypt.

Feroza heard something. The faintest shuffle. An intermittent creak. Sounds so slight that they were absorbed by her rather than heard. They appeared to come from way below.

She froze: she was sure something, aware of her presence, was stealthily climbing the steps.

Feroza's mind again conjured the savage, bestial shapes. The images provoked were frightening enough. Then the shadows around her moved. Some concealed air current caused the dangling bulb to sway gently. A furtive draft keened, sounding eerily human. And her terror, turning its venom upon her like a scorpion its sting, presented her with more fearful images. The dark, impersonal face of the man leering at her in the mirror when she looked up from brushing her teeth, the brutal faces of the men who slyly muttered obscenities in the halls, the dangerous, focused stare of the drug dealer who had loomed whitely out of the recessed doorway on Forty-second Street.

Feroza leaned back against the door on the landing for support. Her body slid slowly down against it. She crouched, still and quiet as a small wild animal. And after a while, like an animal, she sniffed.

Her nostrils picked up the stale, sweet reek and the other odors percolating in the air. But there were no new smells to feed her alarm.

The sounds, too, were becoming familiar. She recognized that old metal and hollow concrete stairwells had their own secret voices. Gradually the space around her became less menacing, and the images her fear made so vivid retreated. She pushed back the new beret that had slid almost to her eyebrows and pulled it about her ears to fit snugly.

At the darkest part of the next flight of steps, just before the bannister curved, Feroza felt something that stopped her breath. A slight buzz inside the palm of her hand on the metal railing, a subtle combination of sensations that were neither built into the steps nor inherent in the construction of the staircase. Somewhere in the uncharted space someone or something had moved closer. There it was again. The faintest suggestion of a quiver beneath her stalled feet; a barely discernible tremor beneath her fingers that, amplified by her tense acuity, traveled up her arm and shot down her spine.

Instinctively she crouched on the steps, carefully pressing her ear to the balustrade. The vibration was discernible, as of someone occasionally touching the railing, taking the steps two or three at a time, swiftly and stealthily, then stopping.

The predatory cunning deployed in the movement, the feel of mass in the vibration of the cement cantilever, convinced her that it was a man. Terror implanted springs into her feet and made her body buoyant. Feroza turned and flew up the steps. She ran up flight after flight of stairs, her heart pounding, her breath rasping in her throat, and when she felt her lungs would explode she flung herself at a door.

She banged on it with her fists and with the palms of her hands and rattled the rod and the handle. She rammed her body into the door and screamed, "Open the door . . . For God's sake, open the door! Can't anybody hear me? Please, somebody . . . "

A form so tenuous that it could be an invention of her terror appeared to be watching her from the patch of darkness where the cement steps angled. She wasn't sure she didn't imagine a movement like a curl of smoke detach itself from the dark, a barely perceptible blur that could be a swarthy man's paler shirt.

Feroza screamed. She screamed like a siren — like an instrument fashioned to scream.

There was a sharp, metallic click. Noises from outside. A voice. Sounds blessedly extraneous to the evil whispers and rustles of the malign stairwell.

The door gave, and Feroza almost fell into the corridor. The sudden brightness smote her distended pupils and turned her eyes yellow. She shied from the shaft of sunlight slanting through a window.

Someone was chattering garrulously in a quarrelsome tone.

Feroza squinted, trying to make out the shape of the person who had opened the door.

Bit by bit an awareness of her surroundings formed about her. She felt the tile floor beneath her feet, her handbag still on her shoulder, the beret again low and hugging her forehead. She saw the green paint on the door, the green walls, the aluminum-framed, sun-glazed window, the shape and face of a Japanese man. He had begun scolding her from the moment he set eyes on her as she tumbled out of the stairwell.

The Japanese man's cantankerous voice washed over Feroza like a fresh mountain stream, like a gentle, dawn-drenched breeze, sweeping her with relief. The look of incredulity and concern that had raised his eyebrows and furrowed his brow when he first saw her was replaced by outrage. The man frowned, glaring at her, and his indignant expression soothed her, immensely reassured her.

Feroza was crying. Great shuddering sobs wracked her body. "Sorry, I'm sorry," she wailed, unconsciously registering the man's gestures, his mannerisms. And though his features and accent were alien, the expressions on his face and the emotions that charged his voice were wonderfully familiar. He could be an uncle, a family friend. He wasn't more than thirty.

Feroza grasped instinctively that the man understood her experience, was reacting to the situation with the fears and fury born of his recognition of her naïveté and ignorance — the sheltered, overprotected condition of her young life as an Asian woman. His rage was protective, fussy, Asian. It poured out in a torrent of warning and dire statement:

"Never do that . . . Never! You could be murdered . . . No one would know. All kinds of shitty people . . . drugs!"

Didn't she know these were fire stairs? Didn't she know the door would open only on the first floor? Did she know she was stupid to lock herself in the fire stairs?

"Sorry, I'm sorry," Feroza wailed again, faint with relief.

Weeping copiously, Feroza followed the stocky figure in the plaid shirt and loose corduroy trousers as he led the way, halting only when he turned to scold or demand an answer.

In this way, she gave him a disjointed account of the events; described the wholesome, helpful woman who had guided her to the stairwell and closed the door after her.

"Who is this woman? Show her to me! Right now you could be raped! You must have your head examined . . . You're not a baby. You got no business in New York if you got no sense."

"Are you alone?" he asked. "Who are you with?"

"My uncle."

Feroza knew they were on the eleventh floor. Somehow, between his scolding and her sobs, she had managed to ask which floor they were on, and the Japanese man had told her.

Feroza had no memory of how she arrived at their room on the fifteenth floor.

She remembered only Manek's face. Ashen, scared. Herself uncontrollably shivering and sobbing. The Japanese man scolding him, scolding her.

As soon as the man left, Feroza crept into bed and covered herself from head to toe with the blanket. The blanket shook with the trembling of her body. Manek stroked the material where her legs were. "It's all right: You're safe now . . . You're safe. Don't worry."

When Feroza awoke some hours later, her body was racked with pain. Her throat was raw and parched from shouting. Her arms, her shoulders, her fingers, her calves hurt.

Manek rushed down and across the street to bring her hot

chocolate, sandwiches, aspirin. He looked wrung out, as though he had been through an equal ordeal.

"Weren't you worried about me?" Feroza asked after she had eaten the last crumb from the cardboard boxes. She was surprised by how hoarse she sounded.

"No. I'd asked you to return by about one-thirty. If you hadn't shown up by two or two-fifteen, then I'd begin to worry."

Feroza couldn't believe she had been marooned in that hell for only half an hour.

The next morning they caught the ten o'clock train to Boston. Feroza was quiet on the train, brooding, unwilling to talk of her experience or listen to her uncle's concerned and worried homilies. Manek buried himself in the *New York Times* and let her alone.

An hour later they were snacking on chicken sandwiches, chips, and chocolate milk, and Feroza, caught up in the excitement of this new travel, captivated by the green, unfolding New England land-scape, buried the horror of the stairwell.

Chapter 9

Manek had moved from a room he shared with a Turkish student at an M.I.T. dorm in Cambridge once he was sure Feroza would visit.

Two weeks earlier, on an unseasonably wintry morning, he had moved into the attic of a large, drafty, two-story, three-bedroom house in a seedy part of Somerville near Union Square. He shared the house and its one-and-a-half ancient bathrooms with five other shivering Pakistani and Indian students. The attic, with a tank of goldfish, had been bequeathed to his charge by the former occupant of the attic, a silken-haired Bangladeshi beauty.

The first thing Manek did after carrying one of Feroza's outrageously heavy suitcases and sundry shopping bags up the steps, dumping them by the mattress on the floor and catching his breath, was to examine the glass tank perched on a narrow china cabinet.

"Shit." A tiny fish, in an aqueous froth of iridescent red and gold scales, floated on the surface. Manek widened his nostrils and lightly sniffed. The murky water, topped by a film of oily patches, gave off a thin, unpleasant odor.

Manek had been away in New York for only a week, but his stock of goldfish, which had persisted in diminishing after the Bangladeshi beauty's departure, looked alarmingly depleted.

"What've you been up to?" Manek asked the lanky Pakistani boy who staggered into the room with Feroza's other obese suitcase and bits of hand luggage. "Eating goldfish for breakfast?"

Fierce strands of black, disheveled hair falling like spikes over his eyes, Jamil merely glanced at Manek. Too winded to reply, he collapsed in a tangle of scraggly limbs on a chair with lumpy stuffing.

Panting close on his heels, Feroza, still wearing the red beret she had bought in New York, threw Manek's backpack and overcoat on her substantive mound of luggage and flopped down on the mattress.

"I fed them every day like you said," Jamil said when he could speak. "But one or two died every day. Maybe you should change the water or their food or something . . ."

Manek solemnly picked up the dead goldfish by its tail and, his perplexed brow creased, laid it to temporary rest in an onyx ashtray.

"I'll bury it when we go down."

A dwindling pot of lackluster ferns by the entrance hall had perked up and flourished ever since its services had been requisitioned as burial grounds.

"Thanks for carrying the stuff up, *yaar*," Manek said apologetically, suddenly remembering to acknowledge Jamil's help.

"No problem."

Pulling down his glasses to rest on the tip of his nose, Manek looked severely over them at Feroza. "The family'd better learn to travel light if they want to come to America. There are no coolies here to carry *memsahib's* trunks up and down on their heads. If Jamil and I develop hernias and premature prostate conditions, it will be because of your ridiculous luggage."

"Come on, *yaar*, it wasn't so bad."

Jamil stole a quick glance at Feroza. Like any well-brought-up sixteen-year-old Pakistani girl, she pretended not to notice.

"I had to lug the bloody things from Kennedy to the YMCA in New York and then here."

Feroza removed her beret and, with a toss of her head, uncoiled the braids she had tied in an untidy knot at the back. "I offered to help. But you always have to prove you're so goddamn strong."

Manek thought Feroza sounded too cheerful and, considering how much he had put himself through for her sake — meeting her at the airport, showing her around New York, carrying her luggage — ungrateful and disgustingly smug.

"And what would you have done? Put your hand on your back, and said, 'Oh, Manek, my back is breaking, the suitcase is too heavy. Oh, Manek, massage my back.' " Manek affected the girlish falsetto and the exaggerated delicacy he favored when he chose to impersonate a spoiled-brat Feroza.

Feroza sprang up to aim a kick at his shins, and her uncle nimbly skipped aside. "Hey! I'm still bruised from your last kick . . . What will Jamil think of your 'hoydenish' behavior?"

None of them was sure what the word meant. Jamil swiftly shifted his darkly admiring eyes from the spirited girl.

"I know exactly how to behave, and how to behave with whom!" Feroza stood hands on hips, tossing her stubby braids and cockily facing her uncle.

To see the determined pose patented by his mother and sister incarnated in his niece, whose behavior had grown alarmingly like theirs in the three years he'd been away, shocked and intimidated Manek. He moved closer to the precariously placed tank of goldfish, crossed his legs, and affected nonchalantly to lean against it. Each muscle tensed in the effort, Manek wondered what surprises his niece might treat him to next.

"You should've seen the kick I gave that fellow at Al-falah Cinema," Feroza continued, oblivious of Manek's complex reaction to her ebullient posture. "He had his collar up — trying to look all smart and *gangee*. A regular Bhattigate type, you know strutting up and down like a hero. He'd pass *that* close to us," Feroza held her thumb and forefinger an inch apart, "and every time he'd go 'pooch-pooch'!" Feroza puckered her lips and imitated the kissing sound. "I kicked him you-know-where! Another fellow there said, 'Oh, you shouldn't have done that!' But all my school friends said, 'Why not? She did absolutely right. He deserved it!' I think they had to take him to Gangaram hospital."

Manek was acutely embarrassed. His niece had not only made the obscene noise and publicly referred to the unfortunate ruffian's anatomy but had also intimated she knew exactly how vulnerable what she'd kicked was. And he was shaken by the chilling endorsement of the brutality by her friends from the Convent of the Sacred Heart. If Pakistani girls taught by nuns were so vicious, what about the rest of the species?

Manek had no difficulty empathizing with the poor fellow. After all the man had only made kissing noises — not actually kissed any one of them. And who could blame the guy for acting a little fresh? It was perhaps the closest he could get to necking with an "uptown girl" in the Bhattigate social context. But for the grace of God, he thought — not, of course, in his sophisticated new American persona but as a callow, pre-America youth.

Observing the painful emotions coloring and contorting Manek's features, and guessing part of the reason for his discomfiture, Feroza folded her knees and abruptly sat down on the mattress. She had gone too far. Finding herself awash in this exhilaratingly free and new culture had made her forget the strictures imposed on her conduct as a Pakistani girl. Reacting typically to her guilt and confusion, she raised her chin, dropped haughty lids over her amber eyes, and, turning scarlet, stared imperiously at the attic paneling.

Languid gaze averted, avid ears nevertheless tuned in, Jamil also blushed. His admiration had quadrupled. Here was the kind of girl he could die for. Join the Mujahadeen in Afghanistan and shoot missiles from his shoulders at the Russian planes for. Dedicate his life to. This girl knew the true meaning of courage and honor the way a girl should!

And she was beautiful.

Taking note of Manek's embarrassment, and appreciating also the reasons for his sensitive friend's chameleonlike changes in color, Jamil made some excuse about preparing dinner and left the attic.

Manek sullenly showed Feroza where to put her things.

While Feroza unpacked, trying to stuff as much as she could in the space he had cleared for her in his makeshift closet and chest of draws, Manek turned his back on her and scowled at the goldfish.

"Manek, look at all the stuff your sister and mother have sent you," Feroza exclaimed.

Manek briefly glanced over his shoulder. There was a pile of books, hand-knitted garments, and parcels neatly wrapped in newspaper. There was Feroza's wistful, almost penitent face looking up at him, aching to make peace.

"Leave it all in one place," Manek directed coldly and resumed his abstracted and glum scrutiny of the fish.

Feroza appeared to have lost the bit of deference he had managed to wrest from her in Pakistan. In the time he'd been away, and in the short while she'd been exposed to the American culture, she'd grown shockingly brazen. She had also been disrespectful and un-niecelike before his friend.

99

And she interrupted him! He thought with chagrin about a fault he had already fretted about in New York. When he'd tried to explain something seriously, she'd cut in with a wisecrack or change the subject. Now, every time he spoke to Jamil, she hijacked the conversation.

Manek regretted his consideration in not drawing her attention to this intolerable habit earlier. He'd thought he must not crowd her with his advice, but she needed to be crowded with as much advice as he could cram into her.

He'd taken the knocks, learned his lessons the hard way, and here she was, being spoon-fed the beneficent fruit of his experience, he reflected bitterly.

Manek recalled the stony expressions of professors as they looked away whenever he tried to correct someone who was giving wrong answers in class. How icily they had looked down their noses at him afterwards. Nobody had told him that Americans felt so strongly about interruptions. He'd had to find it out for himself.

Manek brooded darkly on ways to improve Feroza's manners and tame her behavior. He'd have to guide her, explain things no matter how much she resented it, no matter how persistent he'd have to be. He knew it would no longer do to crack his whip, even figuratively, and say, "You must learn to respect your uncle. You must learn to listen. I've lived six years longer than you," as he could, with a real whip, when they were children. Manek yearned for her respect and, even if he didn't acknowledge it to himself, her awe and admiration.

Manek's eye caught the poster of Bhutto that Feroza had hung from a nail on the paneling. She had removed the landlord's small, framed sketch to do so and was in the process of smoothing out the curl in the paper.

"If you hang that socialist bastard on my wall, I'll tear him to bits," Manek said in a level voice that scared Feroza.

"Okay *baba,* okay," she said and quietly rolled up the poster and tucked it back into its cardboard cylinder.

ಎ

That afternoon, after they had feasted on a dish of lamb-hamburger and peas thoughtfully prepared for them by Jamil, Manek decided

100

to drive his niece across the Charles river in his fifth-hand, two-door 1971 Ford convertible.

The foam stuffing showed through small, angular gashes in the upholstery, and the passenger door was permanently fastened with entwined wire. Jamil vaulted into the back, and Feroza, muffled up in overcoat and scarf, had to slide into her seat from the driver's side.

"So, how do you like my car?" Manek inquired of Feroza.

He sounded so hearty that Jamil, who had wondered if the afternoon's unpleasantness had been smoothed over, relaxed, and Feroza, who knew Manek better, at once became alert.

"I bought it for sixty dollars from the girl who gave me the goldfish."

"We-ell," Feroza said warily, trying to be both honest and tactful, "It's certainly bigger than your room, if nothing else."

"You shouldn't judge things merely by their outward appearance. Appearances are deceptive. Listen to the engine. Even an idiot like you should be able to tell the car's okay for another thirty thousand miles at least. I'm not a fool . . . I've more experience than — "

"Nobody's calling you a fool, *baba*."

"There you go, interrupting again. You won't even let me finish a sentence. I don't know when you *desis* will learn good manners. If there's — "

"What do you mean, 'you *desis*'! What're you? A German?"

Manek lifted both hands from the steering wheel in a gesture combining exasperation and disgust.

Feroza, who had a mind to express herself more fully, curbed her speech.

After a half-minute of absolute silence, Manek said, "As I was saying, if there's one thing Americans won't stand, it's being interrupted. It's impolite. It's obnoxious. You've got to learn to listen. You can't cut into a conversation just as you like. You'll be humiliated. Learn from someone who knows what he's talking about."

And Manek's tone of voice and choice of words finally declared to Feroza all the pent-up hurt within him and the pressures he had been subjected to, not only that afternoon, not only since she'd arrived from Pakistan, but since Manek had arrived in America.

She glanced at him from the corner of her eye. His neck

appeared thin and fragile beneath his curly mop of overgrown hair. His wide, bony wrists stuck out from his shirt and jacket. The lean line of his jaw, covered by slight stubble, looked uncertain.

Feroza's heart went out to him. She could only guess at how he had been taught American ways, American manners. He must have endured countless humiliations. And his experiences — the positive and the humiliating — had affected him, changed him not on the surface but fundamentally.

Manek had told her about the accident late one night in New York. They were both in their respective beds, and Feroza, who thought she would drift off to sleep as she usually did when Manek talked at night, found herself listening.

Manek had spent a weekend with a Pakistani friend in Southbridge, near the Connecticut-Massachusetts border. Walking to the bus stop, which was at a gas station on a country road, he had lost his way in the dark. A car had hit him and sped away. He was severely bruised, his ribs and elbow broken. He had lain there in the snow. The few cars that went past, their headlights shining, did not stop. He had walked six hours to get to a hospital.

This had happened almost a year ago, but he had not written home about it. It would only worry his mother. Feroza guessed that it had been more an assertion of his fierce need for independence — the challenge to cope, to fend for himself — than any inordinate concern for Khutlibai.

Sitting by him in the run-down car, Feroza recalled also how his face had shone when he told her of his travels, hitchhiking across America with a friend. It was his first summer in the States, and he was still at the University of Houston. They'd visited the Grand Canyon, Disneyland, the caves in New Mexico. And the kindness of the people they'd met.

He'd told her about Houston itself, the unimaginable quantities of free food the *desi* students had ingested every evening in Houston's bars during the happy hour.

He'd told her of the unexpected pleasure he had derived from the one opera he'd been dragged to because his friend had a free ticket.

The sheer bliss of telephones that worked come cloud or drizzle, the force of the water in the YMCA showers, electricity that never fluctuated or broke down or required daily hours of "load shedding" were joys Feroza was discovering for herself. The enchantments of the First World.

When she had seen Manek leaning against the railing, waiting for her at Kennedy Airport, his arms and ankles crossed and pantomiming all kinds of exaggerated emotions the moment he glimpsed her, Feroza had believed he was the same old Manek.

She had been misled.

In this moment of insight, Feroza thought about some of the changes she had unconsciously noted since her arrival in New York. Manek was humbler and, paradoxically, more assured and quietly conceited, more considerate, yet she sensed that at an essential level he had become tougher, even ruthless. Her mother had been right when, after that short telephone conversation with him from Pakistan, she had asserted, with tears of happiness shining in her eyes, that her brother had changed.

Feroza vaguely sensed that America had tested Manek. Challenged him, honed him, extended his personality and the horizon of his potential in a way that had made him hers.

She thought of that evening in New York when she had known that Manek would not return to Pakistan. The sadness affected her again.

"Know something — the engine sounds like a Rolls," Feroza said impulsively, convincingly artless and earnest. "I'm sure it will go another thirty thousand miles easily."

But Manek was too upset to be so easily appeased. After an initial moment of silence, he launched into a ten-minute harangue on the virtues of the worn Ford and the astute bargain he had struck. And Feroza drew upon her meager resource of patience and responded to what he said with appropriate exclamations of admiring agreement.

At the end of the hectoring discourse, Manek was soothed. Feroza was driven around Boston. Up Commonwealth Avenue with its stately foreign consulates, through the winding and undulating streets of Beacon Hill, and past the exclusively priced shops and salons on Newbury Street, where a haircut cost two hundred dollars.

They drove along the Public Garden and down Marlborough Street aglow with dogwood, and Boston promptly became Feroza's second favorite city.

When they drove back over the repair-constricted bridge that led them past M.I.T., she found her initial impression of Cambridge reinforced. The squat brick buildings, the peeling frame houses, the seedy-looking shops in Central Square reminded her of the army barracks, servants' quarters, and some of the more unfortunate shopping centers on the once-fashionable Mall in Lahore.

Manek turned into the narrow lane outside Eliot House and sneaked the Ford into a dark space overhung by trees, between two cars parked on the curb.

෴

Manek's life had been blighted the first week he owned the Ford. It stalled at traffic lights, and the engine died on deserted roads. He replaced the battery and the carburetor.

The car's performance improved, but there was another snag. Each time he parked the car it either disappeared or had the dread police ticket tucked under the wiper. And you couldn't bribe the cop with small change; he'd been warned by his compatriots not to try it.

Manek paid more in tow-away costs, fines, and repairs than the Ford was worth. Reeling from the malign rapidity with which the fines were imposed, Manek gloomily toyed with the idea of drowning himself, the dying fish, and the ungainly albatross of a car unloaded on him by the heartless Bangladeshi in the Charles River.

That is, until Jamil, an old hand at bucking the perils of parking in Cambridge, showed him all the secret crevices in which to park a car — even one as wide and long-finned as the Ford — within walking distance of Harvard Square.

With the Ford safely tucked away, they strolled through a narrow lane congested with smart little Japanese cars seeking parking meters and emerged on Massachusetts Avenue. Stores and restaurants lined the street to one side.

"That's Harvard Yard." Hands in his pockets, Manek indicated it with a movement of his head. Feroza looked at the unimpressive masonry peeping through the thick crowns of trees behind a tall brick wall. They crossed Massachusetts Avenue and, through towering wrought-iron gates, entered Harvard Yard.

What had appeared so unimpressive from across the street opened up to display a noble girth of elegantly apportioned space. The atmosphere around them also changed, whisking them off to some loftier dimension that insulated their ears against the din of traffic on the road and freed their minds from the mundane cares of attic dwellers with intractable fish and ornery Fords.

As they sauntered beneath the vaulting spread of newly leafed trees that permitted only a very special light to filter into Harvard Yard, Feroza absorbed some of the sense of the power and intellectual excitement of Harvard. She cast shy darts of admiration at the students, fresh-faced, tall, victorious. Feroza was glad to be wandering among these intelligent beings and felt herself suffused by an exultant glow.

Jamil, a gleaming white scarf tossed about his neck, pointed out the modern science building and the Sanders Theater. Manek remained silent, wearing the benign expression of a man content to see his niece impressed and awed by what impressed and awed him.

It was almost dark when they crossed the street to the Holyoke Center. The square was crowded. Pulling out wicker chairs, they sat at a table in the open. Self-consciously sipping coffee in the American way, without cream or sugar, the three young people felt themselves become part of the privileged throng of boisterous young eaters and drinkers.

The heady sense of freedom, of youthful happiness, deepened in Feroza. Nobody looked at them. If by chance someone did, the glance was incurious and friendly.

Feroza noticed a slender, beautiful girl with short fair hair and transparent green eyes smile at Manek.

"Do you know her?" Feroza asked, surprised.

"No," Manek shook his head, deliberately enigmatic.

"But she smiled at you."

"I looked admiringly at her and she smiled back, that's all."

Warned by the expression on Manek's face, Jamil sat back in his chair and tactfully looked away.

Manek leaned towards Feroza and spoke in a low voice,

"Civilized people don't kick men in the balls just because they happen to stare at them. Imagine what would've happened in Lahore! First she'd kick me, then she'd go whining to the cops wailing, 'O menu ghoor-ghoor ke vekh raha see. He was making big, big eyes and staring at me!' I'd be soundly slapped and hauled off to the police-thanna."

Feroza recalled the stern, watchful eyes of uncles and cousins, ever ready to pulverize young men who dared to look at her with their languishing orbs. She heard her aunt's voice, her mother's, and grandmothers', "Aren't you ashamed, looking at women? How'd you like it if our men stared at your sisters?" or, "Mind your eyes, you shameless! Don't you have mothers and sisters at home?" and other variations on the theme.

Feroza couldn't help drawing comparisons. She concluded there were so few women, veiled or unveiled, on the streets of Lahore, that even women stared at other women, as she did, as if they were freaks.

At around eight o'clock, a jazz quartet suddenly began to play on the far side of where they sat. A trumpet note, loud and pure, spun into the air to greet the fading light, committing the evening to pleasure and beauty. The guitar, in a subtle transition, carried the note where the trumpet left off. Feroza had never expected the melody of an alien music to move her so deeply. The sensual, drawn-out blues notes throbbed in her senses and turned the dusk magical.

Feroza quietly left their table and joined the crowd that had formed round the musicians. Manek and Jamil, busy ogling the girls and exchanging snide remarks, suddenly realized she was not with them. They got up, anxiously looking about, and sought her out.

It was a mellow, spring Friday, and Harvard Square was permeated by a carnival spirit. Streetlights and lights from shops and eating places lit up the cheerful faces of the people thronging the pavement, and they cut across the serpentine streets diagonally from wherever it suited them.

A bunch of Hare Krishna crusaders were prancing about in saffron *dhotis* and saris in front of the Co-op store. Around the corner, on Brattle Street, a lone violinist in a long-sleeved black dress played in the recessed shelter of a small door.

106

And then they stood before a spectacular brown gentleman who was later introduced to Feroza as Father Fibs. Manek and Jamil were full of information about him. Father Fibs was a storyteller. It was rumored that he had given up a promising career at Harvard in order to inspire young yuppies and direct their thoughts to the finer, less materialistic aspects of life. He was reputed to be a Shakespearian scholar and sometimes, when the mood took him, had been known to render long passages from *Hamlet* and *Othello* like a virtuoso. He was a man with a vocation who followed his own heart.

Whatever the truth of the rumors, Feroza was as impressed by the tall and slender middle-aged man as she was by the blue denim outfit he wore. It was his personal uniform, studded with mono-grams, buttons, appliquéd butterflies, birds, and flowers. Despite the flamboyance of his clothes and his sweeping gestures, there was a disarming shyness and sensitivity to his attractive features.

Very few people were listening to him. Father Fibs had been around so long that his novelty had worn off, and the older inhabitants of Cambridge passed him without pausing.

Almost at once his practiced eye lit on Feroza. Father Fibs could tell at once that the girl would be too polite to move away while he was addressing her. His eyes remained on Feroza for the duration of the rambling story, which she found exhausting to follow.

His confidence in her was not misplaced. When Manek and Jamil grew restive, Feroza stood her ground, insistent and steadfast.

At the end of the tale, when even the few remaining listeners drifted away, Father Fibs strolled over and, considerately lowering his towering length onto some steps, started talking to Feroza.

He invited the three of them to Adams House for coffee, and Manek extended an invitation to dinner in his attic whenever it suited Father Fibs.

On the way back to the car, Feroza, unconsciously indulging her Lahori habit of staring at women, was disconcerted when each one of them smiled back. Soon she was smiling at all the women they passed, delightedly greeting those who greeted her.

"What're you doing?" Manek asked. "Don't stare at people like that."

"They don't mind. Everyone's so friendly."

"You're embarrassing them. If you look at them, they have to smile back. It's like holding a gun on them or something. It's rude."

"You don't seem to mind when they smile at you," Feroza retorted, her knowing, foxy eyes reminding him of his mother.

It had become cold, and the wind was swooshing up the narrow byways. Feroza glanced at Jamil. He was walking with his head bent against the sudden gusts, his hands in his pockets. They were, all of them, so far away from home, Feroza reflected, and yet she was happy. Impulsively she tucked her arm into Manek's, and for an instant lay her beret on his shoulder — something she would not have thought of doing in Lahore.

Occasionally sheltering her nose in Manek's sleeve, Feroza continued her uninhibited staring and smiling. Manek was too cold to notice or care. Feroza smiled, as if her cheeks had frozen in their happy contours, all the way back to the Ford.

Chapter 10

They slept late on Saturday morning. Feroza was so cold in the unheated attic that she had snuggled into Manek's long johns and thick socks and pulled the red beret over her ears before slipping into bed with the hot-water bottle thoughtfully provided by Zareen. The bed consisted of a foam mattress that was peeled off Manek's spring mattress every evening. Once the bed was laid on the floor, there was no room to walk or even to sit at the desk.

Shivering in her flannel wrap, hugging her towel and her toilet bag, Feroza followed Manek to the improvised bathroom in the dank basement. The basement was stacked here and there with boxes, furniture, and trash bags filled with stored belongings. Cobwebs trailed from the seams on the roof, and the smell of mold and damp filled the room.

Feroza noticed the antiquated shower protruding two feet from a hole gouged out of a corner. Beneath it lay something that looked like an abandoned kiddy sandbox, decrepit with patches of rust and discolored paint. A wire ran across the corner to hold the shower curtain, which was drawn to one side, its grimy edge sticking to the gray-painted brick wall.

"I can't shower in that!" Feroza balked and stepped back.

"Nobody'll see you once you draw the curtain."

Manek pointed out a plastic bath caddy dangling from the wobbly shower rod. "You can put your shampoo, etcetera, there."

Stubbornly maintaining her distance, Feroza peered into the pit as if looking out for worms that might suddenly rear up to attack.

"I'll get tetanus."

"Don't be silly."

Feroza turned to go back. "I will not shower in that!"

"Then you'll have to sleep outside. You already stink like a goat."

Manek rolled up the sleeve of his navy velour bathrobe and turned on the shower. The rush of water steamed almost at once.

"I'll guard the steps till you finish," Manek said and, before

Feroza could protest, closed the basement door after him.

Alternately blistered by the boiling water and yelping with shock from sudden glacial torrents, Feroza managed to get the shampoo out of her hair.

Feroza dried herself quickly; it was cold in the basement. She pulled her woolen vest over her head and saw a shape emerge tentatively from the hole in the wall in which the shower rod rested.

Feroza froze.

Not sure of its hold, the large cockroach slithered along the slimy edge.

Feroza flung her clothes on in a panicked rush and stormed up the steps. Incandescent with rage she burst into the room and glared at Manek. "You didn't even mind the door!"

Feroza flung herself on the mattress and sat in a huddled, panting huff against the wall.

"I told the boys not to go to the basement. Have a nice shower?"

Feroza turned away her face.

"You look nice and clean. Like a boiled lobster. Ever seen a boiled lobster?"

Feroza flung a slipper and, in rapid succession, a book and another slipper.

"You damn swine!"

"If you'd behaved yourself, I'd have shown you how our shower works. Or taken you to the good bathroom. Don't think you can be smart all the time and get away with it. You behaved disgustingly in front of my friend yesterday. Let this be a lesson to you. There will be many lessons till you learn to behave properly. You have to learn that in America you don't get something for nothing."

"I'm going right back to Lahore!" Feroza was glad she hadn't mentioned the cockroach. At least she wouldn't give him that satisfaction.

Feroza's rigid profile was the color of fire. Her features looked alarmingly swollen, heavy with fury. Knowing her capacity to dig in her heels when confronted and the pride that even as a child had rarely permitted her to cry, Manek felt he might have pushed her too far, and in the wrong direction.

Since he also possessed too much pride to apologize, Manek did the next best thing. He clowned. "Oh," he said in his breathy falsetto, wringing his hands, "Now what will I do? You want to cut off my nose and put it in my hand. You will shame me. How will I show my face to the world if you go back?"

Manek fell abruptly on his knees and, repeatedly lifting and throwing his arms on the floor, absurdly, energetically, and noisily prostrated himself before her. "Oh, say you will not go. Oh, say you will not. My honor and *izzat* are in your lily-white hands!"

Feroza turned her contemptuous, swollen face on him.

"You color blind or something also?"

"Oh, sorry. In your lily-brown hands . . . your lily-brown hands."

Feroza battered his hands with her fleet bare feet. "You lesson-*walla*! You lesson-*walla*! I'll teach you a lesson, you lesson-*walla*!"

Manek made up to Feroza by taking her on a personally guided tour of M.I.T. in the afternoon. He marched her through the long, echoing halls and the auditoriums with the same reverential expression with which he had trotted her, in her high heels, down Wall Street. He held open the doors of his classrooms with a proprietorial and courteous air while she peeped through, and he became puffed up with benevolent vanity at the impression everything made on her. Feroza was profoundly affected to be in this citadel of learning to which her uncle belonged, and Manek was immoderately pleased by her response.

In an excess of self-congratulatory gratification and the affection for his niece the complacent feelings generated, Manek took her to Legal Seafood. So innocuously did he order the boiled lobster that, after a quick look at his face, Feroza decided the choice was inadvertent. Thus Manek gave Feroza her first addictive taste of the succulent Maine lobster. And, glancing at the check, he held his brow to advertise his regret.

⁓

Monday morning returned Manek to a sense of his other responsibilities and set the pattern for the next few weeks. He would awaken, examine the fish tank, and grow mournful at the demise of yet another goldfish. He became obsessed with their welfare and viewed each new catastrophe as a personal failing.

He leafed through books on the care of fish and visited pet shops for advice.

Sometimes when he returned late after working on an assignment in the library bearing little plastic pouches of fish food and fish tonics, he was stricken to discover another casualty. Those were black days, and Manek would bury himself in his books. Feroza knew enough to keep out of his way.

While Manek was out all day, Feroza watched a small black-and-white TV with the fascination of a cobra charmed by the flute, her hooded hand moving hypnotically from the bag of potato chips on her lap to her mouth.

Sometimes Feroza varied her routine and read the Harlequin romances she had discovered at a grocery store, murder mysteries, or the P. G. Wodehouse she had brought from Lahore. Her hand traveled as hypnotically to her mouth with whatever she was relishing as she read as it did when she watched TV.

When she remembered to, she put a few drops of fish tonic into the tank.

She varied her diet: during the commercials she might open a can of cocktail sausages, baked beans or sardines, sprinkle them with lemon juice and red pepper, and, to prologue the delight, ate them in tiny nibbles. For dessert she licked spoonfuls of condensed milk or opened a can of peaches and often combined the two.

Manek had stacked a corner of the wardrobe floor with canned foods and the freezer compartment in his small fridge with pizzas. Judging from his own experience, he knew how much Feroza would relish them.

Manek let Feroza eat her fill for a week and then, looking at the empty space on the wardrobe floor and the nearly empty freezer compartment, announced, "You can open any four cans a day, whether it is soup or fruit or ham or mushrooms. No more than four frankfurters or four slices of bacon, and only one pizza a day. If you're still hungry, you can eat *dal* and rice, or bread and butter. You'll get fat and sick if you eat like this, and I'll get broke and thin. You'll also get fed up."

"Never. I could eat this all my life!"

"That's what I thought too," said Manek. "Now I can't bear the sight of frankfurters and sardines."

Feroza could not believe her good luck where food was concerned. It was an extravagant bonus — like so many of the unexpected delights her visit to America was to provide. She had presumed that canned foods like olives, mushrooms, condensed milk, asparagus, clams, were as precious and rare in America as they were in Pakistan, to be served up only on special show-off occasions.

Feroza was curiously reluctant to venture outside the attic without Manek. She declined his offer to drop her off and pick her up from shopping malls or Harvard Square. For all her brash posturing and tossing of braids, she responded so diffidently to the friendly overtures of the other Pakistani and Indian students inhabiting the lower portions of the house that they reluctantly left her alone.

Feroza became tongue-tied and remote even with Jamil when Manek was not with her. In averting her radiant gaze and by discouraging chatter, Jamil felt she dropped a veil about her person. An intriguing veil that added to her other attractions an element of mystery.

Jamil, and even Manek, wondered sometimes if this demure creature had actually kicked that fellow at the Al-falah cinema. Manek, though, was less uncertain. He guessed that his niece's unexpected shyness and timidity had to do with being sixteen years old and finding herself in such unfamiliar and diametrically different surroundings. But once her exuberance returned, his doubts disappeared, and Manek was sure Feroza was only passing through a phase.

Besides, ever since her experience with the scalding shower, Feroza had become passably tractable, a fact upon which Manek mused with quiet conceit. As for her shield of reserve, he thought it only proper and didn't mind it one bit.

One afternoon Manek finally accepted what had been killing the goldfish. Everyone he consulted had taken it for granted that he changed the water — it was so elementary — and he hadn't. Not since the treacherous Bangladeshi beauty left them in his charge without instructing him to.

That evening, after carefully transferring the few remaining fish to a plastic bag, Manek and Feroza scoured the tank and filled it with fresh water from the bathroom faucet.

Still, the next morning two fish died. Thoroughly depressed, Manek and Feroza concluded that the dead fish had been so contaminated by the toxins in the stale water that they could not recover.

☙

The following afternoon Manek returned with a bottle of wine and a bag of groceries. He had run into Father Fibs, and the storyteller was to dine with them in the evening. Manek had asked Jamil, the students from downstairs, and a few other friends to join the party.

Three fish had expired that day, and Feroza had laid them out ceremoniously on a bed of pink tissue in the ornamental onyx ashtray. Manek slumped into the stuffed chair, defeated, his hand shading his brow, mourning his fish. Feroza sat at his feet, solemnly and silently commiserating.

After a few moments, they roused themselves and gravely set about preparing dinner. Manek, who had never prepared even a cup of tea in Lahore, astonished Feroza by the culinary prowess necessity had brought forth. Not that he cooked anything as fancy as prawn-*patia* or Dhansak lentils. But given the bland taste of the fare available to them and the steady and relentless diet of canned foods and pizza, Manek's cooking tasted almost as good as Kalay Khan's.

Father Fibs arrived. Stooping shyly through the attic door, he was followed by the unexpected and matronly person of his chocolate brown and upright wife.

Smiling genially, Mrs. Fibs handed Feroza a gift-wrapped box of candy. She was a little taller than Feroza, about five feet six inches, and about a foot shorter than her husband.

The other students, looking like pygmies, stood up to greet the guests of honor.

Manek seated Mrs. Fibs on the dining chair Jamil had carried up for the occasion, and Father Fibs was ceremoniously directed to the stuffed chair.

It was a rather small chair for Father Fibs, and he looked as ill at ease in it as a squashed camel. When he stretched his legs, they took up all the walking space in the attic, and Manek and Feroza had to step over them to serve the drinks. When he straightened his arms, his knuckles knocked against the floor. And when, unaccustomed to sit long in any one place, Father Fibs stood up, his head touched the sloping ceiling.

The attic appeared to have shrunk, and Father Fibs, who looked so elegant on the pavements of Harvard Square, suddenly became a lumbering and baffled bean stalk.

Mrs. Fibs talked affably, asking interested questions. But all attention centered on the colorful and alarming person of the willowy giant.

Sensing it, and self-consciously adjusting his booming voice to his restraining surroundings, Father Fibs began to talk. His voice was a husky, hesitant whisper. He told Feroza he liked her manner of speaking, her gentle ways, the movement of her yellow eyes in her brown face. He told Manek he had visited India as a draftee and understood the background of the young men in the room. They must be rich. Only the rich sent their sons to America. Money they would surely make, but what did they plan to *do* with their lives?

When he was a student at one of the universities in this area — Father Fibs declined to tell them which — he had shared a room with a Sri Lankan student. He related stories of their escapades, of rows and hilarious misunderstandings occasioned by their different cultures. He told them what the man, now middle-aged, had achieved and salvaged of his ideals.

As Father Fibs hit his stride and his gestures became more comfortable, his fingers brushed the light fixture on the ceiling, displaced a brass plate recently affixed to the wall, and almost toppled the onyx ashtray. So Father Fibs tried to hold his hands clamped to his sides. His speech dried up. His tapered fingers fluttered nervously and scratched his thighs. Again he sat down, camellike, in the stuffed chair.

At some point after dinner, when coffee had been served, inspired by the expectation on the young faces at his feet, the storyteller suddenly took off on another soliloquy. His hands, like unexpectedly released birds, darted here and there and, after testing the air and adapting themselves to the confined space, coasted with the proficiency of hummingbirds. Again he loomed elegant and splendid, and his presence transformed the shrunken attic into space worthy of his inspired renderings.

"You are like buds," he said, bringing his hands together and loosely cupping his slender fingers. He cast his eyes down, drawing their attention to the colorful flowers, birds, and butterflies appliquéd on his denim costume. The colors appeared to glow, taking on a life and movement of their own. "But like all young things, you will bloom."

Father Fibs opened the tender bud his dusky hands had formed into a quivering flower. The gesture, and his gravelly, almost messianic voice, imbued the tired words with fresh intensity. "You think you are already flying?" Father Fibs paused, looked long at them, and slowly shook his head. "No. You are protected innocents, secure in your chrysalises. When you leave your universities, you will test your wings. You'll fly and fall, fly and fall." His lithe hands weaved and turned, showing beige palms. "It will hurt. You'll be frightened. Don't be. Your wings will become stronger."

Feroza glanced at Manek. His curls had been recently cropped and his lean face looked strengthened, handsome, lit up by the visions Father Fibs's supple hands conjured.

Next to Manek on the mattress, his dark eyes intent beneath fierce spikes of hair, sat Jamil, hugging his knees.

It became clear to Feroza that to be this far from home, to have to cope with strangers and mysterious rites, was itself a test. Manek and Jamil must surely have found themselves in some ways wanting and in some unexpectedly able. Still committed to proving themselves, they would avail themselves of the options America offered. They would stay — no matter how long it took — to test their expectations.

Feroza's perception suddenly ignited when she remembered the smiling blond with the transparent green eyes in Harvard Square and the thought struck her like a jolt — what extraordinary sexual possibilities they would avail themselves of.

116

Might not she, too, wish to prove herself? Even if she was only a girl? Explore possibilities that were beginning to palpitate and twinkle — as yet unrecognizable — on evanescent new horizons?

Father Fibs's arms stuck out at the elbows like fledging wings, his shoulders slightly heaved. "Then you'll want to fly, taste of what Adam tasted," his shy eyes rested for a moment on Feroza, "what Eve tasted, the bitter and the sweet, and discover the places you can fly to and fall from. And once you're no longer afraid to fall, away you'll soar — up, up, to where you need never fall!"

Father Fibs's open-armed and triumphant gesture swept the fish tank off its precarious perch on the china cabinet, and it shattered at their feet.

The fish scattered, barely distinguishable from the patterned carpet and the broken glass, into watery crevices, where they disappeared.

Chapter 11

In the days that followed Father Fibs's memorable dispensation of the fish in the attic, Manek was washed by a tide of relief so intense that he determined never to keep pets. Who needed the onus of tending to pets when nieces like Feroza were packed off to his care? In any case, he felt temperamentally better suited to the charge and guidance of young humans.

Manek guessed, of course, that Feroza was merely the first of the nieces and nephews, the horde in Lahore growing like saplings, ready to be air-freighted to wherever he was, once they shot up.

Youngsters he could cope with. Given his burgeoning sense of responsibility, manifest in the nature of his urges to broaden Feroza's outlook and to improve her mind, who knew but that he might even derive pleasure from his selfless part in shaping their futures.

But once nieces and nephews arrived, could parents be far behind? Manek had an unpleasant vision of ferrying Feroza's parents, not to mention her uncles and aunts, back and forth as they descended on various American airports to blight his life.

Unfortunately the army of Feroza's aunts and uncles (he could never think of the middle-aged brigade as his cousins) took their duties as upholders of tradition and dispensers of wisdom equally seriously. And though he was not prepared to tolerate their obsolete counsel, which as far as he was concerned was a euphemism for interference, he had no notion of depriving his younger kin of the fruit of his experience.

From the moment of Feroza's arrival in New York, Manek had begun mentally to chalk out a program for her future. Although it was not a conscious exercise to begin with, it had bloomed into a full-fledged vocation in a couple of weeks. The call involved not only

Feroza's education and the development of her personality but also her induction into the self-sufficient, industrious, and independent way of American life.

Manek was young, intelligent, and already acquiring a valuable education. He had weathered the trauma of culture shock after culture shock the New World had buffeted him with and emerged toughened.

Disciplined, clearheaded, and worldly wise, who could be better suited to direct the course of an overindulged and overprotected girl's future? Wasn't that why Zareen and Cyrus had sent Feroza to him?

But stuck as they were in the Third World, their vision was limited. They imagined, in their usual woolly manner, that a short visit would suffice to give their daughter the sophistication expected from travel abroad. It was up to him to take Feroza's future in hand, to help her hang on to the opportunities that would otherwise vanish.

Strategically spooned only small and enticing portions of Manek's stirring plans for her, Feroza was not averse to the clear logic of his ideas.

First of all, now that Feroza was already in the United States, it would be illogical for her to go back. Airfare was prohibitive. And as she had seen for herself, it was difficult for a young person to gain entry to the United States, even with a visa. Visa laws were getting stricter every day, and she might not be as lucky next time. Feroza knew how he'd rushed around getting papers certifying this and notarizing that from the university and the banks to sort out the mess caused by her naive and emotional handling of the immigration authority. It was a shame to travel twenty thousand miles and put him through what she had if Feroza's visit were to amount to no more than a superficial jaunt. What could she expect to see of the country or imbibe of its progressive and stimulating culture, in a couple of months? How could she discover the opportunities and choices available to her in such a short time?

Secondly, Feroza had already taken her matriculation exams. Fortunately a School Leaving Certificate was a School Leaving Certificate, and no one in America was wise to the standard of education the Punjab Matric implied. She could gain admission to a reasonably good college and that would enable her to get a student visa. Then she could come and go as she wished.

"You'd better go in for hotel management," Manek advised. "It is on the list of 'desirable' courses for which dollars can be sent from Pakistan."

"I'd prefer psychology," Feroza ventured, "or journalism."

"The Pakistan Government won't sanction foreign exchange for that. Your father will have to run around buying black market dollars and then find ways of smuggling them to you so you can pay your fees."

"I see," Feroza was meek and pensive, as impressed by her uncle's endless know-how as he could have wished.

Feroza and Manek both wrote long letters home explaining all this to Khutlibai, Zareen, and Cyrus.

 example

Zareen waited for Khutlibai to put on her dentures. It was significant that she had interrupted their conversation to do so.

The deed done, she faced Zareen.

"I told you, no good would come of sending Feroza to America!"

Although it was the end of April and the afternoons were already hot, Khutlibai's old bungalow with its thick brick walls and high ceilings was blessedly cool beneath the slowly rotating blades of the fan. Khutlibai sat on the bed in her muslin nightdress with the short puff sleeves, her legs crossed, grimly swaying back and forth as if mourning.

"What do you mean no good will come of it! Of course it will be good. A good education is a good thing!" Perched on a stool before her mother, Zareen felt she sounded less than convincing. "Mumma, times have changed," she continued, more cautious. "A lot of people are sending their daughters for education to America."

120

"Who?"

"Some of the best Parsee families in Karachi."

"So you must also jump into the well? God knows what will become of that poor child . . ."

"What'll become of her? She'll come back a tip-top *madam-ni-mai,* and we'll all be proud of her!"

"And when will she marry? Have you thought about that?"

"When the right time comes. It's in God's hands."

"Everything is in Ahura Mazda's hands," Khutlibai rumbled ominously and cast pious eyes to the ceiling fan. "But even He can't do anything if you chop off your own foot with an axe. Good Parsee boys are scarce, and you know how quickly they are snapped up. The right time will come and go, and mark my words, the child will be lost to us! God knows what kind of people she'll mix with. Drunks, seducers, drug addicts . . ."

"You know Manek will guard her like a lion! You know how strictly we have brought her up. She'll never do anything to disgrace us."

"We don't know what kind of friends Manek has. All I can do is pray he won't marry some white tart. But he's a man; he can get away with a lot. But who'll marry a girl who's been up to God-knows-what? Our elders used to say, keep the girls buried at home. Do you know your grandfather would not allow even our pigeons to stray? If one of the birds from our loft spent the night on another's roof, we'd have pigeon soup the next day. He'd have its throat slit!"

"Mumma, that was hundreds of years ago. Thank heavens my Cyrus is not like that!"

"Don't talk about 'your' Cyrus! It's enough to give me a fever just to hear his name. He should stick to his footballs and shuttlecocks. Letting his daughter go tramping round the world as she pleases. He has no more sense or direction than a Ping-Pong ball!"

"Nothing I or my family do is ever right! Nothing pleases you!" Zareen's face was puffy and red. She sniffed and opened her purse with a snap. She withdrew a handkerchief. Zareen knew, if not checked at this point, Khutlibai would start calling her husband alarming names. Her repertoire had recently expanded to include "Hockey-stick" and "Shuttlecock." She wished sometimes that her mother would use really foul language instead.

Zareen turned to blow her nose, and the way she snapped her purse shut made it clear that she was not prepared to hear another word. She drove away without saying good-bye to her mother.

The evening was even worse. They were out as usual, dining at the Iqbals', when an elderly Sikh, wearing a thick turban and a crumpled gray *shalwar-kamiz*, made a late appearance. He was the Indian journalist Khushwant Singh. His Pakistani host, the lawyer Rehman, was accompanying him.

Zareen and Cyrus knew the journalist slightly from a previous visit. As their genial host sprang to his feet to welcome the guests, they realized the journalist's presence was a surprise.

Zareen and Cyrus stood up to form a small group with the newcomers, and Cyrus asked the Sikh, whose gray beard was untidily rolled up round his chin, "What brings you to Lahore, *jee*?"

"Bhutto's hanging."

The room, buzzing with the usual political and business chatter, suddenly became very quiet.

"You're joking," Zareen said.

"No, I'm not," Khushwant Singh looked surprised that they should find the news so unexpected. "I was sent a message from the top that something important was to happen. What else can it be?" He shrugged, spread his hands and joined in the speculation and consternation the news had caused. Singh explained that he was flying to Islamabad the next morning to meet General Zia.

Bhutto was not hanged. It had been a false alarm.

But Khushwant Singh's visit had been climatic for Zareen and Cyrus and their circle of friends and acquaintances. His comments alerted them to the fact that anything could happen at any moment. It prepared them for the hanging.

Chapter 12

Manek deposited Feroza at the Boston Public Library in front of a stack of college guides before going to class.

Feroza picked out a fat book from the stack and studied the information for the colleges listed under A: Alabama, Alaska, Arkansas.

At the end of an hour, her brain rebelled. At the end of two hours, bug-eyed from reading the small print, Feroza had an urge to throw the book through the window. She glared at the catalog and savagely pushed it away.

Manek found her, her head and arms on the large oak library table, fast asleep.

Glancing covertly at Feroza's sullen profile and pink nose in the car, Manek eschewed comment. He drove silently to the McDonald's at Porter Square and, when they were halfway through their soothing hamburgers, asked, "Well, *boochimai*, have you decided which college you'll apply to?"

"I didn't even get though the As. It'll take me ten years to get to Z."

"No, not ten years, only a few days if you put your mind to it."

Feroza took a gulp of Coke from her paper cup, crushed the ice between her molars, and stared stolidly out the window.

A couple were unloading their children from a battered hatchback and strapping them into baby carriages. A little girl with pale, straight hair, obviously awakened from her sleep, was fussing. The mother spanked her, and the child began to bawl.

"The first lesson you learn in America is 'You don't get something for nothing,' " Manek said. "If you want to get into the right college you have to work for it. Nothing is given to you on a plate. You don't know that, because nobody works in Pakistan. Not your father, your grandfathers, or your uncles. They think they work, but compared to America, everyday's Sunday. If you want to be independent and enjoy the good life, you have to get into the habit of working."

Feroza gave him an insolent, hostile look. "Nobody works in the world except you. All the money spent on you was plucked by your grandfathers from trees."

"People here work much harder. Husband and wife both work. Every minute is organized. A wife will say, 'Dear, put the clothes in the washing machine and come back in ten minutes to take our son to baseball practice. I'll be back from the grocery store in thirty minutes to put the clothes in the dryer and take our daughter for ballet lessons.' "

Manek's impersonation of an American housewife was engaging. It drew a faint smile from Feroza and encouraged him.

"In the afternoon they trim a hedge or clean the swimming pool for relaxation. Then the husband cooks a barbecue dinner while the wife vacuums. There is no 'Cook, bring me soup' and 'Bearer, bring me whiskey-*pani*.' At night they go to a movie or to a disco and enjoy life. They know how to work hard, and they play hard. But they do this only on Saturdays and Sundays. On working days they are so busy they have to regulate — "

"Even their breathing," Feroza cut in. "Dear, you breathe in, I'll breathe out, two seconds in, two seconds out . . ."

"That's right. That's what a free and competitive economy in a true democracy demands. That's why the country is prosperous. That's why the Third World is so backward and poor."

"If you say 'Third World' once more, I'll scream."

"You and your Bhutto, with his socialist ideas, are like those lazy Communists."

"Don't you dare say anything about Bhutto. Aren't you ashamed, speaking ill of someone who is facing death just because he's the voice of the masses?"

"All right, we won't talk about that Third World crook . . ."

Feroza screamed quite loudly. Manek was sure faces turned towards them. He looked straight down, his face red. Feroza's was scarlet. After a while Manek said, "You've got a lot to learn. Never mind, I'll teach you."

ల

The museum circuit started again. They visited all the museums in Cambridge and Boston. Jamil had accompanied them enthusiastically a few times and then, saying, "You've seen one, you've seen them all," declined further invitations.

Feroza went into raptures at the sight of the glass flowers in the botanical display at Harvard and had to be torn away from a painting by Ingres at the Museum of Fine Arts of Raphael with his mistress on his lap, a beautiful carpet spread at their feet. Again Feroza showed her predilection to go into a daze before choice artifacts, and again Manek showed his irritation and impatience. Sometimes he strode off on a solitary tour of the other rooms and returned to discover that Feroza had hardly progressed.

"If you don't want me to appreciate art, why do you bring me here?" Feroza protested.

"Of course I want you to, but I don't want to watch your teeth fall out one by one and your hair turn gray while you're at it."

"So? They're my teeth and my hair and what's it to you?"

They both sensed that there was more than just the love of art involved. Each gauged the undercurrent and direction of the other's strength. And though they enjoyed the battle of wits, snug in their customary mode of communication, it was really a test of their wills: of Feroza asserting her independence by contradicting Manek and countermanding his least suggestion, and of Manek patiently plugging away at tempering her rebellious spirit and bending her will to his own.

The more Manek pressed, the more Feroza balked at writing to the universities and junior colleges for information, until Manek, afraid she might back off and miss altogether the opportunity for a superior education in the United States and, just as important, the benefit of his guidance, wrote to them in her stead.

Manek decided to change his tactics. In fact, carried away by a more critical analysis of their relationship and his part in it, he decided to reform.

Manek awoke one balmy morning (perhaps the clear morning had something to do with it) fired by a determination to conduct himself like an exemplary uncle, a tactful repository of patience and wisdom.

Aware of the tenacity of Manek's ingenious will and mistrustful of his motives, Feroza mounted a formidable campaign against both his will and his exemplary unclehood.

But Manek, committed to his resolve and to his ardor to advantage his niece, surprised himself, and her, by exercising heroic though fitful bouts of restraint and patience.

Feroza was surprised by this novel tack and then perplexed by his behavior. She began to find his patience patronizing and his spurts of restraint devious and unnerving. She soon came to the conclusion that she much preferred the domineering, contentious, and devilish uncle she knew to the implausibly tolerant, mercurial, and unsuitable saint he was transforming into.

Manek wondered why, after all he did and was prepared to do for her, Feroza constantly quarreled with him and walked around with a face like a waterlogged mattress. Feroza's growing intractability and ingratitude began to bewilder him and to undermine his confidence in his reformed spirit. It seemed to him as if the more he did for her, the less she respected or appreciated him.

After they were done with the museums in Cambridge and Boston, Manek resolutely drove Feroza to the exhibits of contemporary paintings at the art galleries at Wellesley and Brandeis.

And when Feroza, appropriating for herself all the credit for their unexpected compatibility, began at last to believe that her struggle against Manek's will was beginning to pay off and that he was becoming not only more considerate of her wishes but also more consistent with his forbearance, they visited the Peabody Museum at Salem, the North Shore town in Massachusetts once famous for its witches.

Fate reserves for each mortal hero a last straw that will break his back.

It was Saturday afternoon. The forty-five minute drive to Salem was spectacular with dogwood, and the emerald radiance of a New England spring lifted their spirits. The Ford bounced along as well as it could on its worn shocks, clattering like a contented rattlesnake at fifty-five miles an hour.

Manek and Feroza both lowered their guard. Full of good cheer, they conversed as was normal with them — that is, before they were locked into their recent misunderstandings: bantering, kidding, Manek hectoring, Feroza retorting. Amused by each other's quips and enchanted by their own sharp wits, uncle and niece were relieved to find themselves on familiar turf.

They drove into Salem, a town with small gabled frame houses and the other accouterments of nineteenth-century architecture.

The museum was at one end of a renovated mall. The complex held restaurants, a theater, shops, and a bar.

"Now don't pull the zombie act on me, *boochimai*," Manek warned as they walked across the parking lot. "I'm beginning to lose my patience with you. I don't want to drive back after dark."

"What're you afraid of?" Feroza said, blithely throwing caution to the breeze. "That your old tin pot will break down?"

"Look, I'm not a lady of leisure like you. I've got to plan my time. You can sit in front of the TV till your eyes become square, but I have to work. You're really quite ungrateful," he added, finally revealing the true cause of his outrage. "When did the car last break down? Why do you hate it so much?"

Feroza wished she'd been more tactful. He was still sensitive about the jalopy. She was pleased all the same that she had finally penetrated the unendurable shield of his all-suffering and all-forgiving complacence.

At the tail end of their museum tour, Feroza discovered a room filled with Eastern miniatures and Persian rugs. It reminded her of the museum in Lahore, and she ached with nostalgia for the first time since she'd come to the United States.

Feroza spent a full ten minutes hovering about the Moghul miniatures and, like a besotted lover, settled on a wooden bench to ogle an intricately woven hunting scene on a Persian silk rug.

"There we go!" groaned Manek, eyeing with disgust the lions with their uplifted paws, the decapitated deer, the trailing vegetation, and the turbaned men aiming spears.

"Oh, Manek, you've no eye for beauty. These are priceless treasures. Look at the clear lines in the detail."

An attractive young woman, holding a little redheaded girl by the hand, turned and gave Feroza a discreet smile of complicity.

"I appreciate treasures also," Manek said in a reasonable and convincing manner, playing to the gallery.

However, the minute the alluring gallery stepped out of earshot with her daughter, Manek moved closer to Feroza and hissed, "But I don't sit down like a lump and turn into a pillar of salt every time I look back. If you don't move in the next ten minutes, I'm going."

Manek wandered through the two remaining rooms and came back in a little over ten minutes.

"You're still here?" He was surprised. "Come on. You've seen the rug, you've seen the lions, you've seen the trees. That's enough. Come on." Manek took her arm.

"Oh, Manek!" Feroza shrugged away his hand and turned her rapt and reproachful face to him. "You're nothing but a local yokel, after all!"

"And you? What're you? A fat obstinate mule. Don't expect me to carry you out. Come on."

Feroza ignored him.

"I'm going," Manek warned.

"Go."

Dark shadows crept into the green afternoon outside. The crickets started their strumming. Feroza, cocooned among the rugs and miniatures, sat oblivious.

Some time later she heard a door shut and gave a start. She looked at her watch. It was 4:30.

Feroza went through the rooms looking for Manek. There was hardly anyone about, and her footsteps echoed in the empty halls. She became acutely uneasy. The light coming in through the windows lengthened the shadows.

"Can I help you?" It was the guard. He looked as she would

have expected a museum guard to: tough, middle-aged, and gray. Even his hair looked strong.

"I'm looking for my uncle," Feroza said shakily.

"What does he look like? I'll keep a look out for him."

"He's got curly hair, and he wears glasses. He's dark," she added — rather unnecessarily, she thought at once. The guard would hardly expect her uncle to be white.

"I'll wait where my uncle left me," Feroza said and retreated to her perch on the bench. She didn't once glance at the fine hunting scene that had absorbed her attention all afternoon.

At 4:45 Feroza heard the doors being bolted, and a moment later the guard came into the room, jangling an enormous bunch of keys that looked more lethal than the gun he wore on his hip. Not bothering to conceal the suspicion his inflection conveyed, he asked, "Hasn't your uncle turned up?"

Feroza shook her head and instinctively tried to appear as stupid, innocent, and unlike an international art thief as she could.

"Sorry ma'am, I've got to lock up. The museum closes at five."

Feroza looked at the man pleadingly, artlessly adopting the help-less, hurt-puppy expression practiced by her grandmother.

"You can wait outside," the man suggested, at once kinder, less suspicious.

The guard locked the doors and, hitching up his navy trousers, adjusting his gun belt, sat down next to Feroza on the museum steps.

"How long will your uncle be, you think?" he asked, scanning the parking lot.

Feroza turned her nervous face to him. "I don't know."

In a little while the burly man stood up, readjusted his trousers and gun belt, and said, "Come on, we'll go through the parking lot. It's no use just sitting here. D'you know the license number?"

Feroza shook her head. "No, but I'd recognize the car. It's an old Ford. Blue."

They went through the parking lot in front of the theater and past the ice-cream parlor and a liquor store. The lot was full of out-of-state cars from the Boston area. Feroza remembered that Manek had plan-ned to buy beer. They went into the liquor store but found no uncle.

The security officer and Feroza settled down on the museum steps to wait again. He removed his uniform cap and passed his hand over his ironlike hair in an apologetic and weary gesture. "I have to go," he said. "But I can't leave you sitting here. I'll call the police, they'll help you find the car and look for your uncle. Will that be all right?"

"I guess so," Feroza said. She was close to tears.

The man called the police on his cellular phone.

Almost instantly two patrol cars rolled up, one behind the other, their blue-and-yellow lights blinking in the eerie Salem dusk.

The guard went up to the first car to explain the situation. The policeman from the other car sauntered up to join them and held the front door open for Feroza. He was very young, tough, and mean-looking. He shut the door and got into the back.

The museum guard looked in the window at Feroza. "You'll be all right now." He indicated the policeman in the driver's seat. "Ben'll look after you."

They cruised around the parking lot several times and then drove up and down the narrow, run-down streets leading from the mall.

There were no signs of a 1970 Ford.

The night was darker here than in Cambridge, probably because Salem was a small town and had fewer lights, Feroza reflected. Perhaps the witches preferred to do whatever it was they did in the dark.

"Where do you live?" the policeman in the driver's seat, whom the guard had called Ben, asked, jolting Feroza out of her reverie. He was a little older than the officer in the back. Feroza's heart skipped a beat. He was handsome.

"In Gulberg, in Lahore."

"What's that again?"

"In Pakistan."

"In Pack-iss-tan!" Ben pronounced the word the American way, obviously surprised and hugely amused. "Did you hear that, Jack?" He looked at his colleague in the rearview mirror. "This young lady here says she lives in Pack-iss-tan!"

Feroza liked the way he said it. She glanced at him when they stopped at a traffic light. He had a high-arched nose, an elegant sweep to his cheeks, and a wide chin that jutted at a commanding angle beneath his cap. The friendly, cheerful officer made her feel less afraid.

"I mean, where do you live in America?" Ben asked.

"In Somerville."

"That's in Massachusetts!" Again he sounded surprised, though less so. "We can get you there if we hav'ta, but we sure can't get you back to Pack-iss-tan!" The man laughed and raising an eyebrow, glanced at Feroza flirtatiously. He was really quite young. "D'you have the address in Somerville?"

"I think so," Feroza said.

Her vaulting, susceptible heart distracting her, Feroza rummaged in her leather sling-bag for the white card Manek had given her. The cop switched on the light. Feroza tipped the bag and emptied its entire contents on the seat. She could not find the card with the address.

"Sorry, I think I've lost it," she said.

"Is that all the money you have?" Ben looked inquisitively at the few crumpled dollar bills among the strewn contents of her bag.

Feroza nodded.

"Do you know anyone near here?"

"No."

"Any close relatives in the United States?"

"Only my uncle."

"Do you have any phone numbers at all?"

"No."

"Do you have your passport or ticket or anything?"

"No."

Although Feroza felt utterly foolish and was scarlet with embarrassment and shyness, still it occurred to her how different this interrogation was from the grilling she had been put through at Kennedy Airport.

"Do you know where the nearest Pack-iss-tan Consulate is?"

"No."

They once again drove slowly up and down the narrow streets.

Ben pointed out the famous house with the seven gables and the Witches Museum where, he explained, innocent women were burned at the stake only a few hundred years earlier.

The policeman turned into a narrow street and parked the car alongside the curb. He turned his face to Feroza. The light inside was still on.

"Lemme get this straight. You have no money, no passport. You don't know where you're going, and you have no address. You have an uncle who appears to have abandoned you, and no phone numbers. What're we to do with you?"

He looked at Feroza for a long, disconcerting moment and, as if drawing inspiration from her bewildered, nervous, and apologetic face, announced, "We'll cruise around the parking lot again, and if your uncle isn't there, we'll go to the police station."

Feroza turned helpless eyes to Ben and nodded her agreement.

The officer in the back, Jack, had not said a word all this while.

Ben drove slowly up the narrow streets and once more entered the shopping center parking lot. They cruised up and down the lanes and drove up to the museum.

Feroza spotted the old Ford almost at once. Even in the dark, it was unmistakable. It rolled up from the opposite direction and came to a stop at the driver's window. Feroza saw Manek's face turned to them in the flashing light.

Speaking as if nothing had transpired in the interval he had been away and as if it was quite normal for him to locate Feroza in strange police cars, Manek said, "Come on. Get into the car."

The mean-looking young cop in the back got out. Moving with the aggressive, thick-muscled gait of American police officers, he swaggered over to Manek. "What happened?" he asked.

"Nothing, officer," Manek said matter-of-factly. "My niece is very stubborn. I was only teaching her a lesson."

The policeman was incredulous. He placed his hands on the car's open window and, leaning forward, brought his face on a level with Manek's.

"Teaching her a lesson? In a strange city, with no money, no passport, and no address?"

132

"I wasn't going to lose her, officer."

In the driver's seat, Ben turned his pale and shocked face to Feroza. He pointed his thumb over his shoulder and asked, "Do you want to go with him?"

"Do I have a choice?"

The policeman was looking at her in a way that made her blush. She quickly lowered her eyes and, turning her face away, fiddled with the handle. Ben leaned across her to open the door.

She was quite out of breath. She thanked him. The other policeman escorted her to the Ford. Feroza got in and pulled in her coat.

"You sure you're gonna be all right?" the young officer asked. He sounded doubtful.

"Yes, of course, officer," Feroza said. Jack shut the door and said, "Now, you take care." He gave Manek a long, intense, warning look.

They drove along the dark highway silently. The headlights were not as bright as they should have been, and Manek needed to concentrate on the winding roads. The lights swept past the trees, lighting up the front ranks and making the area behind appear dark and densely forested.

Manek was the first to speak. "So, *boochimai,* you lost the address. Typical Third World carelessness."

Silence.

Five minutes later: "You did quite well, you know. You didn't lose your head."

"Really?"

Manek chose to ignore the sarcasm implicit in her tone. "Yes, you did all the right things. You didn't panic, you didn't approach strangers for help, and you got the cops to help you. You also seemed to be getting along with them quite well. That's pretty good."

"You bastard! You left me alone in a strange city, in a strange country, at the mercy of strange people. You knew I had no money. I didn't even know the name of the state. Anything could have happened to me. Anything!" Feroza was by now screaming. "Wait till

Granny hears about this! Wait till Mummy and Daddy hear about this! Wait till Rohinton *kaka* and Jeroo *kaki* hear about it. They'll never speak to you. I don't believe you did this. I can't believe — "

"Stop making such a song and dance about nothing. I was keeping my eye on you . . ."

"My left foot! If this had happened to you . . . Oh, don't speak to me. Don't say one more word! And you had the brazenness to tell your sister, all goody-goody and sweetie-sweetie, 'Don't worry,' " Feroza made a face, savagely impersonating a grotesquely simpering Manek, " 'I'll look after Feroza.' "

"Some looking after! And you've the nerve to say I'm doing a song and dance? Granny will show you what a song and dance really is! She'll straighten you out. She'll cut you off without a *paisa*. She'll kick you out of her house!"

"You'll thank me for this one day." Manek's voice carried a becalmed, syrupy inflection that thickened it. Feroza felt a chill creep into her body. Her recollection of the incident was vivid.

Manek had helped her up a tree. She couldn't have been more than three or four. She had found herself straddling a scratchy branch sixteen feet from the ground, and, terrified, she had shut her eyes. The limb she clung to was not very thick, and it dipped slightly with her weight.

"Just hang on," Manek said, slowly backing away from her. "Come on, open your eyes, don't be frightened," he said. "See? You can look into everybody's houses. I'll be back very soon. I'll show you a trick."

An unaccustomed calm and sweetness had washed his voice, soothing her, inducing a feeling of affection and trust. Unable to handle her terror after Manek disappeared, Feroza had frozen into some kind of a trance.

Manek had reappeared at the fork of her branch with a handsaw.

"I want to get down. Get me down," Feroza bawled, feeling the ground sway and fall away from her.

"Don't cry." Again that tranquilizing voice quieting her. "I'll get you down in just two minutes if you stop making noise."

Manek began sawing off the branch she was sitting on.

134

The cook, on his way to the servants' quarters, heard Feroza whimper. "What're you doing up there?" he yelled.

Only then did he notice what Manek was up to.

Feroza's childish mind had absorbed only the logic of Manek's actions and his comforting voice. He'd said he'd get her down, and lopping off the branch was as quick a way of getting her down as any.

In the subsequent hullabaloo, Feroza had realized her danger.

For the first time, driving on the night road winding through a faraway country, viewing the incident from the perspective of her young adulthood, Feroza recognized the enormous treachery. How he must have hated her, she thought, suddenly confronting the issue.

Feroza had never, despite everything, acknowledged the darker side of Manek's nature. She had known it in her bones, but she had not allowed it the sanction of consciousness. To acknowledge it would be to accept that she was the cause, the irritant, the inducer of the evil.

"I've taught you a very important lesson: how to look out for yourself." Manek's insinuating voice was superimposed on her thoughts. "You'll have to cope with all sorts of unexpected situations. This has taught you more about America than six months of pampering. You'll see, you'll gain confidence. You can't rely on anyone but yourself if you want to live in this country — not even on me!"

"Who wants to live in any country with you in it? Who wants you to teach me anything? I'd be better off with a *goonda* than with you!"

"One day you'll thank me for this," he said again. Still that ominous sweetness, that glacial calm.

Feroza became quite hysterical. And by the time they entered their driveway, so was Manek.

"Look, you fool," he shouted as he got out of the car and waited for Feroza to slide out across his seat. "I'm only trying to prepare you for life!"

Manek slammed the door shut after her; the heavy car swayed with the impact. "You have to learn to listen to others — to be more considerate of their feelings and wishes. You can't keep people waiting. You can't have everything your way. If you don't understand that, you'll just have to learn to obey and respect your elders and betters."

"Do you listen to your elders! Look — you can prepare yourself all you want, but let me live my life! I know you tried to kill me when I was a child! You bastard!"

They were climbing the stairs, and Manek had to skip out of reach of Feroza's sudden kick. He pinned her to the bannister and held her hands as Feroza furiously tried to pummel him.

Bruised and battered they went straight up to the attic. Neither switched on the light. They sat silent, brooding in the dark, Feroza on the stuffed chair and Manek on the bed, breathing heavily.

"Why did you try to kill me?"

It was that kind of a night for Feroza. She was surprised by how belatedly she had understood the past that Manek's voice had unexpectedly recalled. And almost simultaneously with the understanding had come the sorting out, the acceptance.

"You're a cat. You have nine lives."

"You must really have hated me."

"Yes."

Feroza didn't ask why. Although the answer seemed to come to her only now, she sensed she had known it for as far back as she could remember.

Instead she asked, "Do you still hate me?"

"Of course not, silly," Manek said.

Then he said, "My mother shouldn't have spoilt you like that. I was a child myself; I couldn't handle it. Don't worry, I got over it long ago. Those were childhood reactions."

Feroza believed him. His voice was normal again.

At least, she thought after a while, the dying fish had distracted them from each other.

Chapter 13

Manek's mailbox bulged with information from the colleges he had written to. After going through various brochures and catalogs, assessing the courses, and calculating the fees, Manek thought it would be best if Feroza went to Boston College. She could live in the dorms and visit him over the weekends. He would be near enough to assist and advise her.

Feroza studied the map of America and announced her preference for a college across the breadth of the map, in the vicinity of San Diego.

"But that's in California! You'll be too far away to keep an eye on," Manek protested.

"Exactly. Do you want me to be independent, or not?"

Jamil suggested a compromise: Middlebury, a small college in Vermont, or if she preferred something larger, Dartmouth in New Hampshire. Bates would be a good choice in Maine, as would Colby. Feroza would be far enough away to feel independent and near enough for Manek to be on call in case of an emergency.

Jamil could not disclose how crushed he felt at the thought of Feroza's departure from the attic, but he spent as much time as he could with them, trying to be helpful.

The matter was resolved when Manek and Feroza received three letters apiece from Pakistan in response to their one.

Between them, the six letters expressed so many fears and doubts that Feroza and Manek were briefly swept with self-doubt and then concerned that the family would not permit Feroza to remain in America.

The letters also conveyed the news that Mr. Anwar, the prosecuting attorney in the Bhutto trial and a family friend, had died of a sudden heart attack. Feroza burst into tears and Manek's eyes were red the next day. They penned careful letters of condolence to the widow and their lively daughter Naveed, who had been among the clingers and touchers seeing Feroza off at the airport.

Cyrus had tried to temper the sadness by relating the joke that was making the rounds. The angel Gabriel had summoned first a judge and then the attorney, so that Bhutto's case could continue and the cause of justice be served even after the hanging. Most catastrophes were converted into jokes. How else could ordinary people tolerate what was happening to the country and to them?

es

A couple of days later, the mail brought encouraging news from a junior college in Twin Falls, Idaho. They were willing to offer a stipend that would cover much of the tuition. Living expenses in a small town would be affordable, and Manek knew that Idaho was in Mormon territory.

To Manek, the timing of the letter's arrival appeared providential, and the clauses in the application form, although they were not as austere as he had expected, resolved the issue.

During his summer tour of the United States, Manek had visited Salt Lake City. He remembered the thirst he had not been able to abate with Coke or beer, both forbidden in the state governed by Mormon values. Twin Falls, like Salt Lake City, was in the secure and irreproachable heart of Mormon territory. Even Khutlibai would appreciate the sobriety of Mormon principles.

Feroza liked the name of the city and the distance between it and Boston on the map. Manek felt that the junior college and the size of the city would ease her assimilation into the American way of life.

Manek helped Feroza fill out the application form. "You're lucky I'm not sending you off to Brigham Young University in Salt Lake City," he said severely. "Not only wouldn't you be allowed to drink or indulge in premarital sex, you'd have to pledge to abide by the college dress and conduct codes. Which means you wouldn't be allowed to wear shorts or bikinis. And if you were a boy, you'd be forbidden to grow a beard or keep your hair long."

"I'm not going there," Feroza said with a note of incipient rebellion, "so why are you telling me this?"

That disturbed Manek and deepened his regret. "Maybe you should. It might be worth looking into it."

"As if I'd ever wear shorts, let alone a bikini!" Feroza sounded scandalized, and Manek's doubts retreated.

Manek wrote a long letter, addressed jointly to Khutlibai, Zareen, and Cyrus. He described the Mormon faith in the light of his limited knowledge, and the puritanical laws supporting it in Idaho. The state, he wrote, did not permit the sale of liquor or allow striptease. It banned prostitution and discouraged discos and all forms of provocative dancing. Caffeine, even in its most innocuous forms like tea or coffee, was not served in most restaurants.

Manek was not one hundred percent certain of all this, but from his experiences in Salt Lake City, he was sure he was close to the mark. His letter would go a long way to assuage family fears and phobias. He left it to them to assume that a community that forbade even coffee was not likely to permit promiscuous sex.

Manek concluded the letter by reiterating that Twin Falls was a small, safe, conservative town that cultivated potatoes and that he would go with Feroza during the orientation to see her safely and comfortably settled.

The contents of Manek's letter were indeed soothing and had the desired effect. Touched by his consideration for their fears and feelings and by his concern for his niece's welfare, Zareen and Cyrus agreed to permit Feroza to study in America.

Khutlibai maintained a noncommittal and disquieting silence on the subject.

☙

Since Feroza had applied late, she didn't get word of her admission until early July. The new term started in September, so at the very latest, they'd have to leave for Twin Falls by the third week of August. Feeling rushed, Manek worked out an itinerary. He'd have to prepare Feroza, cram her with worldly wisdom in the short time available to him. It was his responsibility to teach her to be less trusting and more alert before setting her loose in Idaho.

At least he had, through vigilant sniffs, taught her to use

deodorant and, when she was in a pliant mood, succeeded in extracting an occasional apology when she interrupted.

Then there were the little things that had caused him an extraordinary amount of difficulty and embarrassment when he came to America, such as opening milk cartons, which, like Feroza, he had tried to pry open with a knife with the result that the milk had spilled everywhere. It gave him pleasure to show Feroza how easy it was to turn the top into a spout once you knew how.

When Feroza tugged at plastic wrappers and impatiently tore at them with her teeth, Manek said, "You'll only lose your teeth that way!" and showed her the marked place where the plastic tore easily.

And each time Manek saw Feroza wrestle with a jar or juice bottle or tamper-proof vial, he said, "Remember this: If you have to struggle to open something in America, you're doing it wrong. They've made everything easy. That's how a free economy works," and he'd tap, press, pry, or bang the lid against the counter and effortlessly unscrew whatever it was.

Before long, the moment Manek would say, "Remember — ," Feroza would pipe up: "If you have to struggle, you're doing it wrong!"

If Feroza was impressed by the genius of the American free marketers, she never revealed it to Manek.

Manek made a private list of all that Feroza should know, experience, or do before going to Idaho.

Many items on the list were tackled through direct discussions and negotiation. Often he sat her down, face-to-face, and ladled out instructions and advice.

All this Feroza accepted with surprising docility and grace. It was the only way to be rid of an issue on her uncle's mind or on his agenda.

As the list shrank, Manek became less worried. And one Saturday afternoon, cheerfully rubbing his hands, he asked, "What do you say to a free steak dinner at a posh place?"

"Okay," Feroza said.

In dealing with her uncle, Feroza had learned not to become

overly enthusiastic. It gave Manek a perverse pleasure to disappoint her if she displayed her expectations. What made it worse were the homilies he'd tack on. Hence the dry "Okay."

"Come on, then. We'll have lunch in Boston."

The restaurant was decorous with candlelight, silver cutlery, and crisp white table linens. It was also quite full.

Manek developed lordly airs the moment they stepped inside the plush, thickly carpeted interior. He refused to sit at the table in a secluded nook they were directed to and chose instead to lead the captain to one in the center of a group of occupied tables. Other diners had to shift their chairs to make room.

They were served garlic bread and rolls. Feroza spread her starched white napkin on her lap. Manek ordered a beer for himself and an orange juice for Feroza.

They scanned the menu and, after discussion and dithering during which Manek remarked two or three times, "Don't worry about the prices — order what you like," decided on T-bone steaks. Manek ordered medium for Feroza and medium rare for himself.

"If I see any pink in the meat, I won't eat it," Feroza declared, and Manek accommodatingly changed the order of her steak to well done, contenting himself by remarking merely, "You'll kill the taste of the costly meat — but never mind."

Feroza reached for a roll. "You saw the prices. How do you expect to get away without paying? I hope you're not going to embarrass me."

"It doesn't take much to embarrass you when you see *gora-chittas,* does it?"

"Look," Feroza said, "don't try to palm off your complexes on me. If you're going to shame me, I'm going!" She picked up her handbag and raised her bottom an inch off her seat.

"Stop being childish," Manek said quickly, reaching out to restrain her. Feroza could tell he was prepared to use force if necessary. "I'm not going to embarrass you; I have coupons. We pay for one dinner and get the other free."

Feroza was by now accustomed to the special offers at McDonald's, Burger King, and Kentucky Fried Chicken that Manek assiduously kept track of. She was also used to the buy-one-get-one-free meals advertised by the smaller Greek, Middle Eastern, and Mexican restaurants that abounded around Harvard Square.

Feroza buttered her roll with equanimity and absently made a mental calculation. The total she arrived at and the possible impact of the figure on their lives popped into her mind and sounded a warning.

"Just the one meal will cost more than you spend in two weeks on food," she said thoughtfully. "Are we going to fast for the rest of the month?"

"Just eat and enjoy. Do you want a treat or not?"

"Not if we're going to live on *dal* and rice for the next two weeks."

"Why do you argue about everything? I told you we're getting free meals. Trust me."

"Oh God," Feroza said, dropping her head on the heel of her palm. "Now I'm really nervous!"

They polished off all the rolls, butter, and garlic bread. Manek ordered another beer and, for Feroza, another juice.

The waiter set up a round-topped table on a tripod near them. Solemnly he served them the steaks and, as though bestowing jewels, small portions of glazed baby carrots, potatoes, and asparagus.

Feroza's mouth watered as she watched the unfolding drama of the banquet. She fell to eating the moment the waiter turned his immaculate back on them.

"Hey, take it easy. The T-bone won't run away."

"I want to eat it while it's hot," Feroza said.

"Listen, don't eat more than half your steak. It's bad manners."

Feroza looked up from her plate, incredulous. Her parsimonious uncle, who considered it his sacred duty to get his paid-for pound of flesh and preached her a sermon on starving Ethiopians and Bangladeshis every time she rinsed a grain of rice from her plate, was asking her to waste half her steak?

"Just a minute," Manek said, leaning purposefully towards her, fork and knife in hand. And, as Feroza confusedly lifted her hands clear, he neatly sawed off the charred edges of her well-done steak.

Manek pushed the severed pieces to one side and instructed, "Don't touch that."

Feroza looked at his face again and decided it would be politic to relinquish the segregated portions of her steak unprotested.

She noted with curiosity that Manek did the very opposite with his. He ate round the edges of his T-bone and left a reddish stump in the center uneaten.

"Finish up the vegetables," Manek directed.

When Feroza had eaten the vegetables and her allotted portion of steak, Manek raised his hand and snapped his fingers to catch their waiter's attention.

Looking faintly startled and irritated by the uncouth behavior of his customer, the waiter glided forward. Managing to look both servile and supercilious at the same time, he leaned forward:

"Yes?"

"I would like to have a word with the head waiter. Please call him."

Manek had assumed the air and authority of a man used to having his way and paying well for good service.

The man's disdainful demeanor underwent a subtle change: he appeared uncertain. "Yes, sir," he said and quietly slid away.

In a little while an urbane, distinguished-looking man with gray sideburns and shrewd, blue Scandinavian eyes stood before them.

"What can I do for you, sir? I'm the manager."

"Your restaurant was highly recommended to us. I must admit I'm disappointed. The steaks are useless. Look at that," Manek pointed at the charred remains of Feroza's well-done steak. "Burnt. "And this," Manek's finger hovered accusingly above the bloody stump on his plate. "I asked for a medium-rare steak, not raw cow."

"We'll get you fresh steaks, sir." The manager was polite but firm. "You'll have no complaints, I'm sure, sir."

He signaled the waiter to pick up their plates.

"I'm afraid, after looking at this, my appetite's gone," Manek said. "I came here to celebrate my fiancé's birthday, not to feel sick. I won't pay the bill. The happy occasion is ruined."

Feroza wanted to sink through the floor.

The distinguished-looking manager's Scandinavian eyes turned into glacial chips of Arctic ice. They appeared to know exactly what Manek was up to.

"You don't need to pay," the manager said, a dangerous inflection making his voice hum with menace. "Get out."

The manager took a small step, and his hand darted to the back of Manek's chair.

For a split second, Manek looked confused. Then he shot up like a startled goose just as the manager yanked the chair out from under him.

Convinced all eyes in the room had witnessed their humiliation, her face flaming and head bent, Feroza quickly followed Manek out.

"I've never been so humiliated in all my life!" Feroza said as they scrambled into the car.

Manek remained quiet.

It was only after they had merged with the traffic on Sturrow Drive and were coasting along beside the Charles River that Manek deigned to speak.

"The first lesson you learn in life is to be humble. If you weren't so proud, you wouldn't feel so humiliated, and you'd have enjoyed the wonderful dinner."

Manek's profile was as unrepentant and clear as the sunny faces of the students in the boats bobbing on the Charles.

"These people are so damn rich that one little steak won't matter to them." Manek did not sound bitter, only quasi-profound.

Feroza had been the recipient of this quasi-profundity quite frequently of late, and she listened to him with mounting irritation.

"You've got to skim what you can off the system, otherwise the system will skin you. I learned this the hard way," said Manek the Sage. "After the accident, I had only the tuition money. Hardly any insurance. It would've taken our family seven generations to pay the hospital bills. It taught me many things. It's lucky for you I've taken the knocks and you're reaping the rewards. I'm giving you a crash course. It's the best way to get over culture shock. Pampering only prolongs the agony. I didn't have anyone to take my hand and guide me and say, 'Look, sweetie, this is how you open a wrapper, and this is how you open a jar!' But you're young, you can be molded. You'll do all right if you learn humility."

About a week before their departure for Twin Falls, Manek observed Feroza licking the rice off her fingers in an Indian restaurant. He looked at her until she became aware of his gaze. "You've got to stop eating with your fingers," he said. "It makes them sick."

And, in her last three days in Cambridge, he banned the practice even when they were alone, overriding her protests by saying, "It's all very nice and cozy to be 'ethnic' when we're together, but those people won't find it 'ethnic,' they'll just puke."

Had he prepared her enough? Had he overlooked something vital? Could anyone be prepared enough? He'd done the best he could. Once Feroza lived with Americans, she'd recall everything he'd taught her quick enough. She'd learn a lot besides.

Chapter 14

Twin Falls and the local junior college were exactly as Manek had imagined them. The small-town atmosphere on campus was genial, relaxed, and wholesome. Feroza wouldn't find it too difficult to cope, considering the crash-course in American survival she had been subjected to — and the surprising capacity for adaptation she had revealed.

Feroza was hurt. Why did everybody refer to her college as school? Once she had taken her matric exam she had hoped to be rid of school forever. Was a junior college then merely an extension of school and not a college? She was also quite bewildered by the profusion of buildings and roads and had no sense of where she was most of the time.

Manek explained that in America people referred to even Harvard and M.I.T. as "schools," and he assured her she would find her way blindfolded in a few days.

The counselor smiled and stood up when Feroza and Manek entered her small, sun-bright office crowded with files and books. "You must be the new Pakistani student. I'm Emily Simms," she said, extending her hand. She looked admiringly at Feroza's embroidered shirt and came round her desk to examine it. "Now isn't that pretty?"

The alert, short, and comfortably slender woman put Feroza at ease at once. Feroza guessed she must be her mother's age. After a few pleasant remarks, Emily said, "We don't get many foreign students, but we do have a few. We sure are happy to have you with us. Once you've adjusted and know your way around, I think you'll enjoy Southern Idaho College and Twin Falls. It's not a very large town, but it's safe and everybody's friendly." The counselor smiled, responding affectionately to Feroza's eager expression.

"That's why I selected the college for her," said the solemn uncle. "We come from a conservative background, Mrs. Simms, and I think my niece will be happy here."

"We'll do our best," said the counselor. "Anytime you have a problem, just come right in and we'll sort it out."

Emily tucked Feroza's arm beneath her protective wing and walked them to the neat, two-storied brick-and-glass dormitory. Feroza found its simple straight lines elegant and architecturally satisfying.

The counselor introduced them to Jo, Feroza's roommate. Jo had a large, sullen face and a wary, hostile air that prompted Manek to take Feroza aside and anxiously warn, "Watch out for your valuables. Be careful with her. You don't have to be rude, but don't get too cozy right away. She could be a bad influence."

How bad, Feroza was soon to discover. She often wondered what Manek would have done had he known. As it was, Jo had burst into the room a few minutes later to shout furiously, "What the fuck! The damn toilet flooded when I flushed!"

Manek had just left to buy something from the campus bookstore, otherwise Feroza might have had to listen to more words of dire warning.

Feroza was more surprised, though, by Manek's blushing unease in Jo's presence when he took them both to lunch at a small Mexican restaurant. He was diffident and embarrassingly anxious to make a good impression on the large, unsmiling girl. Wisps of blond hair escaping from a ponytail and tickling her face, Jo chewed gum and looked at them with an insouciance that bordered on disdain. "Where are y'all from — Mexico?" she asked eventually and appeared to unbend a little when Manek told her they were from Pakistan. Feroza was flattered to be mistaken for a Mexican.

After this clarification, Jo began responding to Manek's questions with more than just a monosyllable. And when she cracked an unaccustomed social smile, Manek became so touchingly pleased that Feroza realized the dimensions of the *gora* complex that constantly challenged his brown Pakistani psyche. And he'd been so prompt to accuse Feroza of *her* awe of the whites!

Manek spent three days at a motel near the campus, helping Feroza during the orientation. He stood in line to collect forms and helped get her registered. He bought the prescribed books, paid her college and board fees, and opened a bank account in her name. They explored the campus, visited the library and the dorm laundry, checked out the classrooms, and met some of Feroza's teachers. Saying, "Where do you want this socialist crook strung up?" Manek even helped hang Bhutto's large poster on the wall next to Feroza's bed.

After instructing Feroza on all matters he could think of, Manek gravely requested her lumpish and indifferent roommate to look after her. "Could you help her with the laundry if something goes wrong with the machines? I've shown her once or twice, but she is a bit confused. Would you also show her where to get things?"

Jo nodded briefly and said, "Yeah," with all the enthusiasm of a cat charged with training a pup that has not been housebroken.

By the time Manek finally called for the taxi to take him to the airport, it was clear that he had changed his mind somewhat about Jo. His parting words to Feroza were, "You're lucky you've not been palmed off with some Japanese or Egyptian roommate. Jo's a real American; she'll teach you more than I can. Just remember everything I've told you. Don't become 'ethnic' and eat with your fingers in the dorm. And *don't* butt in when someone's talking."

Feroza had occasion to think of his words often.

Jo and Feroza gingerly accustomed themselves to each other's presence. Their initial conversations were hesitant, peppered with long, perplexed pauses, as each unconsciously studied the other's facial expressions and body gestures to determine the more exact meaning of what was said. Every time Jo spoke, Feroza looked at her with startled, anxious eyes. Jo sounded as if she were either quarreling or stolidly holding the lid on her irritation. Feroza took extra pains not to interrupt when Jo was talking — which some-times led to complex and baffling pauses.

Sensing that she might be giving out the wrong signals, Jo took care to keep her expression neutral. This gave Jo's deadpan face an inscrutable quality that made Feroza even more nervous. She took to furtively applying deodorant several times a day.

On the other hand, when Feroza spoke, Jo wondered if Feroza was being sarcastic or pulling her leg by mimicking some fancy British actress on public television. She couldn't believe that people actually said things like, "Do you mind if I turn off the light?" or, "Is it all right if I read? I wouldn't want to disturb you."

Feroza sounded mannered even to herself sometimes. She couldn't help it. It was the only way she knew to speak English with foreigners. The English she used while speaking to her friends in Lahore was informal because it had a mixture of Urdu and Punjabi words tossed in for emphasis, expression, or comic effect. When she talked to Manek, her intonation and accent also changed — not to mention the blithe bounce of the Gujrati idiom that popped into her English. But she could hardly speak to Jo that way. Jo would understand neither the syntax nor the pronunciation and would find her even more "foreign" and tedious than she perhaps already did.

It was almost like learning a new language, and both sometimes wondered if the other knew enough English.

Jo had more of an inkling of what was happening and a notion of what Feroza might be up against, talking and dressing the way she did.

By late October, the cold was beginning to hurt Feroza. She dreaded going outdoors and avoided any excursion that might take her even a few blocks from her dorm or classrooms.

She did not know how to manage her clothes. If she insulated herself adequately by wearing Manek's long woolen underwear, two pairs of socks, and a polo-neck sweater she sweated miserably in the heated classrooms and almost fainted. If she dressed to be comfortable in class, the red overcoat and red beret afforded little protection against the icy gusts that cut through her inadequate clothing to her skin, making her so cold that she got frightening cramps in her chest and legs.

One blustery afternoon as Feroza trudged bent and dismal behind Jo to a Walmart near the campus, she fancied the wind was an enemy that lurked around corners and deliberately sprang at her to make her teeth chatter, her nose drip, and her hands and feet turn numb and blue. It did not seem to affect anyone else the way it did her.

Brooding darkly along these lines, Feroza miserably allowed Jo to open the door for her and went into the store mumbling a bleak, "Thank you." She stamped her feet and, removing her gloves, breathed on her hands and on the glass bangles that felt like icy manacles binding her wrists and forearms.

Once she had thawed herself and removed her coat, they meandered to the warm heart of the store, where the following exchange took place between Feroza and the middle-aged, wiry little saleswoman behind the cosmetics counter.

"Can I have a look at some of those hair sprays, please?"

The glass bangles on her arms jingling, Feroza pointed at an array of hair sprays in a window behind the saleswoman. The name tag pinned to the saleswoman's pink-and-gray striped uniform read "Sally."

"Sure you can, honey. Look all you want," said Sally, busy with the cash register.

Feroza colored and said, "I mean, can I see some of them up close?"

Sally looked her up and down suspiciously as if measuring the degree of her "foreignness." She got off the stool behind her register, performing the feat as if descending a mountain, plonked three brands of hair spray on the glass shelf before Feroza, and climbed back to her busy seat.

Feroza read the labels on each and, holding the can she had selected timidly forth, nervously adjusting the shawl that had slid off her shoulder, ventured, "May I have this, please?"

"You may not. You'll have to pay for it. This isn't the Salvation Army, y'know; it's a drugstore."

Jo had registered the look the saleswoman gave Feroza and her rude behavior and had followed the exchange between them with mounting indignation and an increasingly threatening scowl. Used to Feroza's mode of dress and more accustomed by now to her manner of speaking and asking for things, she felt Sally had been unpardonably ill-mannered and bullying. She intervened protectively,

"Stop pickin' on her just because she's a foreigner! Here, lemme handle this," Jo said, pushing Feroza aside. "How much d'ya want?" she asked and belligerently unzipped her little wallet.

After she had collected the receipt and the parcel, Jo said to the saleswoman, "You got a problem with your attitude. You have to do something about that."

The saleswoman pursed her mouth and grimly turned her face.

Jo, who had set out to provoke her and whose face had brightened at the prospect of a battle in which the customer is always advantaged, drifted off, contenting herself by loudly remarking, "Stupid bitch!" and to Feroza, "Y'gotta learn! You don't have to take shit from trash like her!"

⁊

Jo took to dropping her jaw and saying to Feroza, "Are you for real? You don't have to always tell the truth, y'know!" or "You can't talk like that. They'll stomp all over you," and took charge of Feroza's life.

Feroza's Pakistani outfits and outrageously dangling earrings were banished to her suitcase and her wardrobe replenished by another pair of jeans to supplement the pair she had purchased at Bloomingdale's and some T-shirts, sweaters, and blouses. But no matter what Jo said, Feroza could not bring herself to wear skirts. Instead she bought a pair of pleated woolen slacks for more formal occasions.

"What's the matter with your legs?" Jo asked one evening when Feroza had, as usual, dexterously removed her clothes and wrapped herself up in her robe without revealing any part of her anatomy. "Are they crooked or fat or something? Lemme see."

Jo lunged across the space between their beds and swept aside the flap of Feroza's robe. Feroza sat stunned, legs bared to the thighs, blushing. It required a monumental effort on her part not to draw together the flaps of her robe.

"There's nothing wrong with them," said Jo in surprise. "Why d'you keep them hidden?" She pantomimed Feroza's furtive gestures.

"It's not decent to show your legs in Pakistan," Feroza said. Recalling the Punjabi movie she had seen before leaving, she used it as an example to explain her culture to Jo. The prancing heroine had tantalizingly lifted her sari to mid-calf and, after a coy look, let it fall;

151

the entire audience had burst into a chorus of whistles and catcalls.

From the very first day they started sharing the room, Jo's utter abandon where her large, white body was concerned had alarmed and embarrassed Feroza. When Jo undressed, Feroza would turn away on some pretext to her desk or run her hand over Bhutto's poster to iron out its creases. When Jo talked to her in a state of semi- or entire nudity, Feroza averted her eyes or stared fixedly into Jo's.

In fact, going to the washroom in the mornings was an ordeal for Feroza. Wrapped from neck to toe in her maroon robe, eyes downcast, Feroza darted to one of the unused washbasins with her toilet bag. Acutely aware of the freshly showered, gleaming bodies in various stages of undress, Feroza splashed her face, brushed her teeth, and slipped out as quickly and quietly as she had entered.

Then, at odd hours, towel in hand, Feroza lurked in the lobby leading to the washroom. She bathed only when she was sure she could lock the door and have the entire washroom to herself. Since this requirement could be met only at some unearthly hour of the night, she rarely bathed during the day.

Occasionally Feroza caught herself imagining those pink bodies, gently tracing the silken curves of the breasts, feeling the soft weight of the flesh in her hands. Sometimes she wanted to hold and be held by those soft bodies as ardently as she had dreamed of being held by the fully clothed, hard, brown bodies of the men she had had crushes on in Lahore.

Mortified and shaken by this new aspect of her desires, Feroza tried to suppress these images. She deliberately called up the attractive faces and bodies of various young men and summoned the emotions aroused in her by them. By diligently nurturing the once-familiar passions that had shamed her so much then and now appeared blameless, she succeeded in banishing the baffling and forbidden images from her mind.

At about this time, she also became aware of her different color and the reaction it appeared to have on strangers like that rude saleswoman, and on some of her classmates. Not that her classmates were discourteous. A few tended to avoid her, and these she disregarded. But some, in their anxiety to be civil, were exaggeratedly effusive and awkward in her presence. She sensed she was not accepted as one of them. Dismayed by her own brown skin, the emblem of her foreignness, she felt it was inferior to the gleaming white skin in the washrooms and the roseate faces in the classrooms.

To add to her confusion, Feroza was astonished, confounded, shocked, and intrigued by the behavior of her strange roommate. Not having known anyone even remotely like Jo, Feroza had no standard of comparison and categorized her vaguely in her mind as a "juvenile delinquent," a Western and, more specifically, American phenomenon.

In her effort to understand Jo, Feroza came to various complex conclusions. To begin with, she imagined that Jo had been packed off by a distraught family to this remote and austere "hick town" (Jo's term) to cure her of her various and unbridled appetites. Jo ate constantly and prodigiously and sometimes, when she was in the mood and could get hold of liquor — which she could get even in "dry" Twin Falls — drank herself maudlin. At such times, Feroza felt constrained to protect her, to let her vent her resentments and tears in the safety of her custody, and kept her tactfully closeted in the room they shared. Jo could be expelled for drinking in the dorms.

Jo had taken one look at Twin Fall's small downtown and had decided that it wasn't a place she wanted to visit again. Some of the restaurants were going out of business, and the stores on the main streets had the dusty, dispirited air of businesses buckling beneath the pressure of the new shopping mall closer to campus.

Going to the mall with Jo was a hair-raising experience. She was a slick thief. Jo seldom bought or let Feroza buy necessities. Toothpaste, shampoo, chocolates, razors, lotions, ballpoint pens were purloined as and when required. She occasionally paid for — or made Feroza pay for — a bag of potato chips or some item too bulky to be easily lifted. Feroza was more puzzled when she discovered that Jo's family owned a restaurant in Boulder, Colorado, and was comfortably well-off.

Feroza could never have imagined a girl as bold. To think that she, the hero-kicking "hoyden" of Lahore, was reduced to a wide-eyed, O-mouthed, and dumb little disciple shattered Feroza's confidence. She wondered if Jo's unconventional code of ethics and general behavior were the kind of shocks Manek had in mind when he had wanted her to plumb the American experience. She very much doubted it, even if her association with Jo might benefit her understanding of America and shorten the period of her adjustment and assimilation.

Feroza longed to talk to Manek about her roommate but was afraid. He might be upset and move her from Twin Falls before her initiation into the mysterious rites of Jo's way of life was complete. Feroza, nothing if not inquiring, realized she was going through a rare and unusually enlightening experience. And she was as loath to abandon the challenge, daily unraveling new and unexpected insights, as any of her intrepid and fierce-eyed foremothers would have been.

Jo and Feroza had only two classes in common. Sometimes a whole day passed without their meeting each other except in the dorm at night. Often they ate dinner at the same table, but not always. One evening in the dining room, Feroza asked someone where the "may-o-neeze" was. No one understood what she wanted, until she found the glass jar on a counter.

Jo spent the next Sunday afternoon improving Feroza's pronunciations and taught her to say mayonnaise as "may-nayze" and mother-fucker as "motha-fuka," with the accompanying curl of nose and emphasis. She made Feroza practice saying, "Gimme a lemonade. Gimme a soda," and cured her of saying, "May I have this — may I have that?"

Pretty soon Feroza was saying, "Hey, you goin' to the laundry? Gitme a Coke!"

By the time the first term was over, Jo had come to the conclusion that the constraints of dorm living did not suit her temperament or her allowance. She took a job waitressing at a nearby restaurant and decided to move into an off-campus apartment. She asked Feroza to move in with her. Feroza wrote a prudent letter to Manek, pointing out the enormous economic advantages of moving from the dormitory, with the result that Manek flew to Twin Falls over Christmas.

Manek and Feroza spent Christmas afternoon with Feroza's genial counselor and her family. Manek, who had balked at the thought of a whole afternoon spent amidst strangers on an occasion that was essentially a family affair, was surprised by how much he enjoyed the turkey and the company. When Jo returned from her brief visit home, Manek and Feroza took her on a tour of some of the apartments they felt were likely to suit their pockets and their requirements.

Feroza, nervous about Manek's meeting with Jo, explained to her, "You'll have to be careful with my uncle. He won't understand some of the things we do."

Jo said, "Yeah, I know, he's as square as dice. Don't worry."

And it was all right. If Jo had influenced Feroza, Feroza had, without either of them being conscious of it, influenced Jo.

Manek found Jo much more amiable at their second meeting and didn't get the impression that he was being slighted as often. In fact, he told Feroza in confidence, "You've had a good influence on Jo. She's almost become normal." Feroza noticed that Manek was much more at ease with Jo and less intense around her. She remarked on it, and Manek cryptically commented, "Yeah, I've got an American girlfriend."

They rented a decrepit two-bedroom apartment within cycling distance of the campus for three hundred dollars a month. It had mangy carpets, stained linoleum, fragile windows that were difficult to open, and a heating system entirely dependent on the caprice of the landlord. But it had an attraction. The landlord pointed out that the rooms above theirs were not occupied; they would have undisturbed quiet in which to study. Feroza bought a secondhand bicycle, and Jo a small thirdhand Corvette that required combat with the stick shift to put it into reverse.

Feroza was thrilled at the thought of living on her own with just Jo. Manek helped them move. They scoured the streets on trash day for discarded housewares and the Salvation Army outlet for discarded furniture. They acquired odd chairs, tables, two thread-bare mattresses, pans, a sofa bed, and lamps. Jo bought a color TV at a garage sale, and Manek stocked their cabinets with toilet paper, an economy-size box of Surf, and a broom. He crammed the kitchen shelves with Indian spices, rice, and lentils and covered the chairs with cushions. He wanted to stock their apartment with toiletries, but Jo, who was by now used to kidding him, dissuaded him. "I know where to get these things at a discount. You've done enough. Now you rest, and Feroza an' I'll massage your feet — Pack-iss-tanny style!"

Manek quickly removed his sneakers, lay back on the couch, propped up his legs, and looked at the girls appealingly.

Jo narrowed her eyes, mean and mischievous, and promptly sat down on his legs, rowdily shouting, "You bum! I ain't gonna massage your legs!" And just as promptly, she changed her mind. "Okay, you bum. I'll massage them!" She screamed and gleefully wiggled her bottom.

Manek, red in the face and rubbing his knees, pushed the hilarious girl off and wrestled her to the floor. Feroza came to her surprised friend's aid awkwardly and felt foolish when she suddenly sensed she might be intruding. She couldn't understand why she should feel wounded and excluded, as if they had both betrayed her.

The day before Manek was to leave, Jo brought home two brown bags of groceries and a bottle of wine. Feroza knew that Jo had acquired a false ID that showed her age as twenty-one. "We're going to celebrate," Jo announced and, warning them to stay out of the kitchen, busied herself in it.

"Dinner's ready," Jo shouted, and made impatient by the meaty fumes percolating from the kitchen, Manek and Feroza all but burst out of Feroza's room.

Jo wore high heels and a dress with thin straps. She seldom wore dresses, and it was the first time Manek had seen her in one. "You look nice," he complimented gallantly, and in an aside to Feroza in Gujrati, "A buffalo will remain a buffalo in skirts or in pants."

The attractive way the table was laid, using only paper towels, stolen cutlery, and unmatched plates, was a lesson in ingenuity.

A fresh, leafy salad gleamed in three small wooden bowls before each place setting. A large ceramic dish containing a leg of lamb with sautéed baby carrots, beans, and cauliflower formed the centerpiece. Garlic bread, cunningly folded in a white paper napkin, wafted its enticing aroma. Empty jars sprouting elegant arrangements of twigs and leaves added a classy touch to the atmosphere. They did not require the wine to make them high; the food, the decor, and their ease in each other's company was enough to put them in a superb mood. Feroza in any case left the dry wine alone after the first sip.

℘

After Manek left, Jo and Feroza both missed him, and Jo remarked, "Your uncle's kinda cute. I like him."

Feroza flashed her a keen look. She couldn't imagine Jo as Manek's wife, and even less as her aunt.

"He likes you, too," she said, graciously returning the compliment Jo had paid her uncle; and, her sense of betrayal and exclusion gone, she was proud to have a member of her family approved by her exacting and redoubtable friend.

Jo, abetted sometimes by a petrified and brow-beaten helpmate, purloined the smaller items they required to make themselves comfortable in their new home. On such occasions Feroza wore her loose Pakistani garments and jingling bangles and played her part by distracting the saleswomen with her exotic finery and exhaustive inquiries. She also carried a large sling bag, its dimensions made inconspicuous by the drape of her embroidered shawl.

Considering Jo's various delinquencies, it surprised Feroza to discover Jo's fastidious housekeeping skills and how well-ordered, cheerful, and feminine their apartment always was, despite its debilitated condition. Jo hung lace curtains and pretty framed pictures and tastefully displayed her collection of dolls. Little arrangements of flowers and ferns in odd pots sprang up on tables and window-sills, and intriguing posters, one of them just three pairs of feet, on the walls.

Feroza brought out the small onyx tortoises and elephants, brass knickknacks, and framed family photographs Zareen had put into her suitcase, and laid them out as her contribution to the decoration. Bhutto's poster continued to enjoy pride of place in her bedroom.

Jo scrubbed the floors and kitchen tiles until they shone, and once, quite by accident, Feroza surprised her scouring the bathtub and bathroom tiles directly after Feroza had cleaned them. Feroza realized at once that Jo must often do this and was touched that Jo, considerate of her feelings, had been at pains to conceal this from her.

Jo kept the apartment obsessively tidy. Feroza, who had never needed to fold or put away her clothes, appreciated Jo's domestic talents and tried to help, but each time she cleaned out the freezer or the small living/dining room, she could tell afterwards that Jo had duplicated the task with sponge and brush and a daunting range of fragrant detergents.

Chapter 15

Once they were settled in the new apartment, Feroza discovered a fresh aspect of her roommate's social life and understood more exactly why Jo had felt so cramped in the dorms.

Jo picked up strange young men from stores, restaurants, movie theaters, construction sites, and places where she worked with an ease and lack of discrimination that shocked Feroza. Feroza also found out that the young construction workers and guys from the next town that Jo picked up, and sometimes brought home, were the source of the wine and beer and the fake ID card.

Jo's extraordinary capacity for expletives, which matched her other appetites, soon had Feroza saying "shit" and "asshole" with an abandon that epitomized for her the heady reality of her being abroad, away from home, and, even if she knew it was an illusion, a sense of control over her actions.

Another reason for Jo's move to an apartment was her delight in cooking. She cooked a lot, ate a lot, and was generous in sharing. Feroza, as sampler of the culinary artistry Jo had acquired from her parents and various restaurant cooks, discovered that pot roasts and meat loaves with vegetables and gravy were as good as anything she could get out of a can and a welcome supplement to her steady diet of sardines, baked beans, and sausages.

Feroza ventured tentatively to cook from a book of Parsee and Pakistani recipes that Zareen had thoughtfully provided and doggedly ate the burned or undercooked consequences of her attempts until she became passably adept.

But after Jo had screamed, "I'm on fire!" a couple of times and, eyes and nose streaming, rushed to splash her face at the kitchen sink and drink Coke, Feroza sacrificed red pepper, an essential and cherished ingredient, on the altar of her friend's unaccustomed palate.

Jo was moody, changeable, her persona governed by an internal orbit of its own, which completed its mysterious cycle once every two weeks.

In early February, a month after they moved, Jo brought home a small, striped cat destined for the pound and named him Kim, after her latest crush. But in just two weeks, the cat got on her nerves; she couldn't stand the responsibility or the continuous strain of pilfering cat food and threw him out.

Feroza took the cat right back in, protesting, "How can you be so cruel. Don't you know how cold it is? You're condemning him to death!"

They had their first serious quarrel the next afternoon. Feroza was away at class when Jo took Kim for a long ride in her Corvette and dumped him outside the city limits.

When Feroza returned, she called out to the cat. After tugging open a window, she cried, "Kim, Kim," and then, "Kitty, Kitty," in case the cat had forgotten his new name.

Jo got back from work late in the evening, hollering, "You won't believe what that asshole said! I told him where he could shove his job!"

Feroza listened sympathetically until her tale of woe was done and then, with a worried frown and a lump in her throat, said, "I don't know where Kim is. I've been calling him all evening, but there's no sign of him."

Attempting instantly to put her friend out of her misery, and with characteristic frankness, Jo said, "Oh, Kim . . . He was yowling and jumping all over. I left him near some farmhouses. Someone'll look after him."

"He was no longer your cat; he's my cat!" Feroza shouted. "How dare you do this. He'll freeze to death!" Tears blurred her vision.

"You don't know cats — he's not gonna freeze so easy. He'll find shelter in a barn, and some schmuck'll feed him."

"You heartless hoyden!" Feroza screamed.

Feroza marched into her room and shut the door with a bang she hoped would reverberate all the way to Lahore. It also caused a lump of plaster to fall from the scabbed and discolored ceiling.

An hour later, the small apartment percolated with the fragrance of grilling meat and steaming vegetables. Jo knocked on the door. "Hey, Feroza, I'm sorry . . . You wanna eat?"

"No!" Feroza shouted. "No! No! No!" and, as memories unleashed by her anger echoed her nostalgia, "I'll never eat in this house again!"

"Jesuschrist! Who cares!" Jo shouted and, in her anguish over the sudden rift in their friendship, polished off the entire dinner and a small loaf of nut-and-raisin bread.

In the morning, they were awakened by the most heart-rending mewing, and Feroza rushed to the door to let her cat in. His fur sticking out in icy tufts, his slashing tail and plaintive cries cataloging his complaints, Kim entered awkwardly, with what appeared to be a limp. He saw Jo and, like a ginger comet, streaked into Feroza's room.

Jo relented — with reservations. "S'long as I don't see or hear the monster, you can have him."

The cat was confined to Feroza's room, and she committed herself to his care. Feroza, who because of her foreign-student status could not work outside the campus, had not bothered to find an on-campus job. Now she dashed off to her counselor, and Emily Simms helped get her a job in the registration office. Feroza started working that very day to support her cat. She bought cans of cat food, bicycled home between classes to feed and stroke him, and cleaned out the litter. In fact Feroza took better care of the animal than she did of her room, which was in a state of permanent disorder. Feroza kept her door firmly closed, to keep both the cat and the mess out of Jo's sight.

Kim was an affectionate little stray who liked company and snuggled, purring, on Feroza's lap every chance he got. He also had a habit of mewing and yowling dismally in Feroza's absence, even though a window was kept slightly open for him to go out.

Jo threw a progressively strengthening series of fits at intervals of approximately fourteen days, until it was decided that Feroza could keep the cat only till they found him a suitable home.

That was when it struck Feroza that, like the moon orbiting the earth once a month, Jo's life revolved round a mystifying cosmic agent that orbited on a two-week cycle. Feroza, who had imbibed Zareen's belief in astrology, wondered what madly swift and obscure planet governed her friend's life with such unfailing regularity.

Feroza gradually discovered that Jo had an unexpected conservative side to her personality as well. It was a different genre of conservatism, and it took Feroza a while to catch on that whereas the shortest skirts were permissible by her standards, a strapless dress was not. Otherwise Jo wore the standard all-American uniform: jeans and, in her case oversized, T-shirts and sweaters.

Jo worked hard at finding a home for Kim; a month after the ultimatum had been served, she found a home that received Feroza's reluctant and tearful approval.

After school, Feroza sat glumly in front of the TV nursing her broken heart and her empty lap and thinking about home. She missed her grandmothers, her parents, their friends, her friends, her ayah, the incessant chatter of her cousins, and even the raucous chorus of the Main Market *mullahs* on Friday afternoons. She became unbearably homesick and found it impossible to work on her term paper.

After a week of moping, alone and Kim-less, Feroza finally plucked up the daring and courage to venture out for an evening with Jo.

Feroza sat shy-eyed and monosyllabic before a glass of orange juice, while Jo flirted with boys in ponytails and trendy bobs wearing dangling earrings in one ear; though she never went for them, Jo was not averse to chatting with them. The boys, after tossing a remark or two at Feroza and observing her confusion and her "foreign" reaction, clammed up.

Feroza had no experience with socializing with boys; there is no such thing as dating in Pakistan. It was excruciatingly painful for her to be among so many young people and not know how to respond or behave. She had a good role model in Jo, but she didn't think she could be as casual and sure of herself around boys in a hundred years.

After suffering the agony a few times, Feroza decided she'd rather stay home, even if it was lonely and Kim-less. "I can't handle it," she told Jo. "I feel like I'm spoiling everybody's fun. The next day is spoilt too; I keep thinking of it and feel miserable."

"You aren't used to boys. So, okay — get used to them," said Jo, compellingly forthright. "You gotta learn to sometime. You gotta stick with it."

At Jo's insistence, Feroza asked for a glass of wine the next time and nursed the drink all evening, taking small sips. Feroza discovered that she became less self-conscious, more comfortable, and that it mattered less what impression she made, whether she spoke or was tongue-tied.

Something within Feroza must have changed imperceptibly, because suddenly one spring evening Feroza discovered that the boys were talking to her, making a concerted effort to kid, cajole, and encourage her out of her painful shell. She felt their genuine interest. It occurred to her that they liked and accepted her.

Feroza graduated to two glasses of wine, and she actually started to enjoy the excursions that she had found such a painful ordeal before. And she began to admire Jo's spontaneity more and more.

At the slightest inclination for company, Jo'd say, "Let's meet some guys," or wail, "I wanna drink," and they'd just shoot off, without needing to seek anyone's permission or fear anyone's wrath. Feroza marveled at her friend and felt that Jo's was a truly free spirit. "Don't feel like washing dishes," she might say. "Let's eat out" — usually at a cheap Mexican restaurant. Or Jo might jump up at midnight to say, "Come on; let's find some guys who can get us a drink."

Although the cat had been banished, Feroza still worked in the college registration office. She found she needed the extra income to pay for the occasional glass of wine or some minor treat involving her new social life with Jo. She had also found a valuable friend in Nancy, the cheerful secretary with curly blond hair who supervised Feroza's duties and with whom she felt as much at ease as she did with Jo. Feroza privately thanked Kim for giving her cause to take the job and treasured the $3.50 an hour it brought her.

Feroza never quite got over her feelings of guilt. Every time she went out with Jo and flirted modestly with strange young men, her dusky face blooming and warm with the wine, her eyes bright, she wondered what her family would have to say of her conduct if they knew. At the same time, she felt she was being initiated into some esoteric rites that governed the astonishingly independent and unsupervised lives of young people in America. Often, as she sat among them, Feroza thought she had taken a phenomenal leap in perceiving the world from a wider, bolder, and happier angle.

As the pressure of constraints, so deeply embedded in her psyche, slightly loosened their grip under Jo's influence, Feroza felt she was growing the wings Father Fibs had talked about, which, even at this incipient stage, would have been ruthlessly clipped in Pakistan. Feroza was curious to discover how they might grow, the shape and the reach of their span. This was her secret, this sense of growth and discovery, and she did not want to divulge any part of it, even to Manek.

Manek called once in a while to find out how she, her studies, her finances, and her social life were doing.

"Oh, I go out once in a while to restaurants with Jo and her friends, but mostly Jo works in the evenings, and I sit at home and study."

"You're not lonely or homesick?"

"Not yet."

As for money, she always told Manek she was broke, which she always was.

The risqué nature of the pleasure the guilt afforded — the smoke-filled, twilight spaces inhabited by the boisterous, teasing, and amorously inclined young men — was well worth the gnawing battle with her conscience it also caused.

Late one evening, Feroza committed the cardinal sin. She took a few puffs from a cigarette at Jo's guitarist boyfriend's insistence. Jo had tried to protect her friend. "Lay off. It's against her religion to smoke. She *worships* fire."

But Feroza was a bit drunk on wine, and the boy persuasive. Without bothering to protest Jo's misleading interpretation of her faith, she drew on the cigarette held between the guitarist's fingers. Feroza choked on the smoke, coughed to the intense amusement of the company, and thoroughly enjoyed her role as an ingenue.

That night Feroza hunted out her *kusti* and her *sudra*. She covered her head with a scarf and, holding the *kusti* between her hands as proscribed, said the *Hormazd Khoda-ay* prayer. She whipped the air with its tasseled ends when she came to the part that said, "May the Evil One be vanquished!" and then, winding the *kusti* three times round her waist, knotting it at the front and the back to the accompaniment of the appropriate prayers, symbolically girded her loins to serve the Lord. After performing the *kusti* ritual, Feroza bowed her penitent's head to beg divine forgiveness for desecrating the holy fire — the symbol of Ahura Mazda — by permitting it such intimate contact with her unclean mouth.

Feroza became accustomed to Jo bringing boys home. Jo fell in love with nearly every boy she met — and out of love by the end of two weeks. The affairs ended in sensationally noisy and nerve-racking brawls, and Jo got into the habit of replenishing her drained energies and soothing her anguish by preparing and imbibing huge quantities of food.

Sometimes two boys were invited home. When Jo disappeared into her room with her boyfriend, Feroza sat decorous and embarrassed in their small living room in front of the TV, sporadically making small talk and suppressing her yawns. Although Feroza had come a long way out of her shell and was able to flirt and laugh when in a group, she still became self-conscious and stiff when she found herself alone with a boy.

"What's the matter with you?" Jo asked. "You frigid or something?"

"Yes," Feroza said defiantly, not exactly sure what Jo meant but sensing enough of the meaning to feel unfairly charged. "What's it to you?"

Jo also changed jobs every other week with the regularity of a calendar, and Feroza wondered that there were that many jobs available. Jo would burst into the apartment to announce, "This is it! The job for me. I really like the people. One guy is so fantastic . . ."

A week later the cook or waiter or some customer was an "asshole," and she had quit. She'd go angrily into the kitchen and, amidst a grand banging of pots and pans, shout, "The asshole said I wasn't doing it right! I've been working in this business too long

165

to take that; I got more experience than that douchebag!" and she'd whip up a feast for the both of them.

At the tumultuous end of each affair — twice every month, true to the track of her cosmic cycle — Jo would bounce into the living room, yelling, "Hey Feroza, I wanna tell you something," sprawl on the sofa, light a cigarette, and say, "I met the most gorgeous guy. He's in the marines. This is the man for me. This time I'm really in love. Oh God, I really, really love the guy. He's gorgeous." She had a thing for men in uniforms and would often turn up with a policeman.

Jo would talk about the man late into the night, describing each physical particular — his nose his eyes his hair his teeth — till Feroza, giddy with exhaustion, fell asleep. Jo would shake her awake and prop her up with pillows. Feroza, conditioned by her relationship with Manek to be resourceful, acquired the knack of sleeping with her wide-open eyes fixed on Jo.

Then Jo met Mike, a slight, good-looking dropout, glib, charming, and phenomenally unreliable. He'd phone and say, "I'm coming over right now," and never turn up, while an ill-tempered Jo sat up half the night feeding, fuming, and throwing cushions Manek had provided at the TV in the living room.

Or he'd turn up the next day.

What with the emotional upheavals in her love life and her propensity to quit jobs and drown her sorrows in food, Jo inflated like a white whale right before Feroza's alarmed eyes.

"You eat too much when you're unhappy," Feroza said, ventilating her concern. "Either you learn to stick with a job or you stop fooling around with that Mike. You can't go on eating like this."

"I'm fat," moaned Jo. "I know. Every time I look into a mirror I wanna puke! I don't know how Mike stands me. Oh God, I'll lose Mike . . . I gotta do something."

As if to vindicate her prescience, Mike did not call for two entire days, or return her calls. She left messages on his answering machine and all over Twin Falls.

On the night of the third day, Jo and Feroza drove to Mike's apartment at two in the morning while Jo sobbed, "Oh God, please don't let Mike ditch me. You're right, Feroza, I'm a fat slob."

When she found the door barred, brutally indifferent to her violent knocks, Jo wailed at his window on the second floor from the moonlit stillness on the pavement, "Mike, I love you, Mike — Pleeeease don't leave me, Mike."

Mike's curtained window, with the light coming through it, remained as indifferent to her pleas as the battered door.

Feroza, who had gone on the mission with her distraught friend in the capacity of a sensible and ministering parent, was so embarrassed and humiliated for her friend that she dragged and pushed the hulking girl to the car. Literally forcing her in and locking the door, Feroza drove her back, venting her bottled-up feelings. "Mike's bad news. You're lucky he's ditched you. Thank your stars."

It was the first time Feroza had ever driven a car in America. As she alternately soothed and scolded her hysterical friend, she also kept cautioning herself that she must keep to the right side of the road and not drive on the left as in Pakistan.

After this incident, Jo encouraged Feroza to drive the Corvette under her guidance. Feroza drove to and from the campus, to the fancier stores in downtown Twin Falls, and to the Department of Motor Vehicles to take her driving test. As soon as she got her American driver's license, she jubilantly phoned Manek with the news.

As maddeningly avancular and condescending as ever, Manek said, "Good, good. You're doing great. Just don't drive over the speed limit, or you'll wreck Jo's car and break your neck. Don't drive alone, yet."

"Oh God. I wish you'd stop being such a grandfather."

Which gave Manek just the opportunity to indulge his rusting falsetto: "Oh, Grandpa, I didn't listen to you. Now look at me, stuck in a wheelchair."

Feroza hung up.

Manek called back at once. "Temper, temper. It's very rude to hang up. You've got to learn to control your temper."

"Shut up, douchebag!"

Manek was puzzled and stunned by this new addition to her vocabulary and too disturbed to call back when she hung up again.

Jo took up with the state trooper who had given Feroza's driving test. But so far as she was concerned, it was an uninspiring alliance, despite the uniform.

"He's the first nice guy you've dated," Feroza said. "He's good-looking and he's steady. He seems to really care for you."

"Yeah, I know," Jo said. "That's why I don't care for him. He's boring. I'm gonna stop seeing him."

Feroza decided to keep her mouth shut.

Mike showed up again, as if nothing had happened and he had not vanished for fifteen days.

When the trooper phoned, Jo barely spoke to him, and she wasn't home when he came by. When he eventually got the message, Feroza spent ten minutes consoling him and packed him off saying, "Whatever happens, happens for the best."

Ecstatic at the unexpected reprieve, Jo fed Mike huge meals, washed his clothes, cleaned his filthy apartment, lent him her car, and tolerated his callous unreliability with a stoic resilience that would have done a masochist proud.

Mike was asking Jo for money. Feroza fathomed this when Jo skipped classes, started working two jobs, and borrowed money from her. Mike was almost living off Jo. Feroza also guessed by the way his eyes oscillated, by his sometimes slow and sometimes fluid movements that reminded her of the kid in the bus in New York, that Mike was on drugs.

Then she suspected he was a thief. Things were missing, like the little gold chain with the angel Asho Farohar's winged image she wore around her neck beneath her clothes. She remembered putting it on the TV. Then she couldn't find an onyx bowl in which they kept nuts. Jo's electric clock in the kitchen disappeared.

Feroza sat her friend down late one night and talked to her seriously. Mike had as usual stood her up. "Why're you working your butt off for that creep? He takes your money, borrows your car, and treats you like shit. Can't you tell he's on drugs?" And she accosted

Jo with her latest discovery. "Things are missing. He's a thief."

"You just hate him!" Jo screamed.

After which she broke down. She knew he was on drugs; no matter how much money she gave him, it was never enough. She suspected he did a bit of dealing and was sometimes a fence for stolen goods. Nothing serious or regular, just to make a little cash now and then. She had hocked her watch and her gold bracelet. At times she didn't know what to do. "But he's a good kid, he just needs work. He's basically good. All he needs is a little help." She loved him so much she would change him. He needed her, really needed her, and she could not just let him down like the rest of the world had. He was making progress.

"You're kidding yourself," Feroza said angrily, thinking Jo was as addicted to Mike as he was to drugs. "You'll fail your classes. You're ruining your life!"

Jo bawled.

Early one evening, Mike walloped Jo in the parking lot. Jo thudded up the stairs noisily and came in crying and sobbing and showing off. "Can you believe it? That asshole beat me up!" She phoned the people at her current job and her other friends, saying, "That asshole beat me. I don't believe it. I'm bruised all over. I'm going to report him to the cops."

Jo called her sister Janine, in Los Angeles. Janine was in the habit of phoning Jo, making a big issue out of small matters. Feroza knew Jo felt Janine was everything she was not. Stunningly beautiful, flamboyant, and dramatic, she had run away with a married man when she was fourteen — and had lived off welfare ever since. At the moment she was living with a bookie, producing baby after baby. Jo fondly remembered the names of all the babies and often talked to Feroza about them. She sometimes quizzed Feroza, firing off a question about one of her nieces and nephews, and was offended when Feroza did not remember their names or who had said which cute thing.

She also rang up her other sister, Sally, who was extremely and newly rich. Sally and her husband visited Paris and Rome and lived in Champion Forest, in Houston. They were members of the

Champion Forest Country Club. They had two children, of whom Jo also talked fondly.

And Feroza realized that to a fat girl, starved for affection and attention, being beaten up was a sign that she was as normal as any of them, her life as dramatic and full of incident as her sisters' — as the pretty girls'.

Notwithstanding her penchant for shoplifting, which Jo incoherently explained was as much a duty she owed an unjust society as an adventure, Feroza found Jo honest and open. The reasons she gave for stealing from the affluent stores were not unlike Manek's reasons for "skimming" the system, and Feroza didn't find it too difficult to reconcile the contrary aspects of Jo's personality. Yet, in many ways, Jo surprised Feroza by her naïveté. Jo believed everything Mike said, and she took as gospel everything she heard on TV and radio.

Feroza had learned from her parents, servants, friends, and relatives to question the news, form an opinion only after she had absorbed through word of mouth and the rumor mill other opinions. Given a bit of time, the information sorted itself out, and she would come to her own conclusions, as most people did in Pakistan.

If Jo thought about politics at all it was because a scrap of news, caught inadvertently while flipping channels, might immediately affect or inconvenience her. Like, if she needed an abortion, would it be legal?

Otherwise, the last thing that concerned Jo in 1979 was politics, and Feroza understood that it was so because she had no cause for concern. No matter who was voted in, Republican or Democrat, the political process would run smoothly, and it would make as little difference to Jo's life as it would to American policy. Jo would continue to change jobs and boyfriends and party at will. Regardless of what happened in Vietnam or Afghanistan, or how many refugees wandered the world — like the three million Afghans who, by 1979, had already begun to pour into Pakistan and devastate its ecology and its social fabric — or how many weapons the United States and the Soviet Union manufactured or countries they bullied or bombs they rained down, the theater of war would be profitably maintained and kept remote from their part of the world.

Martin Luther King Jr.'s and the Kennedys' assassinations, the knowledge and abhorrence of which she had grown up with, had grieved Jo, Watergate had shocked her, but the tenor of her life and that of her parents' and acquaintances' lives remained the same: full of opportunity for those with the ambition to grab it, benign even to those with less ambition, but punishing for the citizens the larger cities had turned into the flotsam Feroza had seen at the Port Authority bus station in New York.

In Pakistan, politics concerned everyone — from the street-sweeper to the business tycoon — because it personally affected everyone, particularly women, determining how they should dress, whether they could play hockey in school or not, how they should conduct themselves even within the four walls of their homes.

Despite Jo's political naïveté, Feroza found her an intelligent and sympathetic listener she could talk to of the political travails of Pakistan and the threatened martyrdom of her hero. Infected by her friend's passion, Jo also found the man on the poster, with his glowing face and impassioned outstretched arm, heroic and handsome. Jo was concerned when Feroza pointed out that the news about Pakistan and other Third World countries was one-sided. Under Feroza's influence, Jo began watching the news with her on TV, and she began to realize the extent of the bias and how pervasive it was on all the networks. Then she became gratifyingly provoked, involved, and curious, and Feroza was touched.

Manek was right when he'd told her she was lucky to have Jo as her roommate, that Jo would teach her more about America than he ever could. Feroza felt that living with Jo helped her to understand Americans and their exotic culture — how much an abstract word like "freedom" could encompass and how many rights the individuals had and, most important, that those rights were active, not, as in Pakistan, given by a constitution but otherwise comatose. A person like Jo could ensure her rights through law and, if required, demand accountability of the State. She admired the vigilant role played in all this by the free press but also realized that each network had its own bias.

Like her parents, Feroza had a politically acute and restless mind, precocious for one her age, at least in America. And living with Jo and watching TV also gave her a disturbing insight into America's foreign policy, into the nature of the fissure that existed at the core of America's political heart, which, like divine Zurvan's mythic face, was divided into darkness and light — Black-and-White Right-and-Wrong Good-and-Evil — with no room for the gray that other older and poorer nations had learned to accommodate. But duality existed also in human nature, in nature itself, in her own religion, even in God, so who was she to sit in judgment?

Nevertheless, the schizophrenia she perceived at the core of America's relationship to its own citizens and to those in poor countries like hers continued to disturb her. She eventually came to the conclusion that it troubled her because America was so consummately rich and powerful, and the inconsistencies of its dual standards, the injustices it perpetuated, were so cynical and so brazen. Not that Pakistan or other countries were paragons, but then no one expected any better of Pakistan — it laid no claim as the leader of nations, the grand arbiter of justice and human rights.

And while Feroza was groping to understand America through her friend and her friend was beginning to grasp the reality of a world that existed outside America, an American in Pakistan, in an unexpected encounter, filled Zareen's heart with fear and loathing.

Chapter 16

Zareen and Cyrus were at one of the many dinners they attended. It was a large party, with about thirty couples, and the sliding door to the TV lounge had been opened to create more space. The guests formed groups around four or five sofa sets placed at various angles against the walls and in the corners of the commodious sitting and living rooms. For the most part the men stood, either with the women or in groups of three or four, discussing business or politics and slapping each other's palms as they joked and laughed. Two or three waiters from the Punjab club had been hired for the evening, and they wove between the loquacious guests unobtrusively replenishing drinks.

Zareen, sitting with some women on floor cushions, looked markedly at her watch and raised her eyebrows. A tall woman sitting next to her in a stunning navy-and-silver sari picked up the cue: "Good God, it's already eleven," she said in a shocked voice, as if it was the first time that dinner had been so late. "We'd better tell Farhi to feed us, or God knows when we'll eat."

This remark drew the attention of the men standing near them, as it was meant to, and produced the expected protests: "Dinner already? Don't you people have anything on your minds but food?" and "Ladies, please, give us a break; the night's still young and tomorrow's Friday. Relax."

These were the little ruses the women amused themselves with while trying to wean the men from their evening Scotches and prime them for dinner.

Their short, roly-poly hostess approached, smiling at Zareen. Zareen feigned astonishment and asked, "Dinner's on the table? I can't believe it!"

A good-looking man with prematurely white hair, notorious for having to be dragged to the buffet table, cried, "Have a heart, *bibi*. Let us finish our drinks at least."

"Take your time," said Farhi. "Nobody's bringing out dinner just yet."

The women groaned. Farhi laughed, shrugged to express her helplessness, and then leaned towards Zareen to say, "The guest of honor, an American gentleman, would like to talk to you."

"Me? Why?" Zareen asked, promptly gathering herself to get off the floor, the lift to her ego at being singled out lending a lilt to her voice.

"Why don't you find out yourself?" her hostess said. "He's heard you're a Bhutto fan, that you have strong political opinions."

The wide borders on their colorful silk saris undulating seductively as they moved, Farhi and Zareen walked through the crowded, noisy rooms into the quieter TV lounge. Furrie went up to a large man who sat at one end of a four-piece sofa, an arm stretched out on the backrest. The vast expanse of his chest, his spread thighs, his sloven posture, all bespoke the language of power and possession and the insensitivity that often goes with them.

Zareen's first instinct was to back off. But her hostess was already saying, "Here she is. You wanted to speak to her, no?"

Zareen stood there, teetering on her party heels, because her hostess had stood her there. The man's glance passed her indifferently, and Zareen wondered if he'd asked to see her at all. The guest of honor looked to her like a made-up B-grade movie villain: a pair of thick, brown eyebrows, and then a bald scalp, clean as a plucked chicken's.

A Dutch man Zareen barely knew chivalrously vacated his chair next to the sofa, saying, "Please, sit down." He could barely conceal his relief as he withdrew.

Zareen smiled her thanks and, as she adjusted the elegant fall of her sari, wondered what she had let herself in for. Sitting sideways in her chair, she turned to the American expectantly.

From the recesses of the sofa, his impersonal eyes wandering, the man rumbled something indecipherable and attempted to draw himself forward, as if trying to get to his feet.

"Good God," Zareen thought. It was as if she had put him to considerable trouble in forcing his reluctant attention.

Zareen lowered her disconcerted gaze. The man's chest and

stomach bulged above his belt like a bomb dressed up in an expensive evening shirt.

"You're a social worker?" The man's grating voice appeared to match his other unpleasant attributes. "They tell me you worked with this Bhutto's wife, on some committee or other?"

He made it sound as if social work was despicable and that having once worked with the imprisoned prime minister's wife was something to be ashamed of. Zareen caught herself feeling sheepish and apologetic. Surprised and provoked by her own reaction, she mutinously replied, "I like to help disadvantaged people. I do voluntary work at the Destitute Women's and Children's Home and at two orphanages. I was on many women's committees with Begum Bhutto."

What was she trying to prove? And to whom?

"And Bhutto — what d'you think of him?"

"He's my hero. The champion of the poor, of women, of the minorities and underprivileged people — of democracy."

The man went through the motion of clapping softly. Zareen noticed that his cheeks dimpled when he smiled. It was the last gesture Zareen expected of this cynical, bald, villainous-looking character. She found herself relaxing, less on the defensive. She smiled.

But the instant she met his eyes, her defenses were back in position. There was no point at which they had made contact as two equal people, as she had imagined.

"What d'you think will happen if this 'hero' is hanged tomorrow? Will there be a lot of trouble? Riots? People making trouble on the streets? Killing?"

The question was weighted with the conceit of a man who already has the answers.

Zareen was acutely aware of the man's insolent demeanor, but courtesy and the tradition of hospitality were too deeply ingrained for Zareen to exhibit her chagrin. She looked away, taken aback in a way she couldn't comprehend.

The man rasped, "The people here lie a lot. I don't know what to believe." He raised a shoulder in a disparaging shrug. "Maybe we Americans have to stop being so naive."

Naive? He did not strike her as naive. She felt he had come with preconceived notions about Pakistan and intended only to reinforce them. Nor were some of the other Americans she'd met naive. Nor were the European, Australian, and American hippies who had passed through Pakistan on their drugged pilgrimage to Katmandu before the trouble in Afghanistan had closed the route.

Had anyone told the poor villagers, who fed and sheltered these wanderers and gave them their pitiable clothes, that the world out there had changed? That these strangers were conditioned to look out only for themselves and that the villagers' kindness and canons of hospitality were naive?

The man sat up straighter and looked briefly but politely at Zareen. "Well, what d'you think?"

Zareen found her petrified tongue suddenly loosen, and with her infinite capacity for loquacity and truth-telling, the frightened, desperate words tumbled out: "There will be a lot of trouble. It will be the worst possible thing, the most tragic thing to happen. He is loved by the masses. The repercussions will be terrible. Horrible."

"But what about tomorrow? If he's hanged tomorrow, will there be trouble?" he asked in the same emotionless voice.

Zareen felt the complete lack of compassion the man projected; he was chilling. For the first time he appeared to be really interested in what she might have to say.

"No," she shook her head, thinking hopelessly that all the Peoples' Party leaders, from the mighty to the smallest, were either in prison or under dire threat of some kind or other. Some had been bribed into compliance. "The immediate trouble will be controllable, I think." Zareen said simply, wondering how she knew the answer to a question she had not thought to put to herself before.

❧

At midnight, as she removed her diamond-and-emerald choker and earrings, unwrapped her sari, and unhooked her blouse, Zareen told Cyrus what had happened. "But why did he want answers from me? Who am I?"

Cyrus looked equally puzzled. "I guess you've a reputation for shooting your mouth off," he said. "And you keep on and on about the feelings of the masses, as if you represent them. The fellow must be CIA."

"You know what I hated most?" Halfway to folding the shimmering, six-yard sari, her arms stretched out, Zareen stood still and thoughtful. "The man did not think of me as a person, as somebody. I was not Zareen, just some third-rate Third Worlder, too contemptible to be of the same species."

Cyrus could see her groping for expression, and he was surprised and touched by the eloquence her distress inspired.

"He was so cynical," Zareen continued. "He asked the most simplistic questions, as if the complexity that makes up our world doesn't exist. I've never felt the way he made me feel . . . valueless . . . genderless."

Zareen jerked her arms to bring the sari edges together. "The fool! If he had all the answers, why did he ask me questions? Did he have to make me feel so miserable?"

She finished folding her sari with abrupt movements and flung it over the back of the rocking chair. As she turned, Cyrus noticed her blink. Her eyes, large and dark, made more seductive by the unexpected width at the bridge of her nose, were unnaturally brilliant.

Zareen was always meticulous about removing her makeup, but tonight she merely switched out the light and crept wordlessly into Cyrus's arms. Cyrus stroked her hair, nuzzled her neck, and, holding her close, healed the wounds inflicted upon her voluptuous and shaken womanhood, and to her psyche.

Exactly a month to the day after the dinner, they woke up to the news that Zulfikar Ali Bhutto had been hanged at four minutes past two in the morning. All-India Radio was the first to announce the news to most Pakistanis, at seven o'clock in the morning. He had been hanged in the Rawalpindi jail.

On the morning of the news of Bhutto's death, their phone rang constantly. Everybody was agitated, asking, "Heard anything new?" or saying, "I've just heard — "

Like thousands of distraught citizens all over Pakistan, Zareen disbelieved the news. They would not dare hang him in the face of the appeals from Amnesty International, other human rights organizations, and leaders of countries all over the world!

In her crumpled sari, Zareen drove her Christian ayah and the sweeper's, gardener's, and cook's wives up and down the streets leading from the Gulberg Market traffic circle. They passed other small bands of distraught women who were also looking to join one of the larger processions that surely must exist somewhere to protest the injustice: to establish a martyr's claim to his martyrdom.

The men drove in cars and trucks and ran here and there on the streets like headless chickens in similar scattered batches to join their voice to the national howl, if they could find the others. But there was no main crowd, no large procession they could become a part of, no avenue to vent their rage, hurt, and grief.

The larger tragedy was that General Zia had the support, open or covert, of all the major political forces in the country and all the country's major institutions — the military, the civil bureaucracy, and the judiciary.

In the long, bitter letter Zareen sent to her daughter she wrote: "I realized then that there is no such thing as a 'spontaneous uprising' unless it is sanctioned!"

Chapter 17

It is believed that troubles come in threes. They can also come during an ominous moment in the Panchang, an astrological calendar in which the Parsees generally believe, in fives.

Jo and Feroza's decrepit apartment, which had been tolerable mainly because of its relative quiet, suddenly developed the most ominous creaks and thuds. Without any warning the apartment above theirs had been rented to what sounded like a family of horses.

This invasion of their peace of mind, Feroza fathomed in retrospect, was the harbinger of their subsequent tribulations — the start of their particular ominous moment.

The girls were startled awake at dawn by the galloping above them of hoofed creatures and, in the lengthening spring evenings, rained upon by peeling paint and chunks of plaster.

Jo called their landlord.

The landlord said he'd have a word with his tenants.

She called him again. And again.

He crustily counseled her to go upstairs and tell the new occupants to stop whatever they were doing and banged the phone down.

Jo stormed up the stairs, followed by a glowering Feroza, and pounded on the door. It was opened by a lissome, athletic-looking young woman wearing mauve jogging shorts over a black leotard. Obliterating the rest of the view with a massive pink torso and overdeveloped biceps stood an irate-looking man in a jockstrap.

Jo's bearing was anything but that of a neighbor dropping by for a friendly chat. The lissome woman, whose brown hair was tied in a severe ponytail, hastily squeezed to one side to allow the muscled creature behind her center stage.

"What d'ya want?" the man said.

"We wanna know just what the hell's going on up here."

"What d'ya mean?"

"I mean the jumping an' all that shit. What're you guys doing, running a bloody stud farm? The living room plaster and paint's falling. If this goes on the ceiling'll crash."

Feroza was more explicit. "On our heads!"

"It ain't none of your goddamn business! Sandy an' Mary here do aerobics." Hearing the shouting, Sandy had poked her cropped blond head out between the biceps and torso. She quickly withdrew it to reveal another muscular and jock-strapped presence in the background. "And Andy an' me pump iron — and we ain't gonna stop," said the bodybuilder and slammed the door in their faces.

Feroza and Jo exchanged alarmed looks and clattered down to their apartment to huddle in a conference. In about ten minutes, while they were conjuring strategies to force the landlord to evict the hulks, there was a dull thud above them, as of a heavy object being carelessly released. A chunk of falling plaster barely missed Feroza's head.

Jo yanked open the door and shouted up, "Stop doin' that you fuckin' assholes!"

The upstairs door banged open. "Shad-up you fucking freaks. Go join a circus, fat-girl!" The door slammed shut.

There were more frightening thumps from upstairs, then a hail of plaster and peeling paint. Another large fragment of plaster fell on the sofa right where Jo had been sitting a moment before and bounced to shatter on the floor. The living room floor, drapes, tables, and furnishings were shrouded by the accumulated debris.

"Don't touch anything! Leave it just as it is!" Jo gasped excitedly, like a detective instructing an underling not to disturb the arrangement of the body or weapon. Feroza, who did not have the slightest inclination to clear the mess, or venture out of the corner she was cowering in, nodded obediently.

Jo cast her eyes to the ceiling, and, as the look of exasperation on her face turned to an expression of incredulity and horror, Feroza looked up too. There was a bulge radiating from the center of the ceiling. It looked as if their ceiling had sagged.

"Come on," Jo said, and without bothering to lock the door or put on their jackets, they hurtled down the steps.

Jo brought her jalopy to a squealing halt right in front of their landlord's small frame house. She punched the horn several times and, having shattered the serenity of the neighborhood with the blasts, proceeded to savagely pummel her landlord's door. "Our ceiling's falling! D'ya hear me? Those dumb hulks up there are dropping weights! If you don't do something about it soon and we get hurt, we're gonna sue your ass."

The landlord opened the door and glowered at the outraged girls. Their distraught appearance and the paint and plaster on their hair and clothes appeared to have an effect: "Don't holler," he opened his mouth exaggeratedly wide to whisper testily. "The ceiling is not going to fall. I'll take a look."

The girls sat tense and panting in their living room while the landlord went upstairs. They listened to the sounds of an altercation, the angry words muffled by the closed doors. The shouting subsided. After a while, the landlord rattled down the staircase and poked his head in for the briefest moment, "I'll have the ceiling fixed on Sunday. I've warned those guys upstairs. They won't bother you again."

Instead of the handsome construction workers Feroza and Jo expected on Sunday, the landlord appeared. He came staggering through the door carrying a stepladder and tools and dragging a large canvas tarpaulin.

Feroza and Jo grumpily sipped the beer they had procured in anticipation of a good time and sullenly ate the roast beef sandwiches Jo had prepared. Regretting the pains they had taken to look good, they watched with skepticism the elderly handyman's efforts. They did not offer him even a glass of water.

The landlord eventually succeeded in attaching a tarpaulin to the four corners of the ceiling. He stepped down the ladder to inspect the canvas. It drooped like an overloaded hammock. He wiped his face and helped himself to a Coke from the fridge. He climbed up again to hammer in more nails along the edges.

The landlord stepped back finally and surveyed his handiwork with satisfaction. He looked at the girls and noting their dismayed expressions, told them that he'd have the ceiling properly fixed once he had the money; there was no way he could afford it from the rent they paid. In the meantime they were not to worry, the structure was sound, and the tarpaulin would keep the paint and plaster from messing up their living room.

The next day Feroza and Jo heard the news of Bhutto's hanging on CBS. It was the second misfortune in the series of their five tribulations.

At first Feroza did not believe it. "Rot! Absolute rot!" she said. "If he's dead, why don't they show his body? I bet he's alive . . . I bet he's escaped from jail and they are saying this to hide the truth!"

"If it's on TV, it's gotta be true," Jo said and, remembering Feroza's tutorials regarding her blind faith in whatever she heard on TV, added, "Shit, I mean, they wouldn't say something like *that* if it wasn't true."

As the inevitability of the martyrdom, presaged by the distress of Bhutto's sister at Data Sahib's shrine, sank in, Feroza's eyes began to smart and her face to turn red.

"Assholes! Douchebags! Fools! Donkeys!" Feroza shouted, her voice breaking, and, repeating the swear words again and again, began to weep.

Jo, also shocked by the terrible fate of the handsome man on the poster in Feroza's room, let loose a sympathetic repertoire of curses to augment her friends inadequate vocabulary.

The following morning it was as if the school had suddenly discovered Pakistan — and recognized Feroza as the country's sole representative. Feroza's face was covertly studied. When it was found to bear the puffy eyes, the red nose, the quivering mouth, and the other signs of grief, the students' sympathetic expressions, and the consideration they showed Feroza, touched and comforted her. Jo accompanied her carrying a square box of tissues and supplied the details and answers to some of the questions when Feroza was unable to speak.

Feroza's counselor, Emily Simms, sought her out in the afternoon. She knew how emotionally involved Feroza was with Pakistani politics, particularly Bhutto. She plied Feroza with coffee, tissues, and cookies and told her, "I know just how you must feel, honey, being so far away from your family and home. But please think of us as your family. We're very fond of you; we love you."

The teachers in Feroza's classes stopped to have a word with her. Students she had never seen smiled at her, said, "Hi, how're you doing?" and grouped round to ask questions and say, "Oh, shit," and how sorry they were.

Just as Feroza's celebrity was beginning to wear thin, Zareen's letter, full of groping evaluations, fanciful conjectures, and the reactions of the Parsee community, their dinner party friends, servants, and shopkeepers, arrived.

The length of the letter and the details with which it was packed, gave Feroza a clear idea of the grief Bhutto's hanging had caused Zareen and many others like her in Pakistan.

She related their tiny ayah's whispered confidence that Bhutto would arrive at the right moment from across the border in India riding a white stallion. Zareen ended the letter saying that she had had the same news whispered in her ear so often by the poor people that she did not have the heart to contradict it.

ന

It had been an exacting day. Feroza spent the free time between classes scribbling out an assignment for her American history class and spent a grueling hour after school with the teacher who was trying to coach her in chemistry.

Earlier that afternoon, she had discovered a flat tire and had walked her bicycle to the campus store to have it fixed.

It was almost dark by the time Feroza returned home. She threw her backpack on the bed, grabbed a can of Coke, and plunked herself on the sofa, as she always did when she was exhausted, to watch TV.

There was no TV on the TV table. Feroza gazed at the clean space on the dusty table where the TV should have been. She wondered what Jo had done with it. She lay on the sofa annoyed, missing the mindless, almost narcotic effect of the voices and images.

With no TV before which to unwind and too irritated to sleep, Feroza decided to work on her term paper. She discovered that her typewriter, too, was missing. It was as if something vile suddenly brushed against her. She went into the living room cautiously. She looked more carefully this time. Sure enough, Jo's stereo system and speakers were not where they should have been. She quickly opened the door to Jo's room. The computer and the large monitor that squatted on it were not on her desk. Their apartment had been burglarized.

It was terrifying to be alone in a place that had been intruded upon by God knows what kind of sinister strangers. The space in their familiar apartment became menacing. She quickly put on her jacket and, banging the door shut behind her, tore down the stairs. The area around her block was deserted.

Feroza turned around and ran back up two flights of stairs to the apartment of the hulks and knocked on the door. They were out. She clattered down the steps again. She knew the restaurant where Jo was working; it was only a couple of blocks down their road. Feroza got her bicycle out of the small storage room near the land-ing and, peddling recklessly, her bicycle wobbling, raced down the darkening street.

Feroza stood panting and flushed just inside the entrance. She spotted Jo in an apron and a cap, expertly carrying four dinners in her hands and serving them. As soon as Jo was through, Feroza dis-creetly called to her. Startled to see Feroza, who even in the dim restaurant light looked agitated and flushed, Jo guessed that some-thing was wrong.

"We've been robbed," Feroza panted as soon as Jo came near her. Feroza's knees began to shake, and she sat down abruptly on a chair at an empty table.

"Here, have some water," Jo poured water into a glass, and after Feroza had drained it, Jo asked, "What's gone?"

"The TV, the music system, your computer, my typewriter, and other things."

Jo called the police. She gave them the address and breathlessly told them that her apartment was being burglarized. She called Mike's number and left a message on his answering machine.

A couple of police cars were parked in front of their building by the time Feroza and Jo drove up. Feroza had left her bicycle at the restaurant. They took the stairs two at a time. The door to their apartment was slightly open. They hesitated and then cautiously stepped into the living room; the lights were not switched on. Slight muffled sounds were coming from other parts of the apartment. Crouching to one side they gingerly pushed open the door to Jo's room. One behind the other they peered in and received the shock of their young lives. A figure stepped out of the shadows, holding a pistol with both hands, and said, "Freeze."

Jo and Feroza promptly froze.

Another cop rushed into the room and blinded them with his flashlight. The policemen lowered their weapons at the sight of the petrified girls clinging to one another and switched on the lights.

"You occupy these premises?" the taller of the two policemen asked. He had a red, beefy face and a stocky body to match.

"Yeah," Jo said.

"You told us the burglary was taking place," he accused.

"My roommate came home, and the door was unlocked. She felt something was kinda wrong. She saw that the TV wasn't on the table. She was sure someone was still around and she wasn't going to hang out!" Jo said, stoutly defending her position. "We called from the restaurant where I work."

Jo and Feroza went over the apartment with the policemen, making an inventory of the stolen items. Some of their clothes were missing. Their shoes lay in a mismatched jumble, and Feroza could not see her new Nikes. Books were strewn on the closet floor in Jo's room where the cartons containing them had been tipped over by the robbers hoping to find something of value. Jo suddenly let out a shriek. "Oh, my notebook! They took my term paper! I've worked three months on it and they've stolen it!"

"Don't be silly, Jo," Feroza said. "What on earth would they want to steal your term paper for!"

They found the notebook on the floor beneath her desk.

"There are no signs of a break-in," said the younger, kinder-looking cop. "Could it be someone you girls know?"

"Nah," Jo said. She sounded hurt. "Our friends aren't that type."

"I suggest you think about it some more," said the older man.

"There's nothing to be worried about, but it's always a good idea to keep the doors locked. If you think of something or someone, let us know." He winked at them both.

After the police left, Jo wept as she looked at the empty spaces that had once been occupied by her computer, her printer, her stereo, and her TV. She missed them horribly and, like Feroza, felt uncomfortable in the apartment; their space had been violated. "I wish we could sleep someplace else. Let's spend the night at a motel."

Feroza was readily agreeable.

It took Feroza till late next afternoon to air her suspicions.

They had both been delighted by their stay at the Travel Lodge. They watched TV till two A.M., slept late Saturday morning, indulged themselves with a sumptuous breakfast of mushroom omelettes and hash browns at a snack bar, and had left with their small overnight bags stuffed with the motel's towels and toilet paper an hour after checkout time.

Back at their abandoned apartment, they were again overtaken by a sense of bereavement. They flung open all the windows and drew the curtains. Fiercely, Jo set to scrubbing the kitchen tile and vacuuming the floors. Feroza dusted and polished their furniture obsessively, tidied up their rooms, and watered the plants.

A couple of hours later, Feroza switched on all the lights and flung herself on the living room sofa in an exhausted torpor. The vigorous activity was cathartic, as if in dusting and tidying up, she had reclaimed her space in the apartment and made it safe.

As Feroza absently watched Jo, who was on her knees washing the fridge with a dishrag and a bowl of suds, she felt a great swell of affection and gratitude for her friend. How many girls did she know in Lahore — or anywhere — who could decide, just like that, to move out of their homes to spend a night in a motel? To Feroza it was an unimaginable feat accomplished, a lottery won.

At the same time, she wished she could be of more use to Jo, do something splendid for her, protect her friend better. Ever since she had gone with Jo to Mike's apartment, she had felt driven to safeguard her strangely vulnerable apartment-mate.

Half an hour later, pushing back strands of hair that had come

186

loose from her ponytail and holding a large glass of Coke, Jo sank into the lumpy sofa beside Feroza.

"I've been thinking," she said, pensively looking into her Coke and stirring the ice with her finger.

"Uh-huh?" Feroza said.

"I think we've been paid back for my sins."

"What sins?"

"The shopliftin' and stealin' . . . and stuff."

Silence.

"I'm gonna stop that shit."

"That's a good idea," Feroza said cautiously, reflecting with remorse on her own timorous complicity.

They remained quiet. Feroza, sitting in corner of the sofa with her legs tucked beneath her, stole a glance at her friend. Jo, abstracted by her thoughts, sipped her Coke absently. Then, holding the glass in her lap, she lay her head back wearily and shut her eyes.

"Feeling better?" Feroza asked at length.

"Yeah," Jo said and then irritably added, "I don't know where Mike is . . . I've left messages on his answering machine . . . The asshole hasn't called back."

"Are you still seeing him?" Feroza asked, trying to keep her tone neutral.

"Only a couple of times since he beat up on me." Jo turned her head to look at her friend curiously. "Why d'ya ask?"

"He has a key to our apartment."

"Yeah, I gave it to him. I oughta take it back."

"You should've taken it away from him. I don't think he's gonna call you," said Feroza.

The implication in the choice of words, and the tone in which they were spoken, sank in.

"You're telling me Mike stole our stuff?" Jo raised her feet to the sofa and turned to face Feroza. Her incredulity and rage were explosive. She was too much on the defensive.

Her attitude strengthened Feroza. "I don't see who else could have. The place wasn't broken into. The policemen thought it was someone we knew."

"I can't believe you're saying this!" Jo shouted, shifting jerkily and spilling part of her Coke. "The poor kid's a mess, but he's not a thief! He wouldn't steal from us! He's a good kid, basically."

Feroza kept quiet.

Jo began to snuffle quietly into her glass. She wiped her eyes with the back of her hand.

Mike showed up a week later. Both girls were in the living room looking at an old black-and-white TV loaned to them by Jo's current boss.

"I got your messages," Mike said to Jo. "You guys had some stuff stolen?" He was looking paler and thinner and, to Feroza, transparently guilt-ridden.

"Yeah," Jo said and then mournfully listed the missing items.

Mike shook his head. "Too bad. You call the cops?"

"You didn't expect we'd hang around for you, did you? Didn't you get the messages I left on your machine? Why didn't you call?"

"I've been kinda busy," Mike said, dismissing the charge lightly.

"Oh yeah?" Jo said. "I'm kinda busy too, but I'd go help a friend who'd been robbed!"

"I'm sorry, I wanted to see you, but it's been, like, one thing after another."

Feroza was distinctly cold and minimally civil. After five minutes of haughty, monosyllabic participation in the conversation, she withdrew to her room. But her attitude had rubbed off on Jo, and some time later she heard Jo and Mike argue loudly. Mike left the apartment before dinner.

Mike again started dropping in at odd hours. Feroza noticed, though, that Jo was more guarded and wary when he was around. She did not believe everything he said anymore, either, and startled him by frequently declaiming, "I don't believe you," about some trifling assertion.

Mike came over late one night, asking to borrow Jo's car.

"You can't have it," Jo said flatly.

"Why not?" Mike was surprised.

" 'Cause I need it tomorrow. I've got a busy day."

"I'll get it back to you by morning," Mike said. "Promise."

"Why don't you use your own car?"

"I've got to go a long way, and it won't hold out."

"I bet it'll hold out if you fill it with gas."

"If you don't give me your car keys right this minute, you'll be sorry!" Mike shouted.

Mike was drunk. Jo wondered how he'd managed to conceal it so well. "Get outta here," she shouted, and Feroza, who had heard most of their conversation, barged into the living room to stand by her friend.

"I know what you want the car for," Jo yelled, drawing courage from Feroza's presence. "You're gonna deal drugs or fence stuff that's stolen. If you think I'm gonna allow you to use my car for shit like that, you're crazy!"

"Gimme the keys, or I'll kill you," Mike said, advancing dangerously on Jo. Feroza quickly inserted herself between Jo and Mike. She stuck out her elbows defiantly, but she was shaking. Mike felt his pockets and his waistband as if searching for a knife. He didn't appear to find what he was looking for and, yelling, "You wait here; I'm gonna kill you," dashed out of the apartment.

Feroza and Jo rushed to lock the door after him. Jo stood trembling against the locked door, and Feroza sat down panting on a chair. A few moments later they heard Mike's car tires viciously scrape gravel as he wheeled into reverse and, with a wrenching of gears, roar away.

Jo phoned her sister in California with the news of the threat. Janine advised her to get a gun at once.

"Please don't," Feroza said. "He's only threatening you. If you get a gun, I'm not going to live in the same house with you. You'll shoot me by mistake."

The next evening, Mike came to the restaurant and created a scene when Jo again refused to let him have the car. In the ensuing brawl, Jo finally accosted him. "I know you stole the stuff from our apartment!"

"Yeah? So what?"

Jo was shocked and dismayed by his admission and the cool and insouciant way in which he said it. "I want my TV back!" she yelled. "I want my computer and my stereo back, you asshole!"

"I've hocked 'em. So what're you going to do?"

Jo's burly boss, a meat-cleaver in hand, rushed Mike out of his restaurant.

After a month Mike again turned up at the apartment to announce, "I'm getting married." He looked subdued and sober in a clean, striped shirt and washed jeans.

"So, when's she due?" Jo asked.

"Oh, Jo, you think I'd only get married if I got the girl pregnant? She is pregnant, but that's not why we're getting married."

Jo looked at Mike with pitying contempt. "You poor kid. You don't realize that becoming a father means more than being a dildo with a sperm count!"

Feroza didn't understand what "dildo" meant, but she sensed from Mike's stunned reaction that Jo had said something quite profound. Feroza's already soaring regard for her friend climbed a notch higher.

Just before the end of the term, a little, short-haired, bandy-legged dog trotted up to Jo as she was washing her car and, for no apparent reason, growled and suddenly nipped her ankle.

Observing the rites of the American spring, Jo, like millions of girls all over the country, was wearing shorts.

"I've had it," Jo announced as Feroza applied the mercurochrome — farsightedly provided by Zareen — to her roommate's tiny, perforated wounds. "I've taken about as much as I can stand! This crummy town is jinxed! I'm getting out! You can stay if you want, but I'm going!"

"Where to?" Feroza asked, suddenly very frightened, wondering how long their bad luck would continue.

"Somewhere, anywhere, so long's it's not Twin Falls. Even the dogs here are nasty. The jealous little mutt bit me 'cause his legs're short and mine are long!"

Both girls laughed. After all, it was spring, and even Jo had to admit that Twin Falls looked spruce and green. Above all else, vacation loomed, and Feroza was going to spend the summer with Jo and her family in Boulder.

The dog bite was the last problem bequeathed by the Panchang.

Chapter 18

Meanwhile Manek was returning to Pakistan after an absence of four years.

A phalanx of perspiring relatives awaited Manek's arrival at the Lahore airport. Jeroo and Behram, who required only an excuse to visit Lahore, had driven down from Rawalpindi for the occasion. Their fourteen-year-old son Dara and his younger sister Bunny were charged with protecting the rose and jasmine garlands hanging from sticks.

Anxious for news of Feroza, Cyrus and Zareen flanked Khutlibai behind the iron paling that separated the crowd of receivers from the arrival lounge. Khutlibai stood entrenched at the central position she had fought through to occupy earlier, grimly hanging on to the handrail.

The arrival lounge was also the baggage claim area, and the aluminum-framed French windows and glass doors that formed one wall — about twenty feet away from them — were guarded by two armed security police.

Khutlibai had insisted on coming well before the plane was due, so in deference to her wishes the family had hauled itself to the airport an hour earlier. Other families — predominantly Muslim and a few Christian — milled behind the railing, their children propped up in their arms like wilting bouquets. The ceiling fans hanging from the vaulted roof were remote and ineffective.

The arrival of the 747 from Karachi was announced, and a few moments later the passengers started trickling into the baggage claim area. The congenitally short-sighted Parsee adults squinted in an effort to peer through the glass doors and urged the few lucky youngsters with normal sight to put their 20/20 vision to salutary use. The glare from outside made it still more difficult to look in.

"Can you see Manek? Can you see him?" Khutlibai asked frequently, and the moment the youngsters' attentions wandered she alerted them with a sharp "What're you doing? Look in front!" If they were within striking distance, she thumped or pinched them to encourage their attention.

The other adults also kept a check on the brood, but the children's eyes, smarting from staring at the dazzling windows, kept wandering to less tedious vistas.

Khutlibai and company were able to make out only a thickening blob of shirts and shalwars as the passengers poured into the arrival lounge. Occasionally one of them clearly saw a figure in the foreground or spotted a porter in a khaki uniform, but there was no sign of Manek.

In a country of paradoxes, where bold women of a certain class often wield as much clout as pistol-toting thugs, Freny could be relied upon to use the advantage. "Here," she said and gave her bright red patent-leather handbag to her husband to hold. "I'm going to find out what's happening."

"Old mare, red bridle!" quipped Khutlibai, offering up the sly adage with a fresh twist.

A mischievous bubble of merriment burst about her. Not used to such levity, Rohinton pursed his mouth and averted austere eyes. He had discovered a few days back that the youngsters had nicknamed his wife "Allah-ditta," or "God-bequeathed," in an obvious allusion to his spouse's bountiful endowment of bosom. He added a thunderous frown to his astringent mouth, and the giggles at once subsided. Rohinton folded his thick arms across his chest and the handbag swung from his wrist defiantly.

Meanwhile, holding up and displaying hands innocent of bombs, guns or knives — and an equally innocent pair of out-thrust breasts that could not possibly conceal a weapon behind the tight fit of her sari-blouse — Freny barreled forward like a squat and unstoppable tank. Before the surprised guards could intervene she had plastered her chest and glued her nose to the glass. Using her empty hands as blinkers, she peered into the arrival lounge.

Two minutes later, offendedly muttering, "Okay *baba*, okay. I'm going," Freny charged past the agitated security police to the waiting relatives. "I've had a good look," she told them. "Manek isn't there."

"Maybe you didn't recognize him," Zareen ventured. "He must have changed."

"Don't be silly." Freny was irritated. "I'd recognize him even if he'd turned into a monkey!" Pointedly looking away she addressed the others. "I don't think all the passengers have come into the lounge yet. We'll just have to wait and see. There's a whole bunch of Sikh pilgrims, it's a wonder the airplane wasn't hijacked." Freny was referring to the two Indian Airline aircraft that had been hijacked by Sikh Separatists in the past few months. The planes had circled the Lahore airport for hours and had been permitted to land only when the fuel ran out. "One of the Sikh pilgrims had his face all covered up like a bandit," Freny continued. "I couldn't tell if it was a turban and beard-wrap, or bandages."

Deep frowns appeared on the faces of the reception committee. Furtive glances were cast at Khutlibai. There was a bit of subdued *khoos-poossing*.

Pale as mountain mist beneath her discreet dusting of powder, Khutlibai looked from concerned face to concerned face and slowly raised a shaking hand to her heaving heart. Appealingly helpless and bewildered, she whispered: "*O baap ray!* Oh dear Father! What's happened? Why hasn't he come?" And, summarily dismissing every-body's hasty assurances that Manck would turn up at any moment, devoutly enlisted Ahura Mazda's help and the angel Behram Ejud's protection.

A clutch of businessmen — overnight travelers carry hand luggage — came out of the glass doors and vanished into the waiting throng. An elegant woman, trailed by three children and a porter trundling a loaded cart, was followed by a sedate trickle of other first-class passengers. Then came the disorderly procession of a hundred squeaking carts piled with mountains of suitcases, bed-ding rolls, and crates, and the accompanying flood of economy-class passengers with bawling infants. The passengers' eyes searched the receiving throng like orphans hoping to be claimed.

The hairy Sikh pilgrims came out next, looking perplexed and anxious, and were immediately greeted with shouts of "Taxi! Taxi!" Their colorful turbans and beard wraps could be seen bobbing as they were dragged away by the rapacious taxi-wallas.

"It's Manek!" A keen-eyed youngster squealed excitedly. "He's all bandaged up!"

Everybody craned their necks. All but hidden behind the crushing line of emerging passengers, his head and most of his face swaddled in white bandages, they recognized him.

"*O mahara baap!* Oh my Father!" Khutlibai gasped, thumping her chest, and Zareen simultaneously screamed, "Oh God, it's Manek! Oh God!"

They had failed to recognize him earlier because he wasn't wearing his glasses and only a tiny portion of his brown face showed through the white cocoon of his bandages.

There was no holding them back. The family broke through the cordon. The security men were as ineffectual as cotton-wool-stuffed gunny-sacks deployed to plug a breached canal. Manek's startling appearance and the stampede of his anxious relatives, yielded him a passage; sympathetic passengers stood back to let him pass.

Manek was instantly absorbed into the family fold and steered to stand before Khutlibai. He bent forward accommodatingly. Khutlibai placed a heavy rose garland round his neck, a touching mix of concern and happiness shining in her brimming eyes. She circled the air round his head with her hands, at the same time sprinkling him with rice, and energetically cracked her knuckles on her temples. Having prudently warded off stray evil and envious eyes, Khutlibai hugged Manek tenderly. She kissed those portions of his face spared by the bandages and, with an audible sigh, briefly lay her head upon her youngest son's chest.

As soon as Khutlibai released him, the men thumped Manek heartily on his sweat-soaked back and said, "What's the matter, *yaar*? You look quite fit . . . Why the bandages?" But the women, eyeing the unfeeling men with reproach, placed fragrant garlands round Manek's shoulders and solemnly held him to their copious bosoms. Making indulgent noises, they asked affectionate questions and stroked his arms.

A pair of solicitous hands grabbed Manek's heaped cart. Other hands divested him of his duty-free packages, hand luggage, and overcoat. In a protective throng, with Manek conspicuous in its center with his garlands and his alarming bandages, they crossed the road to the parking lot. Car trunks flew open to swallow the luggage.

All four doors of the Toyota were hospitably open. The old Pathan driver with the vivid blue eyes salaamed, made anxious inquiries, and gingerly embraced his pitifully bandaged employer. Manek was ushered into the front seat, and the long-legged Cyrus crushed into the narrow slot between Khutlibai and Zareen; he sat hunched up, his handsome chin almost touching his knees.

By this time, even Khutlibai had realized there was nothing seriously the matter with her son. However, maintaining a sympathetic pretense of concern, she lovingly kneaded his shoulders and was pleased by the feel of his strong new muscles. As the caravan of air-conditioned cars honked their way out of the airport, she leaned forward to ask, "What happened to you, my son? May I die for you; tell me how did this happen?"

There was a dramatic pause occasioned by Manek's deliberate silence.

Khutlibai inserted an arm between the front seats and, her elbow jabbing the driver's ribs, placed her palm flat on Manek's chest. This gesture transmitted many messages. Besides expressing a readiness to sooth her son and imbue him with the courage to bear his pain, it also conveyed an understanding of his mute ordeal. But, most importantly, it reestablished the web of ties that traditionally bind son to mother, the sacrificial and protective nature of maternal love and its claim to Manek's everlasting devotion and sense of duty.

With her usual adroit sense of timing, and in a choked voice, Khutlibai heightened the dramatic potential of the moment: "God knows how much pain my quietly enduring child is suffering. But then he was never one to make a fuss! Does it hurt a lot?"

Manek started to undo his bandage. Khutlibai and Zareen immediately began to help and squashed Cyrus further. Cyrus pressed back against the seat and raised his knees to protect himself from their heedless arms and elbows.

Relieved of the bandages, Manek broke his silence. "I've hurt my jaw." Choosing to express his feelings in the colorful Gujrati idiom used by older Parsees, he continued, "Speaking this wretched English all the time has worn away my jaws. Don't anyone dare talk to me in English!"

"Get away from me!" Khutlibai said, laughing with relief and giving his shoulder a shove. "Now I know why you haven't picked up an American wife! Say what you like, but ours are ours! Didn't I tell you — in the end one is comfortable only with one's own kind!"

"*Sala badmash!* Scoundrel!" Zareen swore, messing his sweat-drenched and flattened curls, "You had us all worried for nothing. And we thought your stay in America had improved you!"

"Still the same old actor, *yaar*," commented Cyrus, shaking his long face from side to side with disbelief and amusement, and at the same time giggling with a hiss that sprayed his brother-in-law with a fine mist of spit.

Partaking of the general feeling of relief, and belatedly reacting to the jab of Khutlibai's elbow to his ribs, the driver applied his brakes behind a cyclist and, with inches to spare, blared his horn into the unfortunate man's ears. As the startled cyclist wobbled and turned to glare back, the driver shouted, "If you want to die, you black man, go and die beneath some other car!"

The sun had set, and in the lingering afterglow made opaque by the dust and sooty emissions from the buses and mini-buses, it was impossible to tell the cyclist's color. But, then, had Snow White been the cyclist she would have been called "black man" also. The comment was not pertinent to color or sex. In the hierarchy of Pakistani traffic, truck and car are king; the cyclist, as possessor of an inferior vehicle, is treated with contempt. By the same token the pedestrian, whose only means of locomotion are his shoes, is more lowly. The lowest are the shoeless beggars who skip nimbly from the path of the Toyotas driven by snobbish drivers. The racist overtones were provided by the legacy of the Khan's service in the British army during the days of the Raj.

The family sat up late that night in Khutlibai's air-conditioned drawing room. Manek looked comfortable in a starched white shalwar and kurta-shirt that Khutlibai had kept ready for him. His shampooed curls sprung in a fakirlike halo, Manek regaled his audience with boasts of the wonders of America. "You think we eat well because we're rich? You should see how the poor in America eat! Everyday chicken! Everyday baked-beans, ham, and sardines! What the Americans throw away in one day can fill the stomachs of all the hungry people in Bangladesh, India, Sri Lanka, and Pakistan for two days."

Manek quoted staggering statistics about the inexhaustible supply of gas, water, and electricity. "You can drink water straight from the tap without worrying how many cholera and jaundice germs you're swallowing. You can have tub-baths ten times a day if you want to: there's no shortage of water. The landlord usually pays for it, and for the electricity. Everybody keeps their lights and air conditioners on all the time. Huge football stadiums and offices and shopping complexes are air-conditioned all summer. You have to wear a cardigan indoors, one forgets what summer is: it's as if you are always at a Hill Station. The same thing in winter; everything is centrally heated and you can walk about in shirtsleeves."

They had heard some of this from their America-returned uncles and cousins, but they had heard otherwise also.

"What about their shameless morals?" demanded Freny, and though she sat back in the crowded sofa she sounded as if she had mentally placed her hands on her substantial hips. "But you must have enjoyed all *that* part of it!"

There was a raucous burst of laughter, followed by suggestive hoots and lewd smiles. Manek managed to look like a smug cat who has swallowed nine mice but does not wish to advertise the fact.

"Yes, but," Jeroo chimed in, and winding a long string of pearls round a manicured finger, she stayed with their main concern, "what about schoolgirls and boys having sex as casually as if they're shaking hands? And the terrible muggings and rape? *Na, baba,* I'd prefer to keep my Dara safely in Pakistan, foreign-education or no foreign-education!"

The round-shouldered, bespectacled, and serious fourteen-year-old, sitting next to his father, looked startled and dismayed, his dreams of travel abroad abruptly shattered.

"Don't listen to what everybody says," Manek said, considerately looking at both Jeroo and Behram. "You can live as morally or immorally as you want. I'll tell you something though — "

Manek leaned forward conspiratorially and cast furtive eyes at the door. Behram at once locked the door. The family, too, edged forward on their chairs and sofas, and those tucked away in corners took quick strides to settle cross-legged on the Persian rug at Manek's feet. Satisfied that no undesirable person was likely to overhear him, Manek parted with his breathless secret:

"America is Paradise!"

The expression on his face, the awed tone of his voice, the energy that seemed to emanate in a glow of happiness from him convinced them of the truth of his statement and, without him needing to spell it out, communicated his fear: that the riffraff would take any means of transport available and fly, sail, swim, walk, or ride to swamp the New World by the millions from China, India, Pakistan, and Bangladesh once they knew how wealthy America was, and in how many ways a paradise.

"Now wait a minute," interjected Cyrus's portly brother Rohinton, his attitude still hostile from the quip about his wife's red handbag and the crude allusions to her marvellous bosoms. "I have also been to the United States. You are reacting like a new convert, exaggerating the good points and ignoring the faults."

Rohinton looked round the room, gathering with his challenging eyes a consensus for his opinion. His glance came to rest on Cyrus. Cyrus sat with his long legs casually stuck out. He acknowledged his brother's gaze pleasantly but with reserve. How could he validate Rohinton's statement: he had never been to America. Besides, it had been a long day and he was not up to rocking the overloaded family boat.

"But you haven't lived there," Manek said. He stood up from his perch between Khutlibai and Zareen to take up the challenge. Sliding his hands into the side pockets of his comfortable kurta, he said, "You haven't gone to college there. You are only speaking of impressions!"

Freny nudged her husband to keep quiet. It was Manek's

evening, and he was still glowing from the secret he had divulged for their benefit.

"Of course, you have to know the system," Manek continued and, shifting his eyes from Rohinton, turned on his heels to survey his audience and be surveyed by them. "You have to learn to function within it, otherwise you can have a hard time, like I did in the beginning. But if you want to understand what makes America tick, if you want to 'succeed,' you have to go when you're young and get your higher education there. It's difficult for an old dog to learn new tricks — you'll be like a fish out of water and lose all your money like thousands of other middle-aged and muddled-headed *desis* already have!"

Manek was by now speaking from the heady confidence of his just-returned status, the feel of his hands in the pockets of his starched kurta, and the lightheadedness of jet lag.

The older dogs pursed grim mouths, projected defiant jaws, and prepared to bare their fangs. But they were quickly restrained by warning looks and surreptitiously applied pressures and nudges from their various wives.

Judging that he might have been a bit tactless, Manek smoothly shifted gears and gave an account of the mistakes he had made and the hardships he had endured. He told them about his accident in New England and that he had not written home about it in order to spare his mother. And when the approving murmurs had subsided, Manek gave an account of the humiliation and privation he'd endured in the South as a Bible salesman.

None of them had any idea how impossible it was to live on the income the State Bank of Pakistan allowed a student. Manek knew that at the conversion rate of fourteen rupees to the dollar, it was a princely sum by Pakistani standards. The family probably thought he was living like a prince in America. Not at all. He was living like a pauper. Why else would he, who was considered a heathen in the Bible Belt, sell Bibles? Perjure his soul by lying that he was a Christian? And sometimes risk his life against attacks from farm animals? "You can't imagine how tight-fisted and difficult some of those farm people are," he explained.

Manek had taken an intensive three-day sales course in the basement of the Peach Tree Hotel in Atlanta one summer. The course
was offered free, and he had toiled with forty other ambitious
potential Bible salespersons and shared a cramped motel room with
one of them.

What had made his discomfort intolerable was the ubiquitous
and intrusive presence of the Indian family of Patels who owned the
motel. Manek knew that the Gujrati Indians, almost all of them
named Patel, owned sixty percent of the motel business in the
South; it did not surprise him that one of them should own the
one he was staying in.

In fact, because of the shared last name and the staggering number of motels owned by the Patels, the police in California had at
one time suspected that they were an Indian version of the Mafia.
Why else would anyone bother to acquire an unrewarding chain of
seedy motels?

A year of surveillance had revealed to the California Crime
Detection Agency that the Patels were a particularly docile community. They often pooled the money they brought from India to
buy the motels and, by working long and hard hours, turned a
modest profit from the business. The only violence they could be
accused of were stray and unverifiable instances of self-inflicted
injury — harmless but rather vicious-looking wounds and neatly
fractured bones — that enabled them to file claims and live off
insurance for a while. They were not above an occasional case of
motel arson for the same purpose. For the most part, their crimes
were petty and limited to the white collar variety: fiddling with
accounts, pilfering from cash-boxes, and cheating on tax. Some
indulged in a bit of pimping to supplement their frugal motel
incomes.

The moment Manek opened his mouth and spoke, the Atlanta
Patels could tell from his distinctive accent that he was a Parsee.
Their well-meaning interest in a stranger who shared their language
irked Manek. Especially in view of his strained circumstances and

the duplicitous nature of the path he was embarked upon as a Zoroastrian selling Bibles.

Exhausted at the end of the second day of the course, Manek pretended a headache to avoid another invitation to supper.

"It will be a simple, vegetarian meal," the older Mrs. Patel had declared the night before. Manek had no reason to doubt her word.

But the announcement of a headache misfired. It brought a pack of six Patels flocking to his aid, vocalizing between them six different kinds of medical advice, and Manek's headache threatened to bloom into a full-blown attack of neuralgia.

The eldest Mrs. Patel declared that a headache could be caused by an empty stomach; it would disappear after dinner. If it didn't, he should rub his temples with Tiger Balm or Deep Heat. The youngest Mrs. Patel cross-examined him to see if he had assaulted his stomach with junk food.

Manek confessed he had eaten a cheese and bacon hamburger.

A firm believer in an Aruvedic theory that the root of all ailments lay in abused and malfunctioning stomachs, the younger Mrs. Patel offered to bring him easop-gol. "It's a miracle fiber," she declared, touting the redoubtable virtues of the humble husk. "Mix one tablespoon of the husks in a glass of water — it'll turn into a kind of jelly — and drink it at once. It'll cure you if you have a runny tummy, and it'll cure you if you are corked."

One reflective patriarch, caste marks accentuating the lines on his forehead, counseled that the best cure for headaches was to walk barefoot on the grass in the early morning dew, and a rakish fellow in baggy jeans suggested that there was nothing as effective as a strong dose of Scotch.

Their Indian slippers slapping the hall floors, there arrived a twittering and contentious pair of middle-aged Patels. Talking alternately and together, their mouths red with the betel-leaf paans they were chomping on, they advised Manek to:

Soak his feet in warm water.

Cold water.

Tie a handkerchief tight round his head.

Place a hot water bottle on his forehead.

An ice-pack over his eyelids.

Take an aspirin and lie flat on his back in a darkened room.

However, the Patels all agreed that the worst possible thing was to retire on an empty stomach.

By the end of the unforeseen consultation, Manek had a raging headache. Unable to withstand the onslaught of the pain or the Patels, he docilely sat down to dinner and wondered if they would rely on friends and kin instead of doctors even when one of them was mortally ill.

At the end of the course, relieved at last to be finished and also rid of the Patels, Manek drove a beat-up truck to sundry small towns and farms in Georgia and the Carolinas with the gilt-edged Bibles.

At each town, Manek called on the parish priest, ferreting out the names and incomes of the families most likely to buy the Bible and the locations of motels not owned by flocks of Patels.

Armed with nothing but his briefcase and the information he had garnered from the ministers, Manek braved a hellish menagerie of farm dogs and stray bulls to push the door bells of his wary and bleak-eyed potential customers.

Once the door was opened, Manek wedged his toe in the threshold as he'd been advised to and disarmed the hostile potential customer by asking, "Are you Mrs. So-and-so? The Reverend So-and-so, of this-or-that-church, told me that you were a family of practicing Christians with good Christian values, and that I might call on you."

If he was not invited in at this point, he would ask for a glass of plain water.

Once he was ensconced in the kitchen with his briefcase and his glass of water, Manek might inquire: "How is little Jim (or Bill or Barbara) doing? Have you started him on solids?" Or remark: "The Reverend told me Kevin is a mighty smart boy for his age." And, as the mother (or mother and father) preened, he'd drive the nail home with a coy, "Like his parents, I believe . . ."

At some point, Manek would say: "I took the God-given

opportunity provided by this Bible (a casual wave of his hand in the direction of his briefcase) to drive through your beautiful countryside and meet you good folk."

After dropping this enigmatic hint, Manek would talk of everything — the drought, the flood, their children, the produce, local politics, farm subsidies — of everything but the Bibles. The more time he spent with the confused, bemused, and bewildered family, the more hope there was of a sale.

At strategic moments Manek might request another plain glass of water and be rewarded by a hearty meal instead. He chalked this up as a plus, second only to a sale. But sometimes the door was heartlessly slammed in his face, and he was left to fend off the farm dogs as best as he could with his briefcase and the bulls by leaping over fences. A pit bull had latched on to his haunches in Arkansas, and a terrier to his ankle in Louisville.

*

Sometime past midnight, when the women in Khutlibai's drawingroom began to sniff and discreetly wipe the tears from their eyes and even the men were not dry-eyed, Manek once again skillfully shifted gears and talked to the assembly about his triumphs.

It is to Manek's credit as a raconteur and as a compelling purveyor of dreams that no one yawned. With rapt and serious faces, the family listened to his plans for his future in America. And when Manek solemnly announced that he had come to Pakistan to marry a Parsee girl and take her with him to America, the familiar faces brightened and their smiles and nods conveyed the measure of their gratification and approval.

"I've told my Dara, and I'm telling him again in front of all of you," Jeroo declared, showing the pale palms of her hands and speaking in English. "When he goes for foreign education he can have whatever fun he wants. But when he wants to marry, it must be to a Zarathusti. He will be happy only with a Parsee. Isn't that so?" Jeroo, the assiduous supervisor of her children's homework, had been reassured by Manek's views on marriage and had undergone another change of heart. She looked appealing at Manek.

Khutlibai, in her role as matriarch, felt duty-bound to buttress her daughter-in-law's sentiment. "Even if we have to drill this into our children's heads a thousand times, it will never be enough."

Manek nodded, looked gravely at the round-backed adolescent squirming on his seat beside his father, and said, "I'll keep an eye on Dara when he comes to the Yoo Ess of Ay — as we say in America. Don't worry."

Jeroo made the traditional circling motion with her jeweled hands and cracked her dainty knuckles on her temples to ward off any evil to the paragon. Reverting to Gujrati, she said, "May I die for you. You might be the youngest, but you're such a good influence on the children; a fine example for them to follow."

The faces circling Manek beamed with admiration and racial pride, their faith in the future of their minuscule community affirmed by the decision of this scion of the Junglewalla family, the unlikely standard bearer of noble tradition. And with his ready offer to keep an eye on Dara, Manek was proving himself a champion of their community's future.

The sleepy-eyed cook, Kalay Khan, refilled the empty glasses. The wide-awake and excited kinsmen and kinswomen raised frothing beer mugs to their lips and drank loud and flattering toasts to Manek's courage and wisdom in breaking new ground and exploring noteworthy frontiers, and they inwardly congratulated themselves that he had, after all, turned out quite well for one who had shown so little promise.

The very next morning Khutlibai and Zareen launched a discreet search for a suitable wife for Manek. A week later Manek was whisked off to Karachi and surreptitiously shown several girls at weddings, *navjotes,* and parties. The girls, pretty in their good-occasion saris, eyed him with flattering interest. His family connections and his education at M.I.T. made him quite a catch, and his decision to live in America was icing on the cake. Most girls at these functions hoped to be whisked off to America, the land of their dreams, by this young knight in shining armor (represented by a suit from Sears) and a bright future. The bolder ones talked to Manek, while the less bold grabbed any handy child to twirl around and hug and kiss. Others addressed each other in cooing voices and giggled loudly in his presence. He noticed them all and was surprised how eligible he was.

Khutlibai and Zareen sent out feelers to the families of the girls Manek had liked. Of the five feelers that were sent out, two tactfully rejected the tentative offer, but three showed definite interest. Of these three Manek chose a slight, velvet-eyed, fair-skinned girl with a nightingale's voice and a ready smile.

Aban was distantly related to the Junglewallas.

Chapter 19

While the search was on for a suitable girl for Manek, Feroza was visiting with Jo's family in Boulder, Colorado. When she read the letters she received from Zareen and Khutlibai about the excitement and fun she was missing, the strategies and huddled conferences, the hilarious consultations with Manek and his witty comments on the candidates, Feroza was torn by conflicting desires. She wished she had gone with Manek to Pakistan, and at the same time she knew she could not have borne to miss the escapades and adventures she was enjoying with Jo and her family and finding so incalculably enlightening.

∾

Jo's father could trace his lineage to a stock of sturdy English farmers from the Midlands, her mother to thrifty vine growers in the south of France.

Thrifty and steady though her lineage was, Jo's mother was a compulsive gambler. As inclined to hop a plane to Las Vegas or Atlantic City as she was to dip into their restaurant's cash register, Mrs. Miller was the cause of the ever-present and gnawing anxiety of Mr. Miller.

Mrs. Miller was also given to sneaking off to Denver in her Thunderbird for the races whenever she could manage it. Twice, against the expressed preference of Mr. Miller, she took the two girls with her on a sporting spree. Since horse-racing in Pakistan had been banished to the out-skirts of the cities by General Zia, thereby discouraging the less rabid frequenters, Feroza enjoyed the sport with all the zest of one partaking of forbidden fruit.

Picking a sadly gaunt and docile-looking brown animal out of compassion, Feroza and Jo won a hundred dollars each on their joint bet of five dollars. Mrs. Miller sighed, shrugged, looked at the girls pityingly, and said, "You wanna know something? It's the worst thing that could happen. When luck favors you like this the first time round, it's only to snare you! But enjoy yourselves while you can."

They did.

As they drove back through Denver's downtown, Feroza caught her breath at the sight of the soaring skyscrapers suddenly twinkling with lights, and her heart lifted as it had in New York. This was the America she had imagined herself in; not the dreary, alternately frozen and slushy byways of Twin Falls with its squat structures and inhibiting outlook.

Feroza turned to look back. Beyond the skyscrapers was the jagged wall of mountains, spectacular in the sunset, dwarfing everybody and everything with its billowing mass.

Feroza fell in love with Denver.

A couple of weeks later, when Jo, at some glancing reference by her father to Twin Falls, remarked, "I'm not going back to that dump! I'm gonna look around; maybe at the University of Denver," Feroza decided she would do the same.

The University of Denver was one of the few colleges in the United States that offered an outstanding undergraduate course in hotel management. And just as Manek on learning of Feroza's acceptance to the junior college at Twin Falls had felt it was providential, coming as it did on the heels of the anxious spate of letters from Khutlibai and Zareen, so Feroza felt her switch to the University of Denver was ordained by divine decree.

Both girls filled out forms and applied for admission to the course.

Jo's mother indulged her passion for gambling without noticeable neglect to her responsibilities. She was the restaurant's cashier, cook, waitress, and solicitous hostess. Jo's father shared the duties. He evidently enjoyed the time he spent at work more than did Mrs. Miller.

Since the restaurant did not serve breakfast, Mr. Miller opened the kitchen at around ten o'clock. He locked up around midnight, after the last customers had left and after placing the cash in the safe. Theirs was a small family business, employing a staff of three or four people who had been, for the most part, with them since the restaurant's inception. Millers' Home Cooking was known for the taste, standard, and predictability of its wholesome meals; they had a regular and faithful clientele and an increasing circle of new customers.

Mr. Miller had survived a short stint in Vietnam. Within three months of his enlistment, he had sustained an injury skidding on a slice of cucumber in the army canteen. He had been laid up in the hospital for a month and, a few months later, discharged from further duty. Mr. Miller had required extensive surgery on his left knee, which had left him with a pain in his leg and a tendency to limp when he was tired.

Feroza found Mr. Miller kind and generous. When work was slack, as it was later in the afternoons, he brought the girls slices of strawberry pie and always managed to lead the conversation to complaints about his gambling wife and the money she was siphoning from their cash register. Often he would limp into the girls' room, strawberry pie in hand (he made the pies himself), and say, "You won't believe this . . . Guess how much she took today? I went out to get the paper and when I got back, the cash register was empty, cleaned out — nothing but small change. I wish we'd have a real live holdup — a robber with a loaded gun. At least I'd have a fighting chance! But with Teresa, I can do nothing."

"She doesn't neglect anything, does she?" Jo said once. "So why complain."

Mr. Miller kept a loaded pistol beneath the cash register in the restaurant in the wistful hope that his fantasy about the holdup might be fulfilled some day.

Feroza found Jo's parents preternaturally understanding and unobtrusively hospitable. It was refreshing. The hospitality of her aunts and uncles in Karachi and Bombay could become cloying and oppressive, and, of course, everybody considered it their bounden duty to offer up advice on how to conduct every aspect of your life, undeterred by lack of qualification, expertise, or experience.

Although she had long ago guessed from Jo's unrestrained behavior that the Millers did not meddle in their children's affairs, or impose restriction, it nevertheless amazed her to observe them at such close quarters and discover the way they associated with each other.

The Millers exercised what she could not help but consider a remarkable discretion and forbearance. It astonished her that they were on speaking terms at all with their daughter and that their relationship worked so smoothly and without traumatic scenes featuring heart attacks and lachrymose bouts of sustained melancholia. She could almost see her grandmothers (not to mention stricken aunts and uncles) collapse, with hands on hearts and wounded looks, if she had exhibited a fraction of Jo's blithely independent attitude and disregard for their opinions — opinions and advice that they considered not only their duty to dispense, but also an unalienable right, considering their long years of worldly experience and their even longer memory of traditional wisdom and ways, the centuries-old legacy of their revered forebears.

Feroza's parents, her aunts, and uncles, for all their assertions of being broad-minded and modern, would expect unquestioning obedience on certain matters, like the relationships between various family members, and between boys and girls, and would view with consternation any straying from the established path.

And, surprisingly, even though Feroza found the Millers' way of life admirably tolerant and eminently desirable, she could not imagine it transposed to any community, whether it was Christian, Muslim, Hindu, Sikh, or Parsee, in her part of the world. What would life be like in her family and in Lahore without the extravagant guidance and dire warnings, the endless quoting of homilies, and the benign and sometimes not so benign advice, inquisitiveness and interference?

Unnatural.

Impossible and, in a way, given the intricately woven context of their social and familial fabric, dreary even to contemplate.

It was only after Feroza met Jo's sister Janine — who flew in from California for a week — and her brother Tom that Feroza grasped the astonishing truth that far from being the star delinquent of the family, Jo was, in fact, the most balanced, ambitious, and promising star on the Miller horizon. It soon became apparent that Jo was her parents' confidant and the one on whom they pinned their hopes and aspirations for the growth, perpetuity, and inheritance of Millers' Home Cooking.

Jo's sister Janine had straight ash-blond hair that swung thick about her shoulders, large green eyes, and a lavishly contoured and sensual mouth. She was as beautiful as Feroza had imagined — except when something happened to ignite her combustible passions. Then her face turned fiercely melodramatic, and it terrified Feroza to look at her. Feroza made a point of never being alone with her. Janine also had a whining grating voice that got on everyone's nerves — but got her her way — and a fund of expletives so fantastic that even Jo pricked up her ears and, quietly attentive, learned from her guru.

Jo had a strong sense of family, as was evident from the way she remembered each of her nieces' and nephews' names, preferences, and caprices, and one Sunday afternoon, loaded with presents — some pilfered and some purchased from their race winnings — Jo took Feroza with her to Denver to visit her brother Tom.

Tom's was the only shabby home in a well-maintained, upper middle-class neighborhood of smooth lawns and trim, glossy-leafed trees.

They turned into the drive, and Feroza at once saw the large man with a graying stubble, sprawled in a chair beneath an anemic fruit tree. The yard was overgrown with weeds. The house badly needed a coat of paint.

Tom was drinking beer out of a can, and the gritty soil near his long legs was strewn with empty beer cans. His navel, and the pink hairy bulge above it, showed through a missing button on his red-and-brown plaid shirt. The shirt and shorts were stained where beer had dribbled.

Approximately halfway between the man and his house an unruly tree hung gloomily over a large car. Feroza could tell by the car's long ugly fins that it was an ancient model, older perhaps than Manek's Ford back in Cambridge. Feroza noticed a small grubby face peering out of its shadowed interior.

In fact the yard was littered with children who were either bawling or brawling. A pale child with a runny nose and strawlike hair flung herself at Jo. Jo swung her up, then down between her legs, and, twirling round and round with her niece, clasped her in a huge hug. More nieces and nephews crowded round Jo, clamoring for her attention. Feroza noticed that two or three of the children were not familiar with Jo and stood at a small distance, wistfully sticking their fingers in their mouths, as Jo dished out the kisses, hugs, and presents.

Jo managed to find presents for them, too.

A harried woman with sparse, frizzy hair came out shouting at the children. She wore a skimpy, sleeveless top over baggy draw-string pants. The door gaped behind her, and the dim space inside appeared to be cheerless. Although she saw Feroza and Jo, and was having her sister-in-law visit after more than a year, the woman did not greet them. Their presence unacknowledged by her, the distracted woman scolded, spanked, and dragged a howling child indoors.

Jo and Feroza hung around for about an hour, making desultory conversation with Tom. On closer inspection Feroza thought he was good-looking, and although she was probably seeing him at his worst, there was something appealingly vulnerable about him. He talked in a defensive way, rubbing his nose with his thumb every short while, as if challenging Jo to contradict him. He had fancy business schemes and plans in mind and was about to implement them with the help of partners. He apparently knew a lot of rich people who wanted to do business with him.

But for most of the visit, Jo played with the children. They saw and heard the woman at intervals, and Feroza was surprised that they had not been offered even a cup of tea.

Jo explained that some of the kids were foster children. Feroza at once felt she might have misjudged the couple and had come to hasty and judgmental conclusions. They must be kind-hearted beneath their gruff and rough exteriors to provide care for the abandoned children.

When they were about to leave, the man shouted, "Elly, they're going! Are you gonna haul your ass out or not?"

Elly came out, wiping her hands on her shapeless cotton pants.

She offered them an abstracted, unwilling, little smile and said to Jo: "Oh, you're going? Too bad you can't stay. How're Mom 'n' Pop?"

On the way home, Jo told Feroza that the children had been farmed out to Tom and Elly by the county for a fee.

Feroza couldn't understand the way the family unit she had just witnessed was structured, or how it sustained itself. Obviously Tom was not a steady provider, and she suspected that he drank too much. She was tormented by what she had seen. What would happen to the children? It was so unlike anything in Pakistan. She had never heard of children being sent to foster homes. If a man could not for some reason provide for his family, usually because of sickness, death, or some other calamity, his wife and children would be provided for by relatives. Children were not given up for adoption or "farmed out," so long as there were family members alive. Men didn't go to seed the way Tom had because of drinking problems: few Muslim men drank. She had heard of very few cases of alcoholism, and these existed only among the fashionably wealthy, who could afford the black-market rates demanded by their affliction. She wondered, was this the price one paid for the non-interference and the privacy she was beginning to find increasingly attractive?

After a few days spent in aimless vacation leisure, Feroza and Jo received letters stating that their applications had been accepted by the University of Denver and that their credits were transferable. Feroza and Jo leaped and pranced with a sense of release and exhilaration. Jubilant, they packed small bags and shot off on a tour of the Grand Canyon.

A little before the new term began, the girls rented a small basement apartment in a building near the campus. From her very first day at the University of Denver, Feroza sensed she was in the right place, that her life would develop in unexpected and substantial ways. For one thing the cosmopolitan variety of students — black, Hispanic, Arabic, Irani, and some unmistakably Pakistani and Indian — filled her with suppressed excitement. Besides, after Twin Falls, Feroza found the sheer size and complexity of the University exhilarating.

No one, though, would have guessed it from her conduct. Paradoxically, she was for the most part confused and awkward and so overwhelmed by the activity going on around her, the waves of confident new students' faces and the maze of buildings, that she retreated like a timid clam into her haughty shell.

She latched onto Jo fiercely, like a child, and even regressed sometimes to holding her hand or hanging onto her shirt. Jo, with her innate familial and domestic impulses, was indulgent and tolerant.

For the first few weeks, the girls went to Boulder over the weekends, but soon Jo became less and less inclined to visit her parents. One fall weekend, Jo took her sleeping bag and backpack and went camping in the mountains to view the foliage with some new friends. Feroza had been transported by the fiery colors of the trees. She had not expected this blazing beauty in trees that had looked so commonplace in summer. She yearned to steep herself in the magic of the leaves and abandon herself to the wilderness with Jo. Jo had invited Feroza to go along, but shy at the thought of exposing her sensibility to strangers, resentful of their claim on Jo's time, Feroza made an excuse and backed out at the last minute. Jo did not press her as she might have in Twin Falls. Feroza, though she did not admit it even to herself or fathom the jumble of reasons why, was terribly hurt.

One afternoon the following week, Jo burst in through the apartment door, excited as of old, hollering, "Feroza! Feroza! Hey, listen to this. I'm goin' on a diet!"

"So, what's new?" Feroza asked, shuffling dispiritedly into their tiny living room, blurry-eyed and in her robe. She had in mind Jo's recurrent resolutions to go on a variety of diets in Twin Falls. These resolutions had followed a cyclic orbit something like this:

Fantastic new guy, a fireworks of passion, pledges of eternal love. Diet.

Eternal love waning by the end of the month; Prince Charming transformed into a douchebag. Diet kicked in the teeth.

Compensatory eating binges, horror about weight gained, frenzy of passion with fantastic new love. New diet.

"This time it's different," Jo said, triumphantly hoisting a large packet from Walgreens above her head. "I'm gonna stick with the plan. I've just seen the doctor. He's gonna help me."

"This time you must," encouraged Feroza.

Jo stuck with the diet: little packets and potions of protein drinks, and pathetic morsels of prescribed foods. By the end of the month, Feroza was impressed by Jo's persistence and her regular visits with the doctor and became more encouraging.

Feroza found herself on her own much of the time as a perceptibly shrinking Jo cavorted with new-found confidence and new friends. Had it not been for Shashi's determined advent into her life, Feroza might have clung longer to the umbilical cord by which she had attached herself to Jo.

A sinewy and outrageously gregarious youth from India, Shashi was a year ahead of Feroza in the hotel management program. Intrigued by the attractive new girl from his part of the world and by the challenge her haughty reserve represented, Shashi had persisted in talking to her after the English class they shared twice a week.

Shashi had a lean, handsome, dark brown face and a tangle of straight eyelashes that cast a deceptively somnolent veil over his inquisitive eyes. He penetrated Feroza's reserve in a matter of days, as he knew he would. Not that Shashi came by this confidence through any conceit; it was only natural for people to respond to his indefatigable interest in them. Shashi's readiness to accept people without reservations made him a cherished companion, and he collected friends as one gathers bouquets of wildflowers from mountain slopes in springtime.

Shashi gave Feroza his notes and copies of the assignments and term papers he had completed the previous year. He also introduced her to his spiraling circle of Bangladeshi, Sri Lankan, Tibetan, Pakistani, Indian, Middle Eastern, Far Eastern, black, and white friends.

For Feroza it was like stepping through Alice's wonderful mirror. Each day brought the gift of a tentative new friendship, a provocative bit of knowledge, a mad burst of pure laughter. It wasn't that Shashi or his friends were so funny; rather, something locked within Feroza opened up, allowing her access to happier places within herself.

And this shift in perspective was taking place in her mind as well. Her impulse to acquire knowledge, to figure out things, was stimulated by her studies, challenged by discussions among her new friends, by the books Shashi recommended or loaned her. She ventured into psychology, into philosophy, into literature.

She read books by a variety of new influences: Naipaul, Bertrand Russell, Styron, Desai, Plato, Rilke, Heller, Achebe, Forster, García Márquez.

Feroza found her days filled with excitement, joyous activity, and ascending wonder. It was as if her combat with Manek and his efforts to instruct her, her year in Twin Falls, and her exposure to Jo, were a preparation for the way her new life was unfolding. Otherwise she would have been too shy to embrace the new encounters, too timid to delve into unexplored ideas or grasp the opportunities suddenly falling about her like gifts from the sky.

It was the first time Feroza found herself making friends on her own, without Jo. And the feeling she'd had about Denver and the University — that she was in the right place and that her life would bloom — now appeared affirmed.

It gave Feroza pleasure to introduce Jo to her new friends. Shashi took to dropping in at their apartment as frequently as did Jo's merry-go-round of steadies, and the three of them established an easy camaraderie that included their various friends.

And though Feroza and Jo didn't know how to express it, or even feel the need to, each accepted that the other had enriched her life, extended it to harmonize with and revel in the exotic.

It did not take much to persuade Feroza to transcribe some of the assignments Shashi had given her and hand them in as her own work. Without this lapse — which she understood was not too rare, among the Pakistani and Indian students at least — she would not have been able to cope with her blossoming social life, or read, or consider the assortment of jobs available. Feroza's expenses had increased commensurate with her expanding social commitments. It was also costlier to live in a big city.

Feroza considered waitressing, working in a bar, becoming a

215

salesperson or selling tickets at an amusement park. These jobs were within her range — if she took the chances the other foreign students took — and was prepared to work for less than minimum wage.

Feroza found the very concept of these jobs breathtaking, beyond the compass of the possible in Pakistan. There were no waitresses in Pakistan, only waiters. Since there were no bars, there were no bartenders. Even had the jobs been available and the stigma attached to them had not existed, Feroza would have found working at these professions in Pakistan intolerable. Her slightest move would attract disproportionate attention and comment, for no other reason except that she was a young woman in a country where few young women were visible working.

This focus would always isolate her, keep her removed from the variety of human contact she felt was at the very heart of living. The liberating anonymity she had discovered within moments of her arrival at Kennedy airport, when no one had bothered to stare at her and the smoky-eyed American she was talking to, still exhilarated her. In Lahore these contacts would have been noticed and would have drawn censorious comment. Within the heady climate of her freedom in America, she felt able to do anything.

In this respect, Shashi's lack of inhibition fascinated her much as the young American's consummate unself-consciousness had.

With Shashi's encouragement, Feroza started working in a bar close to the campus (no one asked her for her age when she applied for the job) as assistant to the bartender, who was also a student. Feroza enjoyed the convivial, dusky atmosphere, the strangers who spoke to her so readily and her fleeting contact with them. She delighted in serving the colorful drinks with fancy names like piña colada, screwdriver, margarita, and strawberry daiquiri.

Shashi, and the friends she had met through him, dropped by for an occasional chat. They couldn't afford the drinks, but sometimes they ordered one to share. If Shashi was alone, he lent a hand as they chatted, and the bartender usually slipped him a drink.

Like thousands of other Hindu families, Shashi's had fled Lahore at the time of the Partition of India in 1947. They had been allotted some land as compensation for the urban property and business they

216

had left behind. With the money and jewelry they had salvaged, the family set up a small cloth shop in New Delhi. Given their background and the necessity that drives refugees and new immigrants, their business had prospered.

The spirit of enterprise that drove his family was in no way lacking in Shashi. Feroza saw him in action once. In the snow-packed Denver winter, he sat blue-lipped and shivering in the entry of a suburban shopping center, an almost transparent white *dhoti* tied between his legs like an exotic diaper. Partially visible through the white sheet thrown across his shoulders his ribby brown torso looked stiff and cadaverous. His feet were unshod.

The chattering of Shashi's teeth, like woodpeckers drilling, could be heard a block away. Americans in hooded goosedown parkas and fur-lined boots were aghast at the sight of this touchingly young and emaciated version of the saintly Gandhi so perilously close to freezing. Only the movement of the whites of his eyes beneath his somnolent lids, and the chattering of his teeth, betrayed any indication of life.

Next to him, propped up in a empty bottle, was a stick with a scrap of paper glued to it. The paper fluttered when people went in and out of the doors. Those who were in a hurry, or who lacked the means to help such desperation, scurried past, eyes guiltily averted, counting on others to help.

There are always kindhearted and generous people, and sooner or later, one of them would stoop to read the lettering on the paper. The message was printed with a marker: "Not received money from home in 3 months. Floods have swept away my village and buffaloes. No clothes and no food — kindly HELP."

Since there had been news of recent floods in Bangladesh, the message, combined with the horrendous condition of the youth, achieved immediate credibility.

Feroza suspected that the communique on the note varied according to the nature of the latest catastrophe, which in some shape or other could always be counted on to afflict their part of the world.

Once the near-cadaver was resuscitated, and usually it was by

someone who could afford to resurrect him, Shashi, with his glib
tongue and persuasive ways, got not only whatever he required
but also what his brand-name-conscious relatives in Delhi wanted.

Shashi went on a Spartan diet each year after Thanksgiving, and
staged the drama every winter. Horrified Americans, shopping for
Christmas, bought him enough sweaters, jackets, shirts, and slacks
to see him through spring, enough garments appliquéd with alliga-
tors and Polo ponies to satisfy his kin.

His benefactors also wrote checks to the University of Denver to
pay for his tuition, with an added amount thrown in to make them
feel they were doing something noble in the name of their vague
and cherished notions of Gandhi.

In return, Shashi showered them with gratitude and a touching
profusion of bizarre blessings picked up from Delhi street beggars
rendered into English: "May you live long, sir/ma'am. May you
have many sons and grandsons. May they prosper and look after
you. May God part the skies to pour wealth upon you."

Feroza felt that Shashi earned every ounce of the clothes he
acquired, every morsel of the food he shared with his friends.
Having absorbed the attitudes about money and the exploitative
"system" preached by Jo and Manek, Feroza appreciated Shashi's
methods. She knew that Shashi received very little money from
home; the State Bank of India barely allowed any foreign exchange
to go out of the country. His family could have transferred "black
money," but they didn't. They had complete confidence in his
resourcefulness.

Shashi had a sharp, quick, probing mind, and Feroza's relationship with him was airy, flirtatious, fun. It was easy for Feroza to be
with Shashi precisely because he was so at ease with her. Feroza
came to realize that Shashi's interest in women was powered more
by curiosity and an appreciation of their otherness — their softness,
beauty, and gentler ways — than by the tempestuous urges that
appeared to ravage his more susceptible compatriots.

Shashi's temperament did not permit him to be possessive. This
lightness, this freewheeling congeniality, rubbed off on Feroza; she

understood that freedom, dear as its discovery in America was to her, was also an essential condition of any relationship.

Feroza had grown up, like most young girls in the Subcontinent, believing that everything she expected of life would be hers after marriage. The denial of even her most insignificant wish was followed by comments like: "You'll reign like a queen in your husband's house. You can do as you wish once you're married."

Statements like this made marriage seem to all the girls to be the ideal condition of existence. Their marriages would unshackle them, open their lives to adventure and knowledge of the world, give them the freedom that is each individual's due.

Chapter 20

Manek Junglewalla was married in Karachi the following summer.

Khutlibai and Zareen, complaining at every step that Manek was running them ragged, were in a glorious frenzy of preparations for the wedding. Khutlibai's house took on a festive air. There were many ceremonies connected with the wedding to be arranged for, many sets of clothes to be prepared as gifts for relatives. Khutlibai's house was overrun with children on vacation while their mothers spent their days preparing for the celebrations.

A tailor was engaged. He sat on a white cloth spread in one corner of the veranda floor before a table fan, whirring the handle of his sewing machine. A pious woman, distantly related to Soonamai, was making scores of *sudras* from the finest muslin. She occupied the guest room and could be heard ripping the material into half-yard pieces from the forty-yard *thaan*, wrapped around a board. Rohinton had bought it from a factory in Kot Lakpat and saved Khutlibai almost two hundred rupees.

In fact, the zip of cloth tearing became intrinsic to the exuberant spirit of the house as the women made small cuts with scissors and, curling the edges, ripped the cloth apart. They divided some of the *thaans* into bedsheets and pillowcases, and the silks and satins into blouse pieces and petticoats.

Jeroo, who had a flare for anything to do with precious metals and gems, flew in from Rawalpindi to help select the jewelry sets for Aban and her mother from among Khutlibai's heirlooms. She also assisted Zareen with the shopping and the matching of petticoats and blouses for the sari sets.

Freny firmly helped the more dithering members of the family arrive at decisions and generally threw her officious and solid weight around, as was her wont.

Two weeks before the wedding, the advance party of relatives and their children boarded the air-conditioned coaches of the Tezgam train to Karachi.

In Karachi, Freny took charge of the large triple-storied bungalow in Clifton provided for their use by Khutlibai's widowed
cousin. Freny managed the servants and, with the help of a slender
stick she occasionally waved about, the children. She was promptly
bequeathed a new title, General, which she accepted as graciously
as she had her nickname Allah-ditta. Even the servants started calling her General Sahib.

Behram Junglewalla was urgently summoned to Karachi by
Jeroo, arriving with Bunny and Dara a few days before they were
due. His presence was required to shore up his wife's shaky
authority.

Left to the mercy of her in-laws and being temperamentally
unsuited to stand up to the more powerful personalities around her,
Jeroo had been reduced to a state of stammering and trembling.
When not weeping in her room, she went about her business with
pink rims round her eyes, tight-lipped and dour.

Behram staunchly championed Jeroo and had a stern word or
two for Freny and Zareen. Zareen, finding herself at a sudden disad-
vantage, summoned Cyrus to shore up her authority.

After discharging their duties, the brothers-in-law hung about
the house enjoying the waves of chatter and laughter, the discussions and emergency consultations, the rainbow display of saris
being folded and unfolded so that they appeared to flow like silken
rivers from one room to another.

Some evenings, Cyrus and Behram were invited for drinks on
a Greek ship by a hospitable cousin. The ship was docked in the
Karachi harbor, and the cousin catered for the shipping line in
Karachi.

As scheduled, Rohinton arrived with his and Cyrus's mother,
Soonamai, a week before the wedding. He had not been summoned
because Freny felt quite competent to stand up to anyone and maintain her own authority.

While Soonamai Ginwalla, whip-slender and considerate, dignified the ceremonial occasions with her discretion, Rohinton played
his part by swelling the crowded rooms with his portentous presence. Soonamai's counsel was sought by everyone because she
knew the niceties of traditional rites and, with her tactful ways and

sympathetic outlook, was able to smooth out friction before it escalated into an all-out war.

When a wedding loomed, most families went to Bombay, the sari and jewelry Mecca. Zareen warned Manek that his bride and her mother would have to make do with what was available in the shops in Karachi and Lahore, since he had not given them enough notice to get visas, nor time to travel across the border.

"She's marrying me, not the saris," Manek retorted succinctly, and his wise and witty words (attributed to his education at M.I.T.) were repeated with gusto among his relatives and friends.

The quip also made the rounds of the girl's family, and Manek's intelligence and sagacity were volubly admired, while Manek's family tactfully camouflaged any pride they took in the comment with playfully disparaging remarks.

Aban's mother, a gentle, docile creature, was diligently quoted. She approved the boy's sentiment utterly. What use had her daughter for saris when she was getting such an educated and well-brought-up husband? Her daughter had enough saris.

Pleased by the comment, and not to be outdone, Khutlibai was heard to observe that *khandani* families always showed their good-breeding no matter what. Her daughter-in-law would be welcome if she came with nothing but the clothes on her back. She would cover Aban with diamonds. She had set aside a flawless three-karat solitaire for her youngest son's wife.

That was very generous of her, the girl's mother was reported to remark. But no jewel could compare with the diamond Aban was getting in the person of her handsome and educated bridegroom.

∽

Manek returned to America a married man. He phoned Feroza, smugly saying, "Well, *boochimai*, what've you been up to?"

Feroza screamed with joy at the sound of his voice. She had missed his calls. She wanted to be told every detail of his marriage, what had happened, who said exactly what to whom in the inevitable dominoes of one-upmanship within a family of so many cousins, each related to the other in three different ways, and what had transpired between the girl's family and theirs.

Khutlibai had lost her cool, Manek said, and had given him a dressing-down in front of everybody on the day of the *madasara* ceremony; he had merely stated his skepticism about the mango he was being coaxed to plant in their garden to ensure his fertility.

The petty skirmishes between Zareen and Jeroo had exploded atom-bombically on the morning of the engagement. Freny had added fuel to the fire by waving her hands about and loudly siding with Jeroo, and his mother had fainted in the drawing room when her entreaties for peace on the propitious day had gone unheeded.

The subsequent flap, during which Soonamai applied cologne-watered handkerchiefs to Khutlibai's head and Behram massaged the soles of her feet, brought a contrite end to the sisters-in-law's inauspicious quarreling.

The bride's parents had conducted themselves with exemplary civility and docility, but her two moronic sisters had been inappropriately rowdy. They had pushed him fully clothed into the Karachi Sheraton's swimming pool at the end of a party given by the bride's uncle.

Cy had been full of his usual frivolity —

"Who's Cy?" Feroza interrupted.

"Your pop."

"Cyrus-*jee*, to you," corrected Feroza, tagging on the honoring suffix "*jee*" to express the extent of her censure. "My father would slap you if he heard you call him 'Cy' and 'pop.' "

"No, he didn't. But he foamed a bit at the mouth and threw a fit."

"You don't have to be so damned American."

"When in America, be American. Haven't you — "

"Oh God! I'm going to hang up or throw up!"

"Okay, okay . . . As I was saying, Cyrus-*jee* was full of his usual foolishness. But I was surprised by Rohinton's behavior."

The normally sober and prudent Rohinton had abetted his brother's frivolity. They had arranged for Manek and Aban to ride in a decorated horse-drawn coach to the Fire Temple in Saddar Bazaar after the nuptials. The gaunt and elderly horse pulling their carriage had balked at the attention of a mischievous crowd of street urchins and *goondas* who ran alongside hooting and making smacking noises. Manek said that he was waiting for the day Feroza got married to return the compliment.

"I'd like to see how Cy reacts when his own daughter and son-in-law are ridiculed on their wedding day!"

"Oh my God," Feroza exclaimed, "I think really missed something!"

"Yes, you did," commented Manek laconically. "But I must say, I didn't hear a peep out of anyone saying they missed you. Not even from your grannies."

Of course she didn't believe him. "Jealous? Is someone's bottom burning?" Feroza said, translating the Gujrati idiom into English.

Manek and Aban had received enough practical gifts and *pareekas* of cash to set up house in America. If Feroza had her eye on the three-karat blue diamond, she could forget about it. Her grandmother had given it to his wife; also the diamond and emerald bracelets.

Feroza groaned, "Oh God, you must be really mad to think I'd mind. For your information, Granny told me she'd kept them especially for your wife. You don't know what she's kept for me!"

"I know, a kiss and a kick!"

"Oof," Feroza said, pretending to fan herself at the other end of the line. "It's so hot — somebody's bottom *is* burning!"

"Not mine. Must be yours."

Manek had left his wife patiently waiting beside her packed suitcases back in Karachi. She would join him in a few months, after he got his doctorate and had found a job.

Chapter 21

The citizens of Denver sat beneath the leafy crown of trees on freshly mowed and fragrant summer grass. They smiled at the spectacle of the programmed sprinklers watering lawns already being rained upon. An almost anorexic Jo abandoned her hotel management course and moved in with her uniformed boyfriend, Bill.

To Feroza's protests at her leaving school when she was already halfway to graduation, she said, "I don't need all this theory. I could teach them a thing or two about the restaurant business. I know more than enough to run my family business."

Bill was a reliable young man with an appreciation of good food and the sundry other appetites necessary for the well-being of Feroza's former roommate. He also had a promising future in the United States Air Force, and he was stationed at the air base in Denver.

Feroza moved into an apartment with Rhonda and Gwen, one white, the other black, and both of them strikingly beautiful. The dusky girl, Gwen, was older, almost twenty-five.

Gwen had the longest legs dangling from her cut-off denim shorts. The skin covering them was a glossy mahogany, and Feroza could not help noticing the way her legs stood out, delicate and beautiful, amidst the crisscross stampede of pale or pink legs freshly bared to the summer sun. After a period of association with Gwen and Rhonda, Feroza finally mustered up the courage one sweltering noon to get into a spare pair of Rhonda's shorts. Both her roommates applauded and assured her that she looked just great.

Gwen's tuition and living expenses were paid by a middle-aged white man. Although Feroza and Rhonda believed in his existence, they never saw him. They heard about him, but they never heard him.

Invisible and never heard, their roommate's lover waxed mysterious and romantic in their imaginations. They did not know the make or color of his car, although they knew he sometimes picked up Gwen. Gwen did not reveal his name either, or tell them what he did. She referred to him mostly as "he" and sometimes as "J.M."

Rhonda and Feroza got the impression that J.M. was rich and influential. They believed he was a WASP. Every time they spotted a fancy European car on campus with a male white Anglo-Saxon at the wheel, they excitedly speculated that it might be J.M. Rhonda, herself a WASP, helped a curious and intrigued Feroza recognize the species, but it took a WASP to recognize a WASP, and Feroza wondered if she'd ever be able to tell them apart from other whites.

When Feroza had arrived fresh from Pakistan, she would have considered the arrangement shocking. Even now, more than two years later, she was troubled, but she had a better understanding of the prevailing mores in America and a more accommodating view of the relationship between men and women.

Feroza learned from chance remarks Gwen let slip what it was like to be a young black woman, how difficult it had been for her to attend college, and how much she valued her education.

Gwen was guarded about her past. She did not volunteer information about her family, but if asked, she answered without obvious reluctance. Feroza sometimes found the answers to even her most casual questions unexpected and surprising. She soon felt that she was intruding without meaning to, and she started to be more considerate of Gwen's privacy.

Feroza knew as much about her roommate as Gwen wanted her to, and Feroza felt it was enough. She knew that Gwen came from a large, loosely structured family in Atlanta and that they were poor. Gwen's mother worked as housekeeper to a wealthy family in Marietta, and, being the eldest, Gwen had looked after her younger siblings. Although she seldom mentioned them or seemed to have any contact with them, Feroza got the impression that she was deeply attached to them. At times, when her mother was sick, Gwen had substituted for her. She told Feroza she hated it and that was when she decided that she did not want to spend her life mired in a cycle of poverty and domestic service. Once, unasked, Gwen had told her that she had been discriminating in her relationships with boys and that she had been careful not to get pregnant. "You know how it is," she said, "you can get suckered into something like that!" Although Feroza acted as if she was used to hearing homilies like this and weighing similar considerations, she was taken aback and realized that Gwen's life had been very different from hers.

Gwen had been a conscientious student, but she had not done well enough to earn scholarships. She had been too busy with responsibilities to give enough time to her studies. It had been something of an achievement that she had graduated from high school at all and had not dropped out like many of her peers.

Gwen met her white lover when he was visiting his cousin's in Marietta. It was one of those occasions when she was standing in for her mother. She had moved to Denver because he asked her to.

Gwen spent alternate weekends with J.M. in hotels, or they camped in the mountains and toured the countryside. They had flown to Hawaii for a week once and had spent ten days in the north of Italy when her lover had been invited to a conference at the Villa Serbelloni at Bellagio. He attended the conference for barely a day, and they spent the rest of the time frolicking on Lake Como, eating pasta and trout, and touring the spectacularly scenic playground of the rich. It had been one of the high points of Gwen's life.

"Do you love him?" Feroza asked, agog when Gwen displayed a platinum ring encrusted with diamonds.

Gwen looked at her, surprised and defensive. But she saw that no censure was implied. The question had been asked in innocence. She shrugged her wide, slender shoulders. "He's good to me. He doesn't want me to date anyone while I'm with him. It's not much to ask." Gwen had a musical lilt to her throaty voice that delighted Feroza's ears.

Feroza saw much less of Rhonda than she did of Gwen, and their relationship was consequently less complex and more affectionate.

Rhonda was a blond with a lovely face and dreamy blue eyes, naturally red lips, and a warm, slow smile. She was kindness and consideration personified. Rhonda was not tall, at least not for an American, though she was an inch taller than Feroza. She had a cuddly, feminine body and a most arduous dating schedule.

Rhonda found it embarrassing and unkind to refuse dates. She accommodated even the more persistent of the less attractive boys pestering her. She preferred going out in a group.

The phone rang incessantly for Rhonda. She and Feroza shared the line. Once in a while, an exhausted Rhonda would flop into their threadbare living room in an oversized man's shirt and crankily announce, "I'm not home!" and Gwen and Feroza would handle her calls.

Feroza had her own hectic social life. Given the quantity and the variety of her friends, she was invited to at least four parties every weekend. It was almost like a junior level replica of her parents' parties back home. On alternate weekends, Gwen went along with her.

Shashi found Gwen, her reticence, her secret life with her white lover, and her knowing ways fascinating. He was full of small gallantries in her presence and was considerate of her at the larger parties, making sure she was not bored. Not that he was any less attentive to Feroza. But often when he dropped in at their apartment, he spent the time talking to Gwen. Gwen was laid-back, a good listener, full of insinuating and expressive laughter, and wicked repartee. She had an innate gift for the right compliment.

One overcast evening, Feroza took some papers to be photocopied, and Gwen accompanied her. When Feroza was through paying for the work, she noticed Gwen talking to a Sikh student who worked evenings at the campus Kinko's. What struck Feroza was the way the boy was looking at Gwen, like a hypnotized and charmed chicken. Feroza heard him say, "You know, I feel I've known you all my life. It's . . . as if we're related, you're family. What's your name?"

The expression on the boy's face was revealing. His defenses and social reserve gone, he stood exposed, his soul bared, exhibiting the measure of his homesickness and loneliness, his need for kind words, understanding, fellowship.

Feroza had talked to the boy casually before and had been flattered by his attention, attention that, as a woman from the same part of the world, she considered her due. But this was astonishing.

She knew he was aware of her presence, but she was at the periphery of his consciousness. What was inside him, his naked need for a friend, his devotion, was focused on Gwen.

Feroza could not fathom it. What had passed between him and Gwen in the brief moments she'd been occupied to make him respond like this?

Feroza was not unaware of the interest Gwen aroused in Shashi. Knowing Shashi's incorrigible curiosity, it had not bothered her unduly. But now she took to observing her roommate with a more speculative eye. She wished to probe Gwen's personality and discover the enigma of her compelling attraction.

Although she knew Gwen was likable from her own experience, Feroza now noticed that she generated instant friendships, smitten countenances, warm responses in even the most casual contacts. Feroza sensed it involved more than just her self-possession, her easy, responsive ways or her expressive voice. Although she was pleasing to look at, even striking, there was no particular feature one could focus on and say it was pretty — it was more the way the shape of her face and head and the structure of her long, slender body came together.

Understanding dawned on Feroza gradually, and it had more to do with intuition than observation. The interest that lit up Gwen's brown eyes, the unexpected flicker of shyness that suddenly swept her small features, the brief, almost imperceptible gestures, the movement of her body as it shifted a step back, a step sideways, were charged by a subtle flattery, if one could call it that. Combined with her choice of words and the range of inflection in her voice, her tranquil presence, with its armory of compliments, cast a spell on whomever she was talking to, made that person feel good about himself.

But even then, Feroza could no more grasp the elusive quality of Gwen's magic than anyone could the intriguing and chameleon nature of her own blend of shy, haughty, impulsive, and warm appeal.

Feroza found herself becoming uncomfortable and watchful when Shashi visited and the three of them were together. Not that she could really fault either of them. Shashi did not try to ask Gwen out or be alone with her, and it wasn't as if Gwen was flirting with Shashi or setting out to be winning.

Gwen seldom wore makeup or bothered much with her clothes. The short hair, cropped to form a sculpted whole with her fine jaw and the outlines of her oval face, frequently outgrew its shape and stood out in neglected, wiry tufts. And when Shashi was present, the elusive flattery, as much a part of Gwen as her quiet breathing, was not so much in evidence. As if sensing Feroza's wariness, Gwen reined in her sorcery.

Despite the heavy lids that gave Shashi's eyes their sultry look, his relationship with Feroza was more romantic than sexual. They kissed when they were out alone and indulged in light and playful petting. But Feroza never felt as though she might be swept away by a grand passion, or that Shashi might want her to be. This restraint was also supported by the taboos that governed the behavior of decent un-married girls and of *desi* men.

Some protective instinct within Feroza, without her being con-scious of it, knew that Shashi's attitude about their petting was more experimental and curious than passionate, so that when Shashi cajoled Feroza to be more intimate, she found it easy to slap his hand or to push him away. Their intimacies were a teasing romp, Feroza's kitten to Shashi's tom, a ritual of coaxing and refusing that unraveled amidst laughter and provocative chatter but was neverthe-less dictated by Shashi's cooler rhythm.

At first, Feroza had not been resentful of Shashi's enjoyment of Gwen's company. He had imbued her with too much confidence in himself for that. As time passed, however, she found Shashi's atten-dance on and constant talking to Gwen more and more upsetting. Her hurt began to show in the haughty set of her face, in the ner-vous abstraction of her eyes. And, in becoming so concerned over Gwen's intangible magic, Feroza lost some of her own.

Gwen took to staying in her room when Shashi dropped in. But he would miss her company and, shouting, "Hey, what're you doing hiding yourself away like this?" barge into her room, chuck away the magazine or book she was reading, grab her hands, and pull her to her feet.

Feroza began to sulk. She made up excuses when Shashi suggested a movie or an evening at a disco. Shashi became confused and then concerned.

Feroza hinted he was paying too much attention to Gwen. But Shashi brushed aside the charge as too ridiculous even to countenance. Feroza knew he was telling the truth, but she became surly and sulky with Gwen when they were alone, or chattered with an unnatural brittleness that did not suit her. She avoided Gwen's eyes.

"Hey, what's bothering you? Anything the matter?" Gwen finally asked one day when Feroza set about preparing an omelette, her face hostile. Gwen suspected what the matter was, but she wanted Feroza to broach the subject, express her feelings her way. It was not Gwen's nature to be impulsive or imprudent when dealing with people's feelings.

Feroza's pent-up furies exploded. She accused Gwen of flirting with her boyfriend, of being cunning, of not leaving them alone when he visited, of being a dissembling flatterer, of interfering. Her rage spent, confused and contrite, she lay her head on the chipped kitchen table and began to cry. She knew she was accusing Gwen unjustly, not being strictly honest.

"You know I'm not the least bit interested in the guy. Heavens, he's like a kid brother," drawled Gwen with convincing emphasis, "and he isn't interested in me in that way, either."

"I'm not so sure," Feroza said and began to sob.

"But you're not really serious about him, you know," Gwen suggested, the nebulous question floating in the air.

"I am," Feroza cried, "but he isn't!" and she got up from the kitchen table and flung herself on the lumpy, worn sofa to weep more.

Gwen petted her, saying kind things to her in her comforting voice, affectionately allaying her fears and soothing her unhappiness.

When Feroza, her storm spent, stopped crying, only sucking in her breath with an occasional shudder, Gwen pulled her to her boyish chest and gently rocked her. "He's not your type, baby," she said. "You know he's not your type."

Feroza could feel Gwen's heart throb against her temple. Her chest was shallow, her ribs surprisingly birdlike, a cage too brittle to contain the vigorously pulsating organ. Feroza had a touching

231

impression of the fragile girl's vulnerability then, of all that Gwen might have gone through, of the strength required of her to be where she was, where she wanted to be. And she understood the courage of the heart beating so stoutly in its bony cage, even as the monotony of its throbbing filled her with its tranquility.

Feroza could have lain there, drawing on its strength, but Gwen leaned back and held Feroza by her shoulders. Supporting her so that Feroza had to sit up, the older girl's small, wise eyes looked close into Feroza's. "You can't allow yourself to be hurt like that by Shashi," she said, shaking her head. "It's like being bruised by the breeze. The guy just circulates — he can't help it anymore than the breeze."

✂

Feroza did not stop seeing Shashi. She could no more stop seeing him than she could the mirrored library building. In any event, one did not sever ties with Shashi; he wouldn't allow it.

Shashi gauged the irreconcilable shift in Feroza's feelings. It made him unhappy, and he regretted it. He could not clearly understand why it had occurred and was confusedly, vociferously repentant. But Shashi, being the evanescent, adaptive creature he was, soon accepted the situation and in doing so merely changed the grip, the nature of the tie that bound them, so that they would remain good friends.

After all, Feroza was in his bouquet of mountain wild-flowers. She didn't wish to be torn from it nor did Shashi want her to be. The flowers bloomed and distilled their fragrance in the currents of the friendship Shashi generated, in the quick-witted air in which he circulated, and Feroza's place in the setting was secured by the friends she had made and the ideas and discussions to which she contributed.

Feroza's insatiable excitement about the various knowledge Shashi had made her alive to, bound her to him in a way their romance never could have.

Shashi had graduated in hotel management but could not yet see his way to abandoning his college life and earning his living. He had enrolled in the master's program in business management. He was also taking classes in psychology, philosophy, and creative writing.

The fall term was coming to a close, and the campus was filled with activity. The students were taking exams, handing in their papers, preparing to leave their dorms and rented apartments for the winter vacation, and making plans for Christmas.

Feroza had decided to spend her holidays in Lahore. Her family had been sending clamorous letters for over a year and were anxious for her to visit.

In any case, Gwen and Rhonda would be gone. Jo, who was phoning less and less frequently, would not be in Boulder. Feroza might have visited Manek, but he was busy moving to Houston, finding a place to rent, and settling into the position he had accepted with NASA.

Manek received his doctorate. The family in Pakistan did not know what a landmark occasion it was in America. And it was only after the event, when he saw how many relatives of students had descended on M.I.T. for the ceremony, that Manek himself became aware of it. He called Feroza the day after, "You didn't even come for my graduation!" he said bitterly and hung up.

Feroza had tried to reach him many times on graduation day just to have the pleasure of saying, "Oh, Dr. Junglewalla, how is your pulse this morning?" but he had not been in his room.

Manek's work on his thesis in chemical and structural engineering and the recommendations from his professors were excellent. The engineer at NASA who interviewed him hinted about sponsoring his citizenship if things worked out as satisfactorily as he expected. Manek was already in touch with a lawyer, and he would soon be in a position to apply for his green card.

Chapter 22

Feroza became increasingly excited as the date of her departure drew near. Thoughts of Khutlibai, of Cyrus and Zareen, of her relations and friends, came to the forefront of her mind and hovered there. She wondered how she had borne being away from them so long. Her mind was already traveling, preparing her for the quantum change, transporting her to Lahore before her arrival.

Feroza was received at the airport with garlands. The portals of the house had been strung with a perfumed chain of red roses and the floor before it made auspicious with stencils of fish, flowers, and lettering in English reading "Welcome."

After her stay in the New World, with everything in it scintillating and modern, Feroza was struck by the mellow beauty of their ancient door. Like her father, she had considered her mother's pride and happiness in the acquisition a piquant oddity. But now she stood in awe before the two worn panels, wide open in their carved and painted frames. She had been instructed to wait as Zareen and Freny rushed inside to fetch the ingredients of welcome.

Freny, stouter than Feroza remembered her and as assertive as ever, held the ceremonial silver tray while Zareen circled an egg seven times round Feroza's head. She sacrificed the egg by cracking it on the floor, its contents neatly spilled onto newspaper placed to one side of the threshold.

Feroza held out her hands to receive the coconut. She leaned forward so that Zareen could anoint her forehead with the red paste and press rice on it. Zareen invoked Ahura Mazda's blessings, which, except for variations occasioned by Feroza's travels, were the same as on all her birthdays. Zareen ended by proclaiming, "May you go laughing-singing to your in-law's home soon; may you enjoy lots and lots of happiness with your husband and children."

Again Feroza leaned forward, this time to receive the lump of crystallized sugar Khutlibai popped into her mouth.

Khutlibai drew circles over Feroza's head with her arms, loudly cracked her knuckles on her temples, invoked more blessings, and stood to one side blinking back the tears of happiness flooding her eyes.

Zareen poured a little water from a round-bottomed silver mug onto the tray. Divested of egg, coconut, and sugar, it held only residual grains of rice. She circled the tray seven times round Feroza's head to banish the envious eye and tipped its contents on either side of the door.

Protected against evil and welcomed by propitious spirits, Feroza stepped through the rose-scented entrance of her home.

The family surrounded Feroza affectionately, much as they had Manek. There were a great many questions and a vigorous exchange of views. Fresh details of Manek's marriage came to light and led to a string of hilarious anecdotes. The family feasted, laughed, and gossiped late into the night.

After the initial wave of euphoria, Feroza perceived that many things had changed. Time had wrought alterations she could not have foreseen—while her memory had preserved the people and places she knew, and their relationships with her, as if in an airtight jar.

It hurt her to see both her grandmothers look significantly older. Perhaps her concept of what age looked like had changed in a country where seventy-two-year-olds jogged like athletic young things. Khutlibai had stopped dying her hair and though her short, gray hair looked thicker and fluffed handsomely about her head in jaunty waves, it made the wrinkles on her face seem more resigned. Her back, however, still emerged sturdy and dependable from the monumental pedestal of her rump and hips.

Ill-mannered though it might appear and disagreeable as it was to her, Khutlibai visited her son-in-law's house often to see her granddaughter. She held the girl's hand in both of hers and pressed it to her eyes. Her gaze lingered on Feroza's vibrant face, and her shrewd eyes were luminous with pride and love. She saw life and intelligence shining in her face, but there was too much life there, she thought with a trace of unease, too much intelligence — more than might be good for her granddaughter.

Khutlibai and Zareen went into convulsions of laughter at the funny way Feroza had of describing her adventures in America.

Zareen was astonished at the change in Feroza. Was this flaming, confident creature, who talked so engagingly and candidly and had acquired a throaty, knowing, delectable laugh, the same timid little thing who had refused to answer the phone?

As the days passed, Zareen wondered if she hadn't made a mistake after all in sending her daughter to America. But seeing that Cyrus was quite at ease with the transformation in their daughter, she kept her thoughts to herself and even checked her mother from voicing her misgivings.

Soonamai's cataracts were ripening. It broke Feroza's heart to see her self-contained and dignified grandmother groping for things, having to rely on the negligent care of others.

People appeared to have forgotten Bhutto and his martyrdom. The concerns that had mattered to her, and had once again risen to her consciousness, had been replaced by other pressing issues. Something called the Hadood Ordinances had been introduced by General Zia in 1979 without anyone knowing what they were. The Federal Shariat Court, to oversee the Islamic laws, had also been established.

The new mischief in their midst had sneaked up on them unawares and surprised them one day when they read about the Famida and Allah Baksh case. The couple, who had eloped to get married, had been accused of committing adultery, or *zina*, by the girl's father. They were sentenced to death by stoning. On an appeal to a higher court, the charges were dismissed. Fortunately, stoning to death was declared un-Islamic because there was no mention of it in the Koran.

But the shock that provoked the massive wave of public indignation came with Safia Bibi's case. The blind sixteen-year-old servant girl, pregnant out of wedlock as a result of rape, was charged with adultery. She was sentenced to three years rigorous imprisonment, fifteen lashes, and a fine of a thousand rupees.

Safia Bibi's father, in bringing charges against her assailant, had been unwittingly trapped by the *Zina* Ordinance. It required the testimony of four "honorable" male eye-witnesses or eight female eyewitnesses to establish rape. The startled women, who had enjoyed equal witness status under the previous law, realized that their worth had been discounted by fifty percent.

Since it was scarcely possible to produce four male eye-witnesses given the private nature of the crime, the blind girl's testimony against the assailant was not admissible. Being sightless, she was not considered a reliable witness. Since rape could not be proved, she was charged under a subcategory of rape: "fornication outside the sanctity of marriage."

Safia Bibi was not punished, thanks to the pressure of the legal community and the women's and human rights groups. The women came out on the streets, burning their veils, voicing their protests, and beating their breasts, and Zareen was among them. The verdict was rescinded.

Jehan Mian, a pregnant eleven-year-old orphan, was similarly charged. In view of her "tender age," the judges reduced her punishment to ten lashes and one year rigorous imprisonment, to go into effect once her child was two years old.

Feroza found the judges' compassion revolting, a society that permitted such sentencing, criminal. The addition of *zina* altered the entire legal picture of sexual crime. The victim of rape ran the risk of being punished for adultery, while the rapist was often set free.

Yet there were many apologists, upright men learned in jurisprudence, who agreed with the letter of the law, if not its spirit. They produced a litany of precedent and dire argument to support the verdicts. The gender bias was appalling.

All this had been set in place shortly after Bhutto's hanging. "You should have sent me newspaper clippings," Feroza said to her mother. "I want to know what's going on here. After all, it's my country!"

Zareen did not mention the innuendo, the odd barb, that had suddenly begun to fester at the back of her consciousness. The insinuation that her patriotism was questionable, or that she was not a proper Pakistani because she was not Muslim. What was she then? And where did she belong, if not in the city where her ancestors were buried? She was in the land of the seven rivers, the Septe Sindhu, the land that Prophet Zarathustra had declared as favored most by Ahura Mazda. What if, on the strength of this, the 120 thousand Parsees in the world were to lay claim to the Punjab and Sindh? The absurdity of the idea kindled Zareen's smile.

But such comments were a passing thing, she thought, discounting the remarks made by people who did not matter to her or Cyrus, blaming them for the zealous Islamization fostered by General Zia, which encouraged religious chauvinism and marginalized people like her — the minorities — and made them vulnerable to petty ill will.

Some of Feroza's school friends had entered the Kinnaird and Lahore Colleges and were preparing to graduate. Some had disappeared into their ancestral villages, and a few had married in Lahore. They talked about babies, husbands, and sisters-in-law and took her unawares by their gossip about people Feroza didn't know and their interest in issues she couldn't follow. Feroza felt she had grown in different ways. Her consciousness included many things they had no concept of and were not in the least bit interested in.

When Feroza talked about the condition of blacks and Hispanics, the poverty, and the job insecurity prevailing among even the whites in America, her family and friends looked at her with surprised, unsparing eyes. They had their own vistas of uncompromising poverty and could not feel compassion for people in a distant, opulent country that had never been devastated by war, that greedily utilized one fourth of the world's resources and polluted its atmosphere and water with nuclear tests and poisonous pesticides that could serve as well to obliterate Third World pests like themselves.

After seeing the filthy conditions in the tattered *jhuggees* that had sprung up on the outskirts of the Cantonment and between Ferozepore Road and Jail Road, Feroza understood their reaction. Poverty had spread like a galloping, disfiguring disease. Every kind of poverty in the United States paled in comparison.

Yet it did not mean that the condition of the poor in America was trifling, or the injustice there less rampant. Feroza tried to clarify her thoughts. Poverty, she realized, groping for expression, was relative.

A friend who was now at Kinnaird College described a house she had visited in one of the poorest ghettos in Harlem the summer before. The family had electricity, running water, a fridge, and a car. The concept of refrigerators and cars stood at the very limit of extravagance and, in comparison to the people who dwelt in the rag-and-tin lean-tos and in infested, stinking *jhuggees* without bathrooms or electricity, undeserving of sympathy.

Did that mean they should care less for people's suffering elsewhere if their degree of deprivation appeared to be less? Were compassion and caring rationed commodities that could not bridge national boundaries? A car in America did not signify riches, she explained. It was like an extension of the body; to be without one was like missing an arm or a leg. She spoke from experience, she said. She didn't have a car, and she felt crippled.

Feroza, who had been scathingly critical of America, of its bullying foreign policy and ruthless meddling in the affairs of vulnerable countries, in her discussions with her roommates and the new friends she had met through Shashi, found herself defending it in unexpected ways. Which other country opened its arms to the destitute and discarded of the world the way America did? Of course it had its faults — terrifying shortcomings — but it had God's blessings, too.

Feroza was disconcerted to discover that she was a misfit in a country in which she had once fitted so well. Although Zareen had not mentioned the slighting remarks, having dismissed them as too cranky and trivial to countenance, Feroza's subconscious had registered subtle changes in her mother's behavior. She could not have put her finger on them, but they were there in the wariness that sometimes flickered across Zareen's face and in a barely noticeable hesitation in her choice of words. Feroza, absorbing the undercurrent at some hidden level of her consciousness, found her sense of dislocation deepen.

And there was the question of marriage. Zareen hinted at it casually and then broached the subject unequivocally. There were some wonderful boys she had in mind.

"How can I give up my studies at this point, Mum?" Feroza

protested. "There're only two years left. Let me graduate at least."

"What's this new graduate-shaduate nonsense? We send you to America for a few months, and you end up spending almost three years! Your father and I offered you our finger and you grabbed our whole arm! Enough is enough! You have to listen to us. It's time you settled down."

"I'm not settling anywhere without a career," Feroza said. "I don't want to be at the mercy of my husband. If I have a career, I can earn a living, and he will respect me more."

"Respect you? Nobody'll marry you if you're too educated. I'm not educated and I don't have a career, but I'd like to see your father disrespect me! Or your uncles disrespect your aunts!"

"You've never worked, Mum. You don't know how thrilling it is to earn your own money. And spend it."

Zareen looked at her daughter, surprised at what she had said. It occurred to Zareen that in her many more years on earth, she had missed out on some things. Feroza had said "thrilling," but she understood that she had meant more. The money Feroza earned and spent must give her a sense of control over her life, a sense of accomplishment that Zareen had very little experience with.

"Okay, *baba,* finish your studies," Zareen said. "I know how obstinate you are."

Khutlibai and Soonamai, each in turn, and together, stroked Feroza's arm and expressed the wish dearest to their hearts. They wanted to see Feroza married and settled before they passed away. Couldn't she give it a thought for their sakes?

"Of course I will," Feroza said, trying to stifle her smiles at their earnestness. "I refuse to die an old maid! It's only a matter of a few months; a year at most. When I'm back I'll have a good look at all the boys, and I'll marry the handsomest!"

"Hand-som is as hand-som does," Khutlibai said in her inimitable English. Her eyes twinkled in triumph at having hauled up the proverb so appropriately.

"Now where on earth did you learn that from?" Feroza asked and, delighting in Khutlibai's pleasure, hugged her grandmother.

Shortly before she left, Feroza realized with a sense of shock that she had outgrown her family's expectations for her.

Chapter 23

Feroza was a week late for school. The days in Lahore had simply flown and everyone had told her it was absurd to travel all the way to Pakistan for such a short visit. Behram and Jeroo had come with their children over the long Christmas weekend — which was a holiday because it coincided with the anniversary of Jinnah's birth — and Aban flew in from Karachi at Khutlibai's behest.

Aban was barely three years older than Feroza, her niece through marriage, and the two of them at once forged a strong bond. From her very short experience of married life, Aban already felt the need of a potential ally. Feroza looked forward to having family in the United States, and a lasting and pleasurable alliance was formed between them.

Her relatives were reluctant to let Feroza go. Between them, her friends and relatives gave an endless chain of welcome-home lunches, teas, and dinners that merged seamlessly with the farewell lunches, dinners, and even breakfast parties, without anyone being very surprised.

Feroza was touched. All the attention warmed, gratified, and flattered her; yet she was also anxious to get back to Denver.

Once she was airborne, Feroza opened the envelopes, anointed with the red paste and with grains of rice still adhering to them, and counted the loot. Her family had given her a little over seven hundred dollars, painstakingly procured in dribs and drabs from savvy Americans who knew they would get a better deal from acquaintances than from the banks.

Feroza was jubilant. She gave a small involuntary cry of pleasure, and the old woman who had been quietly watching the activity going on in the seat next to hers adjusted the shawl covering her head as a preliminary signal to opening a conversation and said, "*Khush ho* — Happy?"

Feroza laughed and nodded. She would at last be able to buy a decent secondhand car. Her hints to the family had yielded a sizable harvest. She thought of all the things she could do and places she would go and debts she could repay by running errands for her friends. And, as at the onset of her journey to Pakistan, her accommodating mind transported Feroza to her destination before she actually got there.

Feroza arrived in Denver late in the evening. At the apartment, Gwen and Rhonda greeted their exhausted and overloaded roommate with menagerie-like cries of welcome. Their small apartment rang with sounds of delight. "We missed you . . . We thought you weren't coming back!" they exclaimed.

"Me too. Oh, God . . . I can't believe I'm back!" Feroza cried, her exhaustion banished. Dropping her hand luggage she hugged them happily and, sitting cross-legged on the matted living room rug, began at once to unpack the presents she had brought for them. Onyx pencil holders, ashtrays, plates with mother-of-pearl inlay, carved wooden bowls and bookends with brass inlay, black shawls and cushion covers with shocking-pink embroidery, and white *kurtas* with pastel shadow-work. She showed them the *shalwar*-and-shirt outfit she had brought for Shashi. Sitting on the floor, delving into the suitcases and hand luggage, they chatted until Feroza suddenly fell forward, asleep.

Holding her firmly by her arms, Gwen and Rhonda escorted a hyped and feebly protesting Feroza to her bed. They brought her luggage to her room. As Gwen was leaving, she told Feroza that Shashi had dropped in almost daily to find out if she'd arrived.

Shashi spotted Feroza the next day on campus. Waving an arm and shouting, "Feroza!" he ran across the paved paths and the grassy patches that separated them and flung his arms about her neck. "Oh, I missed you," he said, affectionately rubbing his forehead against hers. "I thought they'd got you married or something and we'd never see you again."

"They almost did," Feroza said, laughing as she recalled her grandmother's pleading. She accepted his prescience without surprise because he was from her part of the world and knew what could happen.

Feroza was on her way to a cooking class but promised to meet him at the cafeteria afterwards.

Shashi was full of news. His brother and sister-in-law had arrived while she was away. She must visit Deepak and Mala this very evening. He'd told them so much about her, and they were looking forward to meeting her.

Mala was going to have a baby. She was due in a month or so, and she expected to have her baby in Denver. Deepak had specially arranged it this way because it would get their child the coveted United States citizenship. It was the least they could do for their firstborn: provide options.

"God knows what things will be like in India by the time he grows up, and it's getting harder and harder to get American citizenship," Shashi said, unaccustomedly frowning, burdened by future responsibilities. "Once the child is eighteen he can sponsor his parents, too. It's good to have some family in America anyway, 'specially for businessmen."

"It looks like you have a farsighted brother." Feroza raised an eyebrow and gave him an ironic look from the corners of her sunlit eyes.

"Businessmen have to be. We're a farsighted family," Shashi said, responding to the sarcasm with a mischievous and wry smile.

"You kept saying 'he.' Are you sure it'll be a boy?"

"They want a son. But it's okay even if it's a girl. They don't have any children yet."

Shashi came to fetch Feroza, and they visited Deepak and Mala's apartment in the evening. They had rented a one-bedroom apartment on the ground floor, near Shashi's.

Deepak had the same dark, heavy-lidded eyes and aquiline features as his brother, but the resemblance ended there. Deepak was heavier, taller, and though he was as alert, his movements were slow. He lacked the airy, inquisitive, easy-going quality that was so charming in Shashi. There was something earthbound about Deepak, his expression wary, less open, calculating, as he sized up Feroza. He probably made friends for reasons other than Shashi's, Feroza thought. She was uneasy in his more worldly presence.

Mala had a soft, passive, melting beauty. She had a waist-length fall of shining hair softened by hints of brown and a complexion several shades lighter than her husband's. Feroza thought she was exactly the kind of wife, docile and simple, she would expect Deepak to have.

Since it was her first child, Mala's stomach was still quite small, and the airline had not objected to her traveling. Of course they had not told the airline she was nearly into her eighth month.

Mala looked tired. An unhealthy pallor accentuated the darker patches of dry skin on her cheeks. Feroza glanced covertly at the protrusion beneath the pleats in her sari; it was larger than she had expected. The skin beneath her short blouse glistened where it stretched taut over the drum of her swelling flesh. She appeared to be in acute discomfort, changing her position and getting up on some pretext or other. Feroza thought they should leave, give Mala a chance to rest. She felt she might space out herself at any moment. She needed to catch up on her sleep also.

A week later, Mala delivered her baby daughter prematurely.

Feroza bought a small arrangement of flowers and visited Mala two days later. Shashi drove her to the hospital. Mala looked much better. Her skin was moist, the dark patches very faint, and now that the strain had left her face, she was radiant with the glow of motherhood.

Deepak was not in the room, and in his absence Mala was winning and talkative. Feroza warmed to her. She felt a surge of gratitude and affection for Shashi. Here was yet another promising friendship to which he had linked her.

"The poor little thing weighs only three and a quarter pounds," Mala said. "The doctor has put her in an incubator. But he says she is well formed, 'complete in all respects.' He says we'll be able to take her home in a month."

Wrapping a Kashmiri shawl over her hospital gown, Mala walked down the gleaming corridor to show Feroza her baby.

Feroza was horrified. The mite lay behind fortifications of glass with her transparent fingers spread, lizardlike, a tube attached to her nose and an IV to her leg.

She glanced at Mala, but Mala was beaming placidly. "Isn't she cute?" she asked, and Feroza said, "Yes, but she's too tiny . . ."

"That's because she's premature. She'll be normal-sized in a month. She'll grow as if she's in my stomach."

Feroza renewed her driver's license. She scanned the classified ads, consulted her friends, and on Rhonda and Gwen's advice made an appointment and went to inspect a two-year-old Chevette stick shift. The feature that struck them as most desirable was that it had been owned and driven by only one person.

That person was David Press.

Feroza got off the bus at the corner of Vine and Cherry at about four in the afternoon. She walked two blocks up East Edison before she located the house. She went to the entrance and was about to ring the bell when she noticed the sheet stuck between the grill and wire netting of the flimsy outer door. The thick red lettering on it, in a fine, sloping hand, read, "If you have come about the car, please knock on the garage door."

At Feroza's timid knock on the garage door, David Press revealed himself, wearing only his ragged shorts and a pair of square, metal-framed glasses. The longish gold-streaked hair that swept his forehead and framed his handsome face appeared, if anything, to enhance the wild effect of his gleaming nudity.

Feroza looked into his vivid blue eyes to avoid looking at the rest of him. Her heart pounding, she blushed and stammered something inaudible.

David leaned closer to catch the mumbling. He guessed that this must be the girl who had made an appointment to see him in response to his ad in the college newspaper. He also imagined that the sensitive creature was embarrassed by the spectacle of his mediocre musculature that refused to bulge satisfactorily despite his efforts, and his offensive near-nudity.

David turned crimson and, saying, "Hold on a sec," gently closed the door of the converted garage in her face.

He reappeared a few seconds later buttoning a long-sleeved blue flannel shirt with a high collar. He stuck out his hand. "I'm David Press."

Feroza raised her hand hesitantly, giving the impression of a timid animal trusting its paw to a stranger.

"How did you get here?" David asked, noticing there was no car except his Chevette parked on the road.

"I took a bus," Feroza all but whispered as David stooped to catch her words. "Then I walked."

"Come, have a look at the car," David said. His eyes had turned the color of sapphires in the sun, luminous and smiling behind his glasses.

David strode toward the small car parked alongside the curb. Feroza followed the broad shoulders, the compact muscular body, the sun-drenched hair.

David opened the hood and stuck the prop into its groove. He stepped back, placed his hands cockily on his hips, a gesture he had acquired to disguise his phenomenal lack of confidence, and said, "Have a look at the engine."

Feroza peered at the intricate mechanism of steel and tubes as intelligently as she could. "What about the carburetor?" she asked, remembering that Jo had once needed to replace it in her car.

"She's only gone forty thousand miles. I don't think the carburetor should give you any trouble."

David had rolled up his cuffs. The sun gilded the hair on his forearms and set off minute sparks against the darker hue of his tanned skin.

David pulled out the oil stick to examine the viscous substance coating it, showed it to Feroza, "Oil's okay," and closed the hood.

His movements had a controlled, graceful fluidity. He reminded Feroza of the Khazak dancer she and Jo had seen leaping about in a televised performance of the Bolshi Ballet. Feroza liked the way his head sat upon his shoulders, the width and strength of his neck which was like a reined-in stallion's.

David held the car door open for Feroza. "Like to try her out?"

He couldn't be more than twenty-two or twenty-three, Feroza guessed. He was obviously very proud and fond of his car. But why did he refer to it as "her"? Feroza experienced an irrational twinge of jealousy, as if the Chevette posed a threat.

She settled in front of the steering wheel and placed her large string-bag on the gear box.

David strutted round the car with the self-conscious gait of a person who wishes to appear taller and settled into the bucket seat next to hers. He picked up the bag and laid it carefully on the floor, moving his feet to one side.

"Ever driven a stick shift before?" he inquired hesitantly, fearful of giving offense.

Feroza nodded and glanced at him. Whereas her eyes had clung to his before, she now found looking into them unendurably disturbing. It was like viewing a solar eclipse without protection. She lowered her eyes to the shift stick in confusion.

"Put your foot down on the clutch," David said, and as Feroza pressed the clutch, he shifted the gears, saying, "This is first. Straight down, second. Back to neutral and up, third. Down again, fourth."

Feroza watched his hand. It was a tough, square hand and, like the rest of him, well formed and compact. The nails were wide and clean. The sun, attracted to him, poured through the window, igniting the hairs on his knuckles, forming a nimbus round his head, refracting off the metal frame of his glasses.

Feroza's eyes were smarting, her face on fire. He was altogether too dazzling to look upon. She hoped, with whatever remaining faculties she could muster, that the transaction would be completed before she made a complete ass of herself.

Feroza turned on the ignition and put the car into first gear. In the flashing moment of lucidity that the diversion afforded her she decided to stop looking at David.

Feroza drove away from the curb, the small Chevette bucking like a recalcitrant goat. She could feel the nervousness and tension mount in the man sitting next to her. She knew, almost intuitively, what he would say and at which point.

"You let go of the clutch too fast," David said.

Feroza looked straight through the windshield, her heart threatening to leap out of its cage, determined not to meet his eyes.

David glanced at her profile. It was impassive, imperious.

"N-never mind," he stammered quickly. "I-its all right." And then, "You could shift into second now."

Feroza changed gears. The car lunged forward. The engine roared in her ears. There was not a peep out of David. Feroza wondered at the roar and, with a start, blushing furiously, realized she should have shifted into third. She slowed to turn west on University Boulevard and, drawing assurance from the deserted stretch of road ahead, smoothly accelerated into top gear.

Feroza could feel David relax. As they cruised along the deserted road, Feroza all at once recalled what her grandmother had once said about the kindness and wisdom of Jamshed Metha.

Jamshed Metha's photograph, that of a slight, humble, and ascetic-looking man in a Parsee coat and *feta,* adorned Khutlibai's prayer table. In trying to convey the impact of the philanthropist's personality to Feroza, she had said, "One could not look at him."

"Why?" Feroza asked, surprised.

"Why?" Khutlibai appeared confounded by the question; as if what she had said was self-evident and needed no explaining. "You'd fall down!"

Noticing the astonishment wreathing her granddaughter's features, Khutlibai explained, "One could not face the power of his eyes." Then, groping to define the essence of a man who had attained a formidable divinity, she continued, "I was about twelve; we used to stand in front of him when he talked about our religion, and he would tell us, 'Look up. Raise your eyes,' but none of us dared raise our eyes above the third button on his coat. We knew we'd crumble."

David was like that, Feroza thought. Not to be gazed upon.

The mountains rose in smoky billows, tier upon tier, their spectacular crown of clouds kindled by the setting sun. This scenic grandeur contributed its own exquisite tumult to Feroza's already tumultuous heart. She wanted to head for the hills — drive like this into the heart of the mountains, lose herself in their profound solitude with David.

On an irresistible impulse, she turned her head slightly to glance at David and caught him looking at her dreamily out of the corners of his sapphire eyes. Their eyes ricocheted off each other, the impact of their colliding glances as difficult to sustain as a glimpse of Jamshed Metha's awesome divinity.

Feroza had a vision of driving David through a crowded street as people fell on either side of them like walking sticks, struck down by the dazzle of his eyes.

But the bright-eyed entity sitting by her had visions of its own. It cleared its throat and told Feroza to turn left at the next light. "I know there's a Friday's a little ways down the street," David said and then diffidently, "Feel like a drink?"

Feroza nodded, incapable of speech. Her heart leapt so wildly that it alarmed her and almost squeezed the breath out of her. Then she was swept by an intoxicating wave of happiness mixed with terror.

Feroza swung left into the street and headed for the bar as if towards the blue mountains of her daydream, confusedly wondering if her paralyzed tongue would regain its power of speech.

"We've passed it." David turned to look back and then, as Feroza swerved erratically to shift to the left lane, quickly said, "It's all right, take it easy. You can make a left anywhere. We'll get to it."

How could she have missed the blazing red neon signature of Friday's? Feroza turned into a small shopping arcade and, after crossing a couple of small streets, drove into the bar's parking lot. She found a small space between two cars and nosed the Chevette into it.

"That's the advantage of a small car," David said. "You can park it any place."

Feroza felt more comfortable once they went inside. The atmosphere of the bar was at once warm and familiar, filled with associations of the good times she and Jo had, way back at the bars in Twin Falls and of the spell she had spent working in one.

As the waitress led them to their seats, Feroza was grateful for the convivial buzz of people talking and the dim, reddish light reflecting off the tablecloths and the dark wood of the counters, tables, and floor.

They sat facing each other, holding their menus in front of them. David glanced at Feroza. Her eyes intent on the menu, her face was serene and glowing in the dim light. Their waitress stood, notepad and pen in hand, ready for their order.

"What would you like?" David asked.

David had placed his elbows on the table and leaned forward in anticipation of the musical murmur he expected to catch as it issued from the tawny girl's delectable throat. But, disturbed by his proximity, Feroza slid sideways and back in her seat, and David failed to hear what she said.

David unobtrusively removed his elbows from the table and cleared his throat. "I think I'll have the house beer," he said to the girl who was waiting patiently for their order and, making another attempt, asked Feroza, "How about you?"

This time both David and the waitress caught her answer when Feroza, as if asking a question, said, "A glass of wine?"

David launched a nervous monologue about his Chevette and sounded so desperate to impress Feroza with its virtues that she seriously wondered if something was the matter with the car. "She's been great. Gives me thirty-five miles to the gallon on a clear road, thirty in traffic. No rust on her; spent fifty bucks to have her chassis treated. Not much trouble, except for an oil leak that I fixed myself, and the exhaust that got knocked loose when I jumped a curb. I've really looked after her. She's a bargain at seven hundred, but what the heck, so long's she finds a good owner. You must think I'm crazy, talking like this, but, you know, I've gotten used to her. She's almost human, like a pet or something."

Their beer and wine arrived. David took a long draft from his mug, wiped his mouth with the cuff of his shirt, and continued his monologue.

Feroza took small sips of the wine from her glass, and David switched from talking about the car to explaining why he was selling it and buying a bicycle instead. The wine coursed through Feroza like a mellow happiness. She realized that David was not so eager to make a sale as he was to impress her. Feroza asked for another glass of wine, and David ordered another beer.

David told Feroza about the hard time his dad was having keeping him in school, despite the scholarships he had earned. He told her how much store his parents set by his education and how much they expected of him, though he didn't think he could ever repay them for their love or their unstinting and unmentioned sacrifice.

As David spoke, it gradually seemed to Feroza as if he were spreading a red carpet to invite her to walk into his life, strewing it with intimate minutiae as if with rose petals. Feroza knew these were his innermost secrets, fragrant with his commitment to his parents and his admirable feelings, and that he had never shared them with anyone before.

And while he talked, David's eyes, alight with elation, also spoke. They appeared to say that he couldn't believe his luck in having drawn this beautiful and exotic creature as if by some extravagant chance — like a winning lottery ticket — through his car. Feroza was awash in David's desire to show off, to impress her, and she gained in confidence with each passing moment. It did not blind her to look into his eyes anymore. The bridge created by his nervous words, his admiration, his need to bare his sensibilities, had carried her beyond their dazzle into the blue, oceanic depths in which she swam as easily as a fish. And the few times she averted her gaze it was more to conceal the flamboyance of her sensations than because of the knock-out potency of his glance.

Then David drew her out, asking questions, and Feroza found herself talking freely of her life in Lahore, of her parents and Khutlibai and Manek and her feelings for them. She was amazed at how comfortable she felt with this incandescent being. His sentiments, his aspiration, were so like hers, and those of her family. And yet it was as if she had taken a leap across some cultural barrier and found herself on the other side of it to discover that everything was comfortingly the same, and yet the grass was greener. She never thought she could have felt this complete trust in a stranger to take her across the unchartered terrain of her emotions.

She did not know when exactly her heart was won. Was it when David had said Pack-iss-tan in that wonderful, shy, deep voice of his, exactly the way that handsome officer had said it in Salem when they were searching for Manek in the maniacally blinking blue-and-white light of the police car? Would she have felt the same had the officer put himself out to win her? Were her feelings as giddy as Jo's? Was that all it was, then, a condition of her chemistry as a young woman responding to an extraordinarily good-looking man, or was it something special that only David had been able to establish? Were his feelings for her as strong as she felt they were?

There was music playing, a few couples dancing in a small dark square of floor-space. David looked at Feroza seriously and formally asked her, "Wanna dance?" He seemed to know instinctively how to talk to her, behave with her, and how she would respond. Feroza was grateful to Shashi for teaching her to dance.

On the dance floor, Feroza felt as if she could not sustain herself without David's support. She felt David's heartbeat against hers, sounding loudly in her ears, and she wanted that sturdy heart to beat and beat forever like that, close to her. Its throb and pulse were her natural element, just as the oceanic depths of his eyes were when she had found herself swimming in them like a fish.

When David held Feroza a little away from him to look down at her, Feroza slowly raised her eyes to meet his, and her face was bathed in a shy, yielding amber radiance that reflected his own tumultuous feelings.

❧

One evening in February, Shashi called Feroza and told her to come to his brother's apartment immediately. He was uncharacteristically abrupt. "I'll tell you everything when you get here," he said cryptically and hung up.

Feroza found Mala weeping hysterically. Her hair hung in long strands about her face, as if she or someone had savagely pulled it. Her silk sari was crumpled and disorderly, it's richly woven palu trailing the floor unheeded as she wailed, *"Hai Bhagvan,"* and swayed on the edge of the long sofa.

Deepak, the quintessence of despairing gloom, sat in a chair, head in hands.

"The baby?" Feroza asked in a whisper, not daring to articulate her fear, and Shashi quietly said, "The baby's all right . . . It's just that Deepak's given it away."

"What?" Feroza was incredulous.

"Yes," wailed Mala. "He gave her away because she's a girl! I bet he'd have gotten the money if she was a boy."

"That's not true," Deepak said, dispirited and woebegone.

Shashi took a confounded Feroza outside, and as they walked up and down the length of the building, he told her what had happened.

They were supposed to bring the baby home that afternoon. Deepak had seen the bill and turned the color of ashes. "Fifteen thousand dollars?" he croaked, his voice a hollow husk. "I've never seen fifteen thousand dollars in my whole life!"

"Please, can't you talk to the doctor?" Mala begged. "We're foreigners . . . We don't have so many dollars. If he wants rupees, we can give him fifteen thousand rupees."

"Let me see what I can do," the perplexed receptionist said, turning pale herself, and departed in search of the doctor.

She resumed her seat, her pretty young face beaming with smiles. "Dr. Walden has reduced his bill. You need to pay thirteen thousand."

"Thirteen thousand dollars?" Deepak gasped. "Where do I get thirteen thousand from? I don't even have five thousand."

Deepak began to bargain, starting with five hundred dollars. Mala was horrified by what was taking place. She desperately whispered, "But, Deepak, you could ask your papa to arrange — "

"Thirteen thousand dollars? Do you know how much money that is? You can deliver thirty premature babies for that kind of money in India!"

Each time the receptionist started a sentence with "I'm sorry—," she sounded less and less sorry. Eventually she said, "We're not in the bargain basement at Filene's. I'm sorry. I have other people waiting. If you don't pay the bill, you'll have our collection agency after you. You could end up in jail."

Deepak looked shocked and defeated. "All right," he said with indescribable gloom, "you can keep the baby."

"Then?" Feroza asked.

"Then he walked away."

"But you can't leave it at that, for God's sake!"

Shashi rolled up his eyes piously and spread his hands. "We've left it in Bhagvan's hands."

"Come on, you Bhagvan-walla," Feroza said, grabbing his arm and pulling him towards her car. "Gwen and Rhonda will know what to do."

David was waiting for Feroza at the apartment, talking to her roommates. He was beginning to relax in their company, and although he was still shy and reserved, he sometimes surprised the girls with a nutty streak of humor and his own particular brand of kidding. Both liked him.

As soon as Shashi and Feroza came in, Gwen and Rhonda knew something was wrong. David stood up with his coffee mug in his hand. He had on brown corduroy pants and a tan velour shirt. Feroza's eyes sought his and lit up with the radiance of their growing communion. He looked incredibly handsome to Feroza, like a golden, languishing god.

Shashi noticed the look that passed between them. He wondered that he had not heard about their relationship. He was hurt, but debonair enough to hide it.

Feroza and Shashi told them what had happened at the hospital.

"Deepak said what?" Rhonda exclaimed.

Feroza was solemn. "You can keep the baby."

"I don't believe it!" Rhonda squealed and exploded in a fit of laughter. Gwen doubled over, shaking, body consumed by mirth. David tried to look solemn, but a huge grin broke on his face, and he burst into guffaws.

Breathless and flushed, the girls wiped the tears from their eyes. After the initial shock, Feroza and Shashi saw the humor in the situation and uneasily joined in the hilarity.

"Oh God," Gwen finally managed to say, "that's the only thing to do if you don't carry insurance. You can't throw yourself on their mercy!" She was convulsed again by laughter. Shaking her head she managed to say, "Your brother's smart!"

"What should we do?" Shashi asked, a bit irritated by the frivolity. After all, he had witnessed his sister-in-law and brother's suffering.

"Heavens! What'll the hospital do with the baby?" Gwen flung her arms out. "They don't want it!"

"My uncle's a surgeon at Denver General," Rhonda said, sobering up all at once and empathizing with Shashi's anxiety and aggravation. "Maybe he can talk to Dr. Walden. Let me see if I can get hold of him."

Rhonda went into her bedroom to call her uncle. She phoned several places before she was able to locate him and get him on the line.

The next day Mala and Deepak went to the hospital and brought their little daughter home. Deepak's bill was for a thousand dollars. It pained him. It would have cost a fraction of that at home. He blinked and surreptitiously wiped his eyes. The receptionist and the doctor supposed he was brushing away tears of gratitude and joy, and they were deeply moved by the salutary effect of their benevolence.

*

Feroza learned the rudimentary mechanism of her car, washed and polished it herself, and whizzed about Denver with one hand on the wheel and an elbow stuck out the window, surveying the world through her windshield with the air of a winged creature flying.

Feroza visited Jo and Bill, who were living together but not married yet, at the air force base, and Mr. and Mrs. Miller in Boulder. She ran errands for Gwen and Rhonda and repaid the debts she owed her other friends by offering to pick them up when they needed to go someplace together.

Ever since Feroza had met David and bought his car, every atom of her being seemed weightless, and the very air she moved in was buoyant, and with every breath she inhaled happiness.

It was one thing to love. But to be loved back by a man who embodied every physical attribute of her wildest fantasies, with whom she could communicate even without speech, who understood the sensitive nuances of her emotions that were so like his own insecurities, was akin to a transcendental, fairy-tale experience.

Sometimes when Feroza lay on the sofa and David sat gazing into her eyes till the blue and yellow of their irises merged, and each glimpsed the mystery of the other, it seemed incredible to them that anyone else could feel as they did or be as lucky as they were to find each other.

And after this, it was natural for them to be physically close, to tenderly touch each other, to abandon themselves to the ardent intoxication of their youthful hormones. Feroza was as "swept off her feet" as she could wish, as David wished her to be. And the instinct that had guarded her before, now let her go as David released her from the baffling sexual limbo in which Shashi's cooler rhythm and the restraints of their common culture had set her adrift.

Yet each appreciated the reserve in the other; a certain sexual reticence. David, who might have wandered naked in his room before an American girl, didn't. Feroza dressed and undressed behind doors and beneath bed sheets. David never saw her, except for brief moments, naked, and then her voluptuous warm nakedness, her swelling breasts, were imprinted in his mind as the essence of desirability. Both were intrigued by the otherness of the other — the trepidation, the reticence imposed on them by their differing cultures.

On a Saturday afternoon, Feroza drove with David for a Sabbath meal with Adina and Abe Press. They lived in Boulder, barely a mile up the road from Jo's parents, in an unassuming house with a neat front yard overhung with pine trees.

They welcomed Feroza warmly but with a certain nervous reserve. Feroza could see how attached they were to David. He was obviously their pride, hope, and happiness. She could imagine to what extent their lives must center on him. They were both much older than Feroza had expected.

Abe was fair and lank and retiring, and Feroza thought David was a lot like him temperamentally. Abe worked at Con Edison and was only a few months away from retirement.

Except for his light eyes and hair, David bore more resemblance to his mother. They had the same strong features and compact bodies. Adina was bustling and energetic and, with her earnest talk, compensated for her husband's reserve.

Feroza and David drove back the next evening. Feroza's mind

dwelt on the Sabbath meal. David's father and David had worn a yarmulke: she had never seen David wear the cap before. The table had a damask cloth cover, flowers, fine china, and two brass candelabras with short white candles. Adina had covered her head with a lace scarf, lit the candles, lightly covered her face with the palms of her hand, and silently prayed. Her gestures and the ritual were very like those performed by her mother and grandmother when they prayed before the *atash*. Feroza sat up in her chair, lowered her head, and shut her eyes. She wished David had warned her to take a scarf along.

Then Abe held up the kiddush cup filled with wine and said a short prayer. He passed the cup around so that each of them could take a sip of the sweet wine, uncovered a loaf of golden, braided bread, broke it, and passed it around too. The bread was delectable. Breaking bread, sharing salt — these concepts curled in her thoughts with comforting familiarity — they belonged also to the Parsee, Christian, and Muslim traditions in Pakistan.

Afterwards, Adina had asked her a few polite questions about her religion. Feroza had sensed nervousness and reserve.

It was the first time that Feroza had been seriously confronted with the fact that David's religion was different from hers. So far, she had refused to think about it. She wondered what David's parents had thought of her and what they might have said to their son. How would her family react when they found out? Her mind dwelt on these questions, and she wanted to share her troubled thoughts with David. She also wanted to know more about the Sabbath ritual that she had found moving. But they were both too tired and relaxed and happy for serious talk. There was plenty of time. They would work through the problems later and deal with the issues as they came up. The disturbing thoughts evaporated, and they drove home listening to Beethoven's Ninth.

David was introducing Feroza to Western classical music. Feroza's experience with Western music had been limited to the Top 40 she had enjoyed with Jo. Bob Dylan was her favorite; Shashi had given her a thick book of Dylan's poems. Otherwise she had listened to the cassettes she brought with her, the cassettes of Nayara Nur singing Faiz's poems, of Tahira Saeed, Medhi Hassan, and Abida Parveen.

257

But every music paled in comparison to the way Beethoven's Fifth and Ninth Symphonies affected her at this moment of love. It seemed to her the orchestrated swell of the new harmonies, like her new love, were bestowed on her by the foreign country like a benediction, a grace. Feroza absorbed the music through her pores, and her nerves were vibrant with the beauty of a new energy — a joyous current that connected her to all the sensory images she had found the most beautiful since childhood, the stupendous mountains of the Karakoram, the lake at Saif-ul-Mulk mirroring the glaciers of the Hindu-Kush. Twilight trapped in the pine-perfumed forests of Nathyagali. The white domes of the Badshai Mosque floating above the Ravi at sunset. The unexpected silhouette of skyscrapers as she looked up from the zoo in Central Park. The explosive colors of the Colorado fall that almost made prayer redundant.

Chapter 24

Feroza spent the Christmas vacation of 1981 with Manek and Aban, newly pregnant with their first child, in their new three-bedroom house, whose grassy backyard was protected by a wooden fence. The house was on the outskirts of Houston, in Clear Lake, only a fifteen-minute drive from Manek's office at NASA. He had acquired a loan on the strength of his salary and was able to make a twenty-percent down payment.

Part of the down payment had come from his wife's money. He had said, "Look. If we get a divorce, you'll get half the house by American law. You might as well contribute to it so there will be no hard feelings later."

That night Aban couldn't sleep. After reflecting on Manek's remarks further, she wept and prayed for three days. With a scarf covering her head, she carried a small silver fire altar, fragrant with sandalwood and frankincense, to the four corners of every room in their house, including the bathrooms.

A marriage as far as she knew — as far as her ancestors had believed for five thousand years — was for keeps. Aban had heard ever since she could remember that a wife only left her husband's house feet first, in her coffin. The mention of divorce was not only insensitive, diabolical, and cruel, but also an affront to all that was auspicious and lucky. Such ill-omened words could not help but attract misfortune. Jinx their marriage. If this was what being in America meant, Aban wanted to have nothing to do with America. She would insist they go back to Karachi or Lahore.

Manek had apologized, said he'd only been joking. By the time Feroza arrived the matter had been smoothed over, and the ill omens exorcised by the daily clouds of smoke from the small fire altar. The smoke hung in the rooms like a holy presence and made Manek and Aban's eyes smart with its piety.

They picked up Feroza from the Intercontinental Airport in

Houston. The very first thing Manek did once they were on the highway to Clear Lake was to dig out a business card from his wallet and hand it to Feroza. "What d'you think of this?" he said, so grandly that Feroza knew it was not a question but a boast.

Feroza was at once on her guard. She did not want to start off the visit on the wrong foot. She looked at the card with an appropriately admiring smile and tried valiantly to maintain it as she realized, with a jolt, that he had changed his name from Manek Junglewalla to Mike Junglevala.

She couldn't help it. "Mike?" she asked, her appalled voice conjuring up Jo's unpleasant boyfriend. "You've become a Mike?"

Manek remained calm. "The people I have to deal with at work find it hard to remember Manek. It's too foreign, it makes them uneasy. But I'm one of the guys if I'm Mike."

"In America, be — " and Aban added her voice to Feroza's as they both chorused, "American!"

The tension was at once dispelled.

"I'm sorry," Feroza declared. "I know I can't call you Mike even if I try."

"That's all right," Manek said. "I don't expect you to; Aban only calls me Mike when we are with Americans."

"But it's taken me a while to get used to it," Aban said.

Manek impressed Feroza by his calm and reasonable manner and the air of consequence he had acquired; that of a homeowner, a breadwinner, and a man on his way up the American ladder of success in the pursuit of happiness.

Feroza did not attempt to puncture his profound airs or pensive speech — though she was sorely tempted to — for fear of deflating him before his admiring and smitten wife. Aban would have all the time in the world to be gradually disillusioned. Feroza need not have worried. Aban was sensible, bright, candid and cheerful. She had wisely shed many of her illusions about marriage and romance, some within a few days of their marriage in Karachi, and some in the United States. She had done so with good grace and without undue pain.

Once in a while she would reproach Manek, "Why did you tell

me, 'Your happiness is going to be my life's study,' when your life seems to be devoted to making me miserable?"

"That was before marriage," Manek answered, as if that was the most logical explanation in the world.

For her part, Aban permitted Manek his posturing so as not to disenchant his young, affectionate, and credulous niece. She even gazed at Manek with deferential and adoring eyes too shore up Feroza's regard for him.

Manek took Aban and Feroza to eat out frequently; after all, he was earning well. And, in a reckless exhibition of extravagance, he offered to take them to La Palms on Christmas Eve, saying, "The smallest lobster costs seventy-five dollars."

Aban and Feroza oohed and aahed with delight.

Aban was stacking the dishes in the dishwasher. She was about to step into the living room to fetch the coffee mugs when she over-heard Feroza say, "I hope you're not going to tell me to waste half my lobster and leave without paying."

Aban rushed in, waving the dish-rag she had in her hand, shouting in her glorious contralto, "Oh, my God! Did he do that to you, too?"

Manek's lofty airs and sober affectations vanished that instant and remained suspended for the rest of Feroza's stay.

Aban and Feroza were relieved to see Manek revert to his caustic clowning and retrieve his wicked, high-pitched soprano to mimic them and correct their misguided ways.

The three of them relaxed, horsed around, and enjoyed each other's company much more than they had at the beginning of Feroza's visit.

On the last day of Feroza's stay, Aban, who was an excellent cook like her mother, outdid herself. The prawn patia was delicious and spicy enough to make their noses drip, the fragrant saffron and lentil rice that went with it light and fluffy, each kernel of the long-grained Basmati exquisitely separate.

They ate with their fingers, licking them, smacking their lips in satisfaction. They chewed the food with silent concentration, reaching for the roasted Bombay-duck, mango pickles, and pepper pappadoms as if performing a sacred rite.

After dinner Manek, who was in charge of the dessert, opened a can of Alfanso mango pulp. Aban had bought it from an Indian store she had just discovered in Clear Lake. She marveled at the ubiquity of Indian stores.

Manek spooned the orange pulp on generous portions of vanilla ice cream, and they took their bowls to the living room to watch the news on TV and then "Star Trek."

"Want to see anything else?" Manek asked.

"Nah," Feroza said, "Let's talk."

Aban agreed.

Manek switched the TV off. "You two've been talking nonstop for ten days. My ears are aching. If you don't watch out, you'll develop fat muscles in your tongues, and they'll hang out."

Manek stuck out his tongue, panted, and turned his head from side to side looking perplexed.

The girls laughed at their pantomimed future.

Aban complained, "He always says I talk nonstop. Who else can I talk to? The walls? I'm alone all day. I didn't know I was going to be so bored and lonely in America."

"You'll make friends," Manek said, and they conversed about the Parsees they had met in Houston. There were almost four hundred Parsees, if you counted the suburbs, and the community organized functions almost every month. But it took them an hour and a half to get anywhere. Houston was such a sprawling city, and they lived too far out.

Feroza could feel the evening coming to a close. She had still not disclosed what she'd meant to. She finally gathered up her courage and, her pounding heart making her breathless, told them about David. "I really love the guy," Feroza said and stopped as abruptly.

Manek and Aban had been vaguely expecting tidings of this nature, considering how many times she had mentioned David — and twice had called Manek David. But to vaguely expect something and to be plainly told it are two quite different matters.

For a moment, except for their breathing, there was absolute quiet. Aban remembered that she had to prepare for the morning and sagaciously withdrew. This was a very personal subject, and she did not feel she had been in the family long enough to engage in a discussion on such a sensitive issue.

"He's very nice," Feroza remarked, on the defensive.

Manek still did not speak. He looked at his shoes. Then he said, "I suppose these things are bound to happen when one lives here for long. But I don't think the family will understand that." He paused, marshaling his thoughts, and Feroza remained quiet.

"I think you have to be sure first. Give it time . . . There's no big hurry. He's probably the first man in your life . . ." Manek stole a glance at Feroza. Her face was set in the haughty mold he knew so well. "It all seems wonderful now, but marriage is something else: our cultures are very different. Of course I'm not saying it can't work, but you have to give it time. We'll keep in touch on the phone, see how it goes?" Manek ended on a tentative note, at last looking directly at Feroza. It was a caring look, and Feroza felt a surge of relief and gratitude.

"I wish you'd brought up the subject earlier," Manek said. "I've had a long day, and I'm not thinking clearly. But I and Aban are going to be here. You can count on us."

℘

The girl who had occupied one of the bedrooms in David's house moved out. David thought it might be a good idea if Feroza moved to the vacant room. The house would give her much more space than the cramped basement apartment she shared with Gwen and Rhonda.

Feroza thought about it. David would continue to occupy the converted garage — it wouldn't be as if they were living together. She had met the two girls, Shirley and Laura, who shared the other bedroom, and liked them.

The enormity of the step she had taken occurred to Feroza only after she had moved in. Her living in the same house with David did affect the level of their intimacy. Their feelings for each other became much more intense and their relationship more complex. When sometimes, in an unconscious gesture that seemed to fascinate David, Feroza lifted her hair from the back, twirled it in a knot, and held it in place by inserting a pencil, David would look at her long, vulnerable, and elegant neck in a special way, as if torn between a desire to gaze at it or brush it with his lips. They appeared to each other equally vulnerable as, huskily saying, "Your skin is like velvet," David stopped her from going about whatever it was she was doing and buried his face in her neck.

To be able to see David whenever she wanted to, at odd times of the night and early in the morning, to cook together over the weekends, to discover each other's endearing peculiarities and the odd unexpected moments when each looked most seductive to the other, did amount to living together. Feroza was riven by bouts of guilt. Once when she was sneaking back into her room at three o'clock in the morning with her shoes in her hand, she wondered if she was the same girl who had lived in Lahore and gone to the Convent of the Sacred Heart.

Chapter 25

A brief but fierce deluge following the dust storm the night before had brought respite from the June heat — 116 degrees Fahrenheit in the shade the day before. Otherwise the consternation caused by the letter from America, with the added irritant of tempers and nerves frayed by unbridled temperatures, would have plunged not only Zareen and Cyrus but the entire family into despair and foreboding.

As it was, holding the letter in her inert fingers, the obscene photograph having already fluttered to the bedroom floor, Zareen found it hard to breathe. That Feroza should have chosen to send this photograph, of a man with his legs bared almost to his balls, was significant. Surely she must be aware of the assault on their parental sensibility. A subliminal cloud of nebulous conjectures and a terrible fear entered Zareen's mind. She grasped the basic premise — that Feroza was preparing Cyrus and herself for a change — but a change of this magnitude? She was confronting the "unknown," and she felt helpless in the face of it.

Once she had scanned the first few lines of the letter, her vision became so acute, so superbly lucid, that she felt able to absorb all the crowded lettering on the typed sheet without once needing to move her eyes. And then the sentences ballooned up disembodied, the words individually magnified, until they popped before her blurring sight. She felt a dizzying rush of blood to her head and was as close to fainting as she'd ever be.

After a while Zareen became conscious of the servants chattering in the kitchen, the cook laying the table for lunch, and as the initial shock wore off slightly, the news, with its tumult of ramifications, settled deeper into her sinking heart.

Feeling drained of strength and feeling each one of her forty years — she had crossed the distressing threshold the week before — Zareen hobbled over to the phone at her desk. With wildly wandering fingers she dialed part way through her mother's number and then, thinking of the effect the news would have on Khutlibai, instead dialed her husband's office. She heard three rings and then Cyrus's preoccupied, "Hello."

A wave of relief swept over Zareen at the thought of transmitting her anguish, and she began to cry.

"What's the matter?" Cyrus's panicked voice repeated the question, "What's the matter?"

"I got a letter from Feroza," she said haltingly, sniffing between her sobs.

"Feroza?" Cyrus shouted, "What's happened to Feroza?"

Zareen blew her nose, swallowed, and with a supreme effort of will, suspended her weeping to gasp, "She wants to marry a non."

Cyrus found his wife huddled on their bed beneath the slowly rotating blades of the ceiling fan, her attractive eyes swollen, her elegant nose red. He gave her a commiserating hug and, pressing her beautiful head against his incipient paunch, scanned the letter silently. His eyes automatically focused on the significant sentences, the casual note their daughter had adopted stabbing his heart and guts like so many daggers.

Feroza wrote that she had met a wonderful boy at the University. Like her, he was also very shy. She had agreed to marry him. She knew they would be very upset, particularly her grandmothers, at the thought of her marrying a non-Parsee. His parents were Jews. The religious differences did not matter so much in America. They had decided to resolve the issue by becoming Unitarians. "Please, don't be angry, and please try to make both my grannies understand. I love you all so much. I won't be able to bear it if you don't accept David."

Zareen suddenly reached down, causing Cyrus's reflexes to jump at the thought that his wife had fainted, and retrieved the photograph with the tips of her manicured nails as if the image was contaminated by disease. She showed it to Cyrus.

Zareen's anxious eyes had already detected a sinister cast in her potential son-in-law's blue eyes, a profile that struck her as actorishly handsome, phony, and insincere, and frivolous gold-streaked, longish hair. But what upset Cyrus most were the pair of over-developed and hairy thighs, which to his fearful eyes appeared to bulge as obscenely as a goat's as they burst from a pair of frayed and patched denim shorts.

"You'd better go at once," Cyrus said. "He can't even afford a decent pair of pants! The bounder's a fortune hunter. God knows what he's already been up to."

The last, an allusion to the imagined assault by those hairy thighs on the citadel of their daughter's virtue, was not lost on Zareen. The furrow between her brows deepened and she withdrew into complete silence.

Ten days later, silently mouthing prayers, Zareen was on the Pan Am flight bound for Denver, Colorado.

The young Pakistani student sitting next to Zareen, awed by her handsome profile, the gust of exotic perfume, and the glitter of diamonds on her fingers, made a few desultory attempts at conversation. Finding her distracted and monosyllabic, he leafed through the flight magazine and, fidgeting forlornly in his seat, resigned himself to sleep.

After she had completed the twenty-one *Yathas* and five *Ashem Vahoos* proscribed for such long and dangerous voyages, Zareen relaxed her grip on the crocodile-skin handbag on her lap. It contained two thousand dollars in traveler's checks and five hundred in cash. Just before they left for the airport Cyrus had given her a slim envelope with a bank draft for ten thousand dollars. He had facetiously labeled it "bribe money." She could at her discretion offer it, or part of it, to the handsome, hairy scoundrel to leave their daughter alone.

Alternately smiling, shaking her head, and making mulish faces, Zareen conversed astutely with her imagined adversary. Six hours after the Boeing had taken off from Karachi, her mind was still reeling from the murmur of last-minute advice and instruction imparted to her at the airport. She tried to remember all that Cyrus had said, all that Khutlibai — after she had fainted and been revived that day — had said, and everything that had happened at the clamorous rounds of daily family conferences once news of the letter had spread.

Behram and Jeroo had driven down from Rawalpindi, and Zareen felt enormously grateful at the way her relatives and close friends had rallied about, thankful for the stratagems the community had pondered and debated and for all their well-meant and useful advice.

For the subject was much larger than just Feroza's marriage to an American. Mixed marriages concerned the entire Parsee community and affected its very survival. God knew, they were few enough. Only a hundred and twenty thousand in the whole world. And considering the low birth rate and the rate at which the youngsters were marrying outside the community — and given their rigid non-conversion laws and the zealous guardians of those laws — Parsees were a gravely endangered species.

There had been acrimonious arguments between the elders and the youngsters, who had grown considerably in the four years Feroza had been away, at the first hastily summoned family conference in Zareen's sitting room.

While the air conditioner struggled to cool the horde — and grappled with the fluctuating voltage — the youngsters, candid in their innocence, wondered aloud why the news should strike their elders as such a calamity. They politely informed their parents that times had changed. They urged their uncles and aunts to enlarge their narrow minds and do the community a favor by pressing the stuffy old trustees in the Zoroastrian *Anjuman* in Karachi and Bombay to move with the times; times that were already sending them to study in the New World, to mingle with strangers in strange lands where mixed marriages were inevitable.

Jeroo and Behram's daughter Bunny, who was by now a pert fifteen-year-old with light brown eyes and a dark ponytail she tossed frequently, said, "For God's sake! You're carrying on as if Feroza's dead! She's only getting married, for God's sake!"

This outrage, coming after the insultingly patronizing tone adopted by the rest of the adolescents, was the last straw. The aunts, uncles, parents, and grandparents molded their mournful features into pursed mouths and stern stares, and Jeroo, sensing the mood and consensus of the assembly, quickly quelled her daughter's rebellion by yelling, "Don't you dare talk like that! One more peep out of you, and I'll slap your face!"

Across the room on a sofa, Bunny's round-shouldered and self-effacing brother Dara, now seventeen years old and in his last year at school, sat back between two uncles and disappeared from view. All the other smirking, smug, and defiant little adolescents who had concurred with the girl's sentiments and wiggled eagerly forward to sit on the edge of their seats, now opened their nervous eyes wide and looked at the forbidding presences uncertainly.

"Apologize at once," Jeroo said. "You have no consideration for poor Zareen auntie's feelings!"

The teenagers squeezed back in their seats and, safely tucked into the communal pack looking away from their cousin to the waxed parquet floor covered with Persian rugs, wisely withdrew their allegiance.

Bunny brushed her flushed cheeks with her fingers and without raising her bowed head, meekly said, "I'm sorry."

This promptly fetched her Freny auntie and Rohinton uncle to their feet. Rohinton stepped up to the girl with stately deliberation and stroked her bowed head, while Freny lowered her bulk to share the cushioned stool with Bunny. Putting a placating arm round the tearful girl, Freny held her close and said, "Now, that's my girl!"

After which, feeling called upon to reinforce community values, which were always in the process of being instilled, Freny dutifully said, "I'm sure your mother didn't mean to sound so harsh. It's just that we are so concerned for you. You know Parsee girls are not allowed into the fire temple once they marry out. You know what happened to Perin Powri."

Perin Powri was the latest casualty. Having defied her family to marry a Muslim, she had died of hepatitis four years later. Although she had contracted the disease through an infected blood transfusion during surgery, many Parsees perceived the hidden hand of Divine displeasure. Honoring her last wishes, Perin's family had flown her body to Karachi to be disposed of in the *dokhma,* or, as the British had dubbed it, the Tower of Silence.

Since the Parsees consider earth, water, and fire holy, they do not bury, drown, or burn polluted corpses. Instead, as a last act of charity, they leave the body exposed to the sun and the birds of prey, mainly vultures, in these open-roofed circular structures. In cities like Lahore, where there are too few Parsee to attract the vultures, the community buries its dead.

Perin Powri's body was denied accommodation in the Karachi *dokhma,* and the priests refused to perform the last rites. Without the *uthamna* ceremony, the soul can not ascend to the crucial Chinwad Bridge, which, depending on the person's deeds, either expands to ease the soul's passage to heaven, or contracts to plunge it into hell. Without the ceremony, the poor soul remains horribly trapped in limbo. Perin Powri's body was eventually buried in a Muslim graveyard, and the poor woman's appalling fate was dangled as an example of the evil consequence of such an alliance each time the occasion arose.

The refrain was then taken up by other aunts, who were as well trained as circus horses, and the names of other transgressors were recited, with each offense illuminating a new and tragic facet of the ill-considered unions. The litany followed an established order, and the names of the earliest miscreants were arrived at last.

"You know how Roda Kapakia wept when she was not allowed into the room with her grandmother's body," continued Freny in solemn tones, naming another misguided woman, who had married a Christian. "She was made to sit outside on a bench like a leper! Would you like that to happen to you when your grandmother dies?"

Thus alerted, Khutlibai jumped to her role with alacrity. Sitting across the room on a sofa, on which she had been swaying as if silently praying, she at once hid the lower half of her face in the edge of her sari and, looking at Bunny through foxy and brimming eyes, pleaded, "No, no, don't do that! If you don't attend my last rites, my child, my sorrowful soul will find no peace, and it will haunt this world till the Day of Judgment." And, being Feroza's grandmother as well, she pleaded, "One child is on the verge of forsaking us. Promise me you won't break this old heart also."

Khutlibai had contrived to make her vigorous person look so

crumpled and close to death while she spoke that all the relatives once more glared at the disgraced girl.

Bunny, suspecting her grandmother had adroitly removed her dentures, gaped askance at her collapsed mouth and hurriedly said, "Please don't worry, Granny, I'll never break your heart."

But a distantly related aunt from the Parsee Colony, respected for her forthright and abrasive manner and known as "Oxford aunt" (her husband had spent a year in Oxford learning to repair truck and tractor engines), was conscious that in all this talk to benefit the girls, the boys had been neglected. Inhaling mightily to fill out her chest she burst forth to say, "What do you expect our girls to do? Our boys go abroad to study and end up marrying white mudums. You can't expect our girls to remain virgins all their lives!"

The aunts and uncles at once shifted their severe countenances to stare at the five boys scattered about the room until they squirmed in their seats.

Acutely conscious of her gangling thirteen-year-old grandson's discomfort, the discerning Soonamai stroked the boy's bony thigh and, in her quiet way, said, "You won't marry a *parjat* will you? You must marry a nice little Parsee girl of your own choice. And don't let anyone tell you otherwise. Marry the girl *you* like."

His buck teeth fanning out like white daisy petals, the excruciatingly slender adolescent gulped and tried to look as innocent, obedient, and accommodating as he could, while Soonamai continued to stroke his thigh with her soft, wrinkled hands.

The remaining boys scattered about the crowded room were coerced by similarly affecting dialogues to adopt corresponding attitudes. They dared not do otherwise under the scrutiny of their uncles, whose knowing eyes bored piercingly into theirs, as they displayed by their upright deportment and righteous countenances the resolute mettle that would keep them from marrying white mudums and from other equally alluring and infernal temptations.

These performances for the edification of the youngsters were staged with such regularity that the behavior of both the young and the old was almost automatic, entailing no untoward effort.

Their parts played out satisfactorily, the children were summarily dismissed, together with the white-liveried and crisply turbaned new servant, who was passing the drinks and hors-d'oeuvres. Now the formidable think tank of uncles, aunts, parents, and friends, talking vociferously, settled down to the solemn business of thrashing out a strategy.

All options were considered, angles analyzed, opinions aired. "If this David fellow says this, you say that! If Feroza says that, you say this!"

Zareen was alternately instructed, "Be firm. Exercise your authority as her mother!" and "If you can't knock him out with sugar, slug him with honey."

They further confused her by directing, "Don't melt if she cries. If Feroza throws a tantrum, throw one twice as fierce!" and "But be careful; if you're too harsh, she'll rebel. Once she becomes *naffat,* she won't care if you or I approve or disapprove."

The Pakistani student in the seat next to Zareen's covertly eyed her from time to time. Intimidated by the range and ferocity of her grimaces, he quietly ate his dinner and, once again contorting his body to accommodate it to his narrow seat, fell fitfully asleep. Clutching her handbag beneath her sari, Zareen dozed on and off.

Chapter 26

Zareen awoke near the end of her long journey to the sound of the wheels being lowered with a grinding noise and a shudder. A few minutes later, the plane tipped its wings to circle the Mile High city. Peering at it through her window, Zareen saw the mountainous, almost uninhabited spread of the new country, so different from the crowded vistas of her flights over Lahore and Rawalpindi with the untidy rectangles of flat roof-tops and flat fields. Even from the sky, she could see that this was an extraordinarily clean part of the planet, as if new and little used, and the mountains appeared to have been arranged by landscape artists.

The Boeing lost height rapidly, and all at once they were flying over clusters of toylike skyscrapers, just as she had seen them in photographs; banked up against the mountains, the city looked flattened and dwarfed. Then they were sweeping over a rush of clearly demarcated roads winding round sloping doll's houses and tiny blocks of emerald lawn.

Thus it was that after again praying eleven *Yathas* and five *Ashem Vahoos*, jet-lagged and duty-bound Zareen landed at the Denver airport.

Half an hour later she emerged, groggily steering her luggage, and spotted Feroza right away. Conspicuous in the thick fence of pink faces behind a railing, Feroza's dusky face glowed with affection and delight at the sight of her mother.

A little knot of love and happiness formed round Zareen's heart. She paused deliberately, looked away, and then looked sharply at Feroza to catch that fleeting instant when a loved face, seen after a long interval, reveals itself as to a stranger before settling into the familiar groove of habitual association.

Feroza wore a light brown tank top and, as Zareen had expected, no makeup. Her plump, well-formed shoulders and arms were chocolate dark with suntan, and her body radiated a buxom brown female vitality. But her most striking feature, even at that distance, were her eyes, a luminous yellow-brown, lighter than her skin or the hair falling about her shoulders, lighting up her face. Zareen held her breath. Her daughter was beautiful.

And then Feroza was hugging her and taking her traveling bag from her hands and brushing the tears from her eyes.

A nondescript young man in long pants and a long-sleeved shirt, crowned by an unsparingly short and conservative haircut and wearing steel-rimmed glasses, smiled awkwardly and picked up Zareen's suitcases.

Feroza said, "Mum, this is David, David Press."

The little knot of happiness and love in her heart was nudged aside to make room for a harder substance as Zareen assessed her adversary. The photograph had been misleading. David bore little resemblance to the confident, actorishly handsome image. His shy blue eyes blinked with anxiety to be liked behind the unadorned squares of glass.

"How are you, David?" Zareen said, outwardly calm, coolly holding out her hand with the three diamond rings.

David, divesting himself of the two heavy suitcases and hastily wiping his hands on his pants, took her hand gingerly in his and shook it formally. "Welcome to America," he said and then mumbled something neither Zareen nor Feroza could decipher.

As they followed David to the little Chevette in the parking lot, Feroza whispered, "He's had his hair cut. He's all dressed up in long pants for your sake." She gave her mother a nervous hug.

Zareen decided to postpone any thinking on the matter for the moment and face the situation after she'd had a cup of tea. She glanced at the straight-backed, square-shouldered, muscular young man walking with a self-conscious spring to his step ahead of them and, turning to Feroza, said only, "You've become very dark; your grandmother won't like it. You'd better bleach your face or something before you come home."

To go downtown, Feroza turned south on Monaco and then west on Seventeenth Street, with its large stone and frame houses. She wanted to impress her mother with the more alluring aspects of the city before taking her to her modest home on East Edison.

As they drove past the sprinklers raining on manicured lawns, Zareen talked about family members, relating amusing anecdotes, and addressed herself exclusively to Feroza.

David sat quietly in the back with whatever bits of luggage could not be crammed into the car's small trunk.

Abruptly they were among the tall buildings downtown, and Zareen stopped talking to gape at the looming skyscrapers that had looked so toylike from the airplane.

David suddenly came to life in the pause. "All this is recent construction," he said and, as Feroza drove around a large circle, doggedly pointed out landmarks. "That's City Hall. That domed building — that's the State Capital. That's the Denver Art Museum. It's ugly," David ventured apologetically, and Zareen, who was impressed with the ten-floor-high fortress with pencil-thin slits for windows that looked like gun-turrets and reminded her of the picturesque forts around Peshawar, wondered at his aberrant taste. "I like it." Zareen was curt.

"That's the Denver Center for the Performing Arts," David continued compulsively, and Feroza noticed his voice was a bit shaky. "Where the Denver Symphony plays . . . They have small theaters where plays are performed, dance and ballet."

"Umm," Zareen said. Even the "Umm" sounded terse.

"Can you see the tall building there with all the glass?" David leaned forward and pointed a taut finger at the windshield. "That's the Seventeenth Street shopping mall; the area with the lampposts has been blocked off for shoppers and people who just want to stand around and look."

And then David abruptly discontinued the tourist-guide bit and quietly said, "Look at the sunset."

It was dusk. They had moved a little away from the tall buildings beginning to twinkle with lights, and they saw the mountains and clouds caught in a still and glorious explosion of scarlet, pink, and steel gray. Once again Zareen felt that the city, enormous as it was from close quarters, was dwarfed by the powerful mountains ranged behind it.

But once they were past the awesome sunset and masonry

downtown and Feroza headed south on University Avenue toward the campus, Zareen continued directing her remarks at Feroza and subconsciously registered the unexpected row of mellowed stone houses, the Cherry Creek Shopping Mall, the astonishing cleanliness everywhere.

Soon they arrived in a street lined with bookstores, restaurants, and stores selling athletic supplies, hiking, and mountaineering equipment. David pointed out a stately building of rust-colored stone with small, recessed windows, flanked by two other equally stately buildings of gray stone and said, "That's the University of Denver."

They entered a residential area crisscrossed by a checkerboard of streets, and Feroza turned into a shallow drive, announcing, "Here's where we live."

Zareen realized that "we" included David. She cast a startled glance at her daughter, and Feroza quickly added, "Four of us share, Mum. David lives in the converted garage. Two girls, Laura and Shirley, share a room. They didn't want to be in the way when you came. You'll see them tomorrow."

Zareen regarded the house with raised eyebrows. Coming as she did from a part of the world where houses have thirteen-inch-thick brick walls and reinforced concrete roofs, her daughter's dwelling looked like an oblong shack of wood and cardboard set up to be blown away by the huffing and puffing nursery-rhyme wolf.

But once she stepped inside Zareen was pleasantly surprised by the thickly carpeted interior, the evenly hung drapes, the comfortable furniture, and she fell in love with the large green fridge and matching dishwasher in the spacious kitchen. She touched the shining surface of things with delight, appreciating the materials that could be kept so easily clean without the help of servants. She was quite civil to David, but with an inflection that left him a bit breathless and fumbling, as both he and Feroza showed off the house.

Feroza made a pot of tea, and after a decent interval, David left them to talk. Almost at once Feroza asked, "Mum, what d'you think of him?" She was a little crestfallen when her mother said, "It's too early to tell. We'll talk about it tomorrow."

The next day, refreshed by her sleep, Zareen launched what she believed was a mild and tactful offensive. She lauded the virtues and earning capacities of three marriageable Parsee boys in Lahore. Each of their mothers had expressed an ardent desire to make Feroza her daughter-in-law. Two other worthy mothers of handsome and wealthy boys in Karachi had expressed similar aspirations.

Feroza kissed her mother fondly and teased, "I think I'm too young to settle down with mothers-in-law. Besides," she said, indicating with a shift in her tone that she was serious, "David's mother, Adina, is really quite sweet. I've met her, and we often talk on the phone. She and Abe, David's father, live in Boulder, near Denver. They are not rich, but they are respectable people. His father is a bookkeeper at Con Edison, the electricity company."

This gave Zareen the opening she was looking for. "You're too precious. We're not going to throw you away on the first riffraff that comes your way."

Feroza's shining eyes lost a part of their luster.

"You know what we do when a proposal is received," Zareen continued, ignoring the change in her daughter's regard, warned though that she must be more guarded in her choice of words. "We investigate the boy's family thoroughly. What is his background? His standard of living? His family connections?"

A well-connected family conferred advantages that smoothed a couple's path through life, and not only their own life, but the lives of their children! What did she know of David's background except that his father worked in some Con company? Of David's family connections? His antecedents?

"What do you mean, 'antecedents'?"

"His ancestry, his *khandan*."

"Oh, you mean his pedigree?"

"If that's how you like to put it."

"Don't be absurd, Mum," Feroza said. "If you go about talking of people's pedigrees, the Americans will laugh at you."

Cut to the quick, Zareen plucked a tissue from the box on the kitchen table. "It's no laughing matter. You'll be thrown out of the community! Do you know what happens to girls who marry out?

They become ten times more religious!" And then, like a magician conjuring up the inevitable rabbit, she ominously intoned, "Take Perin Powri. Like most of you girls, she never wore her *sudra* or *kusti*. After her marriage to a non, she wore her sari Parsee-style, and her *sudra* covered her hips! Her *kusti* ends dangled at the back! Till the day of her death, she missed her connection with community. She would have given anything to be allowed into the *agyari*."

"We're having a civil marriage in any case; a judge will marry us," Feroza said. "That way I can keep my religion, if it matters so much to you. Of course you know David and I are Unitarians."

"Unitarians!" Zareen wrinkled her nose disparagingly. "You sound almost as if you've converted! My dear, your judge's marriage will make no difference to the priests. They won't allow you into any of our places of worship, *agyari* or *Atash Behram*."

Zareen moved her coffee mug to one side and placed her arms on the table, "Do you know how hurt and worried we all were when we got your letter? I couldn't sleep. And your father, I never thought to see him so shaken and grieved! Your poor grandmother actually fainted! She told me to beg you on my knees not to marry this boy. You know she adores you. You won't be permitted to attend her funeral rites — or mine or your father's!" She picked out the last tissue and wiped her eyes. "Do you know how selfish you are, thinking only of yourself?"

Zareen blew her nose and addressed herself to what caused her — next to the thought of her daughter's outcast status — the most anguish. "It is not just a matter of your marrying a non-Parsee boy. The entire family is involved — all our relationships matter."

Zareen tried to describe how much pleasure the interaction with a new bunch of Parsee in-laws would bring the family. More wedding feasts, more cozy friendships, more bonding within the community, more prestige. "You are robbing us of a dimension of joy we have a right to expect. What will you bring to the family if you marry this David? His family won't get involved with ours. But that doesn't matter so much . . . What matters is your life — it will be so dry. Just husband, wife, and maybe a child rattling like loose stones in this huge America!"

Feroza despaired of bridging the distance that suddenly yawned between them. "You'll have to look at things in a different way . . . It's a different culture," she ventured desperately.

"And you'll have to look at it our way. It's not your culture! You can't just toss your heritage away like that. It's in your bones!" Zareen thumped the table with conviction and tried to look as if she'd settled the argument.

Feroza stared at her mother. Her face had become set in a way that recalled to Zareen the determination and hauteur with which her daughter had once slammed doors and shut herself up in her room.

"You've always been so stubborn!" Zareen said angrily. "You've made up your mind to put us through this thing. You'll disgrace the family!"

"I'm only getting married. If the family wants to feel disgraced, let them!"

Zareen checked herself. She recalled the sage advice of the assembly; she must not push her daughter to rebellion.

"Darling," she said, "I can't bear to see you unhappy." She buried her face in her arms and began to sob.

Feroza brushed her lips against her mother's short, sleek hair, and putting her arms round her cried, "I don't know what to do. Please don't cry like this. It's just that I love him."

Zareen reared up as if an exposed nerve had been touched in her tooth. "Love? Love comes after marriage. And only if you marry the right man. Don't think you can be happy by making us all unhappy."

"I think I've had about all I can take!" Feroza said, pushing her chair back noisily.

Zareen suddenly felt so wretchedly alone in this faraway country. "I should have listened. I should never have let you go so far away. Look what it's done to you — you've become an American brat!"

David, who had entered the kitchen at this point to get some cookies, decided he could do without them, and silently withdrew to be forgotten in his book-lined garage.

"I don't know how I'll face the family," Zareen cried. "I don't know what my friends will think!"

"I don't care a fuck what they think!"

Zareen stared at her daughter open-mouthed, visibly shaken by the crude violence of her language. "I never thought that I'd live to hear you speak like this, Feroza!" She stood up and walked from the kitchen with the stately bearing of a much taller woman.

After a while, Feroza followed her into the room they shared and hugged her mother. The corner of the pillow was soaked with Zareen's tears.

"I'm sorry, Mum. I didn't mean that," Feroza said, herself weeping. "I don't know what came over me."

Chastened by the storm of emotion they had generated and the unexpected violence of the words exchanged, each called a frightened, silent truce. Neither brought up the subject for the rest of the evening. David had wisely elected to stay out of their way and had left the house altogether. Feroza, though made wretched by his absence, appreciated it. It was best that she be alone with her mother.

They talked late into the night of family matters, of Feroza's progress in her studies, her expenses (that Zareen termed astronomical), of the scholarship she was angling for; and, carefully circling the subject of marriage, each ventured, gingerly, to mention David. Feroza casually threw in a remark about David when the opportunity presented itself, and Zareen just as casually tossed in a question or two to show she bore him no ill will and was prepared to be objective.

"David has wonderful road sense. I don't know how I'd manage to find my way without him," Feroza said at one point. "In fact, he'd love to show you around. He can explain things better than any guide."

"That would be nice," Zareen said carefully, and on a note so tentative that Feroza expected her to continue. She looked at her mother with a touch of surprise, and quickly Zareen said, "But will he be able to find the time?"

"Of course he will. He's planned to keep the weekend free for you."

Feroza had already explained how hard David worked. Besides devoting every moment he could spare to his studies, he held two jobs — one as a research assistant to a professor of computer science and another with a construction firm — to pay for the expenses not covered by a scholarship. Feroza cast down her eyes, "His father can pay his tuition, but he won't." She knew she was stretching a point; Jewish parents set a premium on education, and David's father would have paid the fees if he could. "He feels David must earn his way through the university. Actually that's why David sold the car to me. He travels by bicycle."

"Quite right." Zareen approved the parental decision and David's attitude. "It will teach him to stand on his own two feet."

It was an attitude Parsee fathers would encourage. If Zareen were to believe all the allusions slipped in by Feroza, David had the brains of a genius, the temperament of a saint, and the most brilliant prospects in computers of anyone in Denver.

"He seems like a nice boy," Zareen said graciously, and Feroza, delighted by this quantum leap in his favor, hummed as she brushed her teeth. She heard Laura and Shirley move unobtrusively in their room. She saw the light that had come on in David's garage go out. Hugging her mother good night, saying, "And DO let the bugs bite!" Feroza laughed so raucously at her own stale joke that it infected the small frame house with her joy, and Shirley and Laura, talking softly in their room, suddenly found themselves giggling at the least little thing.

David, who was inclined to bouts of gloom and self-doubt, felt the thunderous cloud that had descended on him after his encounter with Zareen — convinced he had made the worst impression possible — lift somewhat. He smiled in the dark and longed to be with Feroza. He hoped she would slip into his room later.

But hugging her soft American pillow that never rumpled in the narrow camp cot next to her mother's bed, Feroza blew him a silent kiss and fell peacefully asleep.

Zareen, who had to cope with a twelve-hour time difference, was wide awake at two o'clock in the morning. It came as a bit of a shock to her to think that it was already Saturday afternoon in Lahore. Cyrus would be taking his after-lunch nap, undisturbed by the mosque's rowdy stereo system.

Zareen was always amazed, and mildly resentful, at how peacefully her husband slept through the blasts while she shot up in bed, her heart thumping. Sometimes, when one of the family was sick, she sent messages requesting the *mullah* to tone down the volume. Being a frequenter of the mosque, the bearded cook wielded influence with his pals, and Zareen enjoyed the illusion that she exercised some control over her environment.

Zareen found the quiet in her strange surroundings in Denver eerie, the opaque, dawnlike glow of the night sky reflecting the tireless city lights disorienting.

In Lahore at this hour, the pitch dark night would be alive with a cacophony of insect and mammal noises, with the thump of the watchman's *lathi* stick or the shrill note of his whistle. The population explosion in Pakistan having extended itself also to the bird community, some bird, disturbed by a sudden light or by an animal prowling in the trees, was bound to be twittering, some insomniac rooster crowing. Zareen had never imagined she'd actually miss the mosque stereos or the insufferable racket of the rickshaws.

Covering her eyes and her ears in an old silk sari she kept for the purpose, Zareen summoned the imagined presences of her caring kinsfolk and filled the emptiness of her second night in America with their resolute and reassuring chatter. Their voices, trapped in the sari, rustled in her ears, buzzed in her brain, "Our prayers are with you. Be brave. Be firm. We must not lose our child."

Fortified by the strength of their convictions and of their characters, visible in the images floating before her, she evaluated the perilous situation; fraught with difficulties neither they nor she could have possibly foreseen.

For one, Feroza had changed. Not overtly, but inside. For another, David was not as poor as his tattered pants had led them to believe. Besides, he would not be so easy to discredit. Feroza was convinced he was a paragon of all the virtues the community could ever have wished for in its sons — and the little Zareen had seen of the meek-looking fellow appeared calculated to confirm the impression.

She, of course, was not taken in by his docile exterior. She knew he had wicked little ways hidden some place, ready to kick up trouble!

As the remarks and the advice of the familial think tank echoed in her head and the words reconstituted themselves into new patterns that conveyed fresh instruction and new insights into the changed situation, Zareen was gradually soothed. She felt once again able to cope with the unforeseen circumstances. And, if it came to a pinch, living up to the trust reposed in her, she was confident she would improvise.

By the time she drifted off to sleep at about five in the morning, Zareen had glimpsed the rudiments of an idea that had the potential to succeed.

Chapter 27

Feroza awoke her mother with a cup of tea. "It's ten o'clock, Mum. We've planned a lovely Saturday for you. David's ready."

Zareen was at once wide-awake. Refreshed by her sleep, and subconsciously aware of having spent the night in fruitful endeavor, she was in a happier and more adventurous frame of mind. After all, she was in America! The New World beckoned irresistibly.

They breakfasted on omelettes and muffins at Pour La France, a yuppy hangout filled with the aroma of fresh gourmet coffee and the less aromatic presences of bearded professors and students in jogging shorts. David insisted on paying, and Feroza glowed. They lunched at Benihana, where the Japanese chef performed a fierce ballet with his sharp knives and the grilled mushrooms he tossed to their plates. The bill was impressive, and Zareen settled the question of payment once and for all by declaring, "When I'm with you, I'll pay. When you two start earning properly, you can pay."

At night, Zareen sank her teeth into prime rib of beef at the classy Brown Palace Hotel downtown and rolled up her eyes at its succulence. She tasted the Rocky Mountain trout from Feroza's plate. Never had she tasted the natural flavors of meat and vegetables quite this way, always eating them drowned in delectable concoctions of spices at home.

On Sunday, a day as bright and balmy as all the days she was to spend in Denver, they drove along a winding mountain road through pine-wood country made spectacular by rust-colored canyons and boulders, to Georgetown. It was a mining town that had flourished during the gold rush but was now mainly a tourist attraction. Preserved as on the day it was abandoned — and Zareen was sure it had been abandoned suddenly — the pictorial little downtown, with its hotels and saloons hung with Victorian light fixtures, rough wood furniture, and marble bars, excited her imagination.

Guiding her tour with enthusiasm, blossoming beneath the

warmly admiring gaze of his beloved and the interest shown by the sophisticated woman in a sari, David gave Zareen her first taste for the history of the land. So tied up and tangled the day before, his tongue became fluent, and he brought the Wild West vividly to life. His fumbling movements, too, were replaced by a surety that was natural to his compact body. And David, who had despaired in his dark bout of gloom of ever impressing Zareen, was as surprised as she was.

When Feroza, agile in jeans, asked Zareen to climb the steep struts after her into an old steam engine, David tactfully suggested, "You'd better not in that beautiful sari."

"At least you have more sense than my daughter," Zareen said tartly, and intercepted a look between them — of David's delight at winning her favor and Feroza's bemused surprise — that Zareen was not meant to see. Gloating at having scored over Feroza, David had thumbed his nose, and though Feroza tried to look hurt by the sudden switch in her mother's allegiance, it was plain to see she was pleased.

Each day the next week, Feroza dropped her mother off at one or another of the gleaming shopping malls. To Zareen's dazzled senses, they were pieces of paradise descended straight from the sky, crammed with all that was most desirable in the world.

Shooting off on a tangent, she darted between the garment racks and cosmetics counters, the jewelry, linen, toy, shoe, and furniture displays like a giddy meteorite driven mad by the gravitational allure of contending cosmic bodies. Caught in the whirlwind of her frenzy, she blew tirelessly in and out of the stores, attracted as much by the silver plastic slippers as she was by the grand pianos.

Feroza picked her up late in the evening from some designated spot, usually an ice-cream parlor, and eyes glazed by the glory of the goods she had seen and the foods she had tasted, Zareen climbed into the small car, laden with large shopping bags.

The results of her first shopping spree were manifest that very evening. The tops of everything, counters, tables, window-sills, sprouted tissue boxes as if she had planted a pastel garden of fragrant Kleenex. She went from box to box, plucking tissues with a prodigality that satisfied a deep sensual craving and chucked them away with an abandon she never thought to indulge. She was seldom without a small ball of tissue crumpled in her fist or fluttering in her fingers. Some days later, impressed by the magic of scouring potions like Windex and Endust, she sprayed them on the tissues and spent an ecstatic evening cleaning the house.

Feroza's dressing table and bathroom shelves blossomed in a dizzying array of perfume bottles and cosmetics, and the level of the floor of Feroza's two long closets rose by at least two feet in a glossy flood of plastic packages containing linen, china, lamp shades, and gadgets. The hanging spaces were jammed with Zareen's new blouses, pants, and jackets.

Feroza discreetly moved her clothes to David's closet.

Enchanted, Zareen made her daily debut modeling her new clothes in the kitchen and was as delighted as a teenager by the approving glances and flattering comments of whoever happened to be breakfasting. She spent hours chatting with Laura and Shirley. They ferried her around when Feroza or David were busy, and she treated them to ice-cream cones and the tortilla chips, candy, and chocolate fudge colas she brought home. She bought small gifts for everyone.

Zareen was as happy as a captive seal suddenly released into the ocean. Despite her daily shopping forays and weekend excursions, she felt she had glimpsed only the tips of icebergs. Her heart pulsed to the seductive beat of the New World, and her ears, throbbing to the beat, stopped hearing the counsel of her distant Lahori relatives. The plotted course was forgotten; David's presence, unfailingly courteous and anxious to please, touchingly dependent on her opinion and responsive to her slightest need, was accepted, and necessary to this enchantment.

David and Feroza, exhilarated by their success, relaxed some of their self-imposed restraints. David held Feroza's hand, and glancing at her mother, Feroza permitted it to be held. She rested her head on David's shoulder when the ride was long, and occasionally hugged him in a sisterly fashion in front of Zareen.

Light-headed with delight, David let his hair, and even the

stubble on his chin, grow. His confidence, too, blossomed, and with it, his wry sense of humor that had so touched Zareen in the abandoned mining town when he had gleefully thumbed his nose at Feroza. At such moments, Zareen wished David was a Parsee — or that the Zoroastrians would permit selective conversion to their faith.

Zareen found herself seriously questioning the ban on interfaith marriages for the first time. She had often opined how unfair it was that while a Parsee man who married a "non" could keep his faith and bring up his children as Zoroastrians, a Parsee woman couldn't. And it didn't make sense that the "non" non was not permitted to become Zoroastrian; one could hardly expect their children to practice a faith denied to their mother.

But she argued this from a purely feminist and academic point of view. She had accepted the conventional wisdom and gone along with the opinion of the community because she had grown up with these precepts. She had never doubted that she would marry a Parsee.

Till now these issues had not affected her. But with Feroza's happiness at stake and her strengthening affection for David, Zareen wondered about it. How could a religion whose Prophet urged his followers to spread the Truth of his message in the holy *Gathas* — the songs of Zarathustra — prohibit conversion and throw her daughter out of the faith?

Zareen knew there was a controversy raging round these issues in Bombay, as well as in Britain, Canada, and America, where the Parsees had migrated in droves in the past few years.

Bombay had sixty thousand Parsees — fifty percent of the total world population of her community. Zareen had all along believed that the Parsee *Panchayat* in Bombay was the natural center of authority on community matters. She knew it also had an inclination to be conservative.

Tucked away in Lahore, Zareen had not felt directly involved. She was vaguely confident that the controversy would be resolved in an enlightened manner (after all, her community was educated and progressive) and that she could live with its decisions whichever way they went.

She was not so sure anymore and felt herself suddenly aligned with the thinking of the liberals and reformists. It eased her heart to think that a debate on these issues was taking place.

Perhaps the teenagers in Lahore were right. The Zoroastrian *Anjuman* in Karachi and Bombay should move with the times that were sending them to the New World. Bunny's image materialized before her with startling lucidity as her niece tossed her ponytail and said, "For God's sake! You're carrying on as if Feroza's dead! She's only getting married."

Of course. And to a nice boy. Zareen was sanguine. The various *Anjumans* would have to introduce minor reforms if they wished their tiny community to survive.

Although Shirley and Laura occasionally roamed the house in shorts, David, warned by Feroza, kept his hairy legs modestly concealed. There were other strictures they prudently continued to observe, and David, nosing his way timidly on the surface of another culture, was entirely guided by Feroza. Neither smoked before Zareen, and both were careful not to give the slightest hint of their more advanced physical intimacies.

During the second week of Zareen's stay, they hesitantly introduced her to some of their friends from the Unitarian Church Society, cautiously explaining parts of the Unitarian doctrine to Zareen. In her liberal frame of mind, Zareen found their outlook reasonable, and Feroza and David's friends as charming as they found her.

And then, in the third week of her visit, a spate of anxious letters from Pakistan arrived, recalling Zareen to her mission.

By themselves the letters from her family would not have upset Zareen so much. But Freny had enclosed copies of two pamphlets titled "WARNING" and "NOTICE." One was from the Athornan Mandal, which was the Parsee priest's association in Bombay headed by Dastur Feroze Kotwal, and the other was from the Bombay Zoroastrian Jashan Committee.

Zareen scanned them, her fingers suddenly trembling. A terrible fear for her daughter gripped her heart. Her first inclination was to tear up the sheets. Then she folded them into a tight wad and buried them in the bottom drawer of her dresser.

Zareen's sleep became restless. Her dreams were crowded with the presence of outraged kin pointing long, rebuking fingers. As if prodded by an ominous finger, she bolted upright in bed one night, her pulse pounding. She looked at the watch on the side table; it was three o'clock. She felt something was terribly amiss and, with a shock, realized that Feroza was not in her cot. For the first time, Zareen suspected that her daughter probably slept with David. Tying her scarf round her head, she began to pray.

Zareen knew what she must do. However admirable and appealing David was, however natural to the stimulating and carefree environment, he would deprive her daughter of her faith, her heritage, her family, and her community. She would be branded an adulteress and her children pronounced illegitimate. She would be accused of committing the most heinous sacrileges. Cut off from her culture and her surroundings like a fish in shallow waters, her child would eventually shrivel up. And her dread for Feroza altered her opinion of David.

The next day Feroza and David at once sensed the change in Zareen's mood. They were surprised how fragile their happiness was, how vulnerable they were. Linking Zareen's shift in temper to the bundle of letters that had arrived from Pakistan, Feroza wished the mail had been lost.

Zareen's face grew more and more solemn as the morning advanced, and the little frown-line between her eyes settled into a deeper groove. Feroza, after a few attempts to rally her mother had failed, became equally solemn. David's misgivings launched their customary attacks. He skulked about the garage and the backyard, trying to keep out of everybody's way. There were muffled sounds of an altercation from Laura and Shirley's room. Zareen's ill humor and fear had contaminated the house. Zareen packed Feroza off to the grocery store with a list of things to buy and, once she was safely out of the way, phoned Aban.

Aban and Manek called Zareen on the weekends, when the rates were low. Their conversations had been pleasant, restricted to questions about what Zareen had been seeing and doing, how Aban, eight months pregnant, was faring, and to news of the family in Pakistan.

Earlier Zareen had told Manek the purpose of her precipitate visit, and Manek had advised, "Just keep your cool. I'm sure it will blow over." And Zareen, excited by the adventures of shopping, eating, and sightseeing, had been content to let things ride.

This morning, although it was a work day and an expensive time to call, Zareen phoned Aban and poured out her many misgivings. Aban, still not feeling that she could interfere in a matter so personal, listened sympathetically and advised, "It might be better if you call Manek. He understands Feroza and might offer some suggestions." She gave her Manek's phone number at work.

Manek was surprised when his secretary told him that his sister was on the line. "Everything all right?" he asked anxiously, and Zareen started weeping. "I don't know what to do," she said between her sobs. And pulling herself together, she expressed her anxiety and feelings.

Manek listened to her with growing impatience. "Couldn't the matter wait till evening? Do you know how much this call is costing?"

"Damn the cost," Zareen almost shrieked. "It's a question of Feroza's entire happiness. Is that all you can think of?"

"Look," Manek said, "I still think if you leave things alone, the romance will die a natural death."

"I don't think it will," Zareen said with conviction. "You should see the way they're carrying on. I wouldn't be surprised if they eloped and got married secretly."

"Feroza is a big girl now," Manek said. "She's not a fool. She knows what she's doing. If she really likes the guy so much, there's not much you can do. After all, she's spent four years in America. Our young people are bound to marry out. You know so many already have. I can only make a suggestion. I think the best thing would be to accept the fact with good grace. After all, David sounds like a fine man."

"Very good! Very good!" Zareen was outraged. "You come all the way to Lahore to marry a Parsee girl, and you are advising me to let my daughter marry David? I can't believe it. Thank you very much!" she said and banged the phone down.

Zareen waited for David to appear in the kitchen. It was almost four o'clock, and he was accustomed to forage in the fridge for a snack and make himself a cup of coffee.

When he didn't show up, she was sure he was deliberately avoiding her. She strode to the garage door, and after ascertaining that he was in his room, sounding as if she were unmasking a coward, she sternly said, "David, can you come into the kitchen, please? I want to talk to you."

David's spirits sank lower as he caught the elusive inflection that had so disconcerted him on the day of her arrival. Shoving his legs into his long pants, David hurried into the kitchen and sat down before Zareen.

Zareen gave him a quick, cool smile and, dispensing with courtesies, said, "I am most concerned about Feroza. Do you intend to marry her, or are you just having fun?"

David felt the blood rush to his head and cloud his vision. At the same time, meekly lying in his lap, his hands turned numb and cold. "Of course," he stammered. "We want to get married."

"Please speak for yourself," Zareen said, "and let my daughter speak for herself."

David was too stunned to say anything. He looked at Zareen with an expression of surprise and misery.

"Have you thought about the sacrifice you are demanding of my daughter?"

"I'm not demanding anything. Feroza does as she pleases, pretty much." Then, the slightest edge to his voice, he added, "She's an adult."

"An adult? I don't think so," Zareen said. "You are both too immature and selfish to qualify as adults. She doesn't care how much she hurts all of us. I'll tell you something." Zareen's voice became oracular with foreboding. "I look into Feroza's future and what do I see? Misery!"

David could not credit his faculties. The transition was too sudden. He could not reconcile the hedonistic shopper, the model swirling girlishly in the kitchen, the enthusiastic tourist and giver of gifts with this aggressive sage frightening him with her doom-booming voice and a volley of bizarre accusations.

"Could we talk about this later?" he mumbled, tripping over the chair as he stood up. "I'll be late for an evening class."

"Then go!" Zareen was imperious with scorn. "But please think about the sacrifice you are asking of my daughter."

Feroza had just returned and, hearing the loud voices, had cravenly retreated to her room. Nervously bracing herself for a quarrel or, at the very least, a solemn lecture, she was not prepared for the ferocity of Zareen's attack — or its dangerous direction — when Zareen marched into her room saying, "You're both selfish. Thinking of no one but yourselves. And don't think I don't know what you're up to!"

"What am I up to?" Feroza was at once on her guard.

"Ask your conscience that! We have taught you what is wrong and what is right!"

"If you're referring to my virginity, you may relax," Feroza said, attaching umbrage to her haughty voice. "I'm perhaps the only twenty-year-old virgin in all America."

"You were not in your bed at three o'clock this morning! You expect me to believe you?"

"Believe what you want, since you don't trust me!" Feroza said with scathing dignity and strode out of the room.

Zareen followed her furiously. "Don't you turn your back on me! Look me in the eye!"

Whirring round, her face darkly flushing, Feroza shouted, "Examine me if you want!"

They had the house to themselves. In the course of the row, mother and daughter stormed in and out of rooms, raking up old quarrels, wrenching open doors and banging them shut. They locked themselves in the bathrooms and splashing their faces with water, refreshed themselves for the fray. At the end of an hour, Zareen, trembling with rage and exhaustion, raised her hand threateningly, "Don't think you're too old to slap!"

Feroza moved close to her parent and snatched her hand in a violent gesture of defiance. She stared at Zareen out of savage lynx eyes, her pupils narrowed. Zareen felt she had provoked something dangerous to them both. Tears springing to her eyes she jerked her arm free. She walked to the flimsy entrance door, swung it open and swept out of the house.

Zareen had barely walked a block up the quiet, deserted street when she heard the angry whir of wheels as Feroza backed the Chevette out of the drive. A moment later the car whizzed past.

Zareen felt drained and defeated. She turned round slowly and went back to the house.

Zareen sat brooding before the TV, searching her soul. She had acted in a way that would push her daughter into the arms of this David. How could she have been so foolish? She was the mother, and yet Feroza had shown more maturity and restraint in her behavior than she had.

Late in the evening, lying on her bed, Zareen heard Laura and Shirley enter the house. A short while later, she heard the garage door click. David had returned. Feroza must be with him. Quickly opening a magazine, she waited breathlessly for Feroza.

The moments dragged by, and she wondered if Feroza would show up at all. She wanted desperately to effect a reconciliation, wipe away the hurt in both their hearts. Feroza did not come. In fact the house was as silent as if it were empty.

Tears sprang to Zareen's eyes, and she put the magazine away. She plucked a tissue from the box by her pillow and bitterly blew her nose. Three weeks had gone by, and what had she done except go wild and spend all the bribe money? She had only five days left in Denver. She had one of those tickets that was cheaper if you specified the return date at the time of purchase. In any case she had to be in Lahore in time for her nephew's *navjote*, which Feroza had explained to David was like a bar mitzvah.

Zareen absently heard the phone ring. A little later Shirley knocked on her door and shyly, as was her way, said, "Feroza called. She asked me to tell you she is spending the night with a friend. She'll see you after classes tomorrow."

Shirley stepped hesitantly into the room. "Are you all right? Can I get you anything?"

"I'm all right, dear," Zareen said, her voice thick. "Thanks a lot for asking. I'm just a bit tired. I was waiting for Feroza."

"You sound as if you're heading for a cold," Shirley said. "Let me get you a glass of warm milk."

Zareen felt soothed by the attention. She considered Shirley very pretty. Shirley had high cheekbones, a small nose, and long, blond hair. The girls were not a bit like Zareen's preconceived notions of promiscuous American girls, even if Feroza had made that crack about being the only twenty-year-old virgin in America. These pretty girls did not have boys hovering round them.

Chapter 28

Zareen stayed home the next day. She sorted out her shopping and packed a suitcase with gifts. It was expected of her, that she return like a female Santa Claus bearing gifts. She did not see David or either of the girls all day.

Feroza came home at about six in the evening, announcing, "I'm so hungry!" She was in high spirits. Zareen turned off the TV and followed her into the kitchen, saying, "I'm hungry too. I'll make us a spicy *pora*. Would you like that?"

"I'd love it!"

Zareen took out four eggs for the omelette and rinsed a light plastic chopping board with bright vegetable designs on it. She must remember to purchase a couple. No, at least four. Her sisters-in-law and cousins would love them. And knives. A set of those expensive knives that could chop off your fingers if you weren't careful. Potato peelers, cheese slicers. She was temporarily distracted from her worries at the thought of the pleasure the gifts would give.

"Only five days to go. It's Tuesday today, and by next Tuesday I'll be in Lahore," Zareen announced, expertly chopping onions and jalapeño peppers.

Feroza looked up from the mail she was reading. "Is that all? But you only just got here!" She sounded genuinely dismayed.

David had returned. They could hear him moving around in the garage.

Zareen sighed heavily and turned towards Feroza. Holding the knife, which was plastered with cilantro and onion, she passed the back of her hand across her forehead in a weary gesture. "If you feel you must marry that man, I have only one request."

The allusion to the subject was sudden, the capitulation unexpected. Feroza widened her eyes, pursed her full mouth in an O, and affected a visibly theatrical start.

"What?"

This is what she loved about Feroza. Even as a child, after the banging of doors, the red-faced shouting rages and shut-ins, by the time Feroza emerged from her retreat, all was forgotten and forgiven. She rarely sulked. Even after their epic quarrel the day before, she was not above a little clowning.

"Get married properly," Zareen said. "The judge's bit of paper won't make you feel married. Have a regular wedding. Don't deprive us of everything!"

Feroza remained silent and raised her naturally arched eyebrows quizzically.

"If you and David come to Lahore, we will take care of everything."

"Mum, rituals and ceremony frighten David, he's too private a person. We were talking about it last night; neither of us care for meaningless formalities. Anyway, don't you think you should talk to David first?"

Zareen shrugged. "Then call him."

David came into the kitchen looking unkempt, unshaven, uncombed, and grim. Feroza noted the gold chain hanging from his neck, the star of David prominent on his chest. She appreciated at once that her mother, by constantly flaunting their religion, had provoked his reaction.

The top buttons on his plaid shirt were open and part of the shirt hung out of his pants. David pulled out a chair, turned it around, and, straddling it, faced Zareen, surly and mildly defiant. His glasses caught the light in a particular way, and Zareen noticed for the first time his resemblance to the image in the photograph Feroza had sent; something sinister in the definition of his obdurately set jaw and, with his hair grown somewhat, the cold, actorish symmetry of his profile. Zareen was taken aback by his behavior and appearance. His breath smelled of beer.

"Since you two are so sure you want to get married," she said, concealing her nervousness and striving also keep her tone light, "I want you to grant me a little wish."

David looked wary. "Feroza said you want me to come to Lahore to get married?"

"Oh, not only you. Your parents, grandparents, uncles, aunts. They'll all be our guests. I want you and Feroza to have a grand wedding!"

David remained silent and grimly unenthusiastic.

But marriages were the high point in Zareen's community life, and she was talking about her daughter's wedding. "We'll have the *madasara* ceremony first. You'll plant a mango tree. It's to ensure fertility. May you have as many children as the tree bears mangoes. In all ceremonies we mark your foreheads with vermilion, give you envelopes with money, hang garlands round your necks, and give you sugar and coconuts. They're symbols of blessings and good luck."

David, if anything, looked more wary, and the light glinting off his glasses more sinister. Zareen had expected him to at least smile, but his sense of humor had vanished with his courtesy and sensibility. She felt she was seeing him in his true colors. "After that is done, we break a coconut on your head," she said with acid relish.

Feroza laughed. David blinked his bewildered eyes and looked profoundly hurt. "She's only kidding," Feroza said.

"Then we have the *adarnee* and engagement. Your family will fill Feroza's lap with five sari sets, sari, petticoat, blouse underwear. Whatever jewelry they plan to give her must be given then. We give our daughters-in-law at least one diamond set. I will give her the diamond-and-emerald necklace my mother gave me at my wedding."

"Now, don't look so worried," Zareen said, noting David's ghastly pallor and tightly compressed lips. "And tell your mother not to worry either. We'll be like sisters. I'll help her choose the saris. We get beautiful saris in Lahore, Tanchoi, Banarasi silks."

The more defensive, startled, and confused David appeared, the more Zareen felt compelled to talk. Feroza signaled her with her eyes and, when that did not deter her, with gestures of her hands and small amusing protests, "Mum, you'll scare him witless!" And to David, "It's a lot of fun, really!"

"Of course it's fun. We'll give your family clothes — suit-lengths and shirts for the men, sari sets for the women. A gold chain for your mother, a pocket watch for your father. Look here, if your parents don't want to do the same, we'll understand. But we'll fulfill our traditional obligations."

David was angry. He sat there, exuding stubbornness. Not mulish balking but the resistance of an instinct that grasped the significance of the attack. He realized Zareen's offensive was not personal but communal. He knew that a Jewish wedding would be an equally elaborate affair, and though he didn't want to go through that either, he felt compelled to defend his position.

"My parents aren't happy about the marriage, either. It's lucky they're Reform Jews, otherwise they'd go into mourning and pretend I was dead. We have Jewish customs, you know. My family will miss my getting married under a canopy by our rabbi. We have a great dinner and there's a table with twenty or thirty different kinds of desserts, cake, and fruit. Then there's dancing until late at night." David stopped to catch his breath and looked angrily at Zareen. "I belong to an old tradition, too."

"All the better," Zareen said promptly. "We'll honor your traditions."

Zareen felt an exhilarating strength within her, as if someone very subtle was directing her brain, a power she could trust but not control.

His nostrils pinched and quivering, David felt the subtle force in Zareen undermining everything he stood for — his entire worth as a person. He wasn't sure what it was — perhaps a craftiness older people achieved. His mother would be a better match for Zareen. He had seen her perform the cultivated rituals of a closed society, fending for itself in covert and subliminal ways that were just as effective and difficult to pinpoint.

"Next, we come to the wedding. If there is a wedding," Zareen said solemnly. "You'll sit on thrones like royalty, under a canopy of white jasmine, and the priests will chant prayers for an hour, and shower you with rice and coconut slivers."

"I thought you said the priests refused to perform such marriages." David was sarcastic, a canny prosecutor out to nail a slippery opponent.

"I know of cases where such marriages have been performed,"

Zareen said, as if confessing to knowledge better left concealed. "Feroza's grandmother has ways of getting around things — she's president of the *Anjuman*. The ceremony won't make you a Parsee, or solve Feroza's problems with the community, but we'll feel better for it; so will Feroza."

"Feroza's grandmother is what?" David turned to Feroza for enlightenment.

Using the closest example she could think of, Feroza explained, "Grandmother's like a tribal chief."

Zareen was taken aback. As far as she was aware, tribesmen inhabited jungles and mountain wildernesses, observed primitive codes of honor, and carried out vendettas. A far cry from the Westernized and urban behavior of her sophisticated community. But noticing David's flattering interest in what Feroza was saying, she didn't dispute it.

"You'll have a wonderful time," continued Zareen compulsively. "Every day we'll sing wedding songs, smother you in garlands, stuff your pockets with money and your mouth with sweets." She talked on and on. "I can just imagine Feroza in a white Chantilly lace sari embroidered with gold and sequins."

David folded his arms on the back of the chair and let his chin rest resignedly on them. He imagined his mother talking the same way. She'd want him to get married under the wedding canopy in the synagogue in which he'd had his bar mitzvah and with the same rabbi performing the marriage.

David's blue eyes glazed over. Feroza glanced at him and felt bewildered and mortified by her mother's conduct.

Laura came into the kitchen in a boyish night shirt, apologized for interrupting Zareen's animated monologue, and withdrew with her cup of coffee.

Zareen said, "Such decent girls. They don't have boyfriends to distract them from studies. They seem to know there is a time and place for everything."

"They don't need boyfriends," Feroza said complacently. "They're lesbians."

Zareen did not immediately register what she heard. She had

read the word once or twice in magazines but never heard it pronounced. She became acutely uncomfortable.

"Lovers," Feroza added helpfully.

"But why? They're pretty enough. They can get droves of boyfriends."

"Some women just prefer women. Others are fed up. American boys change girlfriends every few months. All boys are not like my David. The girls can't stand the heartache. It takes them months to get over it. Laura says, 'If Shirley gets my juices flowing, why should I mess around with boys?' Either way, they get on with their lives."

Zareen wanted to throw up. She couldn't tell if Feroza was trying to impress her with her newly acquired worldly wisdom, or deliberately insulting her. Feroza had been properly brought up to be respectful, sexually innocent, and modest. That she could mention such things in her presence shocked Zareen.

Above all, Zareen was dismayed at her own innocence. In all the time she had stayed with them, she hadn't suspected the truth. What goings-on! Feroza was living with a boy and a couple of lesbians. She wouldn't dare mention it to Cyrus, or anyone. How could she face the disgrace of nurturing a brat who looked her in the eye and brazenly talked about bodily juices? She tried not to show how hurt she was.

But Feroza gauged the measure of her pain. Not able to do anything about her mother's attitude, for the past two days Feroza had helplessly watched David's slowly mounting perplexity, disillusion, and fury. And suspecting that Zareen had just destroyed their happiness by her talk about diamonds and saris and superior Parsee ways, Feroza had instinctively hit back.

The assaults were too vicious, the hurt too deeply felt, for either to acknowledge her wounds.

Zareen continued talking, but she was distracted. A little later she said, "I've kept you long enough, David. You're almost asleep." She stood up. "Well, good night."

David nodded without looking at her or attempting to sit up. Feroza glanced at him, surprised and reproachful.

When Zareen left, David swung himself off the chair and, avoiding Feroza's anxious and wistful eyes, stretching his back and rubbing his neck, went into his room and shut the door.

Feroza's heart pounded and her body felt dull and heavy. She sat at the kitchen table for a long time, her face red and frozen. The tears came slowly.

Chapter 29

Zareen switched off the bedroom lights. She hoped the Valium would work before Feroza came into the room. Her mind seethed with a tangle of images. She covered her eyes with the sari scarf in a bid to empty her mind.

Just before she drifted off to sleep, a memory floated up of the idea, vague and unformed, that had calmed her on her second night in Denver. The idea had ripened unconsciously, and its subtle force, combined with her recent fear, had directed her actions. A set of words began to synchronize with the rhythm of her easing mind, "If you can't knock him out with sugar, slug him with honey." Except she'd knocked out her daughter as well. But she must, in any event, protect her from the calumny that would destroy her.

౷

In the few remaining days of her visit, the guilt and remorse passed. David's surly behavior and coldly clenched jaw vindicated her guile. She felt that she had exposed the wickedness hidden him, and she hoped that Feroza was noticing his mean and unpleasant behavior.

The day before Zareen was to leave, David started calling Feroza ZAP. The first few times, Feroza laughed her special musical laugh with its infectious undertones and explained to Zareen that ZAP stood for Zoroastrian-American Princess, an innovative spin-off on JAP, Jewish-American Princess. Zareen knew too little of the Jewish-American culture to appreciate its humor.

But after a few repetitions, the clever ZAP spin-off palled. And when David started calling her "Apple of Mommy's eye," Feroza turned her offended face away and gazed resentfully into the middle distance. There were periods when she and David did not talk. A pinched look around her eyes and an uncertainty in them dimmed their yellow luster.

Feroza's eyes had always revealed her feelings. It upset Zareen to look into them now. They reflected her sadness and resignation and betrayed an occasional flicker of fear Zareen had never seen in them before. Why should her fearless daughter be afraid? She was glad she had hidden those ugly pamphlets Freny had sent.

All the lights in the house had been turned off. Zareen, unable to sleep, had a sudden vision of her daughter as she had seen her at the Denver airport. Feroza had been radiant. Zareen recalled the catch in her heart at the sight of Feroza's loveliness, and the same emotion, an almost unsustainable wave of pleasure and tenderness, tinged with the new dread — swept through her again.

And in its wake arrived a sweating and guilty wave of panic.

In her excitement at being in America Zareen had forgotten old ways. Her daughter's unhappiness had been brought about by Zareen herself, and no one was to blame but she. She had forgotten how malign the admiring and loving eye of a mother could be. To admire one's own child so lavishly was to tempt fate — to cast a spell more potent than the evil eye of envious ill-wishers.

Zareen sprang out of bed anxiously and hustled a bewildered and groggy Feroza into the kitchen. She turned on the stove and placed an old griddle on it.

Almost asleep on the kitchen chair, rubbing her eyes, Feroza followed her mother's movements vapidly.

Zareen took out three jalapeño peppers from the refrigerator and steered Feroza to stand by the stove.

"Oh, Mum!" Feroza protested in exasperation and bowed her head as she used to. "I can't believe you still accept this nonsense."

Holding the peppers in her fist, ignoring Feroza's drowsy protests, Zareen solemnly drew seven circles in the air over Feroza's head, all the while whispering a hodgepodge of incantations. "May the mischief of malign and envious eyes leave you, may the evil in my loving eye leave you, may any magic and ill will across the seven seas be banished, may Ahura Mazda's protection and blessings guard you."

Then she cast the peppers on the hot griddle and, with a dark look, watched them sputter, shrivel, and char to cinders.

"Hey, what's going on?" David stood in the door. The room was filled with an acrid stench.

"Mum's removing evil-eye spells," Feroza said, laconic and wry.

"At this time of night?"

Zareen cast a brief, baleful look at David. She removed the griddle from the fire and, bending over in her dressing gown, tapped its edge on the tiled floor and emptied its contents.

The charred remains of the peppers looked like tortured beetles. In a gesture that appeared needlessly vicious to David, Zareen crushed the remains of the peppers beneath the grinding heel of her slipper.

"Oh, God!" David said, contemptuous and aggravated. "What are you? A witch or something?"

Zareen gave him a fierce look. She pointed a trembling finger at him. "You get out!"

David stepped back, scowling and confused, and almost stumbled off the step leading to his room. He closed the door with a thunderous slam that shook the fragile walls and windows.

Zareen had already checked her baggage. She stepped into the security section at the airport and placed her purse, a packed canvas carry-all, and two bulging shopping bags on the conveyor belt. After it passed through the screening, she collected her hand luggage and turned to look at David and Feroza one last time.

David stood in his faded and torn denim shorts, his arms folded, his muscular legs planted like sturdy trees. Standing forlornly by him, Feroza looked pale, insecure, and uprooted.

As Zareen waved and smiled, an ache caught her heart and the muscles in her face trembled. Covering her head with her sari *palu* to hide her crumbling face, Zareen quickly turned away.

Once she was airborne, Zareen opened her crocodile skin handbag. Its three sections contained three thick wads of tissues. She picked one of each color and daubed her eyes. She wiped the tears from her cheeks and, gathering fresh tissues, held their fragrant softness against her face.

The flight attendant served the first round of drinks. Zareen asked for an orange juice and took a Valium with it. As she was putting back the bottle, her fingers touched the tightly folded wad of paper that she had transferred to her change purse just before leaving. She took it out and spread the sheets on her lap. Since the first cursory scan, she had not looked at them. Zareen had a window seat, but the jet, nosing its way through time, had already been swallowed up in the night outside her window. Zareen switched on the light and held the pamphlet up to it. The message was typed in menacing capitals,

NOTICE.
PLEASE NOTE THAT ACCORDING TO THE PARSEE, ZOROASTRIAN RELIGIOUS BELIEFS, PERCEPTS, TENETS, DOCTRINES, HOLY SCRIPTURES, CUSTOMS AND TRADITIONS, ONCE A PARSEE-ZOROASTRIAN MARRIES A NON-ZOROASTRIAN, HE OR SHE IS DEEMED TO HAVE RENOUNCED THE FAITH AND CEASES TO BE A PARSEE-ZOROASTRIAN. THE LAWS OF PURITY OF THE ZOROASTRIAN FAITH FORBID INTERMARRIAGES, AS MIXING PHYSICAL AND SPIRITUAL GENES IS CONSID-ERED A CARDINAL CRIME AGAINST NATURE. HENCE, HE OR SHE DOES NOT HAVE ANY COMMUNAL OR RELIGIOUS RIGHTS OR PRIVILEGES.

There was more in the same vein. It ended by imploring such blasphemers not to desecrate sacred places with their unwanted presence.

On the other flyer, the High Priest, Dausturjee Rattan, had declared that a girl who married outside her faith was an adulteress and her children illegitimate.

Zareen felt a dizzying wave of nausea. She realized that the debate, instead of bringing about the reforms she had thought were inevitable, had only entrenched traditional norms. These educated custodians of the Zoroastrian doctrine were no less rigid and ignorant than the *fundos* in Pakistan. This mindless current of fundamentalism sweeping the world like a plague had spared no religion, not even their microscopic community of 120 thousand.

But the threatening words that had made her hide the flyers and instinctively blot them from her memory, now resonated hideously in her mind: "The Zoroastrian faith forbids intermarriages, since mixing physical and spiritual genes is considered a cardinal crime against nature."

Zareen wanted to spin a protective shield of love around her daughter, defend her from accusations of polluting the genetic structure of their race and dirtying the spiritual genes, if there were such things, and the purity of their religion: mighty charges no young girl could withstand, not even if she professed to be irreligious.

It dawned on Zareen that the exhilarating strength she had felt when confronting David, as of some subtle power directing her brain, was not a supernatural force come to help her as she'd thought, but the reflexive impulse of her own dread.

A child toddled down the isle waving a spoon and smiled at Zareen. Zareen put the papers away. She adjusted her chair, rearranged the pillows for comfort, and lay back.

A picture formed behind her closed eyelids, of Khutlibai and Feroza. Zareen's expression softened. Feroza had been about three years old then. There had been an epidemic of chicken pox among the children in the servants' quarters and Cyrus had contracted it. Khutlibai had whisked Feroza away to her house on Punj Mahal Road. Cyrus had a raging fever and large sores all over his body. He was racked by coughs, almost blinded, and seriously ill. The disease that is relatively benign in a child can be quite serious for an adult. Busy nursing her husband and afraid to contaminate her daughter, Zareen had not seen Feroza for almost three months.

Khutlibai, who had packed Manek off to the Ghoragali Hills boarding school earlier that year, enjoyed having her grandchild exclusively to herself. Her days passed in a blissful orgy of activities centered around the girl and her schedule. Always anxious about her grandchild's welfare, Khutlibai was certain that Zareen neglected her. Now that Feroza was in her competent care, she enjoyed a season of peace.

Khutlibai massaged Feroza with almond oil, bathed her "properly," coddled her in fragrant clouds of talcum powder, tied large satin bows in her hair, clad her in pretty, frilly dresses and matching socks, and kept her always surgically clean and barber-shop fragrant. Feroza was taken visiting and shown-off to her friends, bought toys, and taken to ride the slides and seesaws in the playgrounds of Lahore's lush gardens.

Khutlibai supervised her granddaughter's diet, giving her Kepler's Malt with her breakfast and nourishing chicken soups at every meal. She regulated Feroza's afternoon nap and bedtime routine and spent hours answering her questions and telling her stories.

At the end of three months, with a great deal of fuss about fumigation and other precautions, Khutlibai reluctantly agreed to return her charge.

She chose a propitious day of the month according to the Parsee calendar, a propitious hour of the day according to her Gujrati almanac, and, preceded by an elaborate flurry of packing, arrived at her daughter's house in her stately Studebaker (this was before her Toyota days).

It was fairly late in the afternoon, and Zareen and Cyrus had visitors. The portals of the home were flung open by the salaaming servants. Carrying Feroza, and followed by the ayah, cook, and her handsome chauffeur, who was haughtily holding a new suitcase and frilly little dresses on hangers, Khutlibai passed through the sitting room on a deliberate course to the nursery.

Their guests had stood up, politely smiling, but Khutlibai's solemn demeanor, profoundly pursed mouth and straight-ahead, purposeful eyes, effectively arrested their greetings.

"Passed through" was inadequate to describe their passage, Zareen thought, smiling reminiscently. Sailed past like a galleon on the high seas was more like it. Khutlibai held Feroza with a protective air of significance and gravity that imbued her charge with all the regard due to royalty. Had Bonny Prince Charlie been discreetly hustled through a palace hall after he'd been smuggled into England by an aristocratic lady-in-waiting, their passage could hardly have been more impressive.

Propped up in Khutlibai's arms, Feroza's regal bearing validated the homage paid by her entourage. Her large irises glowed hazel in her brown face as they deigned to acknowledge the standing presences with a demure glance of coy curiosity.

Her bashful glance, the contours of her finely etched features, the noble angle at which she held her neck as though conscious of her role in the domestic comedy, had branded her image in Zareen's memory.

And all that Kepler's Malt and pampering had paid off. Feroza's lightly flushed face appeared burnished — as if cast in bronze — as her imperious profile cut through the air like an exquisitely chiseled mermaid at the prow of that proud, broad-beamed, wave-riding galleon.

And like the ships of old, Feroza would navigate her own course through life, Zareen thought. Not the easy route she would have her daughter follow but the dangerous and alluring trails Zareen had scented in the New World in the short while she was there.

It appeared to be her daughter's destiny, and there was not much she could do to shield her from the pain. She and Cyrus and Khutlibai could provide her with everything but her destiny — and if they could, they would have given her even that.

But her daughter was resilient, courageous in a way she would never understand. Feroza would bounce back, she always did.

And so would she, Zareen, once she was with her family and friends. She needed desperately to be with them, to be assured she had done the right thing.

Chapter 30

David left Denver at the end of the summer term. He had completed his master's in computer programming and accepted a job with a
firm in California. Feroza and he had long discussions after Zareen
left, analyzing her visit, wondering what had gone wrong despite
their resolutions not to let their religious disparity come between
them. But it had — or at least Zareen had convinced David that the
differences mattered.

It was not only a question of analysis and argument, Feroza
acknowledged sadly. It was David. His feelings for her had undergone a change.

The very thing that had attracted him to Feroza, her exoticism,
now frightened David. Zareen had made him feel that he and
Feroza had been too cavalier and callow in dismissing the dissimilar-
ities in their backgrounds. He felt inadequate, wondering if he
could cope with some of the rituals and behavior that, despite his
tolerant and accepting liberality, seemed bizarre. Stuff his mouth
with sweets, break a coconut on his head! And, were he by some
gross mischance accepted to the Zoroastrian faith, which fortunately
was not permissible, he'd have the singular honor of having his
remains devoured by vultures and crows in a ghastly Tower of
Silence.

Even that could misfire; Zareen's great-great-grandparent's foot
had remained uneaten for a month after an epidemic of typhoid in
their ancestral village in Central India. After all, there was a limit to
how much the gluttonous birds could eat.

Zareen had made the horrible details sound like something to
look forward to at the end of her life. He knew she was joking of
course, but her attitude had distressed and humiliated him. Yet, on
another level, he had not realized before how much Feroza's leaving
her faith entailed. It was such a final break, not something she could
change her mind about later and go back to for sustenance.

The mountains Feroza loved so much appeared to have shed some of their splendor and stepped away from her, dimmed and diminished on a somber horizon. It was as if her eyes, robbed of the blue dazzle they had become accustomed to, reflected only dulled and cheerless impressions. Feroza hardly noticed the sunsets they once had driven to distant places to admire together, locations David had discovered especially for her.

Then her pining, thirsting vision began to conjure up mirages in the wasteland of her heartache, and she started seeing David everywhere. She saw him seated in shaded nooks in restaurants, slipping round campus corners and the counters in stores, cycling ahead of her on paths, climbing into buses and riding past, walking away from her, always stepping away from her. Her heart pounding, she raced after him, her smile fading as she confronted strangers.

When her friends heard that she and David had broken up, they flocked to her. Shashi dropped by regularly, attempting to cheer her up with the latest news from Mala and Deepak. They had left for Delhi with the baby — and the baby's brand-new American passport — soon after they retrieved her from the hospital. Gwen and Rhonda brought her flowers and magazines and tried to get her out of bed and comfort her.

Jo called frequently, and she and Bill persuaded her to go to a Chinese restaurant with them one Saturday evening. Feroza was grateful to her friends and welcoming when they visited, but her spirit was extinguished. She was listless; it was like being with a sick person.

Aban and Manek called from Houston every Saturday and Sunday. Aban had delivered a baby girl and was already pregnant again.

David's room was occupied by a tall and lank student with a racing bike. No matter how much she told herself she was being unfair, she considered him an interloper. She resented his reclusive presence in the converted garage and couldn't bear to hear music, or other inevitable noises he made in inhabiting his rented quarters. In fact she resented his very existence.

David called from California occasionally. Their conversations were pleasant and sometimes for Feroza full of hope. Then she became her ebullient and generous self again, and her life seemed full of possibility. But these brief periods were followed by depression as hope sank anew.

"What's this?" Shashi said late one evening, imitating her lethargic posture as she sat at the kitchen table supporting her chin in her hand and vapidly stirring her coffee. And when her eyes welled with tears at the rebuke, Shashi drew up his chair and put his arm round her and nuzzled her face, saying, "It's not the end of the world, you know. I promise, you'll get over it."

He fell to his knees and dramatically bared his chest. Spreading his arms like a film hero, he crooned the songstress Iqbal Banoo's beautiful lament, *Ulfat Kee Naee Manzil Ko Chalay:*

> Embarked on a new mission of love,
> You who have broken my heart, look where you're going.
> I, too, lie in your path.

Feroza said Wah-wah, wah-wah, in the manner of South Asian appreciation and, although she was playing up to his theatrics, was surprised by his ability to hold a difficult tune.

Shashi touched his bowed forehead repeatedly in a deep salaam and, swinging slowly from one side to the other in an arc, saluted the rest of the imaginary audience applauding his *mehfil.*

Feroza collapsed on the floor beside him, laughing.

But the *ghazal,* with its attendant memories of other romantically sweet and metaphysical poems, and the *mushairas* attended by thousands of fans like herself where poets recited or sang their work, evoked an unbearable nostalgia. Feroza wept, yearning for the land of poets and *ghazals* she had left behind, for her friends from the Convent of the Sacred Heart, and for her own broken heart — when it occurred to her that she had thought of both in the past tense.

Her life that had bloomed in such unexpected ways had just as unexpectedly fallen apart. She must put it together again, heal her lacerated sensibility. But she could only do the healing right here, in America. For even in her bereft condition, she knew there was no going back for her, despite the poets and her friends.

311

From her visit to Lahore, Feroza knew she had changed, and the life of her friends there had also changed, taken a different direction from hers. Their preoccupation with children and servants and their concern with clothes and furnishings did not interest her. Neither did the endless round of parties that followed their parents' mode of hospitality. Although the sense of dislocation, of not belonging, was more acute in America, she felt it would be more tolerable because it was shared by thousands of newcomers like herself.

It was not only that, Feroza thought in mild consternation. Like Manek she had become used to the seductive entitlements of the First World. Happy Hour, telephones that worked, the surfeit of food, freezers, electricity, and clean and abundant water, the malls, skyscrapers, and highways.

There was also the relief from observing the grinding poverty and injustices she could do so little to alleviate, the disturbing Hadood Ordinances that allowed the victims of rape to be punished, and the increasing pressure from the fundamentalists to introduce more Islamic law. These and the other constraints would crush her freedom, a freedom that had become central to her happiness. The abandon with which she could conduct her life without interference was possible only because of the distance from her family and the anonymity America provided.

However comforting the interaction of family and friends was, they would fritter away her hours in activities she had grown away from, and their habitual meddling would never allow her control over her life.

In a way Manek was right when he carried on about time. Not that she thought, with his emphasis, that "time was money," but because the waste of time represented to her a loss of privacy. And privacy, she had come to realize, was one of the prime luxuries the opulence of the First World could provide, as well as the sheer physical space the vast country allowed each individual, each child, almost as a birthright.

She realized now that the convenience provided by servants brought its own baggage of responsibilities, a drain on her time she could do without. The technology of the West kept one sufficient unto one's self without the necessity of intrusive human contact. The genii that opened garage doors, the dust-proof, climate-controlled houses, and the gadgets eliminated the need for servants, for dependence on relatives one might need to call upon in a pinch.

She was not alone in her desire for privacy and plenty. A sizable portion of the world was experiencing this phenomenon, on this scale at least, for the first time in human history, and the rest of the jam-packed and impoverished world — no matter how much they might moan about the loss of human contact, privacy, and the dwindling family — also hankered for it.

The thirst for knowledge that the universities and the libraries filled with books had kindled in Feroza and the curiosity that still burned like a flame in her mind — all this she had become accustomed to and couldn't leave. Like Shashi, she wasn't satisfied with her degree in hotel management. She would indulge her choices: anthropology, psychology, journalism, astronomy. The options were endless.

Feroza knew her thoughts would be considered despicable and selfish were she to voice them at home. But it was a selfishness sanctioned by the values of the prosperous new world in which she wished to dwell. Surely she could arrive at a compromise if her conscience troubled her — and even as she thought this, she knew it would. Her deeply ingrained and early awareness of political and state evils and her passion for justice would always make her fight injustice wherever she was.

And, God knows, there was enough cause: in the pious platitudes, in the narrow vision of a world seen through the cold prisms of self-interest and self-pity, in this strangely paradoxical nation that dealt in "death," that sold the world's most lethal weapons to impoverished countries and simultaneously absorbed the dispossessed of the chronically dispelling world.

Yet this paradox was shaping a New World, the future in microcosm, the melting-pot in which every race and creed was being increasingly represented, compelled to live with and tolerate the "other," and she would play her part, however miniscule it was, in shaping the future. She would leave room in her life for the ideals

of generosity and constancy she had grown up with and the attach-
ment to the family and their claim on her. She would manage her
life to suit her heart; after all, the pursuit of happiness was enshrined
in the constitution of the country she had grown to love, despite
her growing knowledge of its faults, and she would pursue her happiness her way.

Feroza applied for and was admitted to the University of
Arizona's graduate program in anthropology.

Just before the end of the winter term, Gwen vanished. She had
packed a bag and gone for the weekend (at least that's what Rhonda
supposed), but she did not come back. A week went by. Most of
her books and clothes were still in her room. She had disappeared
so completely, without leaving a trace, without any warning, that it
frightened all her friends, particularly Rhonda and Feroza. Could a
person just vanish? Drop out of their lives like that? A person as connected and thoughtful as Gwen? They worried and speculated and
wondered and finally informed the police.

For all they knew, the mysterious WASP had murdered her.
Rhonda and Feroza again speculated, as they had in the beginning,
about her secret lover's car, job, age, and looks. They were fearful.
They had heard of snuff films. There were daily accounts of women
being gagged and bound, brutally raped, found dead.

The police located her family in Atlanta, but they said they had
not heard from her in over a year. Although Feroza and Rhonda
kept in touch after graduation and after Rhonda's marriage, neither
of them ever heard from Gwen or about her.

જ

Manek and Aban had been urging Feroza to visit them. "You
haven't even seen your new cousin," Aban complained. "I thought
once I had the baby everybody would flock to see my little Dilshad,
but nobody's come." She tried to sound facetious but could not
camouflage her hurt. "Neither my parents or sisters, nor anyone
from Manek's family, not even you!"

Feroza knew how she must feel. Poor Aban had missed out on
the seventh and ninth month pregnancy ceremonies and the gifts

314

and clothes and family jokes that went with them, and now she would be deprived of her baby's "Sitting" and "First Step" ceremonies. What a fuss and stir little Dilshad would have caused in Lahore or Karachi, the grandparents vying to look after her and the aunts competing for her attention, everybody lavishing gifts.

Feroza spent the last two weeks before the start of her new graduate program with Manek and Aban. She wished she hadn't. The baby had either a cold or diarrhea, and often both. Dilly, as Feroza called her, sniffed and whined night and day. Little wonder the parents were overworked and irritable.

Aban and Manek bickered continuously over little things, blaming each other when something was wrong with Dilshad or when they had run out of some household commodity or kitchen ingredient. They argued about how to look after the baby and even about what the instructor at Lamaze classes had said.

Worst of all, Aban's nightingale voice had turned shrill and contentious as a shrew's. By evening it issued in a pathetic croak of fatigue. Her stomach was already quite large, and Feroza felt guilty just watching her cope.

"You know," Aban said, "Our life's been on hold since Dilshad was born. We haven't eaten out once or gone to the movies. I don't know how we'll manage when the other one arrives."

Later in the evening, when Dilly was asleep and the two of them had a chance to sit over a cup of coffee, Aban said, "I thought coming to America was such a big deal, so wonderful — my Prince Charming carrying me off to the castle of my dreams. Everybody back home thinks I'm so lucky, but I'm tired of coping, tired of doing everything on my own. When Dilly cries so much, there's no one I can turn to for advice. I know my mother and aunts would have known exactly what to do, but I don't. And I can't keep running to the doctor every time. Oh, I miss home. I'm longing to see my family and my friends and longing to talk to them. Just sit and talk to them. Sometimes I wish I'd never come here."

Manek, his coat slung over his shoulder from his little finger, came into the kitchen just in time to catch the last remark. "No, you don't," he said, "Once you're there you'll miss everything we have here."

"Everything I want is in Karachi."

"Will you get thirty-one channels in Karachi? You won't even get two. You have your Thunderbird, your washing machine and dishwasher, and so many other gadgets. And Gerber food and Pampers for Dilly. The Karachi pollution would have her wheezing all day and give her asthma, and the water would give her non-stop diarrhea. You'd be pumping asthma medicine into her lungs from morning to night and scrubbing her diapers with Sunlight soap. And even if you had the gadgets, they wouldn't work because of the shortage of electricity and water."

"Karachi has nine million people; how many do you know with asthma? I would wash all the diapers and dishes in the world to be with my friends and my family. And you think I wouldn't have help?"

"If you're thinking about servants, forget it. They'll be a big headache. You'll be screeching at them all day. Once you get used to doing things your way, you won't be able to tolerate them."

Within moments they were screaming at each other, and Aban stormed out of the room, crying.

Feroza offered to babysit every alternate evening during the remainder of her stay. Although her infant cousin behaved well, almost finishing the bottle Aban had prepared for her and crying for only ten or fifteen minutes before going to sleep, Feroza was relieved when Dilly's parents returned. Her nerves were quite shot each time, but it was worth it to see her uncle and aunt look relaxed and eye each other romantically every other evening.

Feroza wondered if she had the right inclinations for parenthood. She doubted it. David, who like Feroza was an only child, had been keen on having lots of babies, and she had mindlessly echoed his wishes. She wondered if he would have been as keen once the first baby arrived. And, more pertinently, how would she feel? It occurred to her that the whole subject needed a lot more thought. Would she and David have argued and bickered the way Manek and Aban did? If that was what marriage and children and the responsibilities that went with them did to people, she felt she was not prepared for them. She knew she could think this way because she was in America. In Lahore the pressure to marry would have made such thoughts unthinkable.

Before she left Houston, Feroza promised Manek and Aban that she would spend a month of her summer vacation helping them when the new baby arrived.

The first evening on her return to Denver, Feroza dug out her *sudra* and *kusti*. They had been hibernating for the longest time. Before going to bed, she said her *kusti* prayers and stood, hands joined, invoking Ahura Mazda's blessings and favor. All at once the image of the holy *atash* in the fire temple in Lahore, pure and incandescent on its bed of ashes, formed behind her shut lids. Its glow suffused her with its tranquility and strength.

Feroza lay down, resting her head on her stacked pillows, her arms folded on her stomach, calmer than she had been for a long time. There would never be another David, but there would be other men, and who knew, perhaps someday she might like someone enough to marry him.

It wouldn't matter if he was a Parsee or of another faith. She would be more sure of herself, and she wouldn't let anyone interfere. It really wouldn't matter; weren't they all children of the same Adam and Eve? As for her religion, no one could take it away from her; she carried its fire in her heart. If the priests in Lahore and Karachi did not let her enter the fire temple, she would go to one in Bombay where there were so many Parsees that no one would know if she was married to a Parsee or a non.

There would be no going back for her, but she could go back at will. The image of Father Fibs suddenly filled her mind's eye, as he had filled the space in Manek's attic, with his long eloquent limbs and messianic voice. And though with the passage of time his words had echoed with an increasing banality, the emotional impact of his soliloquy had not lost its initial grip on her imagination. Had she flown and fallen and strengthened the wings he had talked about? He had told them not to be afraid. But she was. Her break with David still hurt so much, especially the circumstances surrounding the break. If she flew and fell again, could she pick herself up again? Maybe one day she'd soar to that self-contained place from which there was no falling, if there was such a place.

Glossary

Adarnee: important ceremony before a wedding at which the bride, groom, and immediate family exchange gifts.

Afeemi: opium addict.

Agyari: Zoroastrian fire temple. No one but Zoroastrians are permitted to enter it.

Ahura Mazda: God.

Anjuman: committee.

Ashem Vahoo: prayer in which the Zoroastrian vows to follow and uphold the righteous plan and path of the Lord.

Asho Farohar: the Guiding Spirit, personified by the profile of an angel with five layers of wings, representing the five stages of creation. A circle beneath the body represents the soul. Two curled legs represent Good and Evil, and the tail serves as a rudder to guide the soul. The three layers of tail feathers denote the cardinal Zoroastrian percepts: Good Thoughts, Good Words, and Good Deeds.

Atash: sacred fire.

Avasta: the holy book of the Zoroastrians.

Avastan: extinct Persian language in which the Avasta is written.

Baap: father. "O baap ray!" literally means "Oh, father," but is used to mean "Oh, Lord."

Baba: old man or holy man, in many Indian languages; male infant or small boy, in Gujrati. An expression commonly used in a kind of slang to emphasize a point.

Badmash: scoundrel.

Baijee: a respectful form of address for women, in Gujrati (like *ma'am* in English); Parsee women are known as *bai* or *baijee* in Pakistan.

Battigate: one of the gates allowing entrance to the Old Walled City in Lahore. It is a rough area.

Begum: traditionally a Mogul word for the wife of an aristocrat or a gentleman, now it is used in place of *Mrs.* In India, *Shrimati* is used for married Hindu ladies, whereas *Begum* is reserved mostly for Muslims.

Bhagran: God, in Hindu. *Hai Bhagran* means "Oh God!"

Bibi: a respectful term with which to address a woman; sometimes it is used after the name to clarify gender; Mrs. or Ms.

Boochimai: little girl, in old-fashioned Gujrati.

Burqa: head to toe covering, worn by conservative Muslim women in the subcontinent, with net in front of the eyes to see through.

Bus kar: stop it.

Chaddar: generally longer than a *dopatta* and covers the body more completely.

Chitta: white, in Punjabi.

Choli: a short Indian blouse, worn with a sari, exposing the midriff and waist.

Dhoop kar: shut up.

Dal: red lentils or beans.

Desi: native. Refers to all people of the subcontinent.

Dhan-dar: plain yellow lentils and rice served on auspicious occasions.

Dhansak: a Parsee dish made from a mixture of various lentils, vegetables, and meat. It is so rich it puts one to sleep, hence it is usually eaten on a holiday.

Dhoti: a length of cloth wrapped around the waist with one end pulled up between the legs, worn by Hindu men.

Dokhma: the complex that holds the Tower of Silence and washing and prayer rooms, for the ceremonies and disposal of dead bodies.

Dopatta: a 2¼ meter length of cloth to cover the head and bosom, worn by Punjabi women. It is now only a decorative symbol of modesty among the fashionable: a long chiffon or muslin scarf worn round the neck or thrown across the shoulders to match the ensemble of loose trousers and long shirt.

Doria: money.

Easop-gol: English medicinal term *Esogell.* It is a husk that serves the same purpose as bran, to keep the stomach in good working order. Available in Pakistan and India much cheaper than in Europe or the United States.

Fakir: holy man; also beggar.

Feta: hard, oval-shaped Parsee hat covered with felt.

Fundos: short for *fundamentalists.*

Gangee: recently coined by modern Pakistani girls to mean a lout trying to impress them by dressing like a gangster.

Gathas: songs of Zarathustra. Much of the Avasta was lost when Alexander sacked Persipolis, but the few salvaged *gathas* are attributed to the Prophet and are said to be the heart of the faith.

Ghazal: Urdu poetry couplets, which are two-line verses that have the same rhyme and rhythm pattern but different themes. Because they are metrical, they are often sung to music.

Goonda: a local bully; similar to *goon* in English.

Gora: white, in Urdu.

Gora-chitta: both words mean *white,* often used in this combination by Punjabis.

Gujrati: the language of the state of Gujrat in India, adopted by the Parsees when they came as refugees to India fourteen hundred years ago. A major Indian language.

Gup-shup: chat to pass the time pleasantly.

Gurdwaras: Sikh temples.

Hai: a versatile sound expressing surprise, grief, shock, embarrassment, or a reprimand.

Hai Bhagvan: Oh God!

Haramzada: bastard.

Haveli: a beehive of rooms, two to three stories high, built around a court-yard to house the large extended families of the wealthy chieftains, etc. Some are still being used, but they are not being built anymore.

Heejra: eunuch or transvestite.

Hormazd Khoda-ay: the prayer "Ahura Mazda is God."

Izzat: honor, respect; good name. Involves an entire code of behavior.

Jasa-me-avanghe Mazda: the prayer "Come to My Help O Ahura Mazda."

Jee: a prefix or suffix for a polite and respectful form of addressing someone.

Jhuggee: squalid settlement inhabited by poor, homeless families, with shelters made out of rags, jute matting, and sticks. Thousands huddle together on outskirts of many large Indian and Pakistani cities. They do not have sanitation facilities.

Kaka: father's brother (ie. uncle). Each aunt and uncle has a special name denoting specific relationship. For example, mother's sister is *masi,* mother's brother is *mama,* and his wife is *mami.*

Kaki: father's brother's wife.

Kamiz: a knee-length shift or shirt worn over a *shalwar.*

Kapra: clothes.

Kemna Mazda: prayer invoking the protection of God against the threat of evil.

Khandan: family lineage.

Khandani: of respectable lineage; aristocratic.

Khoos poos: slang for whispering and gossiping.

Khush ho?: Are you happy?

Khutba: sermon at mosque, usually on Fridays.

Kurta: shirt or shift stitched in panels, worn over several forms of Indo-Pakistani trousers and leg-wraps.

Kusti: sacred thread woven from seventy-two strands of wool, girdled around the waist three times, worn over the *sudra.* In this way, Zoroastrian women and men gird their loins to serve the Lord.

Lamb keema: lamb hamburger meat.

Lathi: long stick used as a club by villagers and Indo-Pakistani police.

Lungi: length of cloth tied around the waist to cover the legs, like a sarong.

Madam-ni-mai (or mudum-ni-mai): mother-of-an-Englishwoman. Gujrati slang for extra-Westernized native women who adopt fancy airs.

Madasara: Parsee ceremony that takes place before the wedding, at which the groom plants and waters a mango sapling to ensure fertility.

Mahara: my.

Makan: shelter.

Maulvi: a more prestigious title than *mullah* for a Muslim clergyman.

Mazda: God. Full name is Ahura Mazda.

Mehfil: gathering. The word is also commonly used for a gathering where the music is the main focus.

Memsahib: term coined by the British for their women in India.

Mobed: ordained Zoroastrian priest.

Mudum: white Western woman, in Gujrati.

Mullah: Muslim clergy. The terms *mullah* or *maulana* are used for men who lead prayers in mosques as a profession despite the theory that Islam does not have an established clergy.

Mushaira: a gathering where several poets recite their verse. Each line is recited twice and accompanied by sounds of appreciation from the audience.

Na: no, in several subcontinental languages.

Naffat: shameless.

Navjote: ceremony of initiation into the Zoroastrian faith, takes place before puberty.

Navroze: March 21, the day of the Equinox, is celebrated as the New Year in Iran. Parsees also celebrate another New Year, which keeps shifting because it follows an ancient lunar calendar. The third New Year that Parsees celebrate is the Christian New Year on January 1.

Nawab: Mogul title given to a peer of the empire. A nawab was the equivalent of a duke or an earl, but some nawabs became independent of the Mogul empire towards its end as the British took over.

O baap ray!: Oh Father! or Oh Lord!

O mahara baap!: Oh my Father! *Mahara* means *my. Baap* means *father.*

O menu ghoor-ghoor ke vekh rah see!: Punjabi for "He was making big-big eyes and staring at me!"

Paindoo: yokel, country bumpkin.

Paisa: a Pakistani and Indian coin; money. There are one hundred paisa in one rupee.

Pakora: spicy vegetable fritters.

Palu: the end of the sari that hangs at the back. Because it is displayed prominently, it usually has a more decorative and elaborate weave or embroidery.

Panchang: Indian astrological calendar.

Panchayat: assembly of at least five elders who form an executive body to govern community matters.

Pani: water.

Pappadoms: English term for wafer-thin disks made out of chickpea dough.

Pareekas: envelopes containing money given as presents on formal occasions.

Parjat: not of the community or country; not of the faith.

Pateti: last day of the year, which precedes the shifting New Year of the Parsee calendar.

Patia: spicy sweet-and-sour fish or prawn stew, usually served with lentils and rice.

Pora: Parsee omelette.

Pora-chora: Gujrati slang for wasting time. Literally: wide and broad, sprawling.

Qawals: a group of singers — can be from five to more than thirty men — with one or two lead singers, the rest clap hands to keep time and occasionally form the chorus. They sing mostly devotional songs in praise of God and Muslim saints, who are traditionally their patrons. Some of the famous Qawals are very popular and hold massive concerts.

Roti: bread.

Sagan: a good-luck ceremony. The forehead is annointed with red paste, the garlands are hung around the neck, the person is handed a coconut and given something to sweeten the mouth — all auspicious omens.

Sala: brother-in-law. It is also frequently used as a mild profanity in Gujrati, Punjabi, and Urdu when addressing men.

Shalwar: baggy drawstring trousers, worn in the Punjab.

Shalwar-kamiz: the Punjabi outfit worn by both men and women in Pakistan and India, except that the women add the *dopatta*.

Shandy: a mixture of 7UP (or sometimes lemonade) and beer. A British drink introduced to India during the Raj and considered appropriate for women.

Sharah-e-Quaid-e-Azam-Mohammad Ali Jinnah: road named after the founder of the nation, Mohammad Ali Jinnah. Quaid-e-Azam, which means Great Leader, is the respected title he is known by. Most people still call it the Mall Road.

Shatoose: shawl; also known as ring-shawl, because it can be passed through a man's ring. The material is woven from the fine hair on the underside of the neck of a rare and endangered species of mountain goat.

Sudra: Zoroastrian religious undergarment made of pure white muslin, worn like a slip next to the skin. It has a small pocket at the V of the neck, which is the repository of good deeds. The child first wears it, together with the *kusti*, at the *navjote*.

Sufi: Muslim mystic.

Tanchoi: a particular type of hand-loomed silk sari with a small motif, rich and expensive.

Tandarosti: good health.

Thann: a bale of unstitched cloth from the factory. It comes wrapped around a board.

Thanna: police station.

Ulloo: fool. The owl's expression is considered foolish rather than, as in English, wise.

Uthamna: important Zoroastrian ceremony for the dead body.

Vekh! Vekh! Sher-di-battian!: Punjabi for "Look! Look! City lights!"

Walla: usually attached to signify someone's trade or profession (eg: tonga-*walla* is a tonga driver). Among the Parsees these have become last names. For example, the Ginwalla family must have originally owned a cotton-gin or a still to manufacture gin. The Junglewallas — a fairly common Parsee name — must have either been in the logging business or lived in a place like a jungle, wilderness, or forest.

Yaar: lover, in Urdu. Used loosely by most people in the Indo-Pakistan subcontinent as slang for *friend.*

Yatha: refers to the Yatha Ahu Vairo prayer, which promises God's Good Mind and the Lord's Strength if the person helps others and thus serves the Lord.

Zina: adultery, or fornication by bachelors and unmarried women, as defined by Islamic law.

Zindabad!: long live!

Zurvan: an obscure Zoroastrian concept of Time and Timelessness (eternity), with half his face in light and half in shadow. As a principle, Zurvan is the father of Good (Ahura Mazda) and Evil (Ahriman).

Author's Note

I received valuable assistance from the Bellagio Study Center. Among my fellow sojourners there, I thank Barbara Kirshenblatt-Gimblett for her intense recreation of New York, Penny Eileen Bryan for her descriptions of Denver, and Pat Auster Vigderman, my fellow Bunting Fellow, for details about Boston and Cambridge. I also thank Don and Joanne McClosky for their help with my software, Sissela and Derek Bock for seeing me off at some unearthly hour, John and Dagmar Searle and Lee and Stephen Whitfield for continuing their friendship, and Gianna Celli and the others associated with Bellagio for their unfailing care.

I will remember 1992 for the shadow of grief it cast at my friend Laurie Colwin's tragic and untimely demise.

In this age of technological complexity, there is a whole new series of debts I owe, and my largest debt is to Neville Patel for his instant and constant assistance. I also thank Lois Mervyn and Imad Mirza at the USIS in Lahore, and Jack Moudy, in Houston.

With each passing day, I feel I owe more to my family and friends. Among those friends I have not thanked before, and who are very special, are Jean-Pierre and Fransoise Masset, Afsar and Riza Qizilbash, and Nasreen Rehman. I also thank Rosellen Brown, always generous, for offering valuable suggestions, Marv Hoffman for his sympathetic perspective on our increasingly intolerant times, Robert Baumgardner for enlivening the linguistics scene in Lahore, and in Houston Aban Rustomji and Arna Setna — that rare species who helps everyone. I thank Ann Zimmer for advising me on the American character in my novel *The Bride* when she and her husband were in Pakistan, and Nick and Sheila Platt for their support and encouragement.

A special thank you to Aasma Jehangir for information on the Hadood Ordinance, and Walid Iqbal for his help with translations.

At Milkweed, I thank my friends, starting with Randy Scholes (for his inspired book covers), Teresa Bonner, Beryl Tanis, Fiona Grant, Arlinda Keeley, my discerning and considerate editor Emilie Buchwald, Henry Buchwald who has become almost a part of Milkweed, and the wonderful and generous "Friends of Milkweed."

About the Author . . .

Bapsi Sidhwa, who belongs to the small Parsee community, was born in Karachi, Pakistan, and grew up in Lahore. She graduated from Kinnaird College for Women, Lahore. An active social worker among Asian women, in 1975 she represented Pakistan at the Asian Women's Congress. Sidhwa taught in the graduate program at Columbia University in 1989 and prior to that at Rice University and at the University of Texas at Houston. Married and with three children, she resides in the United States but travels frequently to Pakistan.

Bapsi Sidhwa is the author of *The Bride* (Jonathan Cape Ltd., 1983; St. Martins Press, 1983), *The Crow Eaters* (Milkweed Editions, 1992; St. Martins Press, 1982; Jonathan Cape Ltd., 1980), and *Cracking India* (Milkweed Editions, 1991; William Heinemann Ltd., 1988, under the original title, *Ice-Candy-Man*), and several short stories. Her work has been translated into German, French, and Russian. Sidhwa was appointed Bunting Fellow at Radcliffe/Harvard in 1986-87 and was awarded a National Endowment for the Arts grant for Creative Writing in 1987. In 1991 she received the *Sitara-I-Imtiaz*, the highest honor in the arts that Pakistan bestows on a citizen, and the *Liberatur* Prize in Germany for *Cracking India*.

An American Brat
was designed by Corey Sevett
and typeset by Jodee Kulp Graphic Arts.
Titling is Calligraphic and text is ITC Galliard.
Printed on acid-free Glatfelter Natural
by Edwards Brothers.

More fiction from Milkweed Editions:

Larabi's Ox
Tony Ardizzone

Agassiz
Sandra Birdsell

What We Save for Last
Corinne Demas Bliss

Backbone
Carol Bly

The Clay That Breathes
Catherine Browder

Street Games
Rosellen Brown

Winter Roads, Summer Fields
Marjorie Dorner

Blue Taxis
Eileen Drew

The Historian
Eugene Garber

The Importance of High Places
Joanna Higgins

Circe's Mountain
Marie Luise Kaschnitz

Ganado Red
Susan Lowell

Tokens of Grace
Sheila O'Connor

The Boy Without a Flag
Abraham Rodriguez, Jr.

Cracking India
Bapsi Sidhwa

The Crow Eaters
Bapsi Sidhwa

The Country I Come From
Maura Stanton

Traveling Light
Jim Stowell

Aquaboogie
Susan Straight

Montana 1948
Larry Watson